BURIALS

The Tenth Faye Longchamp Archaeological Mystery
2018—Willa Literary Award Finalist, Contemporary Fiction
2018—Will Rogers Medallion Award
Bronze Medalist, Western Fiction
2018—Oklahoma Book Award Finalist, Fiction
2017—*Strand* Magazine Top 12 Mystery Novels
2017—*True West* Magazine Best Western Mysteries

"This is a highly successful murder mystery by an author who has mastered the magic and craft of popular genre fiction. Her work embodies the truism that character is destiny."

—*Naples Florida Weekly*

"Evans's signature archaeological lore adds even more interest to this tale of love, hate, and greed."

—*Kirkus Reviews*

"Evans sensitively explores the issue of how to balance respecting cultural heritage and gaining knowledge of the past through scientific research."

—*Publishers Weekly*

ISOLATION

The Ninth Faye Longchamp Archaeological Mystery
2016—Oklahoma Book Award Finalist

"Evans skillfully uses excerpts from the fictional oral history of Cally Stanton, recorded by the Federal Writers' Project in 1935, to dramatize the past."

—*Publishers Weekly*

"A worthwhile addition to Faye's long-running series that weaves history, mystery, and psychology into a satisfying tale of greed and passion."

—*Kirkus Reviews*

"Well-drawn characters and setting, and historical and archaeological detail, add to the absorbing story."

—*Booklist*

RITUALS
The Eighth Faye Longchamp Archaeological Mystery

"A suspenseful crime story with just a hint of something otherworldly."

—*Booklist*

"A superior puzzle plot lifts Evans's eighth Faye Longchamp Mystery... Evans pulls all the pieces nicely together in the end."

—*Publishers Weekly*

"The emphasis on the spirit world makes this a bit of a departure from Evans's usual historical and archaeological themes, but it's certainly a well-plotted and enjoyable mystery."

—*Kirkus Reviews*

PLUNDER
The Seventh Faye Longchamp Archaeological Mystery
2012—Florida Book Award Bronze Medal
Winner for General Fiction
2012—Florida Book Award Bronze Medal
Winner for Popular Fiction

"In her delightfully erudite seventh, Faye continues to weave archaeological tidbits and interesting people into soundly plotted mysteries."

—*Kirkus Reviews*

"Working in Louisiana, archaeologist Faye Longchamp doesn't expect a double murder and pirate plunder, but by now she's used to the unexpected."

—*Library Journal*

"The explosion of the Deepwater Horizon rig in the Gulf of Mexico provides the backdrop for Evans's engaging, character-driven seventh mystery featuring archaeologist Faye Longchamp."

—*Publishers Weekly*

"Details of archaeology, pirate lore, and voodoo complement the strong, sympathetic characters, especially Amande, and the appealing portrait of Faye's family life."

—*Booklist*

STRANGERS
The Sixth Faye Longchamp Archaeological Mystery

"Mary Anna Evans's sixth Faye Longchamp novel continues her string of elegant mysteries that features one of contemporary fiction's most appealing heroines. The author also continues to seek out and to describe settings and locations that would whet the excavating appetite of any practicing or armchair archaeologist. Mary Anna Evans then commences to weave an almost mystical tapestry of mystery throughout her novel."

—Bill Gresens, Mississippi Valley Archaeology Center

"Evans explores themes of protection, love, and loss in her absorbing sixth Faye Longchamp Mystery... Compelling extracts from a sixteenth-century Spanish priest's manuscript diary that Faye begins translating lend historical ballast."

—*Publishers Weekly*

"Evans's excellent series continues to combine solid mysteries and satisfying historical detail."

—*Kirkus Reviews*

"This contemporary mystery is drenched with Florida history and with gothic elements that should appeal to a broad range of readers."

—*Booklist*

FLOODGATES
The Fifth Faye Longchamp Archaeological Mystery
2011—Mississippi Author Award Winner

"Mary Anna Evans gets New Orleans: the tainted light, the murk and the shadows, and the sweet and sad echoes, and the bloody dramas that reveal a city's eternal longing for what's been lost and its never-ending hopes for redemption."

—David Fulmer, author of Shamus Award–
winner *Chasing the Devil's Tail*

★ "Evans has written a fascinating tale linking the history of New Orleans's levee system to the present and weaving into the story aspects of the city's widely diverse cultures."

—*Booklist*, Starred Review

"Evans's fifth is an exciting brew of mystery and romance with a touch of New Orleans charm."

—*Kirkus Reviews*

"Evans's fifth series mystery…reveals her skill in handling the details of a crime story enhanced by historical facts and scientific discussions on the physical properties of water. Along with further insights into Faye's personal life, the reader ends up with a thoroughly good mystery."

—*Library Journal*

FINDINGS
The Fourth Faye Longchamp Archaeological Mystery

★ "Evans always incorporates detailed research that adds depth and authenticity to her mysteries, and she beautifully conjures up the Micco County, Florida, setting. This is a series that deserves more attention than it garners."

—*Library Journal*, Starred Review

"Faye's capable fourth is a charming mixture of history, mystery, and romance."

—*Kirkus Reviews*

"In Evans's fine fourth archaeological mystery…the story settles into a comfortable pace that allows the reader to savor the characters."

—*Publishers Weekly*

EFFIGIES

The Third Faye Longchamp Archaeological Mystery
2007—Florida Book Award Bronze Medal
Winner for Popular Fiction

"As an archaeological tour alone the book would be worth reading, but it's the fascinating and complex characters that give the story life and vibrancy."
—Rhys Bowen, author of the Constable Evans mysteries

"The best one yet… A fascinating read."
—Tony Hillerman, *New York Times* bestselling author

"Though Evans has been compared to Tony Hillerman, her sympathetic characters and fascinating archaeological lore add up to a style all her own."
—*Publishers Weekly*

"A thought-provoking tale about people trying to live together."
—*Library Journal*

"A captivating combination of archaeology, Native American tales, romance, and detection. A must-read for those so inclined."
—*Kirkus Reviews*

"Like Randy Wayne White in his Doc Ford novels, Evans adds an extra layer of substance to her series by drawing readers into the fascinating history of ancient American civilizations."
—*Booklist*

RELICS

The Second Faye Longchamp Archaeological Mystery

"An intriguing, multi-layered tale. Not only was I completely stumped by the mystery, I was enchanted by the characters Evans created with such respect."

—Claire Matturro, author of *Wildcat Wine*

"The remote setting engenders an eerie sense of isolation and otherness that gives the story an extra dimension. Recommend this steadily improving series to female-sleuth fans or those who enjoy archaeology-based thrillers like Beverly Connor's Lindsay Chamberlain novels."

—*Booklist*

"Evans delivers a convincing read with life-size, unique characters, not the least of whom is Faye's Indian sidekick, Joe. The archaeological adventures are somewhat reminiscent of Tony Hillerman's Jim Chee mysteries. While the story is complex, *Relics* will engage the imagination of readers attracted to unearthing the secrets of lost cultures."

—*School Library Journal*

"A fascinating look at contemporary archaeology but also a twisted story of greed and its effects."

—*Dallas Morning News*

ARTIFACTS

The First Faye Longchamp Archaeological Mystery
2004—Benjamin Franklin Award for Mystery/Suspense
2004—Patrick D. Smith Florida Literature Award

"A haunting, atmospheric story."

—P. J. Parrish, *New York Times* bestselling author

"The shifting little isles along the Florida Panhandle—hurricane-wracked bits of land filled with plenty of human history—serve as the effective backdrop for Evans's debut, a tale of greed, archaeology, romance, and murder."

—*Publishers Weekly*

"First-novelist Evans introduces a strong female sleuth in this extremely promising debut, and she makes excellent use of her archaeological subject matter, weaving past and present together in a multilayered, compelling plot."

—*Booklist*

Also by Mary Anna Evans

The Physicists' Daughter

The Faye Longchamp Archaeological Mysteries
Artifacts
Relics
Effigies
Findings
Floodgates
Strangers
Plunder
Rituals
Isolation
Burials
Undercurrents
Catacombs
Wrecked

Other Works
Wounded Earth

The Traitor Beside Her

The
TRAITOR
BESIDE HER

A NOVEL

MARY ANNA EVANS

Published by Poisoned Pen Press, an imprint of Sourcebooks
P.O. Box 4410, Naperville, Illinois 60567-4410
(630) 961-3900
sourcebooks.com

Library of Congress Cataloging-in-Publication Data

Names: Evans, Mary Anna, author.
Title: The traitor beside her : a novel / Mary Anna Evans.
Description: Naperville, Illinois : Poisoned Pen Press, [2023]
Identifiers: LCCN 2022052088 (print) | LCCN 2022052089
(ebook) | (trade paperback) | (epub)
Classification: LCC PS3605.V369 T73 2023 (print) | LCC PS3605.V369
(ebook) | DDC 813.6--dc23
LC record available at https://lccn.loc.gov/2022052088
LC ebook record available at https://lccn.loc.gov/2022052089

Printed and bound in the United States of America.
VP 10 9 8 7 6 5 4 3 2 1

This book is dedicated to my bonus children and grandchild—
Erin, Chris, Evan, Rebecca, Lara, and Bruce.
As the years pass, my blessings grow.

"In wartime," I said, *"Truth is so precious that she should always be attended by a bodyguard of lies."*

—WINSTON CHURCHILL, 1943

Chapter 1

The steel beneath Justine Byrne's shins was gunmetal gray, and the metal touched by her welding torch glowed as orange as her hair. Her ears were full of the shrieks and whines of heavy equipment. In every direction, she was surrounded by oceangoing vessels in various stages of completion and by the skilled people building them. She was working at the Washington Navy Yard, the oldest shore establishment of the U.S. Navy, and the atmosphere was charged with the urgent need to build ever more ships and send them out to a world at war.

As Justine knelt on the deck of a half-finished ship, one eye on her work and one eye on a man perched on a scaffold above her, she wasn't just breaking a fundamental rule of welding. She was blasting it to bits. A welder was supposed to keep her mind and her eyes on her work, because welding accidents tended to maim and kill.

Her target was talking to a man working beside him on the scaffold. No, "talking" wasn't the right word. He was whispering. Their faces were so close that they might have been kissing. She wished she could be close enough to hear, but her cover story required her to be right where she was. It also required her to be welding, but the time had come for Justine to cut the gas to her torch before she killed somebody. The time had come to do nothing but watch, without letting anybody notice she was watching.

She sat back on her heels and rubbed her neck as if she had a crick in it. Then she rubbed her temple with a world-weary expression that she hoped said, "I've been working so hard for my country that I gave myself a splitting headache. I just need to rest a minute before I go back to welding together a victory for the Allies." Then she used the hand on her temple to adjust her goggles, sliding them up on her forehead just enough to give her a view that wasn't impeded by their tinted glass.

And there it was, the moment that she'd been sure was coming ever since she was briefed on this job. Her target's lips formed the words, "It's time," as he locked eyes with the other man. Each man held out a hand to offer a handshake, and only someone who had been watching and waiting for this exact moment would have seen that neither hand was empty. Her target was palming a small brown packet that she knew held microfilm copies of naval design documents. The other man was palming a small green packet that assuredly held money. And in big bills, because they had to add up to enough cash to prompt a man to sell out his country for a sum that he could hold in one hand. After the handshake, her target held the green packet of money and the other man held the brown packet of blueprints.

This was an inopportune time for Ronald, the man who worked beside her, to turn solicitous.

"You turned off your torch. Is your head hurting again? I've got some aspirin in my lunchbox."

Justine did not want Ronald's aspirin. She wanted him to back off. She needed to get word to her partner Jerry that the transfer had occurred. And she needed to do it now, before her target hid the money or disappeared.

Now another inconvenient man, her boss Danny, was walking her way. He, too, must have noticed that she was loafing on the job. He was probably coming to tell her to light her torch and go back to welding, but Justine could not afford to let Danny slow her down. She caught his eye, put her hand on her belly, and pantomimed being ill.

Danny took three steps back and waved her away, and this meant that she was home free. Or she would have been if Ronald hadn't been so impossibly hard to get rid of.

"Are you okay, Justine?" he said, putting a hand on her waist as if to steady her. "You don't look so good."

Ronald hovered around all the women, but he was out-and-out handsy with Justine. She cringed at the familiar way he wrapped his hand around the side of her narrow waist and reached his long fingers all the way to her spine. This was his favorite move. He found an excuse to do it every day under the pretext of "helping" her, and she let it happen because she couldn't afford to make a fuss that would get her transferred someplace where she couldn't do her reconnaissance. He'd already done his waist-wrap once that morning, then he'd managed to cozy up to her again during her lunch break, so Ronald was enjoying a very good day. Well, she wasn't going to have to put up with him much longer.

"Don't touch me. I'm sick, and you don't want to catch it," she mumbled through a fake retch, and even that didn't make Ronald back down. As she hurried away, his fingers were still fumbling at the soft flesh where her waist swelled into her hips. It was enough to make her want to actually retch, instead of just pretending.

———

Jerry Jenkins could see that Justine had fulfilled her mission. He'd positioned his wheelchair on the pier where her ship was moored, so that he could have her in his sights at the critical time. His sharp eyes had seen the moment when she lifted her head, and they had caught the motion of her arm when she adjusted her welding goggles. He knew exactly what she was trying to see, because he had been sitting beside her when she got this assignment. He was her partner, and that was what made the thing he was about to do so damned hard.

He had listened as Paul explained the job to her calmly and thoroughly, making it plain that the stakes were high. Paul had told Justine that this undercover assignment, her first, was crucial to stopping the sale of documents that revealed critical vulnerabilities in the design of certain Navy ships. If she could find out who was selling the documents, she would be helping save the lives of the thousands—perhaps tens of thousands—of American sailors who were aboard those ships.

Jerry knew Justine, so he had known from the start that she would do this job and she would do it well. And she *had* done it well. Even from this distance, he could see an air of success in the bounce of the brassy orange curls escaping her navy-blue kerchief. It was in her victorious stance as she stood on the ship's deck above him, her coltish form wrapped in pale blue coveralls and silhouetted against the pale blue sky.

Justine's quiet exuberance was evident in the confident way that she'd adjusted her goggles and in the way that she'd sprung to her feet when she'd completed her mission. She was heart-breakingly young, only twenty-one, but she had the competence of someone twice her age, and she was fearsomely smart. In a lot of ways, Justine was the perfect partner for a government agent who wanted to get the job done and who also wanted to stay alive, and Jerry fervently wanted both those things.

Justine had done everything she'd been asked to do, as Jerry had known she would, and he would do everything that he had been asked to do. He would wait for her to come and tell him that her job was done. And then he would do again what he'd been doing every day since they got to the shipyard.

He would betray her.

Chapter 2

Justine's heart was racing, but she tried not to show it. She wanted to seem confident when she told Paul about the successful conclusion of her assignment. She also wanted to seem professional and unruffled, which was hard to accomplish after long hours of welding and a long bus ride to his office. At the very least, she wanted to seem competent.

In a single honest moment, she admitted to herself that she hadn't seen Paul in a while, so she also wanted to look pretty. Then she pretended like that thought had never crossed her mind.

Justine was painfully aware of just how little training she'd had. Wars didn't allow time for anything beyond the basics. She and her best friend, Georgette, also a new agent, had spent a few days at a firing range with Jerry. They'd had time for just enough target practice to teach them that shooting guns was scary but exhilarating. They'd also learned that they were reasonably good shots for beginners.

Standing beside Georgette at the shooting range with Jerry barking instructions at them was the most fun she'd had since— well, she couldn't remember. The warm sunshine of a Louisiana

October had glinted off Jerry's blond hair and the metal tubing of his wheelchair. It had tanned Georgette's face and burned Justine's cheeks as they'd spent weeks learning to do things that women weren't really supposed to do in 1944.

Georgette's steady, capable hands had easily supported her handgun as she squeezed off one shot after another, most of them hitting the bulls-eye or coming close. Her bayou girlhood had included time spent duck hunting with her father and brothers, but even she admitted that the sleek weapons that Jerry lent them for practice weren't much like her father's old twelve-gauge shotgun. Justine had none of Georgette's experience and only a fraction of her strength, but she'd learned the mathematics that governed ballistics at her mother's knee. Her aim was remarkably accurate for a city girl. There were times when being born to two physicists came in handy.

Justine and Georgette had spent a few days with one of Paul's people who had taught them a few basic tricks of surveillance, which had boiled down to "try to see as much as you can without being seen." Another agent had run them through undercover training exercises and mock interrogations that were designed to make them blow their cover. A third had worked with them on self-defense. After that instructor had left, Jerry had added a few dirty tricks to their arsenal. He called them "ungentlemanly maneuvers."

"I'm not kidding, ladies," Jerry had said. "If you have to knee somebody in the crotch to stay alive, knee him in the crotch. Grab...um...whatever you can reach and twist it. Hard."

Then he'd made them practice kneeing a six-foot-tall mannequin in its wooden crotch while he bellowed, "Knee him harder, Justine, as hard as you can. Now jab him in the throat. Go for the eyes, Georgette!"

In quieter moments, Paul had joined them. The four of them

had sat down together in the evenings, while Justine showed the others what she'd learned about radios from time spent building crystal sets with her father. Jerry had followed this by giving them a rundown on up-to-date equipment like the radios that Georgette would be using in her new job as a communications specialist. All of it had been fun, but none of it had seemed real. In her head, Justine had known that the bullets in her gun were deadly, but she'd felt like a kid playing spy games.

What Jerry hadn't done, and neither had Paul, was be straightforward about who she would be working for and what kind of jobs she could expect to do. To be fair, Justine had to admit that they might not know. She wasn't sure she liked the idea of doing a series of individual assignments with no sense of an overarching goal, but perhaps that would come with time.

The assignment at the naval yard had dropped out of the sky, rather like the bombs that had been pelting much of the world for years. One day, she and Georgette had been at the firing range, flinging hot lead at faraway targets. Paul had arrived and nodded at Jerry, who had taken the pistols out of their hands and wheeled away, beckoning for Georgette to follow him.

Standing there at a deserted gun range outside New Orleans, Paul had said, "We no longer have time for this," which seemed to mean that Justine was as fully trained as she was going to get. Days later, she was at the Washington Navy Yard, welding and looking for traitors. She knew how to weld, but she was in over her head in every other respect.

At least Paul had assigned Jerry to be her partner, although nobody seemed to want to tell her where Georgette was or what she was doing. Justine had drawn a lot of strength during this mission just from seeing Jerry's kind, gentle face around the navy yard from time to time, even if the situation dictated that she had to pretend not to know him.

And now she was face-to-face with Paul for the first time in weeks. Still in her coveralls and still holding her lunch box, Justine stood in front of his desk, trying and failing to deny that he was part of the reason her heart raced. Even after time apart, she was still drawn to the intelligent blue eyes behind his glasses and to the sly sense of humor that he showed so rarely. His lopsided smile still struck her like a fist. She was still attracted to the lean frame beneath his well-cut suit, broad-shouldered but long-legged and rangy. She wanted him to be pleased with her work, but she wanted more than that.

There had been a time when she'd thought he wanted more than that, too, but no trace of those feelings showed now on a motionless face that was as pale as hers, only without the freckles. From the look of him, this man had no feelings at all, and he never had.

Jerry sat with his wheelchair parked beside Paul's desk, his white-blond head cocked at an angle that let him meet her eyes almost head-on, but not quite. He had met her at the bus stop with a warm hello and a congratulatory pat on the back, and they'd come up on the elevator together. He'd greeted her with, "Hey, Justine," then gone silent.

She'd tried to make conversation, asking, "Have you seen Georgette lately?"

All she'd gotten in return was, "Not since New Orleans."

She'd answered, "Me neither," and then the elevator doors had opened.

Paul's office was at the end of a short hall with only one door. That door opened into the office of a middle-aged woman who seemed to be his secretary, since the door behind her desk opened into the larger office where he waited. In Paul's solemn presence, even Jerry lost his ready smile.

Justine looked around for a chair and saw none, so she stood in silence. If this was how agents were debriefed after successful missions, she'd hate to see what happened when they failed.

Dressed like a banker in a sober gray suit, Paul regarded her through horn-rimmed glasses. She missed the wire-rimmed pair that he'd worn before she'd known that he was a government agent. He barely looked like the same man who had worked with her at a New Orleans munitions plant. His coveralls and working man's demeanor had vanished. Now, everything about his appearance was completely buttoned down. The stray lock that had always dangled in his eyes had been slicked back with hair cream until his hair was as motionless as his eyes.

"So," he said, "give me your report."

She didn't know what he wanted to hear, so she started at the beginning. "I reported to the Washington Navy Yard and was assigned to work under a man named Danny, just as you told me to expect. I monitored the behavior of my coworkers, looking for someone who might be planning to sell naval plans and someone who might be planning to buy them. I soon identified two men whose behavior concerned me."

"How so?"

"They had brief, intense conversations periodically—about once a day—but otherwise they ignored each other. It was an odd pattern, as if they were friends, but only sometimes."

"Were you able to get close to either of them?"

"I tried. They both resisted my efforts to strike up a conversation."

Jerry finally cracked a smile. "I can't imagine how they resisted your charm. When you want to be, you're as appealing as a spring morning."

Justine rolled her eyes at him. "Maybe they didn't find me attractive. Or interesting in any way. They didn't seem to want any friends at all, which I thought was suspicious in itself. I decided to just hang back and watch. Today, that strategy paid off."

"How so?" Paul said again.

She was shocked at the complete lack of…anything…in Paul's voice. No approval. No note of congratulations. No emotion at all.

"I saw the money change hands with my own eyes. And the plans." She was humiliated by the note of desperation that she heard in her own voice.

Why was she letting him make her feel this way? She'd successfully identified an enemy spy, just as she'd been told to do.

"Once the transaction was done, I told Jerry. He hasn't said that he failed to stop my target from getting away, so I presume they're in custody now."

"Jerry, did you take anyone into custody today?"

Jerry hesitated, looking down at his lap. Then he flicked a glance at Justine, and she thought she saw an apology in his eyes. "I did not."

"Thank you." There was no apology in Paul's eyes as they drilled into Justine's. "Jerry, will you leave us to speak alone?"

Jerry nodded and wheeled himself to the door without looking at her again. She heard the latch click behind her and knew that he was gone.

"What's happening here?" she asked. "Why are you treating me this way?"

"There was no transaction today. There was no enemy spy trying to get blueprints for Navy ships. There was no traitor willing to sell them to the highest bidder."

"But I saw—"

"You saw what I wanted you to see. You saw two of my agents passing envelopes back and forth, and that is all."

He reached in his breast pocket and pulled out two familiar

envelopes, green and brown. Opening the green one, he pulled out a sheaf of Monopoly money and riffled it in his hands like a man who had just come into a multicolored fortune.

Justine felt blood rush to her face, although she couldn't have told whether it was from humiliation or anger. "Did Jerry know?"

"Jerry knew."

Justine had never failed at anything, not at work and certainly not at school, but she was about to be fired before she even figured out who she was working for. She was going to have to get herself home to New Orleans, find a sad little room like the one she'd left, and start her life over. Again.

"Come here."

Justine didn't like Paul's tone, and she figured that he was only going to be her boss for another thirty seconds or so, so she stood firm. All he got from her was an angry shake of the head.

"Come here, please."

His voice wasn't noticeably warmer, but the "please" softened his commanding tone enough for her to be willing to comply. Her work boots clomped on the dull linoleum floor as she walked slowly around his gray-painted steel desk.

He waved a hand that said, "Closer," so she moved even nearer to the desk chair where he sat. She was so close that she would have been able to feel the heat coming off any other man's body, but Paul seemed to be operating at room temperature. Nothing radiated from him, nothing at all.

He reached for her lunch box. Confused by the gesture, she handed it to him without thinking. Then she kicked herself, because being her boss (for the moment) gave him no right to handle her things.

The metal lunch box clanged as Paul set it on his desk, and its hinges creaked when he raised the lid. He lifted her Thermos bottle out of it, then unscrewed the red cup at its top and uncorked the bottle.

Somehow, this was the arrogant move that prompted her to protest. "That's not your lunch box. Give it back."

He ignored her, holding the open bottle beneath his nose. "Coffee. Nice choice."

Still holding it in his left hand, he used the right one to fish a scrap of waxed paper, wiped clean and neatly folded for reuse, out of the lunchbox. He sniffed it, too. "Tuna fish. Also a nice choice."

Dropping the waxed paper back into the lunch box, he gave the Thermos bottle a little shake while he picked up the white cloth napkin she'd used as a luncheon plate. Justine heard a distinct rattle. Why would an empty Thermos bottle rattle?

Forgetting her humiliation for a moment, she leaned forward to see what was making the noise. Paul held the napkin below the mouth of the bottle and shook out a round wooden disk. It looked like the buttons that closed her coveralls. One hand went to her belly and the other went to the hollow between her breasts. She ran both hands up and down the front of her body, but she felt no gaps. All of her buttons were in place.

"If you'll permit me," he said, reaching toward her waist, but with none of the lasciviousness that Ronald had used to do the same thing. She felt his hand grasp something behind her, and she felt him pull it forward where she could see it. It was one of the fabric tabs that could be fastened to make her coveralls fit tighter or looser, depending on which of the buttons spaced across the waistband that she used. It seemed that she'd lost the button that she usually used to fasten that tab.

No. She hadn't lost it. The person who put it in her lunchbox to taunt her had made sure of that.

She reached for the spot where the button had been and felt

an even bristle of unfrayed threads. They had been cut by the person who slipped the button into her thermos.

Ronald.

"Was Ronald a plant? The man who worked beside me all week. Did you and Ronald set me up?"

"It seems so, doesn't it? You let somebody get close enough to you to poison your coffee and you're still alive, so it certainly wasn't the enemy playing tricks with your buttons."

Through gritted teeth, she said, "Is it really necessary to drag out the humiliation? Why don't you just go ahead and fire me?"

Paul wasn't looking at her, and he wasn't answering her. He was peering into his file drawer. "Where did I put that—oh, there it is."

He handed her a large hand mirror that looked like the ones that hairdressers used to let women look at the back of their freshly coiffed hair.

"And there's the other one." Paul reached back in the file drawer and pulled out a second mirror just like the first. "I'll hold this one just so—"

He held it behind her back, a few inches above waist level.

"—now you can use this one to get a good look at this spot."

With one finger, he gently touched the center of her back, right between her shoulder blades.

She wondered why she continued to obey his commands. Nevertheless, she maneuvered the mirror into place. Unable to believe what she saw, she let out an audible gasp. Paul didn't react and, for once, she was grateful for his impassive face.

Dead center on the torso of her pale blue coveralls was a blood-red blotch the size and shape of a man's hand, the heel of its palm just above her waist and its fingers reaching halfway to her neck.

"The man who did that could have slid his knife between your vertebrae and dropped you to the ground. Forever."

"It was all a setup? Everything that happened at the shipyard?"

"You thought I would send you into danger without making sure you were up to the job? You thought I would risk Jerry's life like that?"

She moved the mirror to and fro, studying the reflection of the stain that marked her back. "I can't believe Ronald did this."

"Oh, Ronald snipped off your button and dropped it in the dregs of your coffee, but it wasn't Ronald who put that mark on your back. And it wasn't anybody working with you on the ship. Think, Justine. Somebody would surely have said something if you'd walked through a sea of coworkers with an apparent bloodstain covering your back. You couldn't have ridden the bus here with your clothes in that condition, either. It had to have happened after you walked into this building."

Her breath left her in a rush and carried a name with it.

"Jerry."

She could feel Jerry's warm, friendly pat on the back as he said hello.

Paul gave her a single nod. "Yes, Jerry."

"Why would he do that to me?"

"Because he cares about you. As do I."

"Doesn't seem like it," she muttered.

"You let two men get close enough to you to stab you to death. One of them could have poisoned you, too. If I were to be so foolish as to let you keep your job, how do you propose to stay alive?"

She didn't have an answer for him.

"You have it in you to be a good agent. The two men buying and selling military secrets were plants, obviously, but you picked them out of a crowd within days. And you did it in the middle of a tremendous amount of activity. Building a ship requires a lot of people and a lot of loud, fast-moving equipment."

"No kidding," she said. "My ears have been ringing since I set foot at the shipyard."

He graced her with a single nod. "Today, you proved that you have the ability to ignore all that and spot the one important thing that you need to find. But that's the problem. You can't afford to ignore everything going on around you. You can't afford to ignore anything. You have to see everything around you, all the time."

"I see a lot. For example, Jerry's left calf is bigger than his right one."

His face was like a stone. He was going to make her tell him why this was important.

"I'm pretty sure that the polio left him more strength in his left leg. If I'm his friend, this tells me how to help him. If he asks for help standing up, I need to give him more help on his right side."

"And if you're not his friend?"

"If he's standing up when I attack him and I want to knock him down so that I can get away, I go for the weak leg. If I want to change his life long-term, I try to do some damage to the strong leg."

"Not bad. Remind me to stay in your good graces. Now—"

Justine was done being well-mannered. "Let me finish. If you're going to embarrass me over things I missed, you need to listen to the things I didn't miss."

He inclined his head as a signal that she should keep talking.

"You took a bad fall when you were very small and busted your chin open. The scar's barely noticeable when you're clean-shaven, but hair doesn't grow in it. At the end of the day when your beard has had a chance to grow, it's easy to see. Since your hair's dark, a bit of five-o'clock shadow makes the white area really stand out. If you pay attention, you'll see that a lot of men have that kind of scar, but I've never seen one like yours. It's not straight. It's bigger than most men's and it's jagged, like a shallow W."

"I was running around like the rambunctious toddler that I was, carrying a china plate. I dropped it, it shattered, and I landed chin-first on the pieces."

"Well, if you're ever in a situation where it's important not to be recognized, you might want to shave twice a day. Or use some eyebrow powder to cover up that scar."

He put his hand to his chin. "I'll bear that in mind. It's never occurred to me that the scar had an unusual shape that could be a problem, probably because I can't see it, not even in a mirror. I probably couldn't see it even with both these mirrors. I'm glad to see that you pay attention to the kind of thing that could torpedo an undercover operation."

Justine set the mirror on Paul's desk next to the one that he had held. She used both hands to feel the back of her coveralls, as if she could see the fake blood with her fingers. "You're not firing me?"

"No, I'm not firing you. You still don't understand what happened today. I gave you an important test, one that everybody fails. Nobody spots the transaction *and* manages to protect against physical threats. Nobody. Ask Jerry what it was like for him. Three of my undercover agents 'died' because of the mistakes he made."

"What was it like for you?"

He put the mirrors back in his file drawer, keeping his eyes on his hands as he gently closed the drawer. His voice barely audible, he said, "This job is made for people with tunnel vision. Give them a clear assignment and no clear danger to worry about, and they will ignore everything that doesn't put them closer to their goal. For their own safety, they cannot be allowed to operate like that."

It was not lost on her that he hadn't answered her question.

"Who exactly do we tunnel-vision people work for? The FBI?"

A little shrug. A little shake of the head. She was going to presume that these things meant no.

"The FBI would have been an excellent option for you. Alas, they don't employ women as special agents."

"But you were doing domestic intelligence work when we met. Isn't that the FBI's bailiwick?"

Another little shrug. A little nod of the head. She read those gestures to mean, "Yes, but what's a bailiwick, anyway? I certainly don't take them seriously."

"Technically, the FBI covers domestic surveillance, but there are several intelligence agencies operating in this country, all of them jockeying for power. The Military Intelligence Division. The Office of Naval Intelligence. The Office of Strategic Services. The Signal Security Agency. The Counter Intelligence Corps. President Roosevelt would like very much to combine at least some of those functions or, at the least, to convince the bigwigs involved to stop bickering, but wartime is not a time for shaking up bureaucrats. In the wake of our successful operation in New Orleans, I've been given much more latitude. And an expanded staff. And a generous budget. And the authorization to…hmm…do critical intelligence work by any means necessary."

"You take special assignments that go over the heads of the FBI. The OSS. And all those other agencies?"

"I'm not sure I'd use the words 'over the head' of the FBI and the OSS and all the others. I think of myself as going around large, cumbersome operations like those."

"Your assignments come from someone very high up?"

"Very high up."

"From the president."

"Very high up."

She looked around at the dull brown walls, the beaten-up gray desk, and the sagging beige blinds on the window behind the desk. "If you were working for somebody who was all that high up, it seems like they'd give you a better office. This is a dump."

There was the laugh she remembered, and the broad charismatic smile, and the even white teeth. She felt an odd sense of accomplishment at catching him off guard.

"Perhaps my work is best done in a dump. Who would suspect that anything worthwhile could happen in this room? Besides, I can't be all that important. When we met, I was doing my own undercover work."

Justine sighed. "I figure you were just shorthanded. Or else you were working on something that was earthshakingly important."

"It was very important. 'Earthshaking' is exactly the right word. And we were successful because of you."

There was an instant of warmth in his gaze, and then it was gone. How did he do that? Was it really possible to turn one's humanity on and off?

Justine reflected that she probably needed to learn to do that, too, if she hoped to do her job and stay alive. "Well, whoever I'm working for, I'm guessing that today's disaster means that I'll be in training for the foreseeable future."

Paul's answer was quick and crisp. "No. We don't have the luxury of time, and I've got a job that only you can do. Please try not to get killed, because this job is of critical importance. I chose the District of Columbia to stage today's debacle because your real assignment is nearby at a former women's college called Arlington Hall, just outside the city. You can be at your desk there tomorrow."

Justine felt like she was standing in an elevator at the instant its cable snapped. "Tomorrow?"

"Yes, tomorrow. Arlington Hall is the site of a massive crypt-analysis operation run by the Army. From the day I recruited you, I had in mind that you would work there, because…well, you were born for that kind of assignment. They hire civilians, so you don't even have to join the WACs. Or pretend to join the WACs. You've got the brains, certainly, but you also already have some knowledge of code breaking, which is a huge help. And you speak German, which has obvious advantages in an operation that was set up to intercept, decrypt, and translate enemy messages."

"You think I have brains? After what happened today?"

"You were set up to fail. *I* set you up to fail, and I'm very good at what I do. And now I'm explaining your next assignment, so please pay attention."

A whisper of surliness crept into her voice as she said, "Yes, sir."

"There are a lot of smart people in the world, Justine, but there's only one you. An assignment to crack codes at Arlington Hall for the duration of the war would have been ideal for your skills. Unfortunately, it's no longer the best use of your talents."

"But I thought you said you were sending me to Arlington Hall."

"I am, but I'm not sending you there to work on decryption. We know that an enemy agent has infiltrated a key operation at Arlington Hall. This person's actions have already resulted in the destruction of a remote pontoon bridge that was important to our ability to supply our Soviet allies fighting in Poland."

He opened the top drawer of his desk and pulled out a bat-tered photograph. He held it out and she took it. It depicted a family of six. A young woman cradled an infant in her arms and a man stood behind her, one hand on her shoulder. Two boys knelt on either side of the woman, their faces blurred as if in motion. A third, approaching his teens, stood beside his father, shoulders squared and chin set.

"This photo looks a few years old," she said. "So the baby must be walking by now."

"It was taken before the war. And yes, she would be walking if she were still alive."

Justine's mouth went dry. She wanted to look away from the photo, but she couldn't.

"The pontoon bridge was located at the site of a ferry that had been run by this man's family for generations. Centuries, probably. It was the obvious site for our troops to cross. Equally obviously, commandeering the site destroyed his business."

"Poor guy," Justine murmured.

"Not being animals, we hired him to do odd jobs for the troops stationed there and to just generally be a caretaker until the war was over and he could resume his business. He was a man with a family," Paul said, gesturing at the photograph. "It was the right thing to do."

"You say that the baby's dead. What about the rest of them?"

"All dead. When the enemy took out the bridge, they killed everyone—this family and everyone we had stationed there at the time. There were no survivors."

"How many?" she whispered.

"Fifteen of ours, plus this family."

She could see a scrape on one of the little boys' chins. If he'd lived, he might have had a scar like Paul's for the rest of his life.

He touched a finger to her chin, raising her face to his. "We believe there is a traitor among the code breakers at Arlington Hall. This person passed the location of the pontoon bridge to the enemy. As a result, this family died, along with fifteen soldiers who have left grieving families. It will be your job to find out who did this, and not just to prevent more attacks like that one. An enemy agent at Arlington Hall could wreak havoc in every theater of the war and at every level. We can't have that."

"That person could steal our codes," Justine said. "Unmask our agents. Put vital military secrets directly into the hands of Hitler and Hirohito. Is that the kind of havoc you're thinking of?"

"Yes. Lives are in the balance, many lives."

Justine could almost feel the red blotch on her back. It marked her failure. Surely, Paul knew someone else better suited for a life-and-death assignment, someone who had succeeded as an undercover spy at least once.

He was still talking. "Are you willing to take this job, knowing that you will be up against someone who coolly arranged the deaths of all those people? And there may be another death to add to those. One of the women working at Arlington Hall was strangled a few weeks ago. The police have a man in custody. The city is overrun with lonely military men, and not all of them are good people. Add that to a huge influx of young women free of their protective parents for the first time and perhaps the police can be excused for presuming that the man who took her dancing that night killed her. But they don't know that the poor woman worked beside a dangerous enemy agent. A traitor. We can't tell them, but she did."

Justine ached for the poor murdered woman. She too had been pursued by a man who was nothing like he seemed. She could almost feel hands around her neck, but she suppressed the urge to touch her throat. Spies couldn't afford to give away their feelings.

"You can say no," Paul said. "As your friend, I encourage it."

Justine was shocked to realize how badly she wanted to say no. The danger had never seemed real before she saw that bloodred handprint on her back. She saw something in Paul's eyes that might have been compassion.

The room was silent. She felt that there should have been some noise coming from somewhere. From the hall outside. From the street below. From other offices, where typewriters clacked and radios chattered and bosses gave dictation. She heard nothing. Perhaps the room was soundproofed.

It was at times like this, when silence descended and time seemed to slow, that Justine thought she could hear the booming guns of a faraway war. The whole world rattled with war. The world stank of death, and she was helpless to do anything about it. Or she had been. Here was her chance to do something that might help silence the guns.

"I'll do it. Tell me what to do, and I'll do it. If you can tell me how to do it and stay alive, that would be a big help."

"I'll do my best." He reached for the phone on his desk and punched the intercom button. "Clarissa, bring a chair back in, please. My guest will be here for a while, and she needs a place to sit. We'll need the pertinent file, as well. And my guest needs a suitable handbag."

His secretary brought in a chair, handed Paul the file tucked under her arm, set a remarkably unattractive black purse on the table, and left.

"Let's start with the purse," he said, opening it and peering inside, "and with your new identity. Starting now, you are Miss Samantha Ogletree, born and raised in Summerville, Georgia. Yes, Summerville is as small as it sounds. You are a minister's daughter, naive and protected, but you surprised your parents by applying for a job to help with the war effort. They've come around to the idea, and they are very proud. Tomorrow, Samantha Ogletree will report to Arlington Hall to take a job as an assistant to Dr. Edison van Dorn, who has taken a leave from his job as a Latin professor at Dartmouth to lead code crackers in the German section, a group of brilliant but unstable geniuses."

"And this is where we believe our spy is working?"

"Exactly. Miss Samantha Ogletree has been hired to do basic secretarial work, and nobody has any reason to think that she would know anything at all about cryptanalysis. Or German."

"So you're hoping somebody might let something slip in front of me, with no thought that I might understand what they were saying?"

"Exactly."

"Then it's a good thing that the nuns made every girl in our high school learn to type. I can pass as a secretary. I'm pretty good at shorthand and filing, too. The nuns made sure of it."

"Of course you are. Shorthand is a kind of code, and so are filing systems. You're hell on wheels when it comes to breaking codes."

"I see by this hideous purse that Miss Samantha Ogletree is not a fashion plate."

He gave the offending bag a rueful glance. "No. Her mother is an upstanding churchgoing woman, and she does all of poor Samantha's shopping. Wait until you see your wardrobe."

"So that's why you sent that woman to take my measurements back when you first hired me? I figured as much. You don't need detailed measurements to buy coveralls. What's going to happen to my real clothes?"

"We'll store them for you. We'll store all your possessions. My wardrobing people keep all of our agents properly dressed and outfitted, and they do an excellent job of it. Everything you need for this job will be waiting for you when you get home to your rooming house. Leave the clothes you're wearing in your room along with all your other things, and I'll send somebody to get it all. You will be taking nothing with you that could reveal that you're not the person you pretend to be."

Justine imagined herself stepping out of her life and into another, like a butterfly bursting open its chrysalis. Which of her possessions were weighing her down? Which ones would she miss? The answer to that last question bypassed her mind and went straight to her lips.

"Please tell them to take care of my physics books. Some of them belonged to my parents. And…okay, this is odd."

"Not as odd as putting your books ahead of everything you own, but I knew that about you already and I like my books, too. What do you want to say that's weirder than that?"

"Tell them to take care of my makeup and perfume. My mother gave them to me for my birthday right before she died."

"When you finish this job, you'll find that your books and cosmetics are exactly as you left them. Until then, you'll have to make do with the cheap makeup that Miss Samantha Ogletree bought at the dime store as soon as she was out of her mother's sight. Samantha's pretty sure that lipstick is sinful, but she's grabbing her chance to wear some."

He pulled a plastic tube of lipstick out of the purse, removed the lid, and swiveled up a column of tomato-red wax. Justine groaned.

"What else did your people put in my purse?"

He pulled out a wallet, opened it, and held out identification papers, including a driver's license.

"Good thing I know how to drive. Well, a little."

"That's why we asked whether you could drive on the very first day." He pulled out two bank notes, a five and a one. "Samantha had to prepay for her room, and it took all the money her parents gave her. She would die before she'd wire them for more. This is all you have left until payday. Spend wisely."

"I always do."

He pulled out an open packet of cigarettes.

"You know I don't smoke. Do I need to learn?"

"No. Miss Ogletree doesn't smoke, either. She bought this pack as part of her I'm-finally-leaving-home rebellion, but she smoked one cigarette and hated it. We have included this in your cover story, so that you can explain having this in your purse." He held out a small wooden matchbox. "Although you really want to avoid letting people see it, because you can't afford for them to ask you for a light when there aren't any matches in it."

Then he removed the matchbox's wooden cover to reveal a tiny metal box, about two-and-a-half inches long by one-and-a-half inches wide. It had a dial on top, a single hole on one side, and a lens on the other side that revealed its function.

"A camera?" she said, taking it in her hands for a closer look.

"Yes." He handed her a sheet of paper. "Here are the instructions. Read them and leave them here. Your camera has a focal range of four-and-a-half feet to infinity, and it's loaded with enough film to take thirty-four exposures."

"You're giving me darkroom equipment and a supply of film?"

"No. You'll be living in a dormitory with no space for a darkroom. Besides, the other women would smell the chemicals. Jerry will be your contact. When you need film developed, give the camera to him. He'll bring back photos and a reloaded camera."

Justine was comforted to know that Jerry would be nearby, despite the day's betrayal.

"There aren't many other surprises in here," he said, reaching into the main compartment for a pencil, two pens, and an eraser. Then he slid another pen out of a slot that seemed designed to hold writing utensils. He laid it carefully next to the other two pens, so carefully that Justine heard alarm bells.

"That's not an ordinary fountain pen," she said.

"Doesn't it look like an ordinary fountain pen?"

"It actually does, but you're acting funny, so it must not be."

He held it out to her on his open palm. She reached for it, but he pulled his hand away.

"You're right. There's nothing ordinary about it. We call it the Stinger. It fires a single .22 round, then it's useless. It will give you one shot—no pun intended—at getting out of a tough situation. Stingers are hard to aim, so your best bet is to get close enough to discharge your one bullet directly into your adversary. I'd go for the jugular, myself. See the pocket clip? That's the trigger."

"Wait. That's all you're giving me to defend myself? One bullet, loaded into a weapon I can't aim. After all that time I spent practicing at the firing range?" She took the purse out of his hand and felt around inside. Nothing.

Then she hefted it and held it up to get a better look. "The weight's wrong. And the interior of the purse is smaller than the exterior."

She rubbed her hand over the bottom of the empty purse's interior until she felt a small knob. A gentle push lifted the purse bottom, revealing a secret compartment beneath it. Surely, this was where an actual handgun was hiding with its familiar barrel, trigger, and grip.

But no. The secret compartment was empty.

"You've got to give me a real gun. I'm going to be up against people who are playing for keeps."

"No."

"Why not? You don't trust me to handle a weapon?"

"I'm giving you the Stinger. It's a weapon. I just can't give you a weapon that might give away your identity and, in the process, let our target know that we are in hot pursuit. In undercover work, safety is constantly at odds with secrecy. There is no world in which Miss Samantha Ogletree would be carrying a gun, and you will not be able to retain complete control of your handbag. Carrying it around with you constantly would be a dead giveaway. Besides, some bosses require employees to lock up personal items, separating you from your weapon for the entire workday."

"Thus rendering even the Stinger useless."

"Unfortunately so. There are just too many ways that someone would notice that your purse was far too heavy or that you were inordinately attached to it. Believe me when I tell you that this is not a job that will allow you to be armed at all times. You are still free to refuse the assignment."

She reluctantly conceded his point. Then she thought again. "Wait. By your logic, the secret compartment is a risk. If someone searched my purse, they might find it."

"Oh, but Miss Samantha Ogletree might buy a purse that would hide her valuables before she moved from small-town Georgia to the big city, so the compartment is a risk I'm willing to take. If things change and we can afford the risk of giving you a weapon, you'll have a place to stow it. Or if you need to hide documents or photographs or film or any number of other things, you'll have a place to do that."

"But no gun."

"Not for now."

As he opened the file that Clarissa had brought, he spread papers and photographs across his desk and said, "Thanks to Jerry, you learned one last lesson today before I have to send you out into the cruel world sooner than I'd like. Can you tell me what this last lesson is?"

"Never let my guard down?"

"That's a good lesson, but it's not the one I want."

"Keep my eyes peeled? Watch my back? Um…"

He cut her off.

"Here's the lesson you should take from this day: trust no one."

———

Paul sat at his desk, alone, looking at the door to his temporary office. Everything in his life was temporary these days.

Justine had just passed through that door as she left him, and the damnable red mark on her back was the last he'd seen of her. The doorknob must still be warm from the touch of her hand.

He had been cruel today, but the world was cruel. He knew no other way to protect her. And he wanted very much to protect her.

He had planned to tuck Justine into a job cracking codes at Arlington Hall, where she could have spent her days solving the kind of puzzles that saved lives without putting her own life at risk. But the war had other plans, it seemed. If putting Justine in danger would help bring peace quickly, then that's what he must do, because he was hearing whispers about a weapon that must never be used. It was hard to believe that there were people willing to deploy a bomb that might set the whole atmosphere aflame, but there were. He knew them.

If it was within his power to help end the war before it came to that, then he had to try. And he had to let Justine try.

Then, when the war machines had gone silent, he could look inside himself to see if he had anything tender and human left to give her. He thought that he might.

Would she still want him when she learned about the things the war had made him do? That was a different matter.

Chapter 3

Justine missed her coveralls and their loose-fitting comfort. Instead, she wore a brown skirted suit, tweedy and sedately tailored, and her equally sedate black dress shoes hurt her feet. Over the suit, she wore a heavy black wool coat. Beneath it, she wore a girdle. The girdle hurt everything between her rib cage and her knees, but its attached garters kept her heavy nylon stockings up, so she supposed that the girdle was necessary. None of these clothes were hers.

A suitcase had been waiting for her when she got home after her encounter with Paul, just as he'd promised. It had been packed full of drab business wear, because her new job required her to dress like this six days a week. Justine firmly believed that nobody should ever have to ride a bus with a girdle's waistband cutting her in two, but the rest of the world disagreed.

Paul swore that the job was real this time. This meant that the danger was real, too. She had memorized the faces of everybody on the bus, hoping that she'd recognize an adversary if one appeared. All of the passengers were women and all of them were dressed as she was. This meant that the bus was crammed full of girdle-wearing people in mild but constant physical misery.

Justine's hair swung into her face when the bus driver slammed on the brakes, and even its strands were disorienting. She'd done as she was told, bleaching her curls to a pale blond in the hours while she waited for the car that would take her to a new life. She was wearing a pair of spectacles that she'd found in the mysterious suitcase, plain glass disks in silver-wire frames that were painfully unflattering. Paul didn't want a hint of her red hair to remain, as he thought it was too easily recognized, so her eyebrows, too, were bleached pale. While she'd waited for the peroxide to lift the natural pigments from her hair, she had plucked her brows into an unfamiliar arch, as instructed. That morning, she had applied dark eyebrow powder to their bleached strands, just as a natural platinum blond would have done. Trying to bleach her reddish-blond lashes might have left Paul with a sightless agent, so she had coated them with dark mascara. Pancake makeup covered her freckles. If she were to stumble across a mirror unexpectedly, she wouldn't know her own reflection.

When the bus groaned to a stop outside Arlington Hall, Justine rose along with everyone else. Her chunky-heeled dress shoes clattered on the metal treads of the bus stairs, and the sound made Justine feel conspicuous. She fervently did not want to be conspicuous. None of the women had given her a second glance, and neither had the bus driver, so she decided to consider her disguise a success.

Arlington Hall, located in Arlington, Virginia, was far more attractive than the office buildings in Washington, DC. Older government structures in the city, like Paul's dark and vaguely Gothic-looking office building, were bursting with employees hired to support the war effort. Rickety newer office buildings, thrown together so that new employees wouldn't have to work outside in the rain, were crowded beside them. Three years of war had stressed the nation's infrastructure to its breaking point.

By contrast, Arlington Hall looked neither Gothic nor rickety. It looked like what it was, a former women's college commandeered by the government through the War Powers Act, now encircled with a perimeter fence that clashed with its inviting, collegial feel. The Headquarters Building, the focal point of its tree-shaded campus, was a broad brick-fronted structure with monumental Ionic columns and a roof full of dormers. Justine reported to one of the guard stations at its gate, making sure to choose the line that led to a broad-shouldered man with an engaging grin and a wheelchair that was just like Jerry's.

This was because he *was* Jerry.

She waited her turn and then she gave Jerry a shy nod. He had more practice in working undercover than Justine did, so he looked at her without the slightest glimmer of recognition. Deep in her Miss Ogletree persona, she gave him the most demure glance possible.

According to Miss Ogletree's fictional biography, she was still a little young to be considered a spinster, but she was so withdrawn that she would probably achieve that status in a few years. Until she'd gotten on the train for Washington, she'd lived with her parents and taught drawing lessons for her pin money. She had never once been alone with a man. Justine decided that the best way to physically embody Miss Ogletree was to look at her toes as much as possible.

She was rather proud of the tremulous stammer she used to address Jerry, who looked very handsome and very male in his work clothes, heavy black coat, and gray homburg hat.

She handed him the folded piece of paper that bore official

confirmation of her work assignment. "Sir? Ex—excuse me, sir? I'm supposed to start work in just a few minutes, and I don't want to be late. Can you point me in the right direction?"

There was no way that Miss Samantha Ogletree would have been able to hold Jerry's gaze, so Justine didn't. Instead, she peered into her handbag for her fake identification papers. Before she could retrieve them, a voice rose above the sounds of a busload of women reporting for work. It trembled in a different way from the stammering quaver that Justine was faking. It trembled from age. It was an old man's voice calling out a name that made Justine's heart freeze.

The name wasn't Samantha, and it wasn't Justine, but it also wasn't a name that she could ignore.

"Isabel!" cried the old man. "Isabel Byrne!"

Her head rose reflexively and turned in his direction. She couldn't have kept her eyes on her toes if she'd tried, not with that name echoing in her ears. For just an instant, she expected to hear a familiar voice calling out to answer him. It was her mother's voice, and she hadn't heard it in three years. Her mother was dead, and Justine would never hear her voice again.

A rotund man zigzagged through the crowd, somehow managing to pay each and every person in his path an Old World gesture of respect.

"Excuse me, madam," he said, nodding at one woman. Justine's ear caught the faintest possible accent in the way he pronounced "madam." Was it German?

"I beg your pardon," he asked of the next person.

"Excuse me. I must see my friend," he murmured to another with a tiny bow.

Finally, he drew close enough to take both Justine's hands in his. He stood there, beaming, as she tried to figure out what was happening.

"Isabel," he said again. Then his brow furrowed. "But...I forgot. I forgot that you're dead."

He put his hand to his forehead in a way that suggested age or fatigue or illness. Then he brightened.

"My apologies," he said, inclining his head in another small bow. "You cannot be Isabel. You are far too young, and now I remember that she is..." His voice cracked. "My dear friends Isabel and Gerard are no longer with us."

The old man's face was very near hers now. It was chubby and pink, framed by thin white hair and a thicker white goatee and mustache. As she watched, his pale blue eyes brightened, and his thin lips twisted into a smile. "But something of Isabel and Gerard is here. You're Justine! Look at you! You could be no one else. My, how you look like your dear mother. And like your father, too, a bit."

Justine suppressed a shiver when she realized that the man was right. Her mother's hair had been blond, and she'd worn silver-rimmed glasses until her sight was fully gone. She had an urge to run find a mirror, so she could see what her mother had looked like before she knew her.

The hands gripped hers and shook them. "I'm sorry for my confusion. It happens to people of my age now and again. Time grows twisted when you have seen a great deal of it. I know who you are now. You are Justine Byrne. And I must reintroduce myself to you. I am Karl Becker. I knew you when you were small, so very small, but it is not possible that you remember. I knew your parents when they were studying in Chicago, and they often came back to visit after they moved to New Orleans."

He shook her hands again, hard. "Oh, my dear. When I asked for an assistant, I had no idea that I would receive one so capable."

Justine knew full well that she was not reporting to a job

assisting Karl Becker with whatever he did. She was to work for Dr. Edison van Dorn in the Signal Security Agency's German section. She was to pretend to be a not-terribly-bright clerical worker so uninteresting that people forgot she was there while they had conversations in a language that they thought she didn't know.

This encounter with Karl meant that she had already failed. They were surrounded by people listening in on their conversation, and he'd just announced that she wasn't Samantha Ogletree right in front of them. She hadn't yet admitted that anything he was saying was correct, but any of these people could be an enemy agent on the lookout for people who weren't who they said they were. She knew for a fact that there was at least one agent embedded at Arlington Hall. It was why she'd gotten this assignment in the first place.

Becker cupped her chin. "I could ask for no better assistant. No child of your parents...no daughter of your mother...could fail to be capable. When you were eight years old, you spoke better German than anyone who works for me now. We carried on extensive conversations about your math homework, all of them in my native tongue. My goodness, how I've needed you here. It seems that I merely had to wait for you to grow up."

And now everyone within the sound of his voice knew that this man was absolutely sure that she spoke German. She needed to abort this mission.

Justine mentally reviewed the contents of her purse. She had nothing to identify herself as Justine Byrne, the name that Karl Becker had just announced to everyone within earshot. Everything she owned, including the papers that confirmed her true identity, was locked up somewhere. It seemed too risky to get through the gate by flashing Samantha Ogletree's driver's license at Jerry and hoping nobody was standing close enough to notice that Karl Becker was calling her by a different name. Doing so would compromise Jerry's cover, as well as hers.

There was only one thing to do. She pulled her hands out of Karl Becker's grip and used one of them to grope around in the ugly handbag she wore over one arm. Turning to face Jerry, she said, "Oh, no. I left my identification at home, so you won't be able to let me pass. I'm so embarrassed. Can you send word to the man I was to meet? Tell him that I'm terribly sorry and that I'll be here tomorrow."

Jerry was still holding the folded paper she'd handed him. He opened it, gave it a quick glance, and quickly folded it again, too quickly for anyone to see that the name on it was Samantha Ogletree, not Justine Byrne. He handed it back to her and she stuffed it deep in her handbag.

Turning back to Becker, she arranged her face in an apologetic expression. "I'm very sorry. I've made a foolish mistake, and I have to go home. I really must catch the bus before it leaves."

Karl Becker was not so easily thwarted.

"Nonsense. I know who you are." He leaned in Jerry's direction, tapping the badge pinned to his lapel. "Young man, the color code on this little badge tells anyone who can see it that I am to be trusted with sensitive information at the very highest level. My judgment can certainly be trusted where this woman is concerned. Take down my name so that you can defend yourself if you're questioned about letting her pass."

He turned to Justine. "To be frank, I know you far better than I know this young man demanding your papers. I've never seen him before. Of the two of you, you are the one I'd trust with our country's secrets."

Justine was grateful that Becker had brought Jerry into the conversation. It gave her an excuse to look at him. Maybe he could somehow signal to her what she should do.

"Young man," Becker said to Jerry, "I must familiarize my new assistant with her job, while I have the very pleasant experience of hearing what she's been doing since she last visited me in Chicago at the tender age of eight. I can vouch for her."

Jerry barely looked at Justine. He certainly didn't do anything overt, like blink a message in Morse code. Yet she somehow felt that he wanted her to go with Becker. It was entirely probable that this strange old man was bluffing when he claimed the ability to admit her into a bastion of utter secrecy just on his word, but Jerry was the gatekeeper. He gave her a businesslike nod.

Karl made a little shooing gesture and said, "Go ahead, my dear." Together, they swept through the gate.

Justine reflected that simply gaining entry to Arlington Hall was probably the most important part of her mission. If this was so, then she was going to deny that she had failed, just because her cover as Miss Samantha Ogletree was well and truly blown. She was going to claim her first success as an undercover agent.

Chapter 4

Even Karl Becker's powers were not infinite. He was forced to cool his heels while Justine sat through an orientation lecture that concluded with a loyalty oath and a secrecy pledge. The lecture included an assurance that blabbing secrets would bring prison or execution, but this wasn't as terrifying as it might have been. Justine had signed pretty much the same paperwork for Paul, so her life was already on the line. Once she was issued her temporary badge, Karl turned into the best tour guide a spy ever had.

He took Justine through every cranny of the Headquarters Building that was open to someone with her low-to-nonexistent level of access to war secrets, plus a few that probably weren't. The graceful old academic building boasted elegant details like a grand staircase and French doors that were incongruous in rooms crammed full of government-issue office furniture. Moving swiftly for his age, Karl swept past the people sitting at all those desks. Up the staircase they went. Then they passed through warrens of hallways as she clattered along behind him in her awkward heels.

Karl talked a lot, but he was vague about what was being done in the rooms that lined those hallways. "Oh, my dear, you will love this work. You will use every bit of your mathematics, your logic, your language...your mind. And all for the best of causes. If they were alive, your parents would be right here working beside us."

Justine was surprised when he led her back down the stairs. She'd presumed that Karl would end his tour at the office where he thought she would be working as his assistant. Instead, he led her out the back door where she was faced with the true scope of the Army's operation at Arlington Hall. The trees and shrubs of the old college campus lay before her, but the landscape was scarred by two huge structures that dwarfed the Headquarters Building she'd just explored with Karl. They looked as new as the rickety buildings clogging downtown Washington.

"Building A," he said, gesturing grandly with one hand. "And Building B."

Building A and Building B were each twice as long as the Headquarters Building that had seemed so large to Justine and, as they rounded the corner of Building A, she saw that each of them had a series of wings protruding from the back side like teeth on a comb or like the letter E with a few extra crossbars. Apparently, it took a lot of people to break codes.

Looking at the tremendous structures, she found herself hoping that Paul would find a way to keep her at Arlington Hall. The scope of the operation there excited her.

Karl ushered her into Building B and said, "Here is your home away from home. It lacks the charm of the lovely old Headquarters Building, but we will be sharing our space with fewer mice."

———

The chrome percolator gleamed like a Byzantine icon. It sat on a small metal table in Justine's new office, which served as an anteroom for Karl's larger office. Her desk was dead center in the room, in front of his office door and facing two chairs. Karl's guests could wait for him in relative comfort in those chairs, but they couldn't get to him without going through Justine first. And they couldn't even get to her without knocking and waiting for her to open the locked door. Karl's world was set up for secrecy.

The first and most critical of her job responsibilities, according to Karl, was keeping him constantly supplied with hot coffee. This could have been mildly annoying, as Justine did not think of herself as a servant, but she was starting to think like an undercover agent. The coffee smelled like an opportunity. (It also smelled delicious.)

In a time of war-driven scarcity, it seemed to Justine that it might be possible to bluff her way into offices that she wasn't cleared to enter, simply by showing up at the door with a cup of coffee and a smile. The fact that Karl seemed to have access to all the coffee he could drink suggested to her that he held an exalted status within the Signal Security Agency or that he was adept at black market negotiations. Or both.

Even better, Karl had made it clear that she should help herself to the coffee and to the sugar that he hid in the bottom drawer of the filing cabinet to the right of the percolator. Justine hadn't had easy access to coffee or sugar since her parents had died. Whoever Karl's sources were, she was grateful to them.

Actually, she was ecstatically grateful, as she sat with her new boss at the conference table in his office, each sipping from a full, steamy cup.

"All operations at Arlington Hall that involve messages originally written in European languages are under my supervision, as are certain operations involving northern African and western Asian languages," Karl said. "Our listening stations relay messages to us over teletype, telegraph, and air mail. Some of them are hand-delivered by agents who have trudged over the Pyrenees to get information out of occupied France. Some have come by homing pigeon."

"Really? Pigeons?"

"Really. Just because modern communication technologies like radio and telephones and telegraphs exist, it doesn't mean that our troops and undercover agents have access to them in a war zone. We don't care how a message arrives, although its mode of delivery is one source of information about its sender, its receiver, and their purposes...which may not be the same as the purposes implied in the message. Wars are won with information. Moving it from people who have it to people who need it, while keeping it out of the hands of the enemy is, quite literally, what the SSA does. 'Signal' and 'security' are right there in our name."

"I understand."

"I'm sure you do." He gave her a fond smile. "Before being relayed here, the messages we work with have, of course, been encrypted by the people on our side who intercepted them, in case they are intercepted by the enemy on their way to us. Thus, I have people—rooms full of people—whose entire job is to strip incoming messages of our own encryption. Others do traffic analysis, trying to learn everything possible about the message itself from logistical details like who sent the message and from where and to whom and when. You'd be surprised at what we can infer from this information."

Justine had heard teletype machines chattering, which was a kind of sensory evidence of the work Karl described. She'd also heard other unidentifiable machinery clicking and humming, so she suspected that Karl's description of Building B operations omitted some kind of machinery that was being used to break codes by brute force, trying endless possible solutions until something finally worked. Building B wasn't loud in the way a newspaper newsroom was loud, with dozens of typewriter keys striking at any one time, but there was a constant hum of activity. The sounds of machines, voices, ventilation fans, and footsteps never truly ebbed.

"Then, of course, incoming messages must be stripped of the enemy's decryption, which is obviously our biggest challenge. A few of the enemy's encryption systems still have not yielded to my people's efforts. We have some of the finest minds in the world trying to crack them, but the work is—it is frustrating. Imagine spending years bashing your brain against a problem that may not be solvable."

"That would break a person."

"Indeed. Part of my job is to take care of my people. Even the finest mind can crack, and the people who work for me are not replaceable."

She noticed that he was looking at his coffee, not her. Then she realized that Karl rarely looked at her directly. He looked at her hairline or at whatever was keeping his hands busy, but he didn't like to look her in the eyes.

"Two of my men—" He picked up a spoon and stirred his coffee for no reason, the metal spoon clinking against the china cup. "The work was too much for them and they cracked. They doubted their ability to do the job and they allowed themselves to think of the people who are dying every day, all around the world. They allowed themselves the luxury of taking the blame for those deaths. Now, those two men are convalescing, and they may never be themselves again. I visit them whenever I can get a day away from this all-consuming job. Take care, Justine. Take care of your mind."

He laid the spoon on his saucer and shook himself. "Where

was I? Oh, yes. Once decrypted, the messages are still usually in German, so they must be translated into English. I play a key role at this stage, as a native speaker. If there is any nuance to be gleaned from the way a Nazi phrased his German—" He gave her a sharp look, then quickly looked away. "Or hers. There are, of course, female Nazis. If there is a drop of nuance to be squeezed from the way a message is phrased, it is my job to recover that drop."

"That's a lot of work and a lot of people for you to—"

"I was not finished."

As an apology for interrupting him, Justine said, "May I freshen your coffee?"

"Thank you, no. I prefer to drain the dregs and then refill. Otherwise, I have coffee that has been 'freshened,' but my coffee is never fresh."

"Except for the first cup."

"Indeed. Your mind is as precise as your mother's." He lifted a cup in tribute to something. Justine? Her mother? Precision? Justine didn't know, so she took a risk and raised her cup, too.

"But back to my fiefdom. From time to time, the Allies have a need to confuse an adversary. For example, this happened prior to an event in June."

D-Day.

"Do you see how useful it might be to send out all the messages that would be sent before an assault on...say...Calais, even though you have no intention to attack Calais? Perhaps you have designs on Omaha Beach, instead."

"I absolutely do. You would have to be sure that your real messages were completely unbreakable. Then you would have to send a whole lot of fake messages about ships that didn't exist, messages that pretended to send those fake ships to Calais. The fake messages would need to be coded, so that your motives weren't completely obvious, but they would be in codes that you knew the enemy had broken. But the enemy would have to be ignorant of the fact that you knew that they'd broken their codes. And all of your messages couldn't be in the broken codes. That, too, would be too obvious."

Justine paused. She could see that even a seemingly casual conversation among Arlington Hall workers could be very complex indeed.

"It would be a tremendous undertaking to create messages that faked an invasion the size of the assault on the beaches at Normandy." She looked around the room. "Is that what all the maps are for?"

All four walls of Karl's office were papered with maps of Europe, western Asia, the Mediterranean, the north Atlantic, and north Africa. Each map was studded with multicolored pushpins. The walls of her own office, too, were lined with maps.

His eyes darted from one to another. "Some of those pins mark real ships and real soldiers and real battles. Real lives. Some of them mark figments of the imaginations of the Supreme Headquarters Allied Expeditionary Force. I know which are which but, my darling, I will never tell you."

———

The sun was setting, the winter air was cold, and Justine was almost asleep on her feet when the bus dumped her at her new home. Her day at Arlington Hall would have been exhausting, even if she'd truly been nothing other than a brand-new secretarial assistant. The crowded, jostling bus ride. The long lines for everything—the bus to work, the security checkpoint to enter the building, the bathroom, the Caféteria, the bus home—these things would have worn her out all by themselves, but then there was Karl's enthusiastic, lengthy tour and the intense orientation speech. Piling those things on top of the mental strain of working undercover had taken her past the brink of exhaustion.

Even worse, she didn't even know whether she'd wasted all the effort it had taken her to get through the day. If Paul couldn't find a way to get her out of Karl's clutches and into the office of Edison van Dorn, her mission had failed on its very first day.

Justine stood where the bus had left her, swaying with fatigue. It had been less than twenty-four hours since Paul had sent a taxi to pick her up from the room she'd been renting near the naval yard. Justine, her newly bleached hair, and her prepacked suitcase had arrived at Arlington Farms, her new home, with no time to explore it.

Arlington Farms was a dormitory complex that had been thrown together for female war workers in response to a growing housing crisis. It was a separate entity from her workplace at Arlington Hall, and they were several miles apart. This made Justine glad for the buses running constantly back and forth.

A cab had dropped her off at her dormitory long after dark the night before, and Justine had fallen exhausted into her narrow twin bed without taking any time to look around. Now, looking at the sprawling campus dotted with multi-winged dorms, she wasn't even sure she could remember how to find her room. She knew it was at the end of a second-floor hall, and the fob of her room key told her that the room number was 223, but the name of the dormitory was escaping her.

Kansas Hall. She thought it was Kansas Hall.

Yes, that was probably right. She knew it was named after a state she'd never visited. Someday, she'd go to Kansas. Justine wanted to see the world, someday.

At the moment, though, she just needed to find Kansas Hall. Surveying the featureless modern buildings in front of her, she mumbled, "Surely I can find someone who'll point me at Kansas Hall."

A friendly woman in a WAVES uniform heard her talking to herself and helped her out. After thanking her, Justine stumbled into Kansas Hall, through its lobby, past a lively lounge full of dancing women and sailors, up the stairs, and down a residential hall lined with rooms where women were listening to the radio and chatting. She was steps from her own room with her key in her hand when she noticed something strange.

Her door was open. She could see the silhouette of a woman on the other side, moving around the room. She checked the room number on her key fob again. Yes, she was in the right place.

Was an enemy agent lying in wait for her? That made no sense. If this woman had bad intentions, wouldn't she be waiting in the dark behind a closed door? Also, wouldn't she lie in wait someplace where there weren't dozens—hundreds?—of people nearby? All Justine needed to do to get help was scream.

Justine flattened herself against the wall of the hallway and peeked around the doorjamb. The woman, standing with her back to the door, wasn't the only surprise waiting for Justine. There was a second bed in her room that hadn't been there before.

A roommate? Paul had specifically said she'd have a private room for security reasons. A roommate might notice something strange about her possessions or her behavior.

Heck. A roommate might hear her talking in her sleep. This wasn't good.

She left her clinging-to-the-wall position, which admittedly wasn't the best way to blend into a cohort of carefree young women. Easing her hand into her purse, she wrapped her fingers around the Stinger, wondering if she was about to expend her one bullet and end her first undercover assignment with a bang. Faking a relaxed stroll, she entered the room.

"Are you my new roommate?" she asked, trying to strike a tone that said she was surprised to see the woman but happy to have somebody to share expenses. "I didn't know I was getting one, but it will be nice to have some company."

Then the woman turned around and said, "Hey, roomie," and Justine's new spy skills failed her.

She dropped her handbag, which fortunately did not cause the jostled Stinger to release its bullet, and reached up to fling her arms around her best friend Georgette's neck.

"I didn't know you were coming!" she whispered, so that nobody passing in the hallway would hear. "I have so much to tell you."

Everything about Georgette, from her neat brunette chignon to her rural Louisiana accent to the kind way she bent to smile at Justine, was comforting.

She gave Justine a squeeze and said, "Glad to see you survived your first day at work. And...everything." She rumpled Justine's newly blond curls and said, "Nice hair. Bet that took some doin'. Come over here and hold the other end of this here curtain rod."

Justine helped Georgette lift the rod onto its brackets, then they stood back to admire the pink-flowered chintz curtain.

"I just finished making it. I thought it might make my room a little more homey. When I got word that I was gonna have to move—" She leaned down and whispered in Justine's ear. "This morning. On two hours' notice. Can you believe the nerve of that man?" Then she raised her voice to a normal level and said, "Well, I took a risk that the curtain would fit, and it does. Mostly. I put too much work into that thing to leave it or throw it away."

Justine figured that Georgette meant Paul when she said "that man," but she was also pretty sure that Georgette didn't know his real name.

"Let's go for a walk," Georgette said, still fondling the chintz curtain.

Justine put on her you've-got-to-be-kidding-me face, but Georgette kept talking.

"It's quiet out there, so we can...um...get to know each other. Real quiet. Nobody closes their doors on this hall, 'cause the housemother's got the heat cranked up so high that we gotta let the air circulate. And the walls are so thin that you can hear the women in the next room chew their popcorn. That makes it real hard for us to chat."

Justine knew that Georgette meant that it wasn't safe for them to speak freely in the dorm, but she said, "Yeah, it would be hard to hear each other over the noise of all those radios."

"Yep. So let's go."

So Georgette had something to say that required privacy. Justine expelled a couple of lungs full of air, as if breathing loudly would wake her up. Maybe she could stay on her feet long enough to hear whatever it was that Georgette had to say.

"Go wash your face. That'll perk you up. And for heaven's sake, get out of them stiff clothes and high-heeled pumps. Put on something you can breathe in and some flat-soled shoes. Let's take a walk."

———

Jazz seeped out of Kansas Hall's lounge as Georgette and Justine walked past. The room was packed with men in uniform visiting the women who lived there, and it would be packed with men in uniform until the housemother kicked them out at eleven. They were enjoying the music, but they were enjoying the female company more.

Unlike their dorm mates, Georgette and Justine were not

dressed to attract admirers. They had both lived their entire lives in southern Louisiana, so they had prepared for a walk on a Virginia winter evening by bundling themselves into coats, hats, and boots. They smiled and waved at the partiers as they walked out of the building.

"You two think you'll be warm enough out there?" cooed a dark-haired woman nestled under one GI's arm as she shared a cigarette with another. "You better go back upstairs and get a couple more coats." The women sitting around her giggled.

"Cut it out, Thelma," said a woman whose fresh face, bobby socks, red-gold braids, and saddle shoes made her look younger than anybody else in the room. "Why do you care what they wear?"

Justine smiled at the bobby-soxer, and said, "Thank you."

"Don't mention it," she said, taking a sip of her Coke.

Justine and Georgette slipped out onto the silent, cold campus of Arlington Farms. Once they passed out of the puddle of light around the single fixture mounted above Kansas Hall's door, visibility plunged. A little light leaked out of the dormitories' windows, but it receded as they moved away. The new moon offered almost no light to keep them from stumbling off the unlit sidewalks circling the dormitories' parking lots.

"I can't tell you how happy I am to see you. Nobody told me you'd be here," Justine said.

"Nobody knew it till today. Good thing Jerry thinks fast. And what's-his-name. He used to say his name was Charles, but I don't believe it."

His name is Paul, but he wasn't supposed to tell me that.

"Are you telling me that Jerry called him after Karl shouted out my real name for the whole world to hear?"

"Just as soon as you two were out of sight. They've decided to let that man Karl keep you as his assistant, 'cause you'll have access to more people and more files and more secrets thataway. But they still need somebody to do the job they sent you here to do."

Starlight glinted on Georgette's teeth, so Justine knew she was smiling.

"You?"

"Yep. From here on out, I'm Miss Samantha Ogletree, so don't forget that when you're with the women at Kansas Hall. Like that Thelma person." Georgette's voice sounded like she wanted to spit out the bad-tasting word "Thelma."

"But what about your own work? I thought you were going to be working in communications, talking on the radio to other Choctaw speakers."

"I've been trainin' to do that, and there's a radio setup at Arlington Hall where I can work if they need me. They call us code talkers. I hear tell that there's Navajo speakers in the Marines, a bunch of 'em, but there's also people who know Choctaw. In the last war, too." She lowered her voice as if the moon were listening. "The way I understand it, they assign the code talkers in battle zones in pairs. One to work the radio and one to talk. I told you how hard them recruiters worked to get all five of my brothers. That's two pairs of men ready and able to work together, plus one extra to receive their transmissions on land."

"But now Robbie's home, wounded."

"Yep, so now a stranger's took one of their places. Well, maybe not a stranger, but not a brother who'll take care of the others, no matter what. Sooner or later, I'll be the one that picks up their land transmissions. Maybe that means the other four will be out there in pairs, so's they can look after each other. Did I ever tell you how we found out Robbie was hurt?"

"A telegram from the government?"

Again, Georgette lowered her tone as if someone were there to hear her voice cutting through the cold air.

"We got a telegram later, but we already knew about Robbie when it came. When they left home, they made their own code. They gave theirselves numbers. Arthur was 'one,' Claude was 'two,' Hubert was 'three,' Joseph was 'four,' and Robbie was 'five.' Say Hubert was writing home. If he knew Arthur was safe or if he hadn't heard any word, he wouldn't use the number 'one' at all. If Arthur was hurt but alive, he'd find a way to work the number one into the letter. If Arthur was missing in action, he'd use it twice. If he was—"

Georgette couldn't say it.

Justine tried to help her out. "If the news was really bad?"

"Yeah. For that, he'd use the number 'one' three times. That ain't never happened, thank the Lord, but that code's how we found out Robbie was wounded. Hubert sent a letter that started out saying, 'We ate beans five times this week, and I think the whole ship is about to mutiny.' We got his letter three days before the government telegram got to us."

"That's a great code. The SSA should recruit your whole family."

"Well, they got one more of us now. Sorta. I guess I work for what's-his-name and I just pretend to work for the SSA, but the SSA sent me to their Vint Hill station to learn all about radio work. Vint Hill's where they intercept a lot of the messages that are eventually gonna come to Arlington Hall to get sorted out. It ain't fifty miles from here. When Jerry put out the word that you weren't gonna be able to be Miss Samantha Ogletree, I was in a car with a suitcase I never saw in my life before I knew what hit me. I didn't even get to say goodbye to the Vint Hill folks. But now we get to work together!"

"Again!" Justine reached out and squeezed Georgette's

mittened hand. "I'm so happy that you're here, and I'm so glad that I'm not being pulled off this job. How much did they tell you about our mission?"

"Enough to know that I'll be in a room all day with folks who are really high up in the code-crackin' world, and one of 'em is a traitor who'd kill me in a heartbeat if I let it slip who I am. I'm sure you can fill me in on the rest of it."

Justine tried to decide where to start. "Well, your new boss is Dr. Edison van Dorn. He's in charge of the German section, a group of geniuses who have a reputation for ignoring pesky things like rules."

"Isn't the SSA an Army outfit? The Army don't really cotton to folks who think for themselves."

"Oh, the people we're talking about are all civilians, because they're way too strange for the Army, or so I'm told. Now that the British are taking over more of the work on German messages, our government isn't going to let those valuable people sit there and twiddle their brainy thumbs. They've been shifted to some special projects, and rumor has it that there's a big one that's coming to a boil right now."

"Just in time for an enemy agent to join the party?"

"Exactly."

"So what's the party?"

The crunch of tires on new asphalt told them that a car was driving nearby. They fell silent, and Justine saw Georgette's eyes rake over the car, checking for open windows and listening ears.

When it passed, Georgette dove back into her questions without missing a beat.

"What is it about the German section that's so important?"

"They're writing all the messages for a major offensive on the Eastern Front. Battle plans. Supply requisitions. Transportation logistics. They're translating them into appropriate languages for our non-English-speaking Allies. Then they're encrypting them according to the latest information on which of our codes have been broken."

"That's an awful lot of information to put in the hands of just a few folks."

"Yeeessss…"

Georgette gave Justine a sharp look when she heard the drawn-out hiss at the end of her "Yes."

"Yes, but what? Is it suspicious that the government has trusted these particular folks with several whole countries' worth of secrets? The same folks you say ain't wrapped up too tight?"

"Suspicious? You could say that, especially since every last message they're writing—and sending, because the operation is underway—is a fake. And the people in the German section are using codes that we know the Germans have broken. Only the Germans don't know that we know they broke them."

"So what's the upshot, Miss Spy Lady?"

"We're trying to fool the enemy into wasting time, energy, and materials to get ready for an attack that will never come. In the meantime, they'll be distracted from anything else we have planned."

"Do they know that the messages are fake? The folks who work for Dr. van Dorn, I mean."

"We believe that Dr. van Dorn does. The people under him don't officially know, but they're smart. They may have figured it out."

Justine thought of the maps on Karl's office walls. He knew which messages were real and which weren't. Karl bore watching.

"It's probable that my new boss, Dr. Karl Becker, knows the entire plan, too. He tells me that the enemy has already started to act on the fake messages, just not in the way anybody expected. They've blown up a pontoon bridge that our side built on a river in Poland."

"We didn't expect that?" Georgette asked. "Then why send the messages?"

"Destroying the bridge tipped their hand about breaking our code for no benefit that we can see. They haven't lifted a finger to do anything else to head off that make-believe offensive. And that's all we know. At least, it's all I know."

Georgette nodded that she understood. "So tomorrow, I—and by 'I,' I mean 'Miss Samantha Ogletree'—will be in charge of all the scut work for the geniuses in the German section?"

"You got it. And I'll be free to walk in and out of the room where you're doing it, because my new boss supervises the whole section and a lot more."

"That new boss of yours must be the smartest genius of 'em all. If the government's put a German in charge of secret stuff, you know it's because they can't find nobody else who can do the job."

"He knew my parents in Chicago, so he's been in this country twenty years, at least. He may have even come over before the last war. I presume he's an American citizen by now."

Why was she defending Karl? Because her parents had liked him? She'd essentially just met him.

"That don't make him any less German. You know how people are about Germans—and Japanese people, too, and Italians—and the government's just a whole bunch of people."

Justine didn't know what to say.

"You know I'm right. This Karl person may be just as off-kilter as the rest of 'em. You be careful around that man."

Maybe it was because he connected her with her parents, but

Justine didn't want Karl to be an enemy spy. He was part of the past life that she'd lost, and she wanted to hang on to him. She fell silent and Georgette let her.

Their steps took them farther into the darkness, and Justine thought of the woman who had been strangled, maybe by her date and maybe by an enemy agent. Would the Stinger in Justine's purse be enough to keep the two of them safe?

"I don't know what I'm supposed to do if I get into trouble. All I've got is a single-shot gun disguised to look like an ink pen." Justine opened her purse and pointed at the Stinger in its special slot. "Did they give you one of these, too?"

Georgette nodded. "They told me that carrying a real gun would be way worse than being unarmed, 'cause the target might see it and know we were after him. Or her. I'm not sure how we'd hide a real gun inside our tight suits and flimsy dresses, anyway."

"Nor how you'd get to it if you needed it."

Georgette nodded. "But if the time came that we had to shoot somebody, we won't never have time to open up our handbags and haul out our weapons."

"It's worse than that. We can't carry our handbags everywhere we go. People would notice." Justine absently patted the outside of her purse, as if to remind herself that the Stinger was inside.

"I'm ahead of you, *chère*. I borrowed a sewing machine from the front desk and told the housemother I needed to alter that curtain I brought."

"I thought you were absurdly focused on hanging drapes."

Georgette punched her arm. "You're silly. That was my cover story. I'm a spy now, so I need those. That curtain gives me a story to tell if anybody wants to know what I'm sewing. Tonight, I'm gonna set pockets in the seams of our skirts, just big enough for an ink pen."

"Or for a gun that looks like an ink pen."

"Yep. And I'm putting pockets on both sides of those skirts. That way, we can keep our real pens and what-have-you in our right pockets where they're easy to get to—" She stopped herself. "You're right-handed?"

"Yes."

"Me, too. Keep your regular stuff in your right pocket and your explodey stuff in your left pocket, where you won't grab it on accident."

Justine felt marginally safer. They walked a few more steps, but then Georgette stopped dead in her tracks, flapping her hands with excitement.

"I forgot the best thing! I know where Gloria is."

Justine hadn't cried when Paul humiliated her with her failure. She hadn't shed tears of frustration when Karl blasted her mission all to hell by calling her by her real name. She hadn't even cried from happiness at seeing her best friend again. But hearing her beloved godmother's name brought the tears.

"I called her today, just before I left my last post to come here. Gloria's doin' good. The government built her a fancy new lab. She's happy. First chance we get, I'm taking you to see her." At the thought of seeing Gloria again, the hot tears spilled out onto Justine's cold cheeks.

———

They'd been walking away from Kansas Hall, but now it was time to go back. Justine turned around and Georgette followed her. They walked down a sidewalk paralleling the main road. It passed under broad-limbed trees that had been spared the ax when the government decided to build this complex to house its women. The trees cast a deep darkness that contrasted with the warmly lit windows of Arlington Farms's dormitories.

As they neared Kansas Hall, Justine saw that the front door was open just a crack, allowing a sliver of brightness to escape. A tall, sturdy figure stood silhouetted in that narrow band of light.

Someone was leaning out the door.

It was their friend with the reddish-gold braids. "I'm glad you're okay," she said, opening the door wider to let them in. "I was worried. You may not have heard, but one of the residents here was murdered a few weeks ago. I knew her. She was sweet, too innocent to know that she shouldn't trust her safety to these guys." She waved a hand at the lobby behind her, crowded with young men talking to young women. "They come here to pick up a woman, any woman. Not a one of them gives a single damn about any of us. All they want is a good time with somebody they never hope to see again."

"Someone was murdered? We didn't know," Justine said, shocked at how easily she lied to this kind person. "Thank you for looking after us."

"When you were gone so long, I felt bad that I hadn't made sure you knew to be careful."

"We're okay, and now we know what to watch out for. Thank you," Georgette reached out to shake her hand "This is Justine Byrne, and I'm Samantha Ogletree."

The young woman took Georgette's hand. "I'm Sally Tompkins. Welcome to Arlington Farms."

She turned to walk back to her seat in the lounge, then she paused in mid-step.

"Are you here to work at Arlington Hall?"

Both women nodded.

"Both of us are fresh off the bus," Georgette said. "I came up from Georgia, and she's come all the way from New Orleans. Since this is our new home, we figured we'd go outside and look around while we got to know each other."

"A lot of Arlington Hall workers live here, especially women from out of town. It's hard to find a place to live in Arlington—anywhere around Washington, really—but we've got room here. And there's more coming. They've got a few wings of Oklahoma Hall shut down, just so they can turn a bunch of single rooms into double rooms."

"Those rooms must've started out smaller than ours here in Kansas Hall," Justine said. "Somebody moved an extra bed in our room this afternoon and abracadabra! We have a double room."

"The government's doubling folks up in these dorms any which way it can," Sally said. "And that'll double the number of people who can be trundled a few miles down the road and put in Arlington Hall jobs. The government runs a special bus for us, but you know that. I saw you on it today." She nodded at Justine. "Everything's better when it's easy to get to your job. Anyway, I think you'll both like your work at Arlington Hall. The work is interesting, and it makes you feel like you're part of a bigger purpose."

Sally turned away again. Her necklaces, three heart-shaped lockets on three chains, swung with the motion. As she walked, her saddle shoes tapped on the floor.

Over her shoulder, so softly that Justine could barely hear her, Sally said, "Be careful, you two. Okay?"

———

Justine and Samantha seemed nice.

Sally Tompkins didn't trust them as far as she could throw them.

Sally was paid to keep secrets, on pain of death, and there were people who would pay her a hefty sum to reveal them. Her friend, Bettie, was dead, strangled, and she didn't know why. None of these things made her eager to trust Justine and Samantha, no matter how nice they seemed.

Being privy to the kind of military secrets that could make a girl rich or get a girl killed had made Sally wary. Jaded. Jaundiced. People would be surprised if they knew the thoughts that festered behind her open smile and beneath her glimmering hair.

Even Thelma didn't know all the things that went on in Sally's head, and they shared a room that was hardly ten feet on a side. When they were safely tucked in that room, it was impossible for them to be much more than an arm's-length apart, even when they were dreaming. This didn't mean that Sally was without her secrets.

Justine and Samantha, too, had secrets, or Sally had missed her guess.

For example, Samantha had claimed that they were fresh off the bus, but Sally had seen Justine roll up in a cab the night before. Maybe Samantha was talking about a bus that had brought Justine to a station in Washington, where she'd picked up the cab. Or maybe Samantha had come on a bus and was just presuming that Justine was as careful with her money. Or maybe "fresh off the bus" was just a figure of speech for her. Sally couldn't be sure that Samantha was lying, but Sally would not forget this moment of inconsistency between the woman's words and the facts as Sally knew them. Thus, Sally would be watching her, looking for a pattern.

Already, she sensed another inconsistency. Watching Samantha and Justine together, she would never have guessed that they had just met.

Again, she couldn't be sure that they were lying. Sally believed in love at first sight. She'd experienced it. It stood to reason that the same kind of compatibility could manifest as friendship at first sight.

Like the code breaker that she was, Sally understood the world as a series of patterns. Its reality was woven together like fabric, with a tight, even warp and weft. When she saw a thread out of place, Sally paid attention.

———

As Justine and Georgette got ready for bed, Justine said, "This feels strange. We're roommates again, but we can't keep up with your...you know..."

Silently, she mouthed "math lessons." Those lessons weren't exactly state secrets, but anyone passing down the hall might hear enough to know that Justine knew a lot more about mathematics than the typical secretarial assistant. It wasn't wise to let the women of Kansas Hall overhear anything that made Justine or Georgette seem unusual.

"For once," Georgette said, "I'm ahead of you, *chère*."

She brandished something wrapped in brown paper and tied with a string. It was rectangular, flat, and smaller than a piece of notebook paper. Handing it over, she said, "Open it!"

Justine untied the string and balled it up in her hand, too curious about Georgette's gift to put the string away properly and too frugal to let it drop to the floor. She carefully pulled the paper open without tearing it.

"A slate! I haven't seen one of those since I was a little girl. Gloria used one to help me learn my multiplication tables."

She admired the thin slab of black stone framed in red-painted wood. Two fabric loops were attached to its side, holding a sponge and a pencil made of slightly softer stone.

"We was still using them at school when I was comin' along. It saved on paper when we did things like practice our cursive or learn our times tables." Georgette ran a loving finger over the slate's wooden frame. "I found it in the service store downstairs. It was on the toy shelf."

"This will keep people from hearing anything we've got to say," Justine murmured. "And we should make a habit of playing the radio whenever we're here, just to help us keep our secrets to ourselves."

"Did you buy that radio?"

"The government bought it. All the rooms come with beds, nightstands, lamps, closets, and a radio. That's why it's so noisy in the hall."

Georgette turned on the radio and twiddled with the dial until she found a strong station. "That's real nice, and it'll make it hard for folks to listen to us."

Then she slid the pencil out of its loop and wrote,

ESPECIALLY WHEN WE'RE TALKING ABOUT SPY STUFF!

Then she dipped the sponge in the glass of water on her bedside table and wiped the slate clean.

Justine took the pencil and wrote,

SO DO YOU WANT TO KEEP DOING ALGEBRA TOGETHER?

She already knew the answer to this question. Georgette was determined to remedy her lack of a high school education, and Justine was happy to help.

Georgette nodded her head, then she flapped her hands like she couldn't spit out what was on her mind fast enough.

"You're way too excited for—" Justine mouthed "algebra."

"I'm excited because I've got a way to pay you back for it. I finally thought of something I know that you don't. And you're gonna want to learn it!"

"You're planning to teach me to sew?"

"No, silly. I mean…I can, if you want to learn. But I want to teach you…"

Her voice drifted off as she used the pencil to write:

CHOCTAW

Few people in the world spoke Choctaw. Justine loved the idea of learning something so old and so rare.

When Justine said, "Oh, please, teach me that," Georgette clasped her hands to her chest and jumped up and down like a ten-year-old on the first day of summer vacation.

"I'm gonna be the best teacher you ever had. Now, you gotta know that I only know how to talk it, so I may not spell the words right. But you'll get the gist."

Georgette carefully wrote three letters on the front of the slate:

OKA

She held the slate up so that Justine could study the word while she wrote something on the back.

"Ready?"

Justine nodded.

Georgette flipped the slate and showed Justine the other side:

WATER

"This is gonna work so good," she said. "I'll teach you a few words right now, then you give me some problems to do. Then we gotta sleep, because you know what we're gonna do tomorrow?"

Justine shook her head.

Georgette wiped the slate and wrote two words:

SPY STUFF

Chapter 5

"We've gotta find another way to talk in private. People are gonna think we're strange if we're all the time outside in December," Georgette said, taking long strides across the Kansas Hall parking lot. "I'm right proud of my idea to buy that slate, but it's little. We can only write so much secret stuff on it."

"At least it's warmer this morning." Justine hadn't even needed her coat. Somehow, though, she was pretty sure that Thelma would still have found something nasty to say about her outfit.

The sounds of hammers and power saws told her that construction workers had already begun their day somewhere on the large campus of government dormitories. She supposed that Arlington Farms wouldn't be finished until the war was finished.

She and Georgette were dressed in skirted suits that were almost identical, except for their color. Justine's suit was a dull blue tweed, and Georgette's was brown. They were hatless, which would have been impossible to imagine before the war made materials so hard to get, but more and more women were going without hats for exactly that reason.

"Good thing I can get hold of that sewing machine whenever I want it," Georgette muttered. "I've gotta do something about these clothes."

"At least you gave them pockets." Justine slapped her right hip, the one that was loaded with not-deadly writing utensils. "Our costumers didn't have time to shop for new wardrobes for both of us. Especially you. Whoever packed for you only had an hour or two to throw some clothes in a suitcase. It's a good thing they even fit."

"I ain't worried about fashion. I'm worried 'cause it looks like we both got dressed out of the same closet."

"Well, we did. More or less. But the people outfitting us must know what they're doing."

"I'm sure they do, sugar. But think about it. They packed your bag so you could dress like somebody's maiden aunt. Then they packed my bag, so I could come be the same person. That's why my clothes look like yours. But you're not supposed to be her now. You're supposed to be you."

"I wonder if it'll occur to somebody that they could just send me my own clothes. I may be on a secret mission, but I stopped being undercover yesterday."

"That would make a lot of sense, but they ain't done it yet. Look at us. Our suits are cut the same. We've got on the same black shoes and we've got the same black purse. Somebody's gonna notice, and we can't let that happen. We especially can't let 'em pay any extra attention to our purses, what with their secret compartments and all."

Justine saw the problem.

"I've got an idea!" Georgette did an abrupt U-turn, heading back toward Kansas Hall. "I can fix the purses right now, but I'll have to be quick about it. If we're not down here when the bus comes, it'll leave us, and then where will we be?"

Justine could hardly keep up with long-legged Georgette as they hustled back through the dormitory lobby and up the stairs to their room. As soon as the door shut, Georgette opened a drawer, pulling out a belt made of a length of gold-tone chain with a matching buckle. Retrieving a pair of scissors, a needle, and some thread from another drawer, she sat on her bed and spread her tools out beside her. First, she cut off her purse's dull silver clasp and unfastened the fittings that attached its black leather shoulder strap. Then, working in her lap, she cut apart the belt's chain and buckle and set to work switching them with the strap and clasp of her purse.

Tying off the thread that attached her purse to its new clasp, she said, "There. They look plenty different now, doncha think? You carry this one with the shiny chain for a strap, since I'm the one who's supposed to be dowdy. Tonight, I'll do something about our clothes, but right now we better hurry on down to the bus stop. In the meantime, you could look a little less dowdy if you unbuttoned the top button of that blouse."

———

Georgette stood beside Justine, vibrating with excitement. They were at Arlington Hall, waiting in line to be admitted to Building B, but it wasn't just any line. The person who would be checking their badges was Jerry, and Georgette was so excited to see him again that Justine wondered whether she should have packed smelling salts in her handbag's secret compartment. Or maybe a flask of whiskey.

They reached the front of the line, which cued Georgette and Jerry to do the easiest spy task ever done. Their goal? Convince the people around them that they liked each other.

Jerry looked over Justine's papers and said, "Dr. Becker left this for you."

He handed over a security badge. Justine studied the color-coded design signaling that she was authorized to enter Buildings A and B, certain parts of the administration building, and all public parts of the Arlington Hall complex. This was her passport to a successful mission. She gripped it hard.

Jerry gestured for her to pass through the gate. Then he turned his attention to Georgette's paperwork.

He handed her a sealed envelope. "Here are your instructions. You'll be working in Room 117, but you won't get the badge that'll get you in there until you've gone through orientation. So you'll want to join that group over there by that tree. Somebody will take you where you need to go."

Georgette took the envelope, flicked her eyes up at him, then looked at her toes as Justine had coached her to do, but she didn't move away. For Miss Samantha Ogletree, this was outrageously flirtatious behavior.

Her gaze might be lowered, but that didn't deter Jerry. He leaned down and made eye contact. "You're new here? Of course, you are." He flashed her a wide, boyish smile. "I'd remember a face like that."

Fully in character, Georgette giggled, but didn't speak.

Jerry studied her identification papers. "I see you're from Georgia. Do you like it here?"

The faux Miss Ogletree managed to utter a few words. "I do. It's a little cold, but that's not such a bad thing. I've never been many places outside of Georgia, so it's nice that Virginia is different from home."

"You'll have to let me show you around town." Then, as an afterthought, "And your friend, too, if she's interested."

Georgette blushed and mumbled something about not

having been properly introduced. Then she stopped herself. In a voice that was newly firm, she said, "There may be nobody here to properly introduce us, but I can do that for myself."

Georgette had told Justine that her embodiment of Miss Ogletree would use more of the formal grammar she'd learned in school, instead of her usual down-home way of speaking. It would have been a losing battle to try to cover her Southern accent, though, so she was just going to have to gamble that they were far enough from Georgia and Louisiana that the people around them wouldn't be able to hear the difference.

As far as Justine was concerned, Georgette was doing a great job of acting her role. Justine took a few steps away, as if to give her friend Samantha a chance to speak privately with an attractive man.

Georgette stuck out a hand and Jerry took it. "I'm Samantha. It's lovely to meet you."

"I'm Alan. I'll be right here at the beginning and end of your shift, every day. If you think you might want to go out with me sometime, just stand in my line and show me that pretty smile."

"I will," Georgette announced in a bold-for-Samantha voice. Then, as if she'd just remembered the things that mothers in Georgia told daughters about playing hard to get, she added, "I mean, I will if I decide that's what I want to do." Waving an embarrassed goodbye, she hurried to catch up with Justine.

And, just like that, they had a way to pass information back and forth with Paul. Jerry was going to come in very handy.

———

Justine left Georgette waiting for her orientation, then headed to her office. Karl had left her some filing to do, so she busied herself until she thought Georgette was fully oriented. Then she waited until Karl stepped out for a meeting and took the opportunity to use his coffeepot as a weapon for democracy. She fired up the percolator and happily sniffed the air while she waited for it to perk.

When the coffee was ready, she poured two cups, sugared them both well, and walked them down to Room 117. Her knock on the door was greeted by the bobby-soxer from Kansas Hall. Behind Sally Tompkins was a white-painted wooden screen that completely blocked the view of the room from anybody standing in the hall.

Justine's smile was genuine, because she honestly was glad to see Sally. She was nervous, and it felt good to see a familiar face. "Hi, Sally. Since I'm new here, I wanted to come say hello to Samantha's colleagues. Also, I brought her a cup of coffee." She held up one brimming cup. "The other one can be yours, if you want it."

"Hi, Justine. Thank you very much for the coffee, but we have a pot and I've already poured Samantha a cup."

Justine's surprise must have shown, because Sally said, "I've got to hand it to the Army. They find a way to get us coffee, which is a good thing, since they want us to work six days a week, every week that rolls. I say you should take those back to your office and drink them both yourself. Karl is notorious for working his assistants to death. He goes through two a year, at least. Karl has a good point, though. He manages to get sugar when nobody else can."

Sally examined Justine's badge. She must have been satisfied with the colors it displayed, because she stood aside and said, "Come on in and say hello to everybody."

Sally ushered her around the privacy screen into a large room full of people bent over their work. At the sight of Justine, every last person there turned the papers in front of them facedown.

The synchronized motion and the shushing of all those papers was unsettling, and so was the silence that fell as all of those faces turned expectantly toward hers.

Trying to figure out her next move, Justine looked around. A row of windows and several rows of pendant lights illuminated the space. A poster hung in a prominent position on the rear wall displayed a string of variations on a line from a poem Justine recognized from school, Elizabeth Barrett Browning's "Sonnet 43."

> *How do I love thee? Let me count the ways.*
> *Let me count the ways that I do love thee.*
> *How many ways do I love thee?*
> *Do I love thee? I shall count the ways.*
> *If you will let me, I will count the ways that I love thee.*

The poster's caption drove home its message:

There's always another way to say it.
Carelessness kills.

Justine knew enough about cryptanalysis to know that repetition gave an undue advantage to the adversary trying to crack your code. Something about the poster and its reminder to be, ever and always, meticulous made her think of Karl's friends who were recuperating from emotional breakdowns. She wasn't sure how long she'd hold up under the stress of knowing that repeating one word one too many times could result in a sunken ship and the loss of all the lives aboard. Even the loss of a single airplane and its one pilot was too much, and that loss could be caused by a misplaced "the."

No wonder the people in this room had a reputation for being eccentric.

Room 117 was long and narrow, and it was crammed with large wooden desks. A larger desk that clearly belonged to the person in charge sat at the end of the center aisle, facing the door. Georgette waved at her from the smaller assistant's desk beside it, which also faced the door. All of the other desks sat perpendicular to those, facing each other to form a center aisle. Some of the desks sported neatly squared piles of paperwork. Other desktops looked like somebody had backed up a garbage truck and dumped a heap of loose sheets on them.

None of the desktops showed much bare wood. These people were drowning in work. Room 117 was an endless sea of white, and all of that white was unblemished, because every last sheet of paper, whether stacked or lying in a heap, was facedown.

Sally's desk was the first on the right, near the door and near the coffeepot. As the youngest woman in the room, she was apparently expected to act as the hostess, answering the door and keeping the coffee drinkers happy, while also dealing with the stacks of work that were always waiting for her. She had swapped her saddle shoes for a pair of black kid Mary Janes, low-heeled and unadorned. Although Sally was dressed in a plain suit that looked an awful lot like Justine's, she still wore her unbusinesslike braids. They swung as she walked, detracting from her efforts to seem grown up. Sally looked like she should be sitting in a high school English class.

As Sally walked Justine toward Georgette's desk on the far wall, she introduced her to the people they passed along the way. Pointing to the desk across from hers, she said, "Here's Nora Moore. She lives with us in Kansas Hall. You'll have to come down to the music room and hear her play the piano sometime."

Nora, a dour woman of about forty with dark hair cut into a no-nonsense bob, nodded without making eye contact. Her skirted suit, gray and boxy, was equally no-nonsense, so plainly cut that it made Justine's look stylish. Her flat-soled shoes were unadorned. She wore no makeup and no jewelry. Even the pencil in her hand was painted black, instead of the more common yellow. In the middle of the monochromatic serious-ness that covered Nora and her desk was a single spot of color, a small bouquet of flowers. The blossoms, pink snapdragons and white carnations, spilled over the rim of a water-filled paper cup. A single stem of yellow daisies gave the arrangement a spot of sunshine. Justine couldn't decide if the flowers made Nora look more human, because she enjoyed something so pretty, or less human, because she looked so starkly plain in comparison.

As Justine walked, she wordlessly offered the cups in her hand to one person after another. No takers. Her plan to infiltrate Room 117 with Karl's coffee was going down in Hindenburg-like flames.

"You met my roommate, Thelma Dickens, at the dorm last night."

Thelma's dark hair was unfashionably straight, but it suited her by being somehow both severe and pretty. Her desk was next to Nora's and across from Sally's. She sat tapping the fingers of one hand on a facedown sheet of graph paper and smoking with the other. As Justine passed, Thelma waved the cigarette at her, but she said nothing.

"And here's Dr. Kowalski. He's from Poland." Sally gestured to a man on her right, across from Thelma. She looked like she wanted to say more, but she didn't.

"Please. Call me Patryk," he said with a smile that lingered in his dark eyes. She thought that he looked like a painting she'd once seen of the composer Chopin, only with lighter hair. But maybe she was imagining the resemblance because Chopin was the only Polish man she could think of at the moment.

"This man right next to Dr. Kowalski is Ike Grantham," Sally said, continuing to move away from the door. "Don't listen to anything he says. Everything's a joke with him."

Ike was tall and thin, with a long, narrow nose and long, narrow hands. He wore a black-and-red knit cap and a navy-blue peacoat, which made Justine stop to think, *Is it cold in here?* She didn't think so, and everybody else in the room was dressed normally. Maybe Ike was from someplace even hotter than her home in New Orleans. Or maybe he just lived up to Room 117's reputation for eccentricity.

"You cut me to the quick," he said, reaching out awkwardly to squeeze Sally's elbow. His left sleeve slipped higher on an arm that was noticeably thinner than the right one, revealing several long scars. "Everything I say to you is deadly serious, Sally. I'm patiently waiting for you to grow up, so I can make you Mrs. Grantham."

"Don't hold your breath," Sally said, but Justine saw her smile.

Ike turned to Justine. "Everybody knows that Sally lied about her age to get this job, but nobody says anything, because she's just so damn good. I'm quite serious. You should see her reading encrypted messages in real time, the way other people read English or music."

"Do go on," Sally said.

"Oh, hell. I just said a curse word in front of a little girl. There's another one. Shit."

Sally swatted him on the wrist that wasn't scarred and wasted, then she moved on.

They were nearing the end of the row of desks, but Sally couldn't make herself leave anybody out of the introductions.

"Beulah and Barbara have these last two desks across from Ike."

Justine was confused, because the desks were empty, but Sally pointed to two women standing behind them. Sally's gesture seemed to indicate that Beulah was the gray-haired one and Barbara was the brown-haired one. Beulah kept her eyes on her work as she murmured hello, but Barbara called out, "Nice to meet you," as her eyes watched Justine's every move.

"They're always on their feet, keeping track of projects we're all working on together, and their work keeps them side by side most of the time. They're busy bees, and their names start with *B*, so we call them The Bees."

The Bees were clipping slips of paper to long strings that were hung between two wooden posts, like they were hanging out stockings to dry. Similar clothesline-like apparatuses lined the room's walls, except for the area around the door, where visitors might see the symbols typed on the papers.

"And here's Samantha, but you know her. And our boss, Dr. Edison van Dorn, sits right here beside her. He runs everything in Room 117."

Paul had told Justine a lot about Dr. van Dorn, since the original plan was for her to be sitting at the desk next to him where Georgette was now installed. He was an Ivy League Latin professor and a champion bridge player. He spoke five modern languages and three dead ones, and he was particularly proud of his German.

He stood to shake her hand, his sandy head looming over hers. "You'll be working with Dr. Becker. That should be… interesting."

She knew enough about academics to know that this man probably bitterly resented Karl and his native fluency in German. Everything about Edison van Dorn reeked of pride and, perhaps, arrogance. Somehow, she thought that Georgette would find working for a man like this one to be…interesting.

Justine set down a cup of cooling coffee and accepted Dr. van Dorn's handshake, which was firm to the point of being painful.

Her father had taught her that a man who gripped her hand with all his strength was trying to make her flinch, so she honored her father's memory by refusing to do so.

Edison van Dorn had the pallid complexion that one would expect from a man of European descent who worked as an academic and spent his spare time at the bridge table. He was of average weight, but there was a softness to his body that did not extend to his watchful face. His hazel eyes were sharp, his lips were firm, and his hair was cut with precision. His suit fit as if it were made for him, and perhaps it had been. Its soft wool had an elegant drape. Either Dartmouth professors were paid a great deal, or Edison van Dorn came from money.

From Dr. van Dorn's end of the room, the volume of paper spread over every desk in Room 117 looked even more dramatic. The walls, too, were paper-white, and so were all the tense faces. This made her angry, but Paul had warned her to expect it.

"Everybody Arlington Hall employs isn't white, but the workers are segregated. The dormitories, too, are segregated. I know that this is not the way it was when we worked together at Higgins Industries, and I know that it will upset you, but I also know that you've seen segregation in action before. Black workers at Arlington Hall cover coded communications between businesses, and their work has proven so useful that they can't be ignored. Some of the higher-ups are…unhappy…about that."

The people in Room 117 were uniformly pale. The blinds were beige, and they were raised to let in the glaring winter sunlight. The floor was light tan. Staring into all that brightness made Justine feel snow-blind. The bright flowers on Nora's desk, Sally's strawberry-blond braids, and the red trim on Ike's knit cap were the only spots of color in the room. The two Bees were the only motion in sight.

Beulah was focused on sorting through a tray of paper slips, some of them hardly larger than confetti and each bearing a short sequence of letters. She methodically lifted one slip at a time and studied it, then either set it aside or clipped it to the clothesline-like apparatus. For a moment, Barbara left her to that work, fetching an armload of paper from a towering stack of paper in a corner of the room. Circulating among the workers, she added sheets to the stacks of work on each person's desk. Justine had hardly been in Room 117 for two minutes, but she'd already seen a courier arrive with another box filled with far more papers than Barbara had distributed. She was falling behind. They were all falling behind.

They would never catch up, not until the guns stopped booming. Something about the way Dr. van Dorn's cool eyes monitored his workers told her that he liked it that way, because it meant he was justified in pushing them hard, day in and day out. When the work crushed these people, would he, like Karl, visit them in the hospital? Somehow, she doubted it.

Was Karl any better than Dr. van Dorn was? He visited his people, but he'd been the one who gave them the work that crushed them.

Perhaps Dr. van Dorn's fierce arrogance wasn't a bad thing in wartime. The privacy screen, the poster with its dire warning, the furtive hands turning classified work facedown, the wary expressions of everyone she saw—these things signaled the importance of the work done under this man's supervision. They signaled the absolute need to keep the things that happened in this room out of the hands of the enemy.

So did the handgun lying on Dr. Edison van Dorn's desk in full view of everyone in Room 117.

Justine had to put one cup of cooling coffee on the hall floor to unlock her office. As she fumbled with the key, Karl opened the door from inside and let her in. He was clutching a thick sheaf of file folders to his chest, all of them overfull.

"Do I see that you are drinking coffee with both hands now? You are a woman after my own heart."

Justine laughed. "I wanted to give my roommate a cup. I guess I should have asked you first. Anyway, she already had one. Would you like this one? It's cooled off some, but I hate to waste it."

"You drink them both. Then you will be well-fortified. We have much to do. Come. Come in, so we can begin. I wish you to review these messages."

He thrust the sheaf of file folders at her.

She wanted to say, "Review them for what?" but she was afraid of sounding ignorant.

He anticipated her questions, which reassured her that maybe he hadn't expected her to walk in the door knowing everything about military decryption.

"These messages are regular, everyday traffic that span a single morning. One message might be a requisition for supplies. Another might be a response that gives the time of arrival for those supplies. Yet another might be a count of the wounded and dead. Most are in English, but some are in German, written by an enemy soldier who is trading information for his own safety. Some of them remain encrypted. Perhaps, in aggregate, these messages reflect the reality of the situation in that part of the European theatre at this moment. Or perhaps each of these messages is a fiction concocted to mislead the enemy."

"And you want me to…"

"This morning, you will read them all and write a summary of what they tell you about the situation in Europe now, today.

This afternoon, I will give you a second set of messages and ask you to do the same thing. Do not expect them to reflect the same reality. In fact, be assured that they will not. At the end of the day, I will challenge you to tell me which scenario is true."

She took the heavy stack of files, and he left her standing there, locking himself in his office. In his way, Karl was as guarded about his secrets as Dr. van Dorn was. She wondered whether he, too, kept a weapon handy to protect the two of them.

Chapter 6

The air coming out of the Cafétéria smelled good, but Justine was too far away to see the food giving off those savory aromas. Wartime Washington, DC seemed to be a city of queues.

She, Georgette, and Sally stood in a line that snaked outside the Cafétéria and into the bright, cool December air. Sally was easy to like, so Justine was happy she'd joined them, but her presence meant she had to remember that Georgette's name was now Samantha.

"Dr. van Dorn knows how long we'll be waiting for our food. It's like this every day," Sally said. "So we won't get in trouble for being late because he's fair, but he won't be happy about it. You can actually see his chest puffing up when he's choking back all the yelling that he wants to do."

"Have you been working here long?" Justine asked, knowing that the answer couldn't be a big number.

"I've been here since the Army took Arlington Hall over and moved its code crackers in. More than two years."

"What were you?" Georgette asked. "Twelve?"

"I bet I'm as old as you. I'm twenty-one."

"Yep," said Georgette. "So are we. Both of us."

Nora got in line behind them, saying, "You'll be glad for that fresh face when you're my age, Sally."

Georgette gave an embarrassed giggle suitable for Miss Samantha Ogletree and said, "Ike says he's waiting for you to grow up, Sally. Maybe you're old enough for him, after all."

"Don't you dare tell him how old I am. I've got him convinced that the SSA hired me out of my sophomore gym class, back when it was still the SIS, and I want him to go on thinking I'm seventeen. It keeps him from getting too handsy."

"Mum's the word," Georgette said. "Ike keeps the air in Room 117 so blue with his dirty jokes that I'm surprised he has time to do any work. It stands to reason that he'd be fresh, too. To tell you the truth, I'm not used to the way men around here put their hands on us. They don't do that back home in Summerville." She paused as if something had occurred to her. "I guess maybe they leave me alone at home because my daddy's the preacher."

That was exactly what the fictional Miss Ogletree would say when she realized that she'd moved into a whole new world. Justine mentally applauded Georgette's improvisational skill.

Sally shook her head. "They probably didn't act that way before they left their own homes, where their mother would hear about it if they were forward with the girl next door. Here? Nobody knows them here, so they think anything goes. Some of them think so, anyway. Also, some of them have strange ideas about women who have jobs and live on their own. The WACs tell me that people say terrible things to them about women in the military. They think the whole point of the WACs and WAVES is so they can...um...take care of the soldiers. You know...in every last way they want to be taken care of."

Georgette was such a good actress that she mustered up a

blank look, followed quickly by a blush. Justine tried and failed to will blood to her face, so she covered her mouth with her hand to mime shock.

"Don't get me wrong," Sally said. "Ike's a little forward and he's got a foul mouth, but I don't think he's a masher. Honestly, I think it's all a big act. Ike's just...well, a romance with him would be a big risk. He's had the kind of hard time that will haunt a man for the rest of his life. A girl would have to be sure he was what she wanted before she started something with him."

"I'm not sure what you mean." Justine chose her words carefully. "His arm. Was he wounded? I can see how that would be a concern."

Nora cut off Sally's response, blurting out, "Yes, he was wounded. He was badly wounded. Ike's a hero, if you ask me." Then she clammed up and wouldn't say any more.

As the Caféteria line inched forward, Nora looked at the concrete pavement in front of her, hesitated, took a medium-small step, and then took a medium-huge step. She wasn't obvious about it but, unless Justine missed her guess, Nora really didn't like to step on sidewalk cracks.

Sally didn't say any more about Ike and his wounds. The line moved forward again, taking them inside out of the cold. The Caféteria floor was covered with freshly waxed brown and beige linoleum tiles laid in a checkerboard pattern. The tiles measured less than a foot on each side, which made Justine fear for Nora's peace of mind. The cracks between the floor tiles were infinitesimal, barely cracks at all, but there were so many of them that Nora would be hard-pressed to avoid them all. The only way to do it would be to take mincing tiptoe steps that would attract the eyes of everybody in the room. She hoped Nora didn't hate cracks enough to let herself look that odd.

Fortunately, Nora didn't seem to be superstitious about

linoleum. She took normal steps and trod all over the infinitesimal cracks between the tiles.

The women fell silent as they neared the front of the food line, where they would have to be ready with a decision about what to order. Justine chose meat loaf, which came with sides of macaroni and cheese and canned green beans, with a thin slice of applesauce cake for dessert. She had no doubt that there was as much filler in the meat loaf—eggs, carrots, onions, breadcrumbs, oatmeal, chili sauce, and who knew what else—as there was beef, but it smelled good. She wasn't sure she remembered the taste of beef that hadn't been stretched.

"Can I substitute an apple for my cake?" Sally said to the Caféteria worker, who nodded and plunked it on her tray.

Sally slipped it in her purse and said to Justine and Georgette, "For later. The afternoons get long around here. You might want to consider keeping some sustenance in your desk drawer."

The group of four paid for their meals, then they paused to look for a place to sit. Or at least three of them did. Without saying goodbye, Nora walked alone to a table with a single open chair, dropped into it without acknowledging the people already sitting there, and dug into her chicken pot pie.

Sally shook her head. "That's just Nora. You have to get used to her. Anyway, let me tell you about Ike real quick. I didn't want to talk about him in front of Nora, because she has the hugest crush on him. It's so obvious, and it makes me embarrassed for her. So do her strange ways."

Nora, buttering her roll in her chair across the room, did not look embarrassed.

Sally spoke in a low voice that drew Justine and Georgette so close that their foreheads almost touched hers. "Ike was the sole survivor when his squad was ambushed in northern Africa. His left leg and arm were shattered. He'll never be able to return to battle. He'll always limp a little, and his arm will never be right, but he's alive and the other men aren't."

"That would be awful," Georgette said.

"The Army didn't have any use for Ike after that," Sally continued, "but he found his way to Arlington Hall pretty fast. He probably aced one of those logic tests we all took before we got offered a job here. To make a long story short, Ike's been working in Room 117 almost as long as I have. He's really talented at cryptanalysis. More than talented, actually. He has an amazing gift. Watching him work is almost spooky."

Justine was trying to follow Sally's train of thought. "So you think Ike is a bad risk, romantically, because of his injuries?"

"It would be terrible of me to feel that way, wouldn't it?"

Justine didn't know what to think. It was Sally's decision whether to tie herself to a man whose body was changed forever. She wondered whether Georgette, who was happily dating a man who used a wheelchair, would think poorly of Sally for rejecting Ike for his arm and leg, but she didn't think that was Sally's actual concern.

Feeling around for the right words, Justine said, "I think you're not worried about his physical wounds."

"I don't think so, either," Georgette said. "Getting hurt like that would mark a man, but knowing that he lived when all those other men died would mark him worse. He may find out that it's hard to live with himself, much less with somebody else."

Relief showed on Sally's face. "So you do understand."

Their conversation about Ike was interrupted by a voice rising over the hubbub.

"Sally! Over here!" The voice belonged to a sweet-faced woman with shoulder-length chestnut hair, parted in the middle and clipped back on both sides. She waved at them from several tables away. "Sally! Come sit with us."

Sally's bubbly personality had lost some fizz when she started thinking about Ike's pain. Now she looked completely deflated. "Linda saw us. I guess we have to go over there."

Justine looked at Georgette, who shrugged. She didn't know what was so bad about sitting with Linda, either.

Through a pasted-on smile, Sally said, "She's always finding catty things to say to me, because she's jealous that Ike likes me. He pays her a lot of attention, but I think he's trying to make me jealous, and Linda thinks so, too. I don't even think she likes him, but she does like being the belle of the ball. It really snaps her cap that I could have him, but I don't think I want him."

Sally led the way to Linda's table and took a seat beside her. "Justine and Samantha, this is Linda James." Nodding to the woman beside her, trim with iron-gray curls, she said, "And this is Patsy Young. Linda and Patsy work in traffic analysis."

Since traffic analysis was directly related to the project Karl had given her, Justine dove headfirst into her getting-to-know-you questions. "Does that take a lot of training? It seems to me like you could map out the whole history of a war—and look ahead at its future!—with nothing but the messages that were sent by both sides."

Sally was shaking her head and mouthing "No," behind Linda's back, so Justine stopped herself in mid-enthusiasm. Was she asking questions that were inappropriate, given their secrecy oaths? Everybody in the Caféteria had at least a base level of security clearance. She'd thought she was keeping things nonspecific enough.

As it turned out, she hadn't violated any secrecy rules, although she resolved to be more close-mouthed in the future. Sally had been trying to warn her about something else entirely.

"I don't know anything about any of that," Linda said in an airy tone, "and I don't care to know. Patsy pays attention to it, but I don't."

The woman next to her turned pink and murmured, "Oh, no, I don't do anything but type." She turned to look at Linda, as if checking to see if she'd said the right thing.

Justine was annoyed. It had been a long time since any of them were in high school. There was no longer any need to curry favor with the popular girl.

Linda was still talking about how proud she was to stay ignorant. "Other people understand what we're doing, and that's enough for me. Patsy types up the labels. I put the labels on the file folders. I sort the messages that come across my desk—and there's a lot of them!—then I put them in the folders according to the filing system they trained me on. That's all I do, and it's plenty."

She paused to smooth her hair into place and reapply her fuchsia lipstick. Justine had the sense that Linda spent a lot of her time making sure that she stayed pretty.

And she *was* pretty. So was Sally, but that was because Sally had nice, friendly eyes and her thick hair grew out of her head that way, not because she wasted effort on any of that. The biggest difference between Sally and Linda, though, was that Linda wasn't very bright. She did, however, like to talk.

"Do you like this shade?" she asked, holding out the fuchsia lipstick. "It's the latest. I try to keep my look current. It's the only way to stand out in the crowd. Men like lips and cheeks with some color to them."

She looked pointedly at Sally's bare face. Patsy, sitting beside her, said nothing, but Justine noticed that she, too, was wearing fuchsia lipstick. It was a good choice for her, contrasting nicely with her gray hair. It appeared that Linda was an evangelist when it came to cosmetics.

"I mean...look around the room," Linda went on, waving a dainty hand. "You'll see a lot of women and not a lot of men.

Unless you want to spend the rest of your life alone, and I don't, you have to pay attention to your face and figure."

Her eyes turned to the plate of chicken and dumplings in front of Sally. Justine saw nothing wrong with Sally's body, which had the look of robust good health that Justine associated with a milk-fed farm girl, but Linda seemed to see things differently. Judging by the cottage cheese and green salad sitting in front of Patsy, Linda had stressed the need for a woman to have and keep a teeny-tiny waist.

Justine wanted to say, "Ignore her, Sally, and eat your food." Instead, she took a huge bite of her meat loaf, and said, "I believe this is the most delicious thing I've ever put in my mouth."

Georgette and Sally must have been reading her mind because they both shoveled a heavy forkful of their own food into their mouths. Linda looked faintly repelled. It was possible that Patsy looked jealous. Or hungry.

The unspoken corollary to Linda's we're-short-on-men observation was obvious: Every woman at Arlington Hall—no, every woman in America—was in competition for the attention of the tiny number of eligible men who weren't off fighting in the war.

Ignoring the calories that Georgette, Sally, and Justine were enjoying with such gusto, Linda kept talking. "These days, spending a little money on makeup and clothes is a girl's investment in her future." She looked with narrowed eyes at the drab suits that Justine, Georgette, and Sally were wearing. "That's why I watch the sales at Garfinckel's cosmetics counter, so that I can save on lipstick and spend it on clothes or at the hairdresser."

Justine wondered if Linda would be more impressed with their clothes if she knew that she and Georgette were carrying firearms in their pockets.

Linda's eyes had moved from their clothes to their hairdos.

"You do know that there's a hairdresser's shop at Arlington Farms, right near our dorm? I heard Sally say that you lived with us in Kansas Hall."

Her tone implied that she also wanted to say, "You should definitely find that hairdresser's shop right away and go get a new hairdo," but even Linda had more tact than that.

"I'm sure she doesn't work for free," Justine said.

"Oh, we're not talking about just one 'she,'" Linda said. "They don't call Arlington Farms '28 Acres of Girls' for nothing. There's thirty hair dryers in the beauty shop, and plenty of beauticians to put girls' heads in them. Right, Patsy?"

"Absolutely. There really are thirty of them."

"That's more than a hair dryer per acre of girls," Justine said. "What's the optimum number of dryers per acre?"

Sally and Georgette giggled. Linda didn't. Patsy's mouth twisted, but she managed not to laugh.

"Even if there's a hundred beauticians waiting to cut and style my hair," Justine said, "after paying for my lunch, I've only got five dollars and change to get me through to payday. I think I'll be doing my own hair for a good long while."

"You can save money by setting your own hair, but it's nice to know that there's a professional nearby, if you need one."

And then Linda launched into an impressive lecture explicating the advantages and disadvantages of various beauty products. Justine liked makeup and pretty clothes just fine, but she had none of Linda's knowledge of setting lotions and permanent waves. Neither did Georgette, and the natural curls escaping Sally's braids said that she didn't, either.

At some point in Linda's monologue, Justine locked eyes with Georgette, eyebrows raised. Sally glanced at that moment of wordless communication and nearly strangled on her dumplings.

Justine felt terrible about making fun of Linda, so she covered by coming up with a cosmetics-related question to ask her. "My mother swore by witch hazel for keeping her skin looking nice. What do you think about it?"

"I'm sure witch hazel is fine, if you were born in the 1800s."

Justine would have been offended on her mother's behalf, if she'd had time, but Linda couldn't give her any time. She had beauty wisdom to impart.

"Cold cream is so, so, so much better for your skin. I keep a jar on my bedside table and cover my face and hands with it every night. I learned that from *Vogue*. I have a subscription. You're more than welcome to borrow a back issue if you want to read up, so come by my room any time. Kansas Hall. Room 294."

Justine was almost seduced into borrowing a *Vogue* and studying up, but she couldn't spare a cent for cosmetics. Well, maybe for a jar of cold cream, after she got paid. Linda had sold her on that. She mentioned this to Linda, which prompted another monologue detailing her carefully considered opinions on various brands of cold cream. Justine took the opportunity to eat her meat loaf and macaroni, which were delicious, and her green beans, which tasted like canned green beans always do.

While she was finishing her applesauce cake, she felt a gentle touch on her shoulder. Turning, she saw Dr. Patryk Kowalski.

"Pardon me, Miss," he said. "I see that you are eating your meal, but I was hoping to make an appointment to speak with you at some future time. Dr. Becker has told me so much about you."

Dr. Kowalski had Karl's Old World formality without his gregarious nature. He was probably around fifty, almost as old as her parents would have been, if they'd lived. Even so, he was at least twenty years younger than Karl. Justine couldn't read his face at all, but she didn't have any sense that he was one of the flirtatious men that Sally would deem "handsy." She was sure that he'd only touched her on the shoulder to get her attention.

"I hope Dr. Becker didn't fill your ears with embarrassing stories about me as an awkward eight-year-old."

"Oh, no. He told me that you have always been prodigiously gifted with languages, which means that you have found the right place here at Arlington Hall for your talents. In particular, he told me that your Polish godmother had taught you to speak my native language."

Of course, Karl would know Gloria. She had been a student in Chicago beside both of her parents.

"My godmother did teach me some conversational Polish, but I've never studied it formally. I couldn't conjugate a verb to save my life."

A smile flitted across a face that was either tired or sad. Justine couldn't tell.

"One need not do any conjugation at all to make oneself understood. I have very few opportunities to speak Polish these days. Would you care to join me for a cup of coffee someday soon? Perhaps Monday afternoon? Surely, Dr. Becker gives you a break from time to time. If he does not, I shall tell him that he should."

"I'd like that very much. And don't worry about Dr. Becker. He's a taskmaster, but he's not cruel."

"Then until Monday." He nodded his goodbye and withdrew.

When he was out of earshot, Linda said, "He's a little old for you, but he's not bad-looking for his age. He might be right for Patsy, though."

Patsy became fascinated by her salad.

Justine was fast losing her ability to be nice to Linda. Was that a problem? Only if Linda was an information source worth cultivating.

A curt, "Must I consider marrying every man who speaks to me?" crossed her lips, but Linda proved impossible to offend.

"No, silly! But you wouldn't want more eligible men to think you were taken."

Georgette and Sally chirped, "You sure wouldn't! Everybody knows that."

Linda, immune to sarcasm, said, "See what I mean? Don't give that old man too much of your time."

She looked to Georgette and Sally for support, but they were gathering their purses and Caféteria trays. Justine grabbed hers and followed them out, with Linda and Patsy following close behind.

Linda continued her chatter about cold cream all the way back to Building B. Far ahead of them, Justine could see Nora, watching the sidewalk under her feet and studiously avoiding every single crack.

———

Patsy supposed that she'd always been invisible, but passing forty had rubbed her face in it. Passing forty while sitting at the desk next to Linda's had only made it worse. She had endured two years' worth of beauty advice, all of it couched in terms designed to make her feel like she had one foot in the grave.

If you're religious about sleeping in cold cream, it should keep you from getting more wrinkles.

A woman your age should probably wear her hair shorter.

Don't smile too much. You don't want to get laugh lines.

Half the time, Patsy wanted to strangle Linda, so she had to remind herself that she had people to sit with at lunch when she sat with Linda. She had somebody to go with her when she wanted to go shopping, as long as she was willing to let Linda be the judge of which clothes made her look matronly. She had somebody to sit with at the movies, provided she dressed in a way that didn't embarrass Linda.

Linda made her want to scream, but Linda was useful.

———

Nora had seen Justine watching her feet, and that was interesting.

Early in her lifetime of avoiding pavement cracks, she had learned how to do it gracefully. She kept her eyes focused five yards ahead of her feet, which was more than enough space to adjust her stride and avoid any upcoming cracks.

Crevices.

Canyons.

Gouges.

She hated them all.

Nora didn't like imperfections, and she especially didn't like stepping on them. She didn't like holes, either, but they weren't so much of a problem. Nobody steps in holes on purpose, but lots of people tread heedlessly over cracks wide enough to send a tremor up Nora's spine.

Since children notice other children who walk funny, Nora had lived with their bullying until she'd learned to focus her eyes five yards ahead of her feet. She'd also learned to grit her teeth and tread on a narrow, forking, spidery crack, if that's what she had to do to avoid a crevice wide enough to feel through the soles of her shoes. This was her nightmare, feeling the abyss as it began to open beneath her.

The need to camouflage her fears meant that she was usually thinking too hard about her feet to do much talking while she walked, but people didn't notice that, not in the way they noticed people who walked funny. Other than her late husband,

Arthur, nobody had ever noticed whether Nora was talking or not, and even he couldn't grasp the things she told him about the way that her world looked and sounded.

Nora saw colors when she played the piano, beautiful colors. The key of *B* rippled in shades of luminous pink. The notes around middle *C* had a special resonance that she described to herself as "hummy" and "golden." She liked serial music that lacked a prevailing key best of all, because the notes and their colors came to her like a surprising string of Christmas lights, and every light had its own texture. Nobody but her dead husband had ever known this, not since a particularly cruel child had spent three years telling people how weird she was. From this, she had learned that people might think that sidewalk crack avoidance is weird, but they understand it, at least somewhat. However, most of them, and maybe all of them, are incapable of imagining Nora's world, where the sound of her own breath painted the air an effervescent, watery blue.

It fascinated Nora that Justine could see through her careful efforts to hide the ways her brain was different from other people's. This meant that Justine's brain was different, too. Nora reflected that she should probably pay some attention to finding out just how Justine was different from the others. She couldn't afford to be around people who could see through her. But who could?

———

Once inside Building B, Justine, Georgette, and Sally walked Linda and Patsy to their desks, side by side in the center of a huge room. The room was down the main hall from Room 117 in the same direction as the office space that Justine shared with Karl, but closer. Colloquially referred to as "Traffic Records," the room's walls were lined with filing cabinets. It was filled with the desks of people like Linda and Patsy, whose days were spent typing letters onto paper, putting paper into cabinets, and, later, retrieving it.

It was a noisy room, but still somehow more comfortable than Room 117. The workers, all women, chatted among themselves. One of them was filing her nails with her eyes fixed on the door in case her supervisor appeared. It was only now, looking at people who could have been sitting in the secretarial pool at any advertising agency in the country, that Justine fully grasped the nightmare of Room 117.

The people in front of her in Traffic Records were not terrified by the secrets passing through their hands, because they did not understand what they were. They didn't need to know, so nobody had told them.

Sally, Georgette, and Justine waved goodbye to Linda and Patsy as they picked their way through rows of workers to reach their desks. As Linda hung her purse on her chair, a spot of color on her desktop caught Justine's eye. It was a paper cup full of pink snapdragons, white carnations, and yellow daisies, and it looked a lot like the one she'd seen on Nora's desk.

Flowers seemed extravagant in wartime, but there was such a thing as being starved for beauty. Justine imagined someone selling bouquets of flowers on street corners in Washington and Arlington to people who couldn't find their favorite foods and who hadn't seen a pair of silk stockings since 1941, but who figured they could, by God, spend a few cents on some daisies.

Chapter 7

"Miss Byrne." Edison van Dorn's voice was cool enough to cut through the friendly post-lunch conversations going on around him.

Justine had thought she was being stealthy, following Sally and Georgette into Room 117 for a moment of post-lunch chitchat that gave her another chance to study its occupants. Unfortunately, this had put her at cross-purposes with the man in charge.

Dr. van Dorn didn't have to say, "Quit wasting time." His tone said it for him. And his words called attention to the interloper who was distracting his staff.

Justine took a quick step toward the door. "I'm sorry, sir. I was just leaving."

"I'll walk you out."

Every head in the room swiveled to watch Justine walk past, with Dr. van Dorn following close behind like a displeased prison warden. Nora watched from her broad desk, bare of everything but paper and her trademark black pencils. Thelma leaned over her work, pretending disinterest, but Justine saw her brush her bangs out of her dark eyes to get a better look at Justine being evicted from Room 117. Ike grinned as they passed. The Bees stopped their quiet gossip to watch her go. Only Dr. Kowalski was so focused on his work that he didn't look up.

Dr. van Dorn ushered her around the screen and through the door, closing it firmly behind him. She stood in front of him waiting for an angry outburst, but she got none.

Instead, he looked down at her with a face that could have been someone else's. The harsh vertical lines between his eyebrows were gone. His mouth wasn't exactly smiling, but its corners were soft and tilted upward. He looked years younger and, although still not handsome, he drew the eye in the way that granite busts of Roman emperors do. She'd thought he was about forty, but now she wasn't sure. He hardly looked thirty. He had a doctorate, so he'd have to be quite a genius to be much under that, but maybe he was. Geniuses were not rare in his line of work.

He leaned, arms crossed, against the door to Room 117 and silently regarded her. When he spoke, even his voice had modulated into something interesting, even intriguing. "How are you liking your new job? You're a lovely addition to our little family at Arlington Hall."

Even in her regular life, Justine hadn't yet figured out how to behave when a man turned flirtatious. While working as a government agent, she was stymied.

If she were simply Justine, not Justine-trying-to-ferret-out-a-traitor, she would have been debating whether to encourage him with a smile or freeze him out with a prim glare. Her decision would have been based on whether she was interested in spending more time with him, and she really didn't think that she was. A minute before, she would have said that the only thing remotely appealing about Edison van Dorn was his obvious intellect, but now he had turned on the charm like it had a switch.

Would she have responded to that charm if she'd been just a young woman face-to-face with a potentially interesting man? It hardly mattered because that wasn't what she was.

This man must know things about the inner operations at Arlington Hall that could be useful to her work. He had access to files that she didn't. He also had access to rooms that she didn't, and to people, too. Even if he wasn't the spy she was hunting, and he certainly could be, he could be cultivated as an asset. This was what Jerry and Paul called people who could be manipulated into doing what you wanted them to do.

Should she try to cultivate Dr. van Dorn as an asset? Yes. She should.

Did Paul see her as an asset? Yes. He probably did. This upset her, so she hoped he was going to absolutely hate it when he found out she was flirting with Edison van Dorn.

She gave van Dorn the tiniest possible smile and said, "I know I just got here, but I already love my new job. Everybody's so warm and welcoming." She leaned a little on the word "everybody," as if to convey that she really meant him and only him.

The man was evidently easy to encourage, because he responded as if she'd invited him into her bed. He leaned toward her, put his hand on her shoulder, and spoke into her ear. "Then let me buy you a welcome-to-cryptanalysis drink. It's the least I can do."

She let her shoulder tremble slightly under his hand in a way that she hoped said that she welcomed his touch. Then she worried that he'd think she was trying to shake it off. Paul should probably try recruiting agents with at least a little experience in seduction. Either that, or he should add seduction skills to the training regimen.

"Oh, and by the way, you should call me Ed."

She was apparently doing okay with the seduction part of

espionage, because Edison's hand moved past her shoulder joint and encircled her upper arm. Then it slid downward as if he were tracing the contours of her deltoid, tricep, and bicep muscles through the tweedy fabric of her jacket.

"The drinks at the Mayfair are cold and strong," he said, "and the acts are top-notch, if you like music and comedy."

"I do."

"Tonight?"

This man wasted no time. She remembered her mother's dating advice, which came straight out of the Edwardian era and was not calibrated for courtships that didn't involve chaperones. Nevertheless, it did seem applicable in this case.

Don't make yourself too available.

On the other hand, it was Saturday, and she was in a new part of the world where she didn't know the rules. She wasn't even sure whether drinks were sold on Sundays. Should she drag her feet on cultivating Edison van Dorn as an asset? Not while the security leak in Room 117 was endangering lives.

She gave him a little smile and added a little flutter of her mascara-stained eyelashes as she said, "Ordinarily, I wouldn't be free this evening."

"Of course, you wouldn't. I imagine your dance card is filled up for weeks."

"Luckily for you, my plans have fallen through."

"I can't believe any man would cancel on a woman like you."

"Chicken pox."

"Poor him. Lucky me."

The hand continued its journey down her arm and lingered on her hand. His other hand brought hers together, so that he could hold them both. This made her feel confined, even bound. He was now touching every square centimeter of exposed skin on her body, save her face and throat. The hallway was empty, so nobody could see them, but this also meant that there were no watching eyes to make him stop touching her.

"Where shall I pick you up?"

"Arlington Farms. Kansas Hall."

"I'll be by at eight. The Mayfair's a dinner club, so prepare yourself for food that's just as good as the show. The chef is French, and the bartenders are heavy-handed."

And just like that, agreeing to meet Edison van Dorn for a drink had metamorphosed into a full evening all alone with him, dining, drinking, and watching a show. And dancing? He hadn't said so, but maybe.

As he turned toward the door to Room 117, she watched the vertical lines between his brows reappear. His jaw tensed. Apparent age settled on his now-stooping shoulders. By the time he turned the doorknob, he looked like someone else entirely.

———

As Justine walked back to her office, she fretted about her upcoming date with Dr. van Dorn. On second thought, she supposed she should think of him as Ed, since he'd told her she should and since she'd be drinking and dining with him within hours.

Did they dance at the Mayfair? If so, what kind of dancing did they do? She could jitterbug a little bit, but Washington clubs might be more stuffy than the nightclubs in hedonistic New Orleans. Maybe her mother's efforts to teach her the fox-trot were about to pay off. The suitcase Paul's people had packed for her had held some dressy clothes, but they were pretty staid. Maybe Georgette could do something with them.

Paul might have wanted her to be dowdy when she was pretending to be Miss Samantha Ogletree, but that was all wrong now. She needed to show at least a little sophistication to spend time with Edison van Dorn. His clothes and manner made Justine feel like a complete rube.

She shoved aside her worries about their date. This freed her mind to consider something she'd noticed just as Ed had escorted her out of Room 117:

Nora had been sitting at a desk that was bare of everything but papers and her black pencils. Her flowers had been gone.

Maybe the flowers on Linda's desk hadn't been the same ones sitting on Nora's desk that morning. Carnations, snapdragons, and daisies were, after all, common and not-too-expensive flowers. Or maybe, despite the fact that her coworkers thought she carried a torch for Ike, Nora had given her flowers to Linda.

———

Justine was failing. Again.

She sat at her desk, drowning in messages. Messages in English. Messages in German. Encrypted messages in both languages. What had Karl expected her to do with this stack of paper in less than a day?

She'd made some headway with the decrypted messages. The ones that were written in English felt like gifts from God. Unfortunately, there weren't enough of them.

The decrypted messages written in German were helpful. She just didn't have time to translate them all into English. Still, even the ones that she didn't have time to translate provided valuable information. They all had headers that gave a date and location, and even a schoolchild could sort messages written in "Oktober," "November," and "Dezember" by people in "München" or "Köln."

When she combined the things she'd learned from all these

messages, she got a sense of an overall narrative being communicated, but important details were missing. It was only logical to guess that those details could be found in the encrypted messages.

But what could she do in a single day with messages encrypted by an unidentified system? Or maybe in a hundred unidentified military systems?

Karl had set her an impossible task. Either she was going to meet his challenge without breaking the encrypted messages, or she was going to fail.

Justine Byrne did not like to fail.

The clock on the wall was ticking down the minutes before Karl would ask for her results. She picked up another piece of paper and bent over it, hoping to glean some meaning from the letters typed on its face.

———

Justine flinched at the sound of Karl's door opening. Even before he cleared his throat to get her attention, she knew he was there.

She looked up from the paperwork, turning her head to look behind her at Karl standing in the doorway between their offices.

"Have you made your determination?" he asked. "I'm sure you have, because I asked you to do so, and you agreed. You are not a woman who fails to keep her commitments."

Justine looked at her watch. Was the afternoon gone already?

She cast an uncertain glance at the papers spread across her desk. Had she been able to meet Karl's challenge? She had a theory, but no unassailable proof. Not yet. Nevertheless, Karl didn't look like he wanted to give her another day to firm up her theory. She was going to have to work with the information she had.

"I'm ready."

"You may have a few more minutes to build your case, if you need them. Make some notes. Copy down the exact text of key messages. Bring a map if you need one, but you know that I have several." He stretched a hand behind him and waved at the map-covered walls of his office. "When you're ready, bring your argument and your evidence to me. There's no need to knock." He disappeared but left the door open.

She was far more nervous about showing her work to Karl than she should have been. It felt almost like showing her physics homework to her parents. They could be trusted to point out all of her errors, but they could be trusted to do it with love. Everything she knew about Karl said that he would be kind when he corrected her. Still, she didn't want him to see her fail.

Karl seemed to think that she didn't remember him at all, but he was wrong. As far as she knew, Karl had never had children. Maybe that was why he underestimated eight-year-olds. And six-year-olds and, to an extent, four-year-olds. Since he'd jogged her memory about who he was, Justine's memories had come back in a slow stream of long-ago moments. She remembered playing chess with Karl. She remembered looking at the yellowed pages of his childhood copy of the tales of the *Brüder Grimm* as he read to her. She remembered her mother laughing at his jokes. She remembered him playing billiards with her father.

She also remembered writing letters after those times they'd spent together, letters that Karl hadn't answered, many of them. Eight-year-old Justine had blamed herself for that rejection. Maybe her unanswered letters to Karl were the reason she was paralyzed by the thought of being wrong in front of him.

Justine let out a sigh, then she kicked herself for letting him hear her frustration. She checked her notes, mainly to calm her mind and not because she'd forgotten his very straightforward assignment. He'd asked her to compare two sets of messages and tell him which ones were real and which ones were faked to simulate an attack that was never coming.

What had she learned?

Not enough to see any difference at all between the messages. None. She was not looking forward to admitting this to Karl. This seemed to be her week to thoroughly experience failure.

She gathered the two stacks of paper that he'd given her, laid all of her other work neatly in the top drawer of her desk, and locked it. As prepared as she could be, she walked into Karl's office, armed only with those papers and her notepad.

"Shut the door behind you and come sit at the conference table with me," he said, and she did.

Karl's face was utterly blank. He was a man who had spent the entire war keeping secrets on pain of death, and he looked like it. Perhaps Karl had been trusted with government secrets even before the war. Maybe he'd kept the country's war secrets back in 1917. She had no idea.

"You've had a full day to work, except for an overlong lunch break."

He waited for her to use the busy Caféteria as an excuse, but she declined, so he went on.

"You made up for that time by taking no other breaks."

So he had been watching her. This wasn't surprising. His door had stayed open most of the day.

"What have you learned?"

She laid the two stacks of paper on the table. "For convenience, I will call the set of messages that I reviewed this morning 'Set E,' because they appear to relate to a planned Allied attack on the Eastern Front." She placed her left hand on this stack. "I'll call the afternoon's messages 'Set W,' because they

seem centered on a planned Allied attack on the Western Front."
She placed her right hand on Set W.

"Understood."

"Once I had both Set E and Set W in hand, I learned that
the two sets were identical in terms of the number of messages.
It quickly became clear that the decrypted messages also cor-
responded in terms of content. There was an exact one-to-one
correspondence. If a message in Set E referenced a fuel ship-
ment that had been received, there was a message in Set W that
matched it word for word. Only the city names were changed."

"You were also provided with undecrypted messages. Were
you able to glean any information from them?"

"Well, if I was supposed to be able to figure out the encryption method in a day, then I failed. I imagine that you've got
machines for that, so it's hardly fair for anyone to think I could
do it by hand."

It was not lost on Justine that the word "machines" made
Karl sit up straighter. She'd struck a nerve.

"I have rooms full of analysts doing decryption here. Maybe
they're just better than you are. What kind of machines do you
think you need?"

Refusing to rise to the bait, Justine said, "My mother was fascinated with cryptography. You know that. She told me about a
man who built an electric-powered machine that could be used
to encrypt and decrypt messages, way back in the Twenties
when she was in graduate school. He ran an advertisement
challenging people to solve his unbreakable cipher. She and her
friends didn't quite manage to solve it, but they had some pretty
clear ideas about the design of his machine and its rotors."

"We are not using some nobody's thirty-year-old machine,
and neither are the Germans. Nor the Japanese."

"No, but that machine sounded like quite a time-saver.

Anybody who got a look at the volume of messages coming through this place would guess that both sides are using some kind of time-saving device to generate them. And, likely, to decrypt them."

"And you think we have magic electric machines? With rotors? And that they work faster than all my analysts put together?" Karl's tone, usually so kind, was biting.

His dismissive questions embarrassed Justine, but not enough to make her back down.

"I suggested that you are working with encryption and decryption machines that use rotors based on facts I learned from my mother, whom we both agree was a reliable source. It's a reasonable hypothesis. There's no need to sneer."

"Your magic-rotor-machine hypothesis sounds more like an excuse for not being able to decrypt any of the messages."

Justine thought of the reams of paper he had given her. The undecrypted pages had been covered with endless sequences of letters, organized in groups of five.

How could he expect her, by herself and in a single day, to do anything with stacks of pages covered with nothing but gibberish like "FDJKM LQWOR MDFVO VVKJZ ASKHD KXWPY UNHYI OXAVR MYGTC GFZIB NRTTE OEBER"? He could not possibly have expected her to crack the cipher. Thus, he had expected something else.

She decided to drop the subject of electric decryption machines and shift to one about which she felt herself to be on firmer ground. "Let me go back to the original question you asked—which set of messages is real and which is fake? My answer is that I think they're both fake."

"Oh, you do?"

"Yes. I suspected it when I could find no difference worth mentioning between Set E and Set W. I decided that the best use of my limited time was to assess whether I thought *either* of them seemed real. To do that, I thought about what I know about the European war theatre, which admittedly isn't much. I only know what I read in the papers and see in the newsreels. I have to think that at least some of the people working on projects like this have access to more privileged information."

"That's a fair point."

"I understand a little bit about the logistics of the Normandy invasion, because I knew somebody who worked at the Higgins factory where they built the boats used for the landing."

In this case "somebody" was Justine herself, but she didn't want to make it too easy for Karl to pry into her recent past. He already knew far too much about her distant past.

"The Higgins boats made it possible to land on beaches. Beach landings, even with specialized boats, only make sense if you don't have access to a deepwater port and you have no realistic chance of seizing one. I'm guessing that this means we didn't hold any of those on D-Day. Thus, I'm going to presume that the Nazis either continue to hold them all or that they destroyed them as they withdrew. It's what I'd do. Wouldn't you?"

She was gratified to see that she'd forced him into a brusque nod.

Encouraged, she pressed on. "Perhaps we've gotten some of the ports back into operation, but we've still got to be short on them. I'd guess that this lack of deepwater ports means that supplies are still tight for our troops in Europe. They'll stay tight until we take more key ports and get them running again."

"You're quite the amateur logistics expert. Maybe you should volunteer for the military."

Karl was openly sneering at her now. Justine didn't like it, but she pushed her anger aside so she could concentrate on what his dismissive tone told her. Karl did not seem like the sneering type, so he was consciously trying to manipulate her emotions with his insults. She decided not to let him do that.

"Sure, I could volunteer for the military but, as a woman, I'd be pretty limited in what they'd let me do. I think I'm better off here."

She held her silence for a moment, waiting for another sneer. She didn't get one, so she plunged ahead.

"Supplies like food, fuel, and ammunition must still be hard to come by in the parts of Europe we occupy, and probably throughout the continent. And the shortages must get worse and worse as you get farther from the coastline where at least some supplies must be coming in at the surviving ports. And from smugglers. I mean, surely we've been bombing the high-ways and railroads for years. All transportation routes in Europe have got to be in bad shape. Torn-up railroads are a good thing when the enemy holds them, but they're a bad thing when we take them back. Right?"

"I can't argue with that."

This was not a ringing endorsement, but at least Karl had stopped sneering.

"The newspapers say that our troops have penetrated France quickly. Combine that with torn-up roads and railroads, and it's obvious that our supply lines are stretched thin. They have to be. Yet neither set of messages gives any hint of that. It doesn't make any sense."

"Do you have other observations?"

"I don't think our problems are limited to moving things around. We also have to move information around. How do we do that? We use radio signals when we can. Well, what does that mean as we expand our territory?"

No answer. She kept talking.

"The farther our people are from each other, the more

messages we have to send. That gives the Germans more opportunities to intercept them. But the Germans are in the opposite position. We're crowding them together, so they don't need to use their radios as much. Also, now they're close to their old territory, where they probably have more intact telephone and telegraph lines to use. This means that we aren't able to pick up as much of their communications, but they can still intercept ours. In the arena of information flow, they have some important advantages. Hence our need for fake traffic to confuse things."

Karl's face was turning pink. Was it because she was right and he didn't like it? Was it because she wasn't making any sense at all? Justine couldn't tell.

"Right now," she said, "they have a few small, specific advantages, but not for long, not if we keep pushing them back. If I were the Germans, I'd be preparing for one last offensive. If they're ever going to have the supplies, they have them now. Their communications are more closely guarded than they have been, so we wouldn't necessarily see it coming. Presuming that weather's an issue as we're heading into winter—and I imagine it usually is—my guess is that an attack is imminent. Now's the time."

Karl lifted both hands and slapped them palms-down on the desk.

"Yes, now is the time. Today is the time. It is as if you have been reading the enemy's strategy book. A few hours ago, the Germans launched a surprise attack on the Western Front. Snowstorms have grounded our planes, and this has devastated our troops' ability to defend themselves or to do critical reconnaissance. Because of that, our knowledge of the situation in Europe is limited, but the situation is grim for the very reasons you describe. I am tempted to say that you know as much as our generals do. It would be an overstatement, but you have described the current situation very well, and you've done it with very little supporting evidence."

"Was I right about Set E and Set W both being fake?"

"Yes, my dear. You were."

"So I get to keep my job?"

"Wild beasts couldn't tear you out of my grip. Go home. Rest that fine mind of yours. Given the situation in Europe, I will need you to use it."

She rose, notebook in hand. "Do you think—"

"I don't think. My own fine mind is completely depleted. Go home and pray for our soldiers. There will be plenty for us to do tomorrow."

———

As he stood in the door between their offices, Karl watched Justine pass into the hallway. And he thought of Gerard and Isabel. Justine had just proven that she really did possess the mind that would be expected of their child.

Why had he let Gerard and Isabel pass out of his life? Isabel, in particular, had tried mightily to hold on to their friendship. She had been a formidable correspondent, writing long letters to all the friends she'd left behind in Chicago when Gerard's work took them to New Orleans. He'd enjoyed her letters. Actually, he'd loved them, and he'd loved the shorter notes from Gerard that she had tucked into most envelopes. Gerard's notes were always worth the effort it took to decipher his shorthand-like scrawl and his telegraphic grammar. It had helped to have a bit of mental telepathy when one tried to read anything Gerard had written.

In later years, there had been notes from Justine. They had been chock-full of big thoughts written in the spidery cursive of a child. He believed that Isabel had finally quit writing because of Justine. How many times could a mother respond to a child who was asking why her letter hadn't been answered? At some point, she would stop encouraging the child to write at all.

But why had he stopped answering their letters?

He couldn't be sure. Anyone who thought they could be sure about their own motivations was a fool. But he thought that his ability—compulsion?—to let people go stemmed from the way he'd left his first home.

He had fled a Germany intent on empire, which he'd seen as a threat to himself. The Kaiser had been hungry for young men to conquer and hold his colonies, and Karl had nurtured no interest in giving over his body as a tool. His parents and siblings, by contrast, had been nationalists to the core. Karl had stayed with them as long as he could, securing a respected position as a professor of physics that had paid him well and made his parents proud, but the day had come when he'd had to walk away. His job, his family, the woman who might have loved him if he'd tried to woo her—none of these things had been enough to keep him. If forced to face facts, Karl would have to say that loyalty was not his strongest quality.

America had offered escape and a fresh start, so he had crossed the ocean and begun again. The revolutionary work of the Curies, Rutherford, Thomson, and their colleagues had eclipsed his more traditional approach to physics, but Karl had not been without salable skills. He had secured a position teaching German language and literature at the University of Chicago. Distance had slowly decayed his bonds with the people he had left behind, and their rabid support of the Kaiser's ambitions had sped up the process. The half-lives of Karl's human relationships had always been oddly brief.

When the Great War came, he had been too old to fight for

his new country, but he'd been well able to serve. He had taken leave from the university to work at Riverbank Laboratories's Department of Codes and Ciphers, providing cryptographic services for the American government. Riverbank Laboratories, a private organization, had been the perfect place to serve his adopted country, which might have balked at his German birth if he'd offered himself to its government. By the time this second war erupted, he had earned the trust of the cryptographic community and his skills had won their respect. These things had brought him to this place, where he believed he was doing important work.

Because the world is strange, the same currents of history had also brought Justine back to him. Why had he ever let her go?

He couldn't say. He also couldn't say for sure that he wouldn't push her away again. It could happen, but Justine was here for now, and she lit up his lonely life. She was also most useful. In a day, she had ferreted out the reasons for a battle that was even now gripping a continent on the other side of the world. Her mind was astonishing.

That mind inhabited a person who was still very naive, though. If she'd had any idea of the value of the work she'd done that day, she would have asked for a raise, a large one, and a position more worthy of her talents. And he would have gotten them for her.

Chapter 8

Justine and Georgette got off the bus, moving through Arlington Farms in a long line of women that shrank every time they passed another dormitory. At Idaho Hall, a cluster of women broke off from the larger group and headed indoors. This happened again at Nebraska Hall and again at Texas Hall, where all the women seemed to be WACs. When the line reached Kansas Hall, it was time for Georgette, Justine, Sally, Thelma, Nora, Patsy, Linda, and The Bees to do the same. When the government hired a woman and referred her to Arlington Farms, the dormitory managers clearly took their work assignments into account when they doled out rooms.

Sally and Thelma lived on the first floor of the same wing of Kansas Hall as Georgette and Justine did, so the four of them said goodbye to the other women in the lobby and headed to the left, where Georgette and Justine headed upstairs. As they climbed, Justine said, "I have a date tonight, and I don't have anything to wear."

"You sound exactly like our new friend Linda. Only you should heave a heavy sigh first. And do this." Georgette laid the back of her hand across her forehead and struck a "Woe is me" pose.

Justine was still laughing when they opened the door and found a note on the floor that said, "Package at the front desk for Justine Byrne."

Georgette turned to leave. "You ain't got time to stand in line for that package. I'll go get it while you start getting ready for your date."

When Justine came back from her shower, hair wrapped in a towel and body wrapped in a fluffy bathrobe, Georgette didn't even say hello.

She just pointed at the suitcase on Justine's bed and said, "What's-His-Name thinks of everything, don't he? Not twelve hours ago, we noticed that your clothes ain't right, now that you're yourself again. And here comes a suitcase that's gotta be packed full of the right stuff, because the dang thing's heavy. Open it up! This feels like Christmas!"

Justine popped the latches. Inside the suitcase, she found a pair of high-heeled work shoes, still a very practical black like the ones she'd been wearing, but much more sleek and stylish. There was an equally sleek purse, which she held up for Georgette to see, saying, "It matches the shoes! But look—it still has room for a secret compartment."

Beneath the purse were a luxurious fur-collared coat and five neatly folded daytime suits, better made and more flatteringly cut than anything in either of their closets. Even better, there was a pair of black satin pumps and a matching clutch purse of quilted satin that would be perfect for dinner and dancing at the Mayfair. There was also a velvet bag of high-quality cosmetics that made her want to throw the waxy dime-store lipstick she'd been wearing right out the window.

"Wouldn't Linda have a flat-out fit if she got a look at that stuff?" Georgette breathed.

Justine sprayed a puff of perfume into the air so that they

could both enjoy it. "She'll be jealous the second she gets a whiff of me."

Along with all that, Paul's costumers had packed three pairs of silk stockings for evening and five pairs of nicer nylons than she'd been wearing, plus a week's worth of underwear that lived up to the rest of her finery.

Everything else in the suitcase was wrapped neatly in white tissue paper. This made her wonder whether the paper was protecting something worth wearing to the Mayfair. Excited in spite of herself, she tore in, while Georgette hovered behind her, too thrilled to speak.

The first five packages that she unwrapped contained simple but elegant silk blouses to wear under her suits. Beneath them was a quilted black satin evening coat that matched the pumps and clutch. Tucked into all that white tissue paper was a tiny puff of black netting that was a fashion designer's answer to the problem of how to make an evening hat when hat-making materials were impossible to find. And beneath the coat lay three silk dresses cut from purple velvet, black shantung, and emerald chiffon.

They were so lovely that, for a moment, neither of them could speak. Then practical Georgette said, "You gotta shake those out and get 'em on hangers before they wrinkle."

———

Justine had fastened all the little hooks and eyes on her fancy new longline brassiere. She'd slid a slip over the long, boned bra and fastened her hose to the bra's garter clips. And all the while, she was wondering whether her date had even started getting dressed. His underwear surely consisted of a single garment that required nothing more involved than sticking his feet into its leg holes and pulling it up. And maybe pulling on an undershirt.

"I hate to bother you," she said to Georgette, "but there's no way I can get this fabulous dress over my head by myself, much less reach around and zip it up."

Georgette, who was stretched out on her own bed, reading and listening to Gene Autry on the radio, said, "I'm always happy to help a friend truss herself up like a Christmas turkey before a night on the town."

Justine threw her a baleful glare. "You're enjoying my misery."

Georgette laughed. "I'd rather help you get ready for your fancy date than go on one myself. I get to enjoy your pretty dress and your splendiferous makeup, but I don't have to spend the evening with hairpins stuck straight into my scalp. I can sit around here in my flannel nightgown while you're out pretendin' like your underwear don't hurt. Lucky me."

"You'd truss yourself up like a turkey in a heartbeat if Jerry asked you to go on a fancy date."

"I can't lie. I certainly would. But it wouldn't fit his cover story. He ain't supposed to have much money, and his cover story is that he don't come from money and he ain't used to fancy things. Just like the real me."

Justine lifted her arms, so that Georgette could slip the dress over them. It was truly gorgeous, but it—and the other truly elegant gowns in her closet—made her nervous, because their very existence asked the question, "What, exactly, is my job?" And also, "Why does this man who acts like he might want to be my boyfriend want me to look this good on my date with another man?"

Georgette said, "There. All zipped up."

Justine smoothed the luxurious fabric over her hips. "Do you think the costumers knew I was going dancing tonight?"

"Don't know. Maybe? If Dr. van Dorn got to braggin' about his date with the new girl, it mighta gotten back to Jerry. All it would take would be a quick phone call from Jerry to What's-His-Name. It seems like he can just snap his fingers and make things happen." She gestured at the grand gowns in the closet and on Justine's back. "Or maybe this is standard-issue for a lady spy who's not meek-minded Miss Samantha Ogletree."

Justine ran her palms over the expertly tailored bodice hugging her body. She was enthusiastic about the intelligence-gathering part of her work. If she got a chance to crack some enemy codes, too, then that would be a bonus. If she got to be part of an operation that took down an enemy agent and saved the lives of a bunch of soldiers, that was good, too. It was just that she'd pictured fighting for an Allied victory with her mind, not her body. Somebody—was it Paul?—seemed to think that her physical charms might help win a war. And Justine didn't like it.

"This dress is way too nice for Dr. van Dorn. Look how pretty your new blond hair looks against that purple velvet. Ain't it grand what a bottle of bleach can do?" Georgette said. "And them satin shoes look like they're dancin' when you're standin' still."

The dress had long, close-fitting sleeves, a plunging neckline, fullness over the bust that was gathered into a set-in waist, and a flared skirt that stopped below the knee, yet still managed to showcase her stocking-clad legs and her shapely shoes.

Justine opened a lipstick and twisted it up to show off the color. "This is certainly a prettier shade of red than the one they're making you wear."

"You mean the one that's the same color as a boiled crawdad?"

"That's a lot more appetizing description than 'Dried Blood,' which is what I would've called it. Now I just need to finish with my makeup and hair before Ed shows up." The casual nickname felt strange in her mouth.

Touching her thumbnail lightly to see if her scarlet nail polish had dried, she said, "Speaking of Ed…"

"Yeah?"

"How old do you think he is? I mean…he's had time to get his doctorate and establish himself teaching at Dartmouth. I'd assumed that he was in his forties, just because of his job, until I took a close look at him. Now I'm not sure he's that old."

"Naw. I'd say he's past thirty, but he ain't thirty-five yet."

"Then he didn't waste any time getting that PhD."

"How old were your parents when they got theirs?"

Justine did the math in her head. "Probably not thirty. I guess you're right. He may not be very old at all."

"If life had treated you different, you'd already be on your way to getting one of them doctor degrees yourself, and you wouldn't be wasting any time about it. Dr. van Dorn is smart. You're smart. He's a good bit older than you and me, but most people are, to tell you the truth."

Justine picked up the velvet bag holding her new government-issue cosmetics, fidgeting with the jet button that held it closed.

"It ain't his age that bothers you," Georgette said. "He may not be any older than What's-His-Name. It's just that you like one of 'em, and you don't like the other one. Ain't a thing wrong with that, but there also ain't no reason to feel bad about a night on the town with Dr. van Dorn when that other gentleman never asked you to make him any promises."

Justine drew in a deep breath and blew it out. "You're right. You're always right." Gripping the velvet bag, she said, "I'll just run down the hall and put some of this goo on my face."

Georgette interrupted her. "Settle yourself on this chair, and I'll hold the hand mirror for you. That way, you won't have to elbow anybody out of your way to get a spot in front of the bathroom mirror."

"Thank you!" Justine flopped onto the chair, dumped the makeup on her bedside table, and set to work. "Tell me if I'm going too heavy on the pancake makeup. I've been covering my freckles up all week, so I've got to keep it up."

"I won't let you go out looking bad. Not that you ever do." Georgette shifted the mirror to a better angle. "Hey, do you want to go see Gloria tomorrow?"

"After work, you mean?"

"Tomorrow's Sunday, silly. It's the only day off we get. That's why the bathroom's so crowded. Everybody's getting ready for their Saturday-night dates."

"Oh, yeah." Justine leaned toward the mirror as she applied the crimson lipstick. "I've only been working at Arlington Hall two days, so it doesn't feel like it should be the weekend yet, but that's because I was finishing up my work at the shipyard on Thursday."

And getting treated like a sucker by your boyfriend and my maybe-boyfriend, but never mind that.

This thought made her so angry at Paul that she could see her cheeks flushing pink in the mirror, even through the pancake makeup. It wasn't a bad look, so she rubbed some rouge on those spots so that she could look that way all evening.

"I'm glad you want to see Gloria, 'cause I already called her at work today," Georgette said, handing Justine a handkerchief to blot her lipstick. "It's probably the easiest way to reach her, since she's living in some kind of government barracks without a phone. Took me a few calls to track her down, but I knew where I saw her, and I knew where her lab was, and I knew the right people to ask. I can't wait for you to see that lab."

"She'll be at work on a Sunday?"

"You know Gloria. Let's see if I can remember what she said and how she said it." Georgette's voice turned cool. It took on something that sounded a little like a Polish accent, and her grammar shifted into something that proved she'd been paying attention in school.

"'Come see me at the lab,' Gloria said to me in that professor voice of hers. 'I spent so many years working with equipment I built out of the equivalent of Tinkertoys and pipe cleaners that I have no time to waste. Sunday is just another day to see what I can do with this laboratory that God and the federal government have bestowed upon me.'"

"Sounds like Gloria."

"I wish you could have heard how happy she sounded, but you'll see it tomorrow."

Justine studied her face in the mirror. "Is this lipstick too loud? I've never been a blond before."

"It's killer-diller. Makes your skin look like porcelain."

"My eyebrows look weird arched like this, but I guess the whole point of makeup is to make you look like somebody else."

"Those brows make you look kinda like Marlene Dietrich, them and the hair. Only you've still got your own ladylike ways. So maybe you're like Marlene Dietrich before she ever had anything to do with a man."

"You mean I look like Marlene Dietrich when she was twelve?"

Georgette looked her up and down. "You know, that ain't a bad way to put it. Maybe he'll keep his hands to himself, if you can hang on to that ice queen look."

Justine felt her new eyebrows rise.

"Now you just look scared. Pretty but scared." Georgette patted Justine on the elbow. "You don't have to go, y'know. You can send me downstairs to tell him you're sick."

"I'm a little scared, but it's not just that. I feel…strange… getting dressed up to go eat a fancy meal and watch a fancy show when there are people dying on the other side of the world. People are suffering, and I'm pretending like I'm helping them by having a fine night on the town."

"You *are* helping. There's a battle going on right now and—" She paused. "You heard anything about how things are going in France?"

Justine shook her head.

"Me, neither. Nothing good, anyway."

Georgette leaned toward Justine and lowered her voice. "Dr. van Dorn may be the person tellin' the Germans about our war secrets. If you go out with him tonight and find out that it's him, What's-His-Name will know how to stop him. You could save a bunch of our boys' lives that way." She took one of Justine's hands in hers. "You don't gotta go, and you sure don't gotta do it for me, but everything we do in these strange new jobs of ours could save my brothers. I'm grateful for anything you do to help." She squeezed the hand. "Even if you have to get all dolled up like a movie star to do it."

"So I should spend the evening sitting in the lap of luxury— and maybe in the lap of Edison van Dorn—for truth, justice, and the American Way?"

Georgette laughed. Actually, she cackled.

"Oh, you absolutely should. So you need to hurry up and put on your makeup. You're smart. Smarter than him, I bet. You'll be just fine." She dropped Justine's hand and waved her own hand at Justine's pile of makeup. "Fluff on a little powder to set that makeup and put some hairspray on that platinum-blond hair. I'll go downstairs and keep an eye out for your buddy, Ed. You don't wanna be down there in the lobby when he gets here, like you can't wait to see him and you ain't got a single thing better to do."

———

Within minutes, Georgette was back. "Good thing I checked. He got here early. He's already down there playing cards with hisself."

Justine jumped to her feet.

"Slow your roll. Didn't your mama teach you nothing but how to speak German and how to do particle physics? You want to ease down them stairs and give a little yawn when you see him, like you're thinkin', 'I forgot he was coming, but I always dress like this. I might as well let him take me out and show me a good time.' Don't run down the steps like you never had a date before and you're afraid some girl's gonna steal him away."

She handed Justine her evening coat. "Here you go. And here's your purse with enough mad money to get you home, in case he gets fresh. And…you know."

This was Georgette's subtle way of reminding her that there was a single-shot gun shaped like an ink pen tucked into the clutch purse.

"Catch your breath and head on down the stairs, because maybe I spoke too soon. Men are in short supply these days. One of them women really might try to steal him away."

———

Georgette wasn't kidding about Edison playing cards with himself. Justine found him in the lounge, ignoring the people drinking, smoking, and dancing around him. He sat on a sofa with several cards fanned out in his hands, hunched over a coffee table that was spread with cards, some facedown and some faceup. He kept his eyes fixed on the cards, moving them around the table until she spoke to him from a few feet away.

He looked up with the glazed expression of a man who was interrupted while he was completely immersed in a task, but this only lasted for an instant. When his eyes finally focused on Justine, he smiled and raked the cards into his hand. As he put them in a small pasteboard box and tucked it in a front pants pocket, he gave the box a rueful grin, as if he knew that it was rude to seem more interested in cards than in his approaching date.

He compounded the rudeness by saying, "I don't suppose you play bridge?" instead of "Hello." She shook her head and said, "Bridge, no. Gin rummy, yes."

"Alas. I've always hoped to find a beautiful bridge partner. But never mind. Tonight is for dancing."

Ed helped her with her coat, saying, "You look glorious in that shade of purple. All eyes will be on you tonight."

This was not what nervous Justine wanted to hear.

He held out his arm, elbow crooked to give her a place to nestle her hand. His crisp black overcoat gave his tall form a presence that it hadn't had before. The coat was open, revealing an equally crisp black suit and white shirt. His silvery tie, like his hazel eyes and ash-blond hair, picked up the colors all around him, without asserting a color of its own. It occurred to Justine that, if it should turn out that Edison van Dorn was not the enemy spy that Paul was hunting, a man with his intelligence, confidence, and chameleon-like looks might be a spy worth recruiting.

———

Ed drove a 1940 Buick Super, black with a heavy chrome grille, whitewall tires, and a long slashing line of chrome from nose to tail. Its ride was so smooth that Justine felt like she was sitting on a down pillow.

Mellow horns and snappy percussion wafted out of the car

radio. "Do you like jazz?" he said, his hand on the radio tuner. When she said she loved it, he pulled his hand back to the steering wheel without changing the station, but not before he rested his fingers on Justine's hand and gave it a gentle squeeze.

"Building B is a better place since you and Samantha arrived." He turned down the radio until the music was just a syncopated hum. "At the very least, it's a more scenic place."

She smiled her thanks at the compliment. "We're both really excited about our new jobs. And about being in Washington. And about everything, really."

"I can tell. Maybe that's why you two seem to have hit it off so quickly. You share the exuberance of extreme youth. It's like you've become fast friends within days."

Justine didn't like the direction the conversation was going. Had she and Georgette already blown their cover by failing to seem like strangers? She tried to forestall this line of questioning by waving away their instant friendship as hardly worth mentioning. "Being small-town girls together in the big city will do that."

"New Orleans isn't that small."

"It's smaller than Washington, DC. It's socially insular. Everything's slower there."

She saw his eyes cut in her direction when she said, "socially insular," but she'd chosen those words by design. Samantha Ogletree wouldn't have said them, but she was portraying herself now, and Justine Byrne was the daughter of two overeducated academics. She was free to let her full vocabulary fly.

"New Yorkers would say that Washington is small and socially insular and slow. Humans are inordinately invested in establishing a social hierarchy." Ed, too, was letting his full vocabulary fly. As an Ivy League professor and a man, it had probably never occurred to him to censor it.

The Jefferson Memorial's dome drew her eye, its shallow curve lit white against the night sky. It was jarring to see something so iconic in person. Monumental architecture was designed to make the viewer feel small, and the Jefferson Memorial's design was working. Justine felt like a country bumpkin dressed up in fancy clothes and plunked down in the big city.

Flailing around for conversation, she circled back around to her friendship with the fictional Samantha Ogletree.

"As I was saying, I feel so very lucky to get Samantha as my roommate. I could have been thrown together with—" She paused.

"With Nora?"

He took his eyes off the road to look at her as he said it. She didn't feel particularly embarrassed, since he was the one who was being a little cruel about poor Nora, but she dropped her eyes like a tenth grader who had been caught repeating mean gossip.

"I'm sure Nora's very nice, but Samantha's closer to my age. So's Sally. She would've been a great roommate, too."

"Honestly, I think the government treats you all like children, encouraging grown women to live like boarding school kids. Oh, I know the reason they gave for building Arlington Farms. All the women coming to town to work in war jobs literally couldn't find a place to sleep. But what was wrong with building apartments where you could have your own kitchen and bathroom? And bedroom? What about privacy?" It did not escape her that Ed seemed very invested in the idea of single women with private bedrooms.

"I just moved into Kansas Hall, and I still like it there. Ask me again later, when I've had time to get tired of the place." She heard herself say "later," and realized that he could presume that this was a signal that she was already interested in a second date. Or more.

Well, let him presume. Maybe dropping provocative hints was just an arrow in a spy's quiver of manipulative skills.

The Washington Monument occupied a white slice of the night. Justine felt compelled to turn her head as they passed, keeping it in her sight as long as possible.

"Have you been to the Mayfair yet?" he asked.

"No. Tell me about it." Justine was relieved that the conversation had moved away from her—where she was from, where she lived, who her friends were, and the unstated question of whether she might be interested in seeing him again. This was how people on normal first dates made conversation, but when Ed did it, she felt like he was tapping on her cover story, looking for holes.

"The Mayfair is a supper club in the theater district, and I think it's top-notch. It opened up as soon as Prohibition ended, so it's been in business a while. The acts are all over the map. Piano jazz. Singers. Dixieland bands. Magicians. Comedians. I even saw a fortune-teller once."

"Did she tell your fortune?"

"The Lady Suzanne said that I had depths I did not show."

"Do you?"

"If I told you about the depths I do not show, they would become the depths I do show."

"And you can't possibly betray The Lady Suzanne by making her wrong?"

"It wouldn't be gentlemanly."

He deftly maneuvered the car into a parallel spot and hurried around to open her door.

Taking his arm, she clasped her evening bag in the other, aware of the pen-shaped Stinger inside. It didn't seem to belong in the same world with her velvet dress or Ed's elegant car or the brightly lit facades of the theaters they were strolling past. She was grateful to the Stinger, and not just because it could save her life if her undercover work went south. She was grateful because it reminded her that this was not just a pleasant evening with a touch of glamour, spent with a man who interested her more than she had expected.

The Stinger reminded her that he could also be an enemy agent prepared to kill her if she stood in his way. And so could anybody else who crossed her path.

Chapter 9

The Mayfair was decorated with painted scenes from around the world, with one wall reserved for a mural called "Flags of All Countries" that depicted flags representing, if not all nations, many of them. Diners were served by women dressed in the traditional costumes of those nations—or at least the American version of those traditional costumes—a fashion choice that nodded to the club's nickname, "The Café of All Nations." It occurred to Justine that this nickname must have sounded different before the world's nations went to war.

"The Mayfair's kitchen boasts chefs stolen from some of the city's swankiest restaurants," Ed said. "When ingredients like filet mignon or Carolina shad are available, those chefs serve it with style. When the war makes luxury items hard to come by, they work miracles with the ingredients they do have."

The entertainment for the evening was a seven-piece tuxedo-clad band playing swing music. Most of the room was filled with black-and-chrome dining tables arranged to allow a good view of the stage, but a small area had been kept open for dancing. The chairs were upholstered in a strong, deep turquoise that combined with the colorful murals and flags and costumes to make the whole room vibrate with color.

The hostess seated them at a table and asked if they'd like cocktails.

"If you enjoy raspberries," Ed said, "I'd suggest the Clover Club. It's one of their specialties."

When she nodded that, yes, she enjoyed raspberries, he said, "The lady would like a Clover Club, and I'd like a Stinger."

Justine tried not to flinch at the word "Stinger." Her eyes wanted to wander to the purse where she had tucked her Stinger, but she turned them to Ed, instead.

"This place is grand," she said.

"Wait until you taste that drink. While we're waiting for it, we should have time for a dance."

Justine stood, bending to put her purse on the seat of her chair and push it in close to the table, as she'd seen other women do. Ed plucked it out of her hand.

"This is tiny. Let me put it in my breast pocket. It'll be perfectly safe there." He removed the soft satin bag from her hand and tucked it inside his jacket.

Now he'd said the word "Stinger" and taken hers within a few short seconds. Unless this was a coincidence, Justine was now in the company of a man who had told her that he knew who she was and then disarmed her. If he shot her to death with her own tiny gun, she would at least not have to face Paul and admit her failure. Again.

———

The raspberry-studded Clover Club was delicious, and so was the meal. The Mayfair had stolen its chefs well. Justine's ham was drizzled with the perfect amount of champagne sauce, and her cauliflower polonaise was elegantly strewn with buttered breadcrumbs and capers.

"I don't suppose I could convince you to learn to play bridge. We would be an unstoppable team."

"I'm flattered, but what makes you think I'd be good at it?"

"Karl says that you have a completely logical mind, and that's half the battle."

"What's the other half?" she asked as she cut a bite of the succulent ham. "A flair for numbers? Experience at playing other card games?"

"Those things are useful, but I think you're focusing on the game play, instead of the bidding. That's natural for a gin rummy player because there's nothing to gin rummy but laying down the cards and seeing who wins according to the game's rules. Bridge favors players with a Machiavellian frame of mind, because the game lets them shift the rules in their favor while they're in the process of playing the game."

"My mother would have called that cheating."

This earned her a surprised chuckle. "It's not cheating if everybody knows what's going on, although card players gave the Machiavellian nature of games like bridge away when they designed them to give victory to the team who takes the most 'tricks.' Let me try to explain without committing the unforgivable sin of pulling out this deck of cards while dining with an elegant lady at an elegant club."

He patted his thigh over the spot where his cards rested in his pocket.

"After the hands have been dealt and before any cards are played, everyone at the table looks at their own hands and makes an educated guess about how powerful their cards are. Then they conduct an auction, bidding for the chance to name the most powerful suit. You know—clubs, diamonds, hearts, or spades. The winner also gets to see his partner's cards, but so does everybody else. It's all fair and square."

"That sounds more like a gambling game, like poker."

"Well, you don't have to play for money. Most of my friends don't. What you're bidding for is control and a chance to shift the rules in your favor."

When Justine heard that Ed enjoyed a card game that centered on "control and a chance to shift the rules in your favor," she wondered if those were the goals he pursued in real life.

He was still talking about bridge. "The important part about the auction in bridge is that you have a partner, so you're bidding on a contract that you're going to have to fulfill together. The contract is a commitment to win a certain number of tricks during that hand, usually a lot of them. But you can't see each other's cards before you make that commitment."

"That sounds like a guessing game, and where's the fun in that? How are you and your partner supposed to agree to a contract without the information you need on whether you can both hold up your end of the bargain?"

He gave her a wide grin, tossed down the last of his drink, and nodded at the waiter to signal he wanted another. Leaning toward her like a co-conspirator, he murmured, "That's the thing. You're not guessing, because the whole auction is conducted in code. A bridge tournament conducted at Arlington Hall would be the most fearsome competition ever, don't you think?"

"There would be intellectual carnage."

"Exactly. A bridge player who knows the game's code can construct a theory of the cards in the hands of every player at the table, just as surely as if they were allowed to do this." He pantomimed reaching for a stack of cards sitting on the table in front of her, spreading them into a fan, studying them, and giving them back to her. "But so can all the other people at the table."

"Because they know the code, too?"

"Exactly. If everybody knows the code, then everything's fair. But if my partner and I are working with a secret code that our opponents don't know, then that's cheating."

Justine was so intrigued by this that she forgot to maintain her icy glamour. She furrowed her brow in thought. "Bridge sounds more interesting than I expected."

"Oh, good. Maybe I can convince you to take a chance on me as a bridge partner. That will make up for the fact that you're working for Karl instead of me. Karl says that I should be jealous that he got such a choice assistant." As if he'd suddenly realized that he was talking to his own assistant's friend, he hurried to say, "Not that I expect to have any problems with Samantha's work. Not in the least. She seems very competent."

Justine wondered if he knew that she was supposed to have been working for him or, worse, whether he suspected the reason for the change. She also wondered if this line of conversation was code for "I know who you are, and I know why you're here." She arranged her features into a calm mask, dabbed her lips with her napkin, and said, "It's a little soon for Karl to be so sure that I'm going to be such a big help to him."

"He's pretty sure. There aren't many bosses who've had the advantage of teaching their employees from the age of eight. I saw him after work, and he told me that your German is excellent and that you have an innate understanding of cryptography and logistics."

Ed had ordered wine with dinner and asked the waiter to leave their wine bottle at the table, which meant that he was able to refill her glass himself as he spoke. This could be the action of a gracious host. It could be the move of a masher hoping to lower his date's inhibitions. Or it could be the strategy of an enemy agent trying to get his target to talk.

She took a bite of her cauliflower and let her now-full wine-glass sit untouched. "I'm surprised Karl has told you anything. I didn't think the two of you got along."

"'It is easier for the prince to make friends of those men who were contented under the former government, and are therefore his enemies, than of those who, being discontented with it, were favorable to him and encouraged him to seize it.'"

"Isn't that Machiavelli? Or, at least, some version of Machiavelli, since it doesn't sound exactly like the translation I remember. And is it a fancy way of saying that it's best to keep your enemies close by, where you can see what they're up to, instead of spending all your time with your friends?"

He raised his glass and said, "Yes, it's Machiavelli, and that's what he's saying. Very good."

She raised her own glass and tapped his with it. "Thank you, Professor. A few minutes back, I noticed that you credited me with a Machiavellian streak. I'm not sure whether to be flattered or insulted." Then she took the smallest sip and locked eyes with him over the rim of her wine goblet. "But I hope you didn't ask me out just to talk professor talk."

She leaned against the back of her chair and crossed her legs, taking her time about it. This seemed to Justine like a pose that Marlene Dietrich might strike when she got to the seductive part of the evening. At the very least, she hoped she didn't look foolish doing it.

"No." He leaned toward her. "Oh, no. I asked you out because I enjoy a woman with a fine mind. And a shapely pair of legs." She felt his palm cup her knee. "But that is absolutely not the same thing as wanting her for a student."

Justine was startled by how quickly and directly he'd

responded to her leg-crossing maneuver. It was too early in the evening to let his hand stay where it was—where would it go next?—but she didn't know how Marlene Dietrich would get a man's hand off her knee.

Flailing around for a smooth, sexy way to do that, she said, "I think we should dance," and rose. If he rose, too, he would have a hard time reaching her knee.

He did rise, although his hand lingered a little too long and rose a little too far before he released her leg. With his palm on her shoulder blade, he steered her to the dance floor and, because the music was slow, into an embrace. He was so tall, and he held her so close, that she could feel her soft handbag in his breast pocket beneath her cheek. Inside it, she felt the Stinger that could put a single bullet in him, or in her, or in somebody.

"Don't believe everything Karl tells you," he said, rocking her gently from side to side in time to the music.

"Should I believe what you tell me?"

"At work? Sure. When two people are on the same side—like bridge partners—and I believe we are, why would they lie to each other? We both want the war to be over, don't we?"

"But aren't Karl and I on the same side?"

Instead of answering, he raised his hand and led her into a spin that left her dizzy and wrapped in his arms, her back to his chest. She could no longer see his face, but he could whisper in her ear.

"But you're probably wondering whether you should believe what I tell you now, when I'm talking about you and me. If you want what I want, then I think you should."

"How can I know what you want unless you tell me?"

He raised his hand again and twirled her around to face him with her entire body pressed to his. Cupping the back of her head in one big hand, he tilted it back. Then, still swaying to the music, he leaned down and brushed his lips across hers.

"You don't need me to spell out what I want, and you don't need me to say it in code, either. You know what I want, but I'm in no hurry. Romance is a game and it's a dance. It moves to its own rhythm, and it takes its own sweet time."

———

Washington still looked like a cross between a fairy tale and a history book as the Buick rolled along its streets in the late-night quiet. The radio still murmured quiet horns over a smooth bass line. Justine was only a little tipsy.

As they passed over the Potomac, Ed said, "Don't forget what I said about Karl. There's a reason he goes through assistants so quickly, but I don't know what it is."

"Does he fire them? Is he so hard to please that they quit?"

"Oh, he's fired a few, although he's so ecstatic over your work that I think you'll escape that. At least for a good long while."

"I've got a lot of perseverance. It would be hard to make me quit."

"I'm not so concerned about the ones he fires or the ones who throw a screaming fit and walk out on him. He's a hard taskmaster. Everybody knows it. There's a reason that the people around Arlington Hall call him 'Killer Karl'—or they did until Bettie's death caused that nickname to stop being funny. I'm far more concerned about the women who work for Karl until they...well, until they disappear."

Her head whipped his way so hard that her neck hurt.

"What did you say?"

"They just leave. We come to work, and we find that Karl's been left to his own devices. And then the word comes from somebody on the military side of things that they've been 'reassigned.' It's happened at least twice. The women don't say goodbye. We don't see them at all. Their roommates say that they come home that day to find an empty closet. The women are just gone. It's happened at least twice that I know of."

"Does Karl know where they went?"

"If he does, he doesn't say."

He downshifted as the car climbed the hill where Arlington Farms sat. Higher up the flank of the hill, the graves of Arlington National Cemetery began. Somewhere, a great war was making more bodies to be buried in more graves.

"He may not know. One of my employees left the same way, and I don't know where she went."

"You're not talking about Bettie, are you?"

"No." His voice wavered oddly, and he stopped talking to clear his throat. "No, Bettie's not missing. She died. We know that for sure."

"She was the one who was—" Her own voice felt unsteady.

"The one who was murdered? Yes. That was Bettie, and we miss her every day. She was soft-spoken and sweet, and everybody in the room considered her their friend. She wasn't as obviously brilliant as you are, but she had everything a code breaker needed."

"Perseverance, careful analytical methods, intuition, and luck."

Ed gave her a sad smile. "You've read Hitt. Yes. Bettie had those things. She broke some messages that saved lives—a lot of lives. It was another of my employees, Mabel Hennessey, who was, according to the Army, 'reassigned,' like Karl's two assistants."

"Do you think she's safe?"

He shrugged. "I don't know. All I can do is hope that it was a simple case of the government moving her someplace where her skills will do even more to help us get to the end of this war. More than that, I hope she's okay."

He parked the car and fumbled in the pocket where he'd put her purse. She presumed that he was going to pull it out and return it to her. Instead, he pulled out a pack of cigarettes and offered her one. "Do you smoke?"

She shook her head.

"Mind if I do?"

"No, not at all."

He lit it, took a drag, cracked the car window, and held the burning cigarette outside the car.

He said, "You intrigue me. I'd like to see you again," as he leaned over to give her a kiss that was a little less brief than the one they'd shared on the dance floor. His lips tasted of tobacco smoke, and Justine was surprised to find that she didn't mind.

Still pretending that she was Marlene Dietrich acting in a not-too-scandalous movie, she reached a hand up as he kissed her, brushed it across the exposed back of his neck, and slid it along his jawbone before he pulled it away. The hand gripping her shoulder said more than the kiss did.

She said, "Yes. I'd like to see you again, too," and it was possible that she meant it.

Now that he had secured the promise of another night of romance, Ed flicked a short length of ash out the window and shifted the conversation to other things.

"Let's see. I've told you to be careful of Killer Karl. What else can I tell you about your new job? Well, there's this." He leaned over to whisper in her ear. "Take great care of your mind."

This advice caught Justine off guard. She'd always been able to rely on her mind, and she'd never given a second thought to its care. Now, in the very same day, Karl and Ed were both insistent that she understand the risks inherent in the work that she was doing for them.

"The work we do—the work we all do—will crush us

eventually. The small successes just don't make up for the day-to-day failures. The frustration of staring at pages of gibberish for days, sometimes weeks, will break us in the end. The SSA doesn't care what the work does to us, as long as we remain able to keep doing it. I know this, because I spend a lot of time propping up employees who are brilliant but not especially stable."

Justine thought of Nora and her refusal to step on cracks. She thought of Ike, wearing his winterwear indoors in a well-heated room and living in a body cruelly damaged by the war. Ed might be exaggerating when he suggested that all of his employees had mental or emotional vulnerabilities, but there seemed little doubt that some of them did.

"Success in our business is about numbers," he said. "How many people with the right mind for cryptanalysis can we find and keep on the job? How many encrypted messages can each of us crack before we crack? How many fake messages can we create to bend reality for the enemy? How many uncoded messages can we scramble before we scramble our own minds?"

"I don't know. Do you?"

He shook his head, blowing tobacco smoke in a half circle around his head. "I think there is no number that will satisfy them. Their goals for us are infinite. We do a meticulous job on each and every task, but nothing we do is ever enough."

A bitter, choked laugh escaped him along with the tobacco smoke.

"It's rather like working for my father. A college degree, a doctorate, an Ivy League job. None of them were ever enough, and a responsible wartime position isn't enough now. 'Why can't you play football? Why can't you make more money? Why can't you pick up a gun and fight for your country like your brother?'"

He sucked in another puff of smoke.

"I can't even tell my father what I do. My country would

execute me if I breathed a word to him. But don't you think he might be able to infer that what I do is important, since it's keeping my body—a body that's young enough and plenty strong enough to be cannon fodder—off the battlefield? I guess that's the real joke. My contribution to the war effort is using logic to infer truths that I can't learn any other way, but he's not capable of inferring that my work is critical to winning this war. I suppose I could make him proud if I died for my country, but I wouldn't know about it, and isn't that a joke?"

He turned his eyes from the red tip of his cigarette to Justine. "But none of that is about you, the very lovely you. If you're a quarter as capable as Karl says you are, he'll spread around some of the work he's using to drown the rest of us. He'll give some of it to you, and then maybe the rest of us will be able to take an easier breath or two."

He took the final drag of the cigarette, sucking the smoke as deep into his lungs as he could. The lit tip of the cigarette reflected in his eyes, revealing something that she'd already heard in the quaver of his voice. He was blinking back tears.

He crushed his cigarette butt in the ashtray tucked under a tiny metal flap on the dashboard, and said, "My guess is that we will breathe a little easier when Karl shifts some of our assignments to you, but only for a while. He'll give us more work, different work, and he'll pile more and different work on you. He'll tell you that the work must be done perfectly and instantaneously, or men will be mowed down by machine guns and blasted apart by bombs. But why must he tell you that, when you already know it, right down to the marrow of your bones? That knowledge, and Karl, will crush you, too. Eventually, Karl and this damn war will crush us all."

———

"Want a couple of aspirin?" Georgette said as Justine trudged through the door. "I got a glass of water waiting for you. And I wrote you out some new things to learn. That's unless you had too many cocktails to learn anything tonight. Hey! Maybe those cocktails mean you'll go easy on me tonight." She pointed to the slate where Justine wrote her algebra problems.

The slate was sitting on the bedside table beside the glass of water, and it was inscribed with Justine's nightly Choctaw lesson. Just to make things fun, Georgette had encrypted it with the private cipher they saved for messages nobody else should read. Justine's head was throbbing, so she downed the aspirin tablets at one gulp. It was possible that she'd indeed had too many Clover Clubs to come up with an algebra lesson for Georgette.

She willed her eyes to focus on the words and phrases that Georgette wanted her to learn. After applying the private cipher, she read:

> YAKOKE
> ANT PISA
> NA YUKPA

Turning the slate over, she read the words' translations.

> THANK YOU
> COME AND LOOK
> HAPPY

Georgette sat in bed reading, her hair tied up in rags and her face oddly shiny and slick. "I went down to Linda's room to find out more about that cold cream she's so crazy about. It felt so good when I rubbed some on my hand that I bought a jar off her. I think she buys it by the case, so she had more than plenty. Why don't you use a little dab of it when you take off that pancake makeup, so you can see if you like it? Just remember that it don't take much. I only used the tiniest bit, but I feel like I rubbed my whole face all over with lard."

Justine kicked off her shoes, peeled off the velvet dress and its underpinnings, put them away, and wrapped herself in a cotton gown. "You're so good to me," she said. "I'll pay you back next time Jerry takes you out. You'll come home to everything you need to keep a hangover away."

"That'll be swell, but you'll be paying me back right now when you tell me all about your evening. Was he nice?"

"Yes. I guess? He was a perfect gentleman. Well, not perfect, but there's no fun in that. He showed me a nice time. Dinner was delicious, and so were the drinks. He was pleasant to talk to, but other than the fact that his work is hard and he doesn't get along with his father and he likes to play cards, I'm not sure I found out very much about him."

Georgette lowered her voice to a whisper. "That sounds like a date with a spy."

Justine whispered back, "I certainly didn't volunteer anything about myself, and I'm a spy."

"I prefer the term 'agent,'" Georgette said in a low, husky voice.

This was Paul's personal motto, and Georgette sounded so much like him that Justine nearly fell off her bed laughing.

"We'll have some privacy to talk more tomorrow," Georgette whispered. "Too many ears here."

"If we're still going to Gloria's, maybe we can find someplace to take a walk. Like a park. A quiet sidewalk."

"Oh, we're going to Gloria's. And we're getting privacy. Just wait and see. Now take this cold cream and wipe off them Marlene Dietrich eyebrows. You look like a dish, but you don't look like you."

Chapter 10

Justine had imagined Gloria and her lab in one of the buildings that had sprung up in downtown Washington in the years since the Pearl Harbor attack. Where else would the government put the fancy, modern lab that Paul had promised Gloria?

It seemed that the answer to that question was not "downtown Washington." According to Jerry, who had arrived bright and early to ferry them wherever they were going, Gloria's brand-spanking-new laboratory was at an abandoned Civilian Conservation Corps camp, way out in the Maryland countryside.

"Get comfortable," Jerry said as he adjusted a set of hand controls that he must have installed himself. "We'll be going about sixty miles, and they're not all highway miles."

Georgette leaned forward and poked Jerry in the shoulder. "Just last night, I told Justine that we'd have some time to talk about secret stuff. I bet she didn't guess that we'd have such a handsome driver while we was doing it."

He barked, "Watch it! I'm driving," and swatted her hand away, but not too hard.

Georgette had left Jerry sitting all by his lonesome in the front seat, so that she could sit in the back and talk to Justine. They didn't have any secrets from him—at least, they didn't have secrets from him that were related to work—but they needed to make the best use possible of this time when they could speak freely. They had so very little of it.

"Now let me tell you what I learned last night while I was gettin' us a jar of cold cream." Georgette brushed her hand over her own cheek as if hoping that Linda's face cream had worked magic in a single night.

"You learned that neither of us is going to be getting a permanent wave, because we can't afford to go to the hairdresser?"

"Yes, I did learn that, and also your hair is curly enough that you don't need one. Lucky you. But I also learned that Sally used to room with a woman named Doris Goldberg. Until… poof! Doris was gone, up and left without a word. That's when Sally moved in with Thelma. Can you believe she lives with that sourpuss? She must really miss Doris. I ain't heard nothing but nice things about her."

"Did Doris have my job working for Karl?"

Georgette looked impressed. "She did. How did you guess?"

"Ed said that at least two of Karl's assistants have left without a word. She must be one of them. Did anybody look for Doris?"

"Karl told people she got transferred. That's all anybody knows."

"That's exactly what Ed told me. He seemed to be trying to tell me not to trust Karl, but he admitted to having a former worker named Mabel who left the same way."

"So Karl and Ed have both lost employees who disappeared?"

"Yes. But Ed told me about it—warned me about it, actually— and that makes him seem more trustworthy. I've been working closely with Karl for two days, and he hasn't breathed a word."

"But maybe Ed told you about it on purpose, so's you'd trust him."

This could be true. Justine had seen enough of Ed to believe that she'd only heard what he wanted her to hear.

"Also, Bettie was working for Ed when she got killed," Georgette pointed out. "Maybe it was a coincidence and maybe it wasn't."

Ed had seemed really sad about Bettie, but did she believe him? Justine felt antsy, like she wanted to ask Jerry to stop the car and let her walk for a while.

"But here's the thing," Georgette said. "On my way back to our room from Linda's, I made it a point to go by the piano room, in case Nora was there, and I was lucky. Well, I don't know how lucky I was, 'cause I think she's in that room every night that rolls."

"That's what I hear."

"I have to tell you that nobody's lyin' about her music. It ain't what the rest of us are used to. But they're wrong when they say she just bangs around. That woman can flat-out play the piano. Her fingers can go a million miles an hour, and the music… how can I say it? It makes you feel things. It even makes you see things, a little. One minute, I saw swans a-floating on the water. The next, I heard a great big tree slam hard to the ground, so sad and so beautiful."

Justine saw Jerry sneak a peek at Georgette, so she knew he was listening to the way her friend talked about music.

"You know what else Linda told me?" Georgette said. "She said that Nora gave up a career as a concert pianist to marry her husband. He died, y'know. She trained for that career for years and years, and now they're both gone, her husband and her music."

"She must have really loved that man," Justine said. "To give up music when she'd worked so hard and for so long for it, I mean."

Georgette didn't answer right away. She just looked out the car window and watched the trees go by. When she finally spoke, she didn't turn back to Justine. She spoke to the trees. "I don't like it that people are mean to Nora."

There was only the slightest twitch of movement to betray Jerry as he swiveled his neck so he could hear what Georgette had to say.

"I don't like it, either, but I can't see that she notices." Justine tried to remember everything she'd said and done. Had she been mean to Nora?

She didn't think so, but she knew that she hadn't been especially kind.

Georgette turned back to her. "I notice. The next person who says something awful behind Nora's back is gonna hear from me."

———

The last stretch of their trip to visit Gloria took them through rolling terrain where they saw no other cars or human beings for miles on end. In the distance, Justine saw a hazy blue ridge of low mountains.

Jerry needed to keep his eyes on the twisting road, so Justine had to listen closely to the words floating over his shoulder. "Before the war, the place we're going was a CCC camp," he said, "so there was already a mess hall here, along with a kitchen, a bunch of cabins, and an administrative building with offices all ready for the brass. When the government took it over as a training facility, it made some substantial upgrades."

"Upgrades?" Justine asked.

"Indoor toilets, for sure. Hot water. Insulation and heat for the cabins and office space. Refrigeration for the mess hall. A dispensary. A classroom building and some barracks. Officers' quarters."

"All the comforts of home," Georgette said. "And more. My folks would be real happy if somebody put a toilet in their house."

"The water supply and waste disposal system had to be upgraded before we could house many people this far out in the woods, but our engineers managed it. We've got flush toilets for all. And electricity," Jerry said. "Our trainers have other ways to make our people miserable while they're at the camp. Like obstacle courses. Mock interrogation rooms. And so on."

"Gloria would need reliable electricity and waste disposal for her lab," Justine said. "And gas."

"She's got it all, even an LP tank of her very own. Gotta keep those Bunsen burners burning. Pretty sure she's got her own generator, too."

Jerry parked the car outside an older log structure that seemed to be the administrative building he'd mentioned, and Georgette moved to the trunk where his chair was stored. Justine knew Jerry could stand up and move around long enough to manage this alone, if he was careful and if he kept a tight grip on the car, so watching Georgette reflexively help him with it gave her the sense that their already close relationship was growing closer. Her simple, wordless gesture, and his refusal to be too proud to let her do that, said that they were partners. More than that, they were friends, just as Paul was his friend when he helped him get his chair in and out of the car. She hoped that she and Jerry were good enough friends that he'd be happy for her assistance when he wanted it.

She wondered where Paul was and what he was doing. She wondered why he thought she shouldn't know.

The administrative building was surrounded by a cluster of cabins, also older and built of logs. Surrounding the cabins was a ring of newer prefabricated buildings that must hold the classrooms, barracks, and dispensary that Jerry had mentioned.

Standing several paces away from the mess hall was a sizable structure with the characteristic arching profile of a Quonset hut. Like all Quonset huts, it looked like someone had slung an ax at a tin can, slicing it in two from top to bottom, and then laid it on its side for people to live in. The LP tank beside it made Justine's heart skip because it told her that she was looking at Gloria's lab.

There was a window in the hut's front door. Through it, Justine caught a glimpse of a shadow in motion. Gloria was hovering there, waiting for her. To prove that this was true, the metal door, set in a metal wall under exhaust vents, burst open and Gloria erupted out of it.

"Justine! My dear." Gloria's arms, strong and skinny, wrapped around her goddaughter's chest, and Justine was a child again. Her mother and father were gone, but Gloria had loved them, too, and she loved Justine. Her godmother's embrace brought them back. Her arms felt like home.

Gloria kissed her hard on the cheek and released her. "And you must be Samantha," she said smoothly to Georgette, whom she knew quite well. Taking both of Georgette's hands in hers, she said, "I'm so glad that Justine has already found such a good friend in Washington." Then she gave Jerry, whom she had entertained in her home several times, the cool nod one would give a stranger. All she said to him was, "Thank you, sir, for bringing them to me. I'm Gloria."

Returning her nod, he said, "It was a pleasure. I'm Alan."

During their phone conversation, Georgette must have told Gloria what she needed to know about their undercover identities, and Gloria was carrying out the ruse perfectly. This only made sense for a woman who was brilliant enough to earn a PhD in physics in her second language at a time when women were not welcomed into the field with open arms, especially when they weren't American. Gloria would always have the wariness of a refugee to temper her trust in other human beings.

Except for Justine. Gloria had never been afraid to show Justine how much she loved her.

The morning sun sparkled on Gloria's salt-and-pepper frizz, tightly braided and coiled atop her head, as always. Her black eyes sparkled, too. A pencil was poked into her braids and a pair of blue reading glasses hung on a chain around her neck. Her face, unlined for a woman in her fifties, was alight.

"You must tell me about your work, and you must come see my beautiful lab." She opened the door behind her and shooed them through it. When it closed, she said, "It is safe to speak freely in here." Then she turned on the overhead ventilation fan to foil anyone who thought they might stand outside and try to listen in.

From outside, a Quonset hut isn't much more than a humble half of a huge tin can. From inside, though, it is a different story. The great arc of corrugated metal that forms both its roof and walls covers a floor that is uninterrupted by walls or pillars or supports of any kind. This gives the humble Quonset hut the kind of uninterrupted interior volume that cathedrals gain from vaults and domes. In the few weeks since Justine had last seen her in New Orleans, Gloria had begun building a cathedral to science in that space.

Four long workbenches made of steel and topped with black slate crossed the room. Each was topped with steel racks, neatly loaded with shining glass flasks, beakers, test tubes, and pipettes. Shelves held bins of electrical wiring, batteries, and clamps. Ventilation hoods and a workbench ran along one wall, and piles of boxes sat in front of them, waiting to be unloaded.

At the rear of the space, behind the benches, was an open area for larger equipment, and Gloria had a whole lot of it. Some of it was still crated, but Justine thought she recognized one contraption, crafted of a curved metal tube and a straight one fastened together in the shape of the letter *D*. It made Justine think of the rainbow-shaped streams of ionized uranium isotopes that had attracted a German spy to New Orleans. Unless Justine missed her guess, Gloria was still following that rainbow-shaped trail, and the American government was paying her to do it.

"Oh, Gloria," she breathed, spinning in place to take it all in. "You must be so happy."

Gloria's face glowed like a hot stream of uranium ions. "Oh, my dear, yes. I am."

"Even my father didn't get to work in his lab all day, every day," Justine said. "He had his classes to teach, although I know he enjoyed his students."

"Oh, I will be teaching. That is why I'm here at the training center. For one thing, I will be part of the training sequences for handling explosives and poisons. When one must handle deadly chemicals, one must know how they work."

Justine couldn't argue with that.

"I will also be training agents who will be building explosive devices in the field. They will come into my laboratory and learn how to do so safely. This is why I have such expansive benches. I must have room for my students."

She pointed to four tables in a rear corner of the lab. "I have space for students to do paper-and-pencil work, as well. And I need it because I have already begun classroom teaching. In those classes, I work with agents who wish to fine-tune their accents and vocabularies when speaking in Polish or German."

She crossed her arms and surveyed her territory. "The U.S. government has been very generous, but I believe they find me useful."

"Yes, ma'am. I know they do," Jerry said. "If I'm ever deployed to eastern Europe, you can expect to find me here, asking for help with my Polish."

Gloria's smile was quick and brilliant, like lightning. "More than anything, I aim to keep my students alive. In return, they keep me young."

She led them to one of the tables, near a coffeepot that sat perking next to a tray of biscuits. "I live in a cabin that I have all to myself, a privilege I owe to the fact that the permanent staff here is all male. Propriety dictates that I not be bunked with them. My cabin has everything that I need, but it does not have a kitchen. Fortunately, I was able to cajole the camp cook to hold back these biscuits for you from breakfast."

After handing around cups of steaming coffee and doling out the biscuits, Gloria sat down and did one of the things she did best. She cut straight to the point.

"I understand, Justine and Samantha-who-is-really-Georgette, that you are both working as agents, undercover and presumably in danger. And yet I have not seen you here being trained. How is this possible?"

She turned her head to stare directly at Jerry. Speaking crisply, she asked, "Who is this cavalier with their safety?" and Justine understood that the "who" was rhetorical. Gloria was speaking of Paul.

It was strange to hear Jerry speak in a defensive tone, but Gloria had that effect on people. "I taught them to shoot and took them out to practice—"

"There has not been time for them to have gained sufficient practice with firearms to be a danger to others. At this moment, they are dangers to themselves."

"Georgette did very well in her training as a radio operator—"

"Again, she has not had time to finish that training."

"Look," Jerry said. "As everybody at this table knows, there's a war on. We needed Justine to be where she is. When an unforeseeable complication arose, we pulled Georgette in."

"Unforeseeable events get people killed. Someone failed to foresee that Justine might be recognizable to the kind of people who tend to be assigned to cryptanalysis. This has put her in a position of considerable risk. And it was avoidable."

"I know for a fact that he has lost sleep over that. I hear him bumping around in the kitchen on the nights when his worries keep him awake. I'm not sure he sleeps much at all these days."

So Jerry and Paul were housemates, as they'd been in New Orleans. Justine hadn't known that for sure. Somehow, she thought she should know more about their lives. If she were to be completely honest, it was Paul's life that she believed she should know more about.

"Pardon me if I am more concerned about the safety of my goddaughter and her friend than I am about how well their superior sleeps."

"We have these," Justine said, reaching into her purse and drawing out the Stinger. "As guns go, they're not very impressive, but they're not nothing."

"Georgette told me about your little Stingers. They are not nothing, no. But they are not sufficient."

Jerry hurried to do some more explaining. Justine wished she had Gloria's ability to unsettle people until they were defensive and vulnerable. Her godmother should be training agents in interrogation techniques. Perhaps that was part of her new employer's long-range plans for her.

"We have to balance the safety they might gain from any weapons they carry against the risk that possessing those weapons will give them away." Jerry looked at Gloria, obviously hoping that these words pacified her. He didn't know Gloria very well.

"Do not speak to me as if I am stupid. I work here," she opened her arms expansively enough to encompass the training facility and the square miles of wilderness surrounding it. "I understand the balance of risks inherent in sending an agent out into the world. I am merely speaking to the apparent lack of concern paid to the relative risks facing these two women. Their safety is very important to me."

Justine wondered if she had been wise to trust Paul's judgment, just because she believed that he cared for her. This didn't stop her from trying to defend him. "Georgette and I both share your concerns, Gloria. We'd like to be better armed, but we're not sure how it would work. Women's office clothes aren't designed to conceal weapons, and the men around us are really handsy. You can slap a man's face for groping you, but you can't erase his memory if he felt a gun strapped to your leg while he was doing it."

"I did make us some skirt pockets," Georgette said. "As long as we carry something in them that don't look like a weapon, like a Stinger, them pockets could help us keep safe."

"You made what?" Gloria's face was rigid with shock.

Jerry, too, was aghast. "You can't do that. The costumers—"

Gloria interrupted him to yell at him. "They would know this, if you had trained them."

Speaking to Justine and Georgette in a more even tone, she said, "You cannot overrule the decisions made by the costumers. You cannot."

Jerry risked Gloria's ire by interrupting her. "There's an art and a science to outfitting an agent for undercover work. People have lost their lives for smoking a British brand of cigarettes while in France. Agents have been unmasked by wearing the wrong shoes or by wearing the right shoes that were scuffed in the wrong places."

"Or that weren't scuffed enough," Gloria said, smoothly regaining control of the conversation. "Human beings sense the tiniest clues that another human being doesn't fit in. This is the way that we are made, and you know it. Anyone who has ever been shunned by a social group knows it."

Justine thought back to tenth grade. She had once worn a dress to school that had been sent to her by one of her mother's friends in Germany. It had been a lovely dress, evidently well-made and expensive, but the popular girls had been able to spot from twenty paces that it was very slightly different from what they were wearing. They had been so cruel with their mockery that she'd never worn the dress again, and she'd never told her mother why.

"Do you live or work among women who know fashion?" Gloria asked.

Justine locked eyes with Georgette, who mouthed the word, "Linda."

Gloria answered herself. "Of course, you do. In any large group, there are people—usually women—who are constantly aware of how they look relative to how others look. These women may well have recognized the brand of your clothes and realized that their design did not originally include pockets. This would lead them to the question of why you needed pockets badly enough to install them. That question leads directly to a hand in your pocket that pulls out your Stinger and shoots you with it."

"I'll sew them pockets right up." Georgette's voice was contrite.

"Have you worn the clothes in public since you added pockets?"

Georgette gave her a slow nod.

"Then it's too late. You cannot be seen walking around with pockets that appear, like Schrödinger's cat, to exist based on random events. Leave the pockets as they are and let me give you some things to fill them."

Gloria fetched a box from a drawer in the nearest laboratory bench. "I have made myself helpful to the engineers who build covert weapons for our agents, and I have received some prototypes as recompense. It will please me very much to know that they are protecting the two of you." Settling herself back in her seat, she opened the box.

Pulling out two pens that looked a great deal like their Stingers, she held them balanced on her palm. "See this clip here? It looks like it is meant to hold the pen in a man's shirt pocket, but no. Like the Stinger, this weapon uses the clip as a trigger, only it does not shoot bullets. It emits pepper spray."

"Not poison gas?" Georgette's laugh was nervous.

"Would I give you something that would kill you along with your adversary?"

Georgette, Justine, and Jerry shook their heads like high school freshmen caught talking in class.

"The pepper spray will disable your adversary—and you, to an extent, but you will be prepared for it. You should be able to affect an escape, despite the tears flowing down your face."

Gloria handed the pepper spray pens to Georgette and Justine, who put them in their purses, since Georgette had only put pockets in their office clothes.

She pulled two more items from the box, both of them small and made of a dull metal. Saying, "For when you need a diversion," she twisted one of them with a small precise motion.

A god-awful racket like a giant's alarm clock echoed off the Quonset hut's metal walls until Gloria twisted the device again to silence it. She held out the two devices, and the women each took one.

"Neither the pepper pens nor the noisemakers can be used to kill you by your adversary, although possessing them gives you away as a government agent. These, however, can be used against you, so bear this in mind."

She pulled two ordinary-looking pencils out of the box and laid one on the table. Holding the other, she gripped the metal cage that connected its worn graphite-stained eraser to its yellow-painted wood. In a single motion, she twisted and yanked hard to reveal a long piece of sharp metal, more like a spike than a blade.

"As you know"—she paused to smile at Justine—"I have always kept my writing utensils close at hand." She brushed her fingers over the pencil stuck in her braids. "Nobody who has ever met me would bat an eye to see me wearing a pencil in my hair. And yet my pencil might have the capacity to render me deadly."

Justine studied the yellow-painted stick in Gloria's hair. Was it just a pencil or did it conceal a deadly weapon? Gloria would never say.

Gloria handed over the pencils. "Take care with these. There is a small amount of graphite in each tip. They will write for a brief time, if necessary to keep them from being recognized as weapons, but they will not write for long."

She leaned close to Georgette and peered at her hair. "Your customary chignon will work as well as my braids to hold this weapon at the ready." Georgette immediately stuck the pencil in her hair. "As for you, my dear—" She reached out to touch Justine's newly blond locks. "You look so astonishingly like your mother these days that I hesitate to suggest that you style your hair like hers, but it would be a good idea. Begin twisting your hair into a bun atop your head and develop the habit of tucking a pencil in it while you're working. You will be able to arm yourself in plain sight."

To Jerry, she said, "If you would like devices like these for yourself, I can arrange it."

"I wouldn't mind it, and I'd be grateful. Thank you, ma'am."

———

Jerry found Gloria fascinating.

He knew that she had seen dark days, but she had come into her own when Paul—prompted by Justine—had recognized the usefulness of her talents and hired her. Now, she was a woman with a firm control of herself and her actions, with an equally firm control on the actions of those around her. Unless he was badly mistaken, Justine and Georgette didn't realize this. Gloria oozed mother-love, and they luxuriated in it. If he were honest with himself, so did he. They were all young people far from home, so why wouldn't they?

He was realizing how powerfully comforting it was to be fussed over by an older woman, and he was not careless about using the world "powerfully." By making them feel comfortable and loved, she gained power and influence. By showing her care for them—and he did believe that she genuinely cared for them— she gained allies who would want her to feel comfort and love.

Jerry could see that she had been using this strategy since she began this new job and to good effect. As they'd finished their midday meal, he'd noticed that the mess hall staff were sufficiently caught in her spell to sneak a tray of snacks into Gloria's hands, just as they'd filched a tray of biscuits for her that morning. He saw that her lab had been built with astonishing speed, and this was not always the case with government contractors.

Most impressively, the engineers who built covert weapons for government agents had been grateful enough for her generous help to hand over rare prototypes that just might save her beloved goddaughter's life.

Jerry had watched many men jockey for power, and some of them had managed it with kindness and empathy, but none of them had accomplished the task in quite the same way. He could see that this feminine approach had its advantages, especially when coupled with Gloria's confidence. And her boldness. These were the things that drew him to her. Justine and Georgette, too, were confident and bold women. He found them rare, and he wondered why that was so.

He was beginning to fear that they weren't rare at all, but that the world beat the confidence out of bold women. When the war was over, he was going to sit his mother down and ask her to tell him some things. He didn't know what things, exactly, but he wanted her to tell him things that she'd never thought he wanted to hear. When he told her that he wanted to give her bold, strong granddaughters, she would tell him.

He sat alone in Gloria's lab as she tucked Georgette and Justine into the back of his car. He imagined her placing the tray of hijacked goodies on the seat beside them and kissing their cheeks. She had asked him to wait inside, as she had one last thing to say to him. Since he found her so fascinating, he was impatient to hear what it was.

Gloria was still waving at Georgette and Justine when she came through the door of the Quonset hut, and she waved at them until she shut it behind her. She walked over to where Jerry sat, handing him a cinnamon roll wrapped in a napkin.

"I saw how much you enjoyed these, so I saved this one for you. Justine loves them so much that she might not realize you wanted another one, and you're too much of a gentle soul to tell her."

"Thank you, ma'am."

"I need to tell you something, Jerry."

"Please do."

Gloria leaned against a laboratory bench groaning with scientific equipment, and she studied him. "Georgette adores you. You are a kind man, and I think you would be happy together, if you both decide that it is what you want."

He wasn't sure how to respond.

"Don't say anything. Your romance is your own business. I only offer my observation. But I have observed other things I must tell you."

Jerry didn't know what else to say, so he said, "Please do," again.

"You and your housemate, the man who likes to keep his name to himself, have recruited the person I cherish most in this world into a dangerous job. You have drawn a person whom I believe that you cherish, or will come to cherish, into the same precarious position. I can see that they have no idea how much danger they are in, and the two of you have done precious little to prepare them."

"We—"

"Yes, yes, you've done your best. There is a war on. I know the reasons, but I also understand the possible consequences. Let me explain some other consequences to you."

Clasping her hands in front of her like a Victorian pupil reciting her lessons, she enunciated her final words to him carefully.

"I like you, Jerry. I admire you. But if anything happens to either of those young women, I will hunt you down, and I will make you and your mysterious friend sorry that I was ever born. Please tell him for me."

Chapter 11

Kansas Hall didn't feel quite like home yet, but Justine had been glad to see the sprawling building ahead after the long drive with Georgette and Jerry.

Georgette had gone upstairs, but Justine had needed to check her mail, so she was navigating the crowded lobby alone. It was mid-afternoon on a Sunday, but men were already clogging the lobby of the dormitory, hoping for female companionship. Justine had only lived there for a few days, but it didn't take long to get tired of being harassed by strangers who thought they should be able to waltz into her home and stay there until some woman decided to be cooperative.

Most of the women tolerated the male attention, and some of them enjoyed it, but the more direct among them made it clear when they'd had their fill. Thelma, in particular, wasn't one who suffered fools gladly. Justine had grown up in a culture where good manners trumped all, so she didn't know how to respond when people ignored the rules of good behavior.

"Hey, baby…" A hand pressed itself flat against her back.

She drew away but said nothing.

Another man's hand was plucking at her elbow. "How come a

pretty girl like you is all by herself when she could spend her day off with me?" She pulled both elbows toward her body, clamping them against her ribcage.

Bettie had been killed by a date she'd just met, and Justine couldn't push this out of her mind. She didn't know these men and, based on their behavior, she didn't want to know most of them. Kansas Hall had stood for more than a year and, for all she knew, only one of the men who had visited it had been a murderer, but it only took one murder to change the way you looked at people.

Even given the constant overfamiliarity of the men haunting Kansas Hall, Justine was shocked when a man wearing full sailor regalia—bell-bottomed pants, neck scarf, and folded-brimmed cap—crept up behind her and ran the fingers of both his hands through her curls. Startled, she exploded like a torpedo embedded in the hull of a battleship.

"Leave me alone! Stop touching me. *Leave me alone.*"

The sailor fled, and all but one of the men in her immediate vicinity—and there were several—recoiled. This should have given her space to collect her thoughts, but the one still standing beside her wouldn't let her be. He grabbed her by the shoulder, prompting her to flail an arm in his direction, yelling, "Stop it right now!"

"What's wrong?" he said.

She kept flailing.

"Did one of these guys scare you? What's wrong, Justine?"

Hearing her name calmed her enough to look the man in the face. It was Ike Grantham, wearing his customary peacoat and knit hat. This made him look a little like a sailor, too, but it seemed to be just Ike's everyday garb, indoors and out. For the first time, she wondered if the hat camouflaged scars from his battle wounds.

"There are just—" She waved both hands at the hubbub around her. "Too many people. Too many men. And too many of them are touching me. I hope it's not like this every weekend."

Ike gave her a smiling shrug. "My friends all say that this is the weekend place to be for a guy who doesn't have a date. There's a reason they call Arlington Farms 'Girl Town.' That sounds a lot better to me than the other name I've heard for this place—'No-Man's Land.'"

Ike's head swung from right to left, taking in women dressed in everything from church frocks to dungarees. "It's like a department store where everything a man could want is in stock."

He misinterpreted her silence to mean that she was entertained by what he had to say. "They tell me this is the first place some soldiers and sailors go when they come back stateside, but I've been taking my time about getting here."

Justine felt like she should be able to figure out how to get a word in edgewise.

"Where's the lounge?" he asked, swinging his head from left to right. "I hear the dancing's good. Sally told me I should stop by sometime and check it out."

She was tempted to start flailing at him again.

"If it sounds so great to you," she asked, "how come it took you so long to get here?"

He took her words as flirtatious and completely overlooked the frustrated glint in her eye.

"Well, maybe I don't have to work as hard as these guys do to find dates. Or maybe you should think about the timing of my visit. Two pretty ladies come to town, and a couple of days later, here I am! Where's Samantha?"

"She's upstairs, waiting for me."

Finally, he bent down and actually looked at her. "You're really upset."

"Look around. This is my home. All I want is some peace and quiet." Justine had worked at a factory where the sounds of grinders and lathes and saws never went away. The noise in the lobby was approaching that level. "I'm sorry, Ike. I think I need to go upstairs."

Ike said, "Wait. I have an idea. And look, there's Samantha over there talking to Nora. Let me get her over here, so I can share my idea with both of you."

Ike's vision was perfect, at least when it came to women, because he'd spotted Georgette across the spacious lobby. Ike reached both hands in the air and gesticulated until she did what he wanted her to do.

"Good to see you, Ike," Georgette said as she approached.

"I've got a great idea, ladies. Here's what I'm thinking. You two are new to town. Why don't we walk across the bridge and take in some sights? We can see the Lincoln Memorial, the reflecting pool, the National Mall, the Washington Monument." He looked down at Justine and, as if remembering how upset she'd been, he said, "Just three friends looking around. Not a date. I'm not like these other guys, honest. Does that sound like fun?"

Georgette cast a sideways glance at Justine that seemed to ask, *What are we doing here? Do we have a plan?*

Justine gave a little shrug that she hoped said, *Heck if I know.*

Georgette hesitated. "It really does sound like fun, Ike, but I just promised Nora I'd go hear her play the piano at her church this evening. But you two go and have a good time!"

Justine weighed the possibilities. Here she and Georgette stood with a chance to learn more about two of their targets, Nora and Ike. It seemed obvious that they should split up and take both of those chances.

"I'd love to see the sights with a new friend, Ike," she said.

"That's a great idea. It's too bad that Samantha can't come, but maybe next time."

"It's cold," Ike said. "Get your coat."

Any hope that she could have a second alone with Georgette was dashed when Ike followed her to the cloakroom, laughing and joking all the way. Within minutes, she was waving goodbye to Georgette. Wrapped in her winter coat, Justine was on her way to see the sights of Washington, DC.

———

Georgette watched Ike usher Justine out of Kansas Hall. She wished for some kind of sign that told her what to do, but the only emotion that showed on Justine's face was jittery nerves. Espionage had a tendency to make people nervous, so this told her exactly nothing.

She had waited a couple of extra heartbeats after turning down Ike's invitation, listening for Justine to say, "Couldn't you go to church with Nora another time? Please come with us."

Justine had said no such thing. She'd stayed silent.

It seemed to Georgette that a spy should pay attention to her partner's lead. Her partner was not urging Georgette to horn in on her time alone with Ike, so she shouldn't do it.

Justine's face was still unreadable as she turned to go. Georgette thought maybe that was a good thing. A spy should have an unreadable face.

She'd never seen anybody with a face that gave away less than the nameless man who pulled her strings and Justine's and Jerry's. She knew that Justine had feelings for the man, a lot of feelings, so maybe she could read him better than Georgette could. Surely she could read him somehow, because how could you fall for a man who never once let you see how he felt?

Speaking of that man, Georgette's gut told her that he needed to know where Justine was going and who was taking her there. Too many women had disappeared, and one of them had died. This was worth a phone call, despite the risk of being overheard.

She sidled into the phone box, a closet-like wood-paneled booth with a telephone and a seat, but no door. As she dialed Jerry's home number, she planned out how to say what she needed to say, using as few words that could be overheard as possible.

She decided on, "Somebody we know is on her way to the Lincoln Memorial right now. She's not alone. I'm going to follow her."

———

Justine walked out of Kansas Hall with a strange man, wondering how worried she should be about her own safety. A short walk conducted in broad daylight sounded pretty safe. Of course, people did like to whisper about other people, usually women, being murdered in broad daylight. (And what was broad about daylight, anyway? Was it ever narrow?) Still, she would probably be safe enough with Ike, despite the fact that he always seemed just a little "off," just a little too awkward with women and just a little too eager. Even if he was "off," it didn't matter. He worked in the German section, so he was, by definition, one of the people she was supposed to learn more about. Justine hadn't planned this time alone with Ike, but this didn't mean that it wouldn't be useful.

Ike cleared his throat. "Thank you for coming with me. How do I say this? I saw how much it bothered you to have all those men in your dorm. I never thought about it, but I get it now. That's your home and you should have some privacy there. But, well—" He cleared his throat again. "I thought maybe it might help your feelings if I could explain *why* they're all there, at least a little bit."

Justine couldn't think of anything to say but, "Sure. I'd like to hear it."

"I'm guessing that a lot of them feel like I do. We're all just tired of being alone. The lobby of Kansas Hall makes you believe that there could be a place where nobody ever has to be by themselves, unless they want to be. It's homey. I live in one room in a rooming house, four walls and a cot. It's not really where you want to be on a sunny Sunday afternoon."

Justine felt her irritation with Ike ease. She was also oddly touched by his claim not to know how to say that he didn't want to be alone. He knew perfectly well how to say it. His problem was that men weren't supposed to feel lonely or uncertain. They weren't supposed to have feelings at all. They were supposed to carry on as if nothing ever touched them.

She heard herself saying, "I'm happy to keep you company. It'll do us both good to have somebody to talk to."

She watched the muscles in his face relax. It was a nice face—a little long, a little wide in the jaw, but nice. Maybe there was nothing "off" about Ike. It wasn't a crime to be awkward with women.

She gave him a smile, and it was not a spy's smile. It was the kind of genuine smile that people give their friends.

"I'm excited to see the Lincoln Memorial up close."

"You're gonna love it. That's what I like to do with my friends. I like to show them a good time."

———

Georgette, head down, waited until Ike and Justine were almost across the Arlington Memorial Bridge before she stepped onto it. There was little chance that either of them would look back and see her, but she was taking no chances. She kept to the shadows of other pedestrians.

She had hurriedly made her excuses to Nora, saying, "Something came up, and I can't come with you to church. I hope it's okay if I come see you play at choir practice Tuesday night, instead."

Hardly giving Nora a chance to answer, she'd rushed away. Then she had "borrowed" a cream scarf and a crimson coat from the Kansas Hall cloakroom. It was a flashy ensemble for someone trying not to be noticed, but Georgette had been in a hurry. She'd grabbed the outerwear that looked the least like hers, so that Ike wouldn't recognize her.

Now, the scarf covered her dark hair and the oversized coat added pounds to her muscular frame. Jerry had taught her some tricks for quick disguises, but the slumped shoulders and drooping head were her own idea. They aged her by decades.

The little girl from Des Allemands who had never before left southern Louisiana slouched resolutely toward Washington, DC. She trudged through a landscape designed to awe—a broad bridge lined by ornate lampposts, the temple-like Lincoln Memorial at its end, and the Washington Monument looming over it all—but it failed to awe Georgette. Her focus was unwavering, and it was on her friend.

———

Justine stepped off the Arlington Memorial Bridge, where the Lincoln Memorial rose like the Greek temples that she'd studied in school. She and Ike circled around the building to get a view of the monumental statue of Lincoln sitting behind its colonnade, and she felt an intimate familiarity with the scene. This view of the Lincoln Memorial had adorned the back of every five-dollar bill printed since she was six years old.

There was no breeze, so the surface of the reflecting pool at the foot of the Lincoln Memorial lay still, like a long, narrow shard of glass. It drew her eye to the shaft of the Washington Monument standing tall in the distance. Justine had inhabited this spot in her mind so often while looking at textbooks and newspapers and newsreels that she was disoriented to realize that her body had never been there before.

"I wish my parents were here." These words crossed her mind several times a day, but she rarely spoke them. Why had they popped out of her mouth now, today, while she stood face-to-face with Abraham Lincoln?

Perhaps it was because she desperately wished she could know how they would feel about the work she was doing. Dead of a car crash before America entered the conflict, they hadn't been able to help Justine navigate the realities of wartime. She had lost sleep, and she would lose more, over the people who had died because of work she'd done while employed at munitions factories. Yet she wasn't sure that she'd had any other options, not after the unprovoked attack at Pearl Harbor and the ongoing atrocities around the globe. Maybe building killing machines had been the most ethical choice open to her. Somehow, she thought that Lincoln, who had presided over an ugly war between Americans, would understand her dilemma.

Now she'd agreed to take this job, gathering intelligence on people who might be executed for espionage as a result of her work. Their deaths would be on her hands, too. But what kind of guilt would she bear if Hitler conquered the world because she didn't do her part? All she could do was muddle along without her parents' sober judgment to help her, doing the best she could.

The patriotic scenery around her was certainly

beautiful—beautiful, serene, and designed to put her in her place, her tiny and insignificant place.

"Your parents have passed?" Ike asked.

"Yes. They passed few years ago. What about your family? Do you have close relatives living nearby?"

He turned away from Lincoln to study the reflecting pool as he shook his head. "No. My father was a coal miner, and miners don't live long in West Virginia. You could say that he coughed himself to death. My mother had tuberculosis, so I guess she coughed herself to death, too. They both died while I was in high school. I've got no brothers, no sisters, no cousins that I care to speak to. Getting mail is a real important thing when you're stationed overseas, and there wasn't anybody to write me any letters."

Now there was mischief in his eyes. "Well, not at first. When I started going on leave and finally got a chance to meet women, that changed. It's not hard to get a woman to write you when she thinks you might get killed any minute."

Beneath Ike's mischief, Justine saw an essential loneliness.

"A lot of the women at Kansas Hall and at work spend their evenings writing soldiers," she said. "They line up at the post office boxes every day and come away with a stack of letters to answer. It's one way to take your mind off—" She waved a hand in the air. "Everything. We all need to take our minds off everything. I'm not much of a letter writer, so I guess I take my mind off things by trying to make friends wherever I am. A few days ago, I didn't know Samantha and Linda and Patsy and Thelma and Nora and Sally."

Still looking at the pond, and thus not meeting her eyes, he said, "Yeah, I tried your strategy. When I was in Africa, I made friends with the men who served beside me. Good friends, some of them. That didn't work out so well."

Too late, Justine remembered what she'd heard about how Ike had gotten his injuries. He got around so well that she'd forgotten for a moment how he'd left Africa, so busted up that an Army at war with half the world wasn't interested in keeping him. She wanted the granite steps of the Lincoln Memorial to crumble into the bowels of the earth and take her with them.

"They—"

"They're dead. Every last one of our unit but me. I woke up in a pile of dead bodies with just enough strength to crawl out into the open. I thought maybe somebody would see me breathing and put me in a hospital instead of a grave. That was presuming I was still breathing when anybody came along. Everything that's happened to me since then has been a flat-out miracle. I don't take anything for granted these days."

Justine couldn't think of a single thing to say.

"I don't remember anything, but I'm guessing a grenade went off somewhere to my left, because the bones in my left arm and leg were all broken. My hip, too. I was in the field hospital until they had to strike the tents and move it to the next battle. After that, they put me in a hospital in Morocco where I slept in an actual building, instead of in a tent. I was there a while. Bones take a long, long time to heal."

"It looks like you healed well?"

"Eventually. And yes, I'd guess you'd call my arm and leg well-healed."

He took off his coat and held up both arms bent to show off toned biceps through the thin shirt he wore underneath it. "I've spent a lot of time working on my injured arm, and I can do plenty with it. I could probably lift you one-handed with it, but then you're small. The bad leg takes me where I want to go. I can even run on it, when I have to. I can't complain."

"I just saw that leg take you across the Potomac."

"You got that right. And it'll take me back, too. I've got a few scars, but I'm okay and I'm alive. I have a place to live and a job to do, and I have that grenade to thank for it."

"The grenade? You're thankful for it?"

He nodded. "It got me off the battlefield and that kept me alive. But I'm thankful for more than that. The grenade brought me here. Right here."

"I don't understand."

"The grenade brought me to Washington. Well, Arlington Hall."

"I hate to admit it, but I still don't understand."

"While I was in the hospital in Morocco, I made friends with my doctors. They really liked working on somebody who was going to go back to a life pretty much like the one he'd had before. I could still see. I could still hear. I had my arms and legs and hands and feet. My brain was in no worse shape than it was before the war. I know there are a lot of people who come all the way back to a good life from terrible injuries, and I admire them, but I'm grateful I didn't have to do that. Compared to the busted-up people lying in the cots around me, I must have been a breath of fresh air for those docs."

"I guess they spend a lot of time patching up injuries that will never really heal."

"Yep. But me? I was just lying there waiting for my bones to knit, so a bunch of them got in the habit of stopping by my bed to chew the fat. They brought me things to pass the time. Cigarettes. Books. Girly magazines."

He cut his eyes in her direction, but she refused to give him the embarrassed giggle he was hoping for.

"One day, a doc brought me a book of crossword puzzles. I like those, so I worked them all. He brought me another. I worked them all in a day. He brought me another. Two days later, I got a visit from somebody high up in the Signal Corps. As soon as I was up and around, they gave me a few tests. Next thing I knew, I got shipped across the ocean. I've been working at Arlington Hall ever since."

"In the German section?"

"The whole time."

"Where did you learn to speak German?"

"You'll laugh."

"Why do you say that?"

"I learned it in college. Can you imagine that? Me. Me, a coal miner's kid. At college."

"You talk like a college boy."

"You think so? I guess that's a good thing." He absently slid his right hand up and down his injured left arm. "I had a scholarship and a job, and I still might not have been able to afford to make it all the way to my degree. The war came along just when I was starting my last year, so now we'll never know. Anyway, history majors have to pick a language. I was interested in the other big war of this century, so I studied German. And Russian, just for fun. I know the Russians are our allies, but the SSA seems real interested in keeping an eye on them. Because I speak those two languages, the higher-ups give me the impression that I've got a job for life."

Justine knew that the people working in Arlington Hall's German section were the cream of the crop. Ike's talents probably didn't stop with a few German and Russian college courses and a knack for crossword puzzles.

"Wanna go pay old Abe a visit?" he asked, leading her up the stairs. At the top was Abraham Lincoln, massive and carved of marble. Sitting in a ready stance, hands active and both feet flat on the floor, Lincoln regarded them with his stolid stone face. Justine explored the memorial's chambers, admiring the murals and reading the quotations chiseled into the walls, but Lincoln kept drawing her back.

In the end, she simply stood in front of him, feeling his stone eyes on her and wondering what he would make of the warring world.

If he could talk, she feared that he would say, "I saved the union for you people. What are you going to do to deserve it?"

The only acceptable answer was, "End this war. End them all."

———

The National Mall was the perfect place for a beginning spy to hone her surveillance skills. No matter where Georgette stood in the grass surrounding the reflecting pool, she could see the entire open area, and she could see Justine's white-blond hair.

Georgette's "borrowed" red coat made her stand out in a very thin crowd. It was just too cold and too late in the day for people to be enthusiastic about walking around outside.

Rather than being a lone woman in red who never moved from one spot on the Lincoln Memorial stairs, she thought she'd be less noticeable if she moved around. She drifted from the stairs to the oval pool near the Washington Monument. There, she pulled a stick of gum out of her pocket, just for an excuse to trudge over to a garbage can to throw away the wrapper. Pausing there, she wondered what else she could do to pass the time without being conspicuous. After a while, she withdrew to an unobtrusive spot under one of the elm trees that surrounded the grassy strip.

Foot traffic around the reflecting pool, never heavy, ebbed as time went by. Once, twice, three times, Georgette watched Justine and Ike walk slowly around the pool. By the time they passed her the third time, the early wintertime sunset was approaching, and nobody else was in sight. Georgette felt the need to be invisible growing, so she put her scarf in the pocket of the crimson coat and stripped it off. Turning the coat wrong-side out to reveal a plain black lining, she threw it into the shadow of an elm. She was cold in just her dark pants and sweater, but now she could fade into the shadows.

Georgette guessed that each lap around the reflecting pool was about a mile long. Ordinarily, she would guess that two people circling it three times were a couple trying to begin a romance, looking for a way to get to know each other that didn't force them to be alone in the dark before they were ready. Justine had not shown a flicker of interest in Ike, and Georgette had never known her to be overly interested in exercise for exercise's sake, either. Ike might be trying to romance her, but Justine would only be trudging around in the deepening cold if she thought he might say something useful.

Maybe he already had. If so, Justine would be extricating herself soon. Feeling antsy about the situation, Georgette hoped her friend would hurry up.

She looked over her shoulder to keep her face out of sight as they strolled past her yet again. Ike and Justine were just two people taking a walk. They were doing nothing worrisome. Nevertheless, Georgette was worried.

After they passed, she raised her eyes and scanned the area. She saw no one looking at Ike and Justine, nor at her, but she was pretty sure that someone was out there watching.

———

Justine had set out on this third trip around the reflecting pool reluctantly. The first time around had been pleasant and novel. The second loop had been a little monotonous, and Ike's increasingly flirtatious repartee hadn't helped. To do it the third time, she'd had to tell herself that she was doing it for her country.

She'd done her best, but she'd gotten no useful information out of Ike. He seemed to be exactly who he said he was, a man who had survived the battlefield scarred but mostly intact.

She adjusted that thought. Ike was mostly intact, physically, but being the sole survivor of an enemy attack had left mental wounds that he hid under a flirtatious veneer and behind constant jokes that weren't very funny. Justine knew that the social convention was that women tittered politely when men were trying and failing to be funny, but she was coming to the end of her ability to do that.

Being a cheerful giggler was hard when she knew that she might be walking beside the person responsible for the death of everyone at that port in Poland. Anybody in the German section could be guilty of that atrocity. How on earth did Paul expect her to ferret out who the culprit was?

And then there was Bettie to consider. For all she knew, this man had killed her.

At odd moments, Ike would set a foot down wrong and the weakness in his leg would show, reminding her that guns and bombs and torpedoes were, at that very moment, blowing up Europe and sinking ships in the Pacific. And all the time a monument to a murdered president loomed over their heads.

Justine was tired of war and death and destruction. She wanted nothing but to fall into bed and pull the covers over her head, but she couldn't say that out loud. Ike would immediately make a ribald joke about women and beds, and she just wouldn't be able to stand it.

As they rounded the far end of the reflecting pool and headed back toward the Lincoln Memorial, she said, "It'll be dark soon. Don't you think we should walk back?"

Justine had made some version of this suggestion twice already, with no effect. She should have stated firmly that she was ready to go home, but women didn't do that. It was a rule as firm as the rule that women giggled when men made unfunny jokes.

This particular woman was fed up, and she was ready to break some rules.

As they walked the final leg of their third lap around the reflecting pool, she had her eyes on the stairs that led up to the walkway toward the bridge and home. When they reached those stairs, she would be climbing them, with or without Ike.

It was still daylight, but not for much longer. It was time to go. The other Sunday afternoon strollers had all left the mall, and the bridge would be just as deserted soon. In a few hundred more feet, she would be on her way.

Ike must have sensed her departure plans because he made his move before she could get away, and he was not subtle. Justine could feel the pressure of his hand through her coat, through her clothes, through the band of her bra. She could feel its slow and lingering downward motion.

"It's getting chilly. Why don't we go grab some beers and get warm?" The hand pressed into her back to guide her body toward his.

She lurched away from him, fleeing the hand. "Keep your hands to yourself. We said that this was not a date."

She almost said some stupid things, too, like, "It's too early to start drinking," and "Can we even buy alcohol on Sunday?" but his suggestion of alcohol had nothing to do with actually finding an open bar. It was merely a signal that he intended to change the terms of their agreement without her permission.

She knew that they were alone in the waning light. She'd watched as everyone else left, one by one. She'd let this happen, because Ike had done a lot of talking about his coworkers, and she needed to find out which one was an Axis spy.

Justine now knew what Ike thought of Dr. Edison van Dorn's cryptanalytic skills. (Not much.) She knew what he thought of Linda. (Sexy.) And Nora. (Not sexy.) And Sally, Thelma, Patsy, and the two Bees. (Sexy, marginally sexy, old, and not sexy at all.)

She also now knew his approach to wooing women, which was to make a play for sympathy by bringing up his injuries as soon as humanly possible. Periodically, he returned to them when he wanted to control the conversation. She had the sense that this sometimes worked, as he had mentioned women from his past, but she noticed that it hadn't worked with Sally and it wasn't working with Linda.

She had felt his sad story tugging on her own heartstrings, until he suggested that poor Bettie wasn't to be pitied, because she had brought her fate on herself.

"A woman who's out at midnight with a man she just met?" he had said with a leer. "She knows what might happen."

As soon as this statement had come out of his mouth, Justine had begun her campaign to get home, counting the steps it took to reach the stairs that would take her far away from Ike.

Now this man who had blamed Bettie for her own murder had one hand on her body and he was reaching for her with the other one. She thought of the weapons in her purse, the Stinger, the pepper spray pen, the noisemaker, the trick pencil with its hidden blade. She could possibly get to them and use them before Ike disarmed her, but ordinary women did not carry guns disguised as ink pens.

Justine couldn't use the weapons of a spy if she didn't want to be labeled as a spy, and she wasn't ready to give up on this mission yet. If she could get away from Ike without them, then that was what she should do.

Her purse itself, loaded with these things, was heavy. She didn't think swinging it at Ike's head would put him completely out of commission, but it might stun him long enough to let her use the self-defense tactics that Jerry had taught her.

"Some people would call these tactics 'ungentlemanly,'" Jerry had said, "because they are intended to disable your assailant by any means necessary. I want you to be ungentlemanly, ma'am, because I want you alive."

Justine eyed some ungentlemanly targets—Ike's groin, eyes, throat, shins, feet, and the side of his neck, but she was innately 'gentlemanly' enough to give him one last chance. For this, Jerry was going to yell at her.

Yanking herself away from Ike, she shouted, "Stop it! Stop touching me!"

This was a mistake, because his response was to grab her by both shoulders and shake her hard. Dizzied, she fell to the ground. Now, the only ungentlemanly targets within her reach were his shins and feet, and the violent shaking had left her so dazed that she wasn't sure she could even find them. But she could try.

Then, once she'd figured out which way was up, she could go for his groin, and she would now be happy to do so. If she survived this fiasco, Justine resolved never to be gentlemanly again.

———

Georgette watched Justine fall to the ground. She was armed with her Stinger, her pepper spray pen, her noisemaker, her hidden-blade pencil, and the roll of pennies that her father had always made her take when she went on dates. With that roll of pennies in her fist, she could pack a heckuva punch, because her brothers had made sure she knew how. The trouble was that none of her weapons could be used from a distance. She had to get to Justine.

Georgette had been focused on staying hidden, and that meant she was on the wrong side of the reflecting pool. As the crow flies, she wasn't far away from Justine at all, but running around the water would take her a half-mile out of the way. Ike could beat her friend to a bloody pulp in the time it would take Georgette to run to her.

Georgette had grown up on the bayou. She had no doubt that she could get across that tiny sliver of water, one way or another, but she didn't know how deep it was. If she had to swim, the Stinger would probably be useless and she didn't know what would happen to the pepper spray pen or the noisemaker.

No matter. She had a blade stuck in her hair. Even without it, the roll of pennies would work just fine.

———

With the word "ungentlemanly" echoing in her head, Justine drew back a fist and landed a hard punch on the knee of Ike's injured leg. He didn't go down, but he howled. This was useful information. His injuries still pained him.

In her peripheral vision, she saw a dark shadow leaping into the reflecting pool, launching drops of water into the air like diamonds. Simultaneously, a figure in blue emerged from the trees just a few feet behind Ike and a shrill, biting sound tried to burst her eardrums. The figure's right arm gestured, palm out, and the shadow in her peripheral vision stopped dead still, crawled out of the pool, and retreated behind a line of trees on its far side.

Ike turned toward the piercing sound, and Justine saw his face change from aggression to stealth. A man in a police officer's double-breasted blue uniform stood right behind him, whistle between his lips and nightstick raised. Ike was tall, but the policeman was taller. His arm, extended by the nightstick, towered over Ike's head.

"She tripped, Officer. Those pretty shoes just slipped on the grass," Ike said, reaching down as if to help Justine to her feet. "I don't know why women wear such things. C'mon, honey. Let me help you up."

Justine gave his hand a withering glare and stood up without taking it. "You could come up with a better lie. My penny loafers get perfectly good traction."

Ike shrugged, palms out. "Women. Am I right?"

The officer gestured for Justine to come stand beside him. "Are you okay, Miss?"

The sound of his voice startled her. She'd been too shaken to see the police officer as anything more than a person in a uniform, his face obscured by dark glasses and a policeman's hat pulled low. When she looked past the disguise, Paul looked back at her.

His face was expressionless, but his blue eyes, as always, were warm and intelligent and, perhaps, a tiny bit mischievous. He was enjoying her surprise at seeing him.

"Are you okay, Miss?" he said again. "Would you like me to escort you home?"

Justine was shaken up, but she was still herself. She wanted so badly to say, "No. How do I know that you're any safer than he is?" just to poke at Paul. Not being stupid, she squelched the urge.

"I would appreciate that very much, Officer."

He shifted his attention to Ike just long enough to say, "You're lucky I don't take you in. Jails are made for men like you, but I don't want this lady to have to go down to the station to make her complaint. You belong in the drunk tank, from the looks of you." He brandished the night stick to remind Ike what would happen if he misbehaved, and then he turned away.

Head high, Justine let the friendly faux policeman in his sober uniform escort her far away from her assailant. The results of her afternoon with Ike were inconclusive, since she still had no idea whether he was a spy, but she had learned that he was not a man anyone should trust.

———

Georgette, wrapped in the purloined coat and wet from the thighs down, moved quietly through the elms, staying ahead of Justine and what's-his-name. She might be a brand-new spy, but it seemed obvious that she shouldn't be seen spying on her roommate. And she certainly shouldn't be seen with this man, because the world didn't need to know she worked for him.

She had to admit that he cut a fine figure in that policeman's uniform. He was capable of a manly swagger when he was playing a role that demanded it, and it was on full display. His uniform coat swung with each long stride, and its shiny buttons and counterfeit badge glittered with his every step. For someone standing up close, someone like Justine, the deep blue uniform would make his blue eyes impossible to ignore.

At times like this, Georgette could see why this man dazzled Justine so. If she were honest with herself, she'd admit that she'd always been able to see it. Anybody could see that he was crazy for Justine, too, no matter how good he was at pretending he was made of stone. This was as it should be. From where Georgette sat, her friend was dazzling, too.

Georgette had hoped that her emergency call to Jerry would bring help, but she'd had no idea what form it would take. She'd doubted that Jerry would come himself. The risk that Ike might recognize him from Arlington Hall was too great. Once on the spot, she'd also realized that there was no ramp in sight for Jerry's wheelchair.

She should have known that Jerry's nameless buddy would be the one coming to the rescue. Was this really the role he wanted to play in her friend's life, the absent lover who showed up when the chips were down but otherwise left her alone?

This was not what Georgette wanted in a man, but Justine was going to have to make her own decisions. Georgette wasn't sure that a life with a dazzling, charismatic man who liked to keep his distance would be a happy one.

One thing was for certain. Her friend would not be choosing Ike Grantham. Georgette wrapped the crimson coat tighter around her chilly shoulders. Trying to ignore the water squelching in her shoes, she stepped onto the bridge, confident that Paul and Justine would be behind her, making sure she was safe.

———

"Was it worth it?"

Justine bristled at Paul's words. "Was what worth it? Did I find out anything from Ike that was worth the effort you just made to pull my bacon out of the fire? No. I didn't. I'm sorry. Are you saying I shouldn't have tried? Isn't it my job to try?"

He took a few silent steps, bumping the nightstick rhythmically against his leg. She wasn't willing to look him in the eyes, so she watched the stick instead.

"That's not what I meant," he said. "It's a question I always ask myself at the end of an operation. 'Was it worth the risk? Was it worth my time? Was it a mission I believe in?' When I can't answer all of those questions with 'Yes,' I'm getting out of this business."

She took some time to think about her answer. The lights on the bridge flickered on. She checked to be sure there was nobody in earshot, and then she told him what she thought.

"Yes. It was worth it, but only because it helped me get a better sense of how Ike fits into the German section. I certainly didn't learn anything that's obviously useful right this minute. I already knew he'd been wounded. I already knew he had talents that had gotten him assigned to the German section. I already suspected he was a heel. Now I know those things for sure, although I wouldn't call those things information that's worth risking my safety for."

Finally, she looked at him. "Or yours. How did you know to come?"

"You thought Georgette was going to let you do something like this alone?"

Paul inclined his head in the direction of a woman in the distance ahead, a crimson coat hanging from her shoulders and a scarf dangling from her hand. Her dark hair was knotted at the nape of her neck in Georgette's familiar chignon.

"Georgette was there the whole time? She followed me?"

"After she called Jerry and sounded the alarm."

"I don't deserve her."

"Yes, you do. You deserve each other."

"Like you and Jerry do."

"I try to deserve him. I doubt that I ever do. You and I are both lucky to have our partners."

She reached for his hand. "Yes. We are."

She felt a twitch of surprise in his hand, an urge to pull away that he suppressed. She had read him wrong.

She released his hand. "You're in disguise. Policemen have sweethearts, you know."

"It's not an acceptable risk."

She whipped her head in his direction, ready with a retort that froze in her mouth. The sunglasses hid so much of his face. All she could see were his cheeks, his jaws, his mouth, and they were motionless. Impassive, even, but they revealed enough. He had been afraid for her, and he wasn't over it yet.

"Risking your safety," he said, "is not acceptable to me."

"And yet you recruited me for this dangerous job."

"I might have miscalculated there." Anticipating her argument, he hurried to say, "It was a personal miscalculation, not a professional one. I don't personally want you in danger, but the government is thrilled to trade your safety for your talents. You have to know that your combination of skills is unique. There cannot be another woman in the country who has acquired a background in cryptanalysis and a fluent command of German, while producing publishable work in physics."

Flattery would get him nowhere. Neither would the appealing smile that beamed gently down at her. He was trying to charm her, and she refused to let it happen.

"There are others. For example, you're forgetting Gloria."

"Does Gloria weld?"

"She does."

"Well, wonderful. I've recruited you both." A brief smile escaped him, and she watched his jaw relax. And there he was, just for an instant, the man she'd fallen for when she thought he was nothing more than a security guard.

"It's good news for America that I've secured the services of both you and Gloria, but I didn't think ahead to how it would make me feel."

He bent his head a little closer to hers, but he didn't take her hand, and she sure as hell wasn't taking his again. Maybe she never would. Maybe they'd both survive the war and work out their differences. Maybe they would get married and have children and grandchildren, and maybe, during all that time, she would never take his hand again.

In all those years, if he wanted to hold her hand, he was going to have to reach out and take it himself.

"I didn't intend for you to have such a dangerous assignment," Paul said. "I thought I could put you in a position that was useful, but safe. If I got lucky, that job would be somewhere near me—someplace where I could maybe see you now and then."

She stopped still and let him stumble forward a couple of steps before coming to a halt.

"What are you saying?" she demanded. "I uprooted my whole life. I left everything I've ever known, except Georgette and Jerry. And you, when you decide to grace me with your presence."

He winced, but she wasn't finished telling him what she thought.

"I did those things so that I could be part of something that might bring peace. I had a good job, building things that directly helped the war effort, but I left it because I wanted to do more. Are you saying that you were willing to take me away from all that and stick me in a job that didn't use my skills to the fullest? Because it would hurt your feelings if something happened to me?"

Justine thought her anger might choke her, but she squeezed out one more sentence. And then another. And another.

"And you have the gall to say that you did this so that you could *see me now and then*? I am not your reward for a hard day's spying. And I am most certainly not your lapdog, waiting around for you to remember I'm alive."

Paul was making little "Be quiet!" noises with his hands, but the nightstick was hampering those efforts. Since there was still nobody nearby to hear her, she had no intention of being quiet.

"Do you know how insulting that is?"

He stood motionless, hand spread and nightstick dangling awkwardly in midair. "I would hate it if somebody did that to me."

"You don't say!"

"As it turns out, you're in plenty of danger, despite my best efforts. Are you happy now?"

Chapter 12

Justine stepped off the bridge, still walking beside Paul, despite the fact that she wasn't speaking to him, and he apparently had decided to stop speaking to her. As the entrance to the Arlington Farms parking lot approached, she reflected that leaving Kansas Hall with one man and coming back, hours later, with another was about to make her a dormitory legend.

Paul still wasn't speaking to her when he abruptly stopped keeping his hands to himself. She felt his palm rest flat on her back where it hadn't been before, where Ike's hand had been before he shook her senseless. Paul was using that hand to steer her to the right.

A second later, she found herself walking down a narrow path between overhanging trees. Wondering what was happening, she saw Paul give the empty path ahead of him a sharp look, then turn to cast an equally sharp look behind him. Satisfied that no one was in sight, he used the hand to steer her off the path and behind a broad tree trunk.

Still silent, Justine stood chest-to-chest with Paul. Both of his hands gripped her shoulders, pinning her to the tree, as she waited for him to explain himself. He was so close that

Justine found herself struggling to hold on to her anger. But she persevered.

"What's your next move?" he said.

"I will be making no more moves on a man who won't even hold my hand."

Sheepish, he said, "I mean professionally. What's your next move in terms of the investigation? Tell me you're not planning to do anything else this dangerous."

She leaned hard into the tree's rugged bark and shrugged. His hands maintained their grip, following the motion of her shoulders.

"I can't tell you that I won't do anything else dangerous. If I could think of something risky that was also useful, I would do it in a heartbeat. Unfortunately, I can't think of much. My best idea is a boring, mundane trip through a whole bunch of paper."

He moved his face so close to hers that his breath warmed her face. "I like the sound of the words 'boring' and 'mundane.'"

"Since Karl is the boss of everybody in the German section, and I'm his assistant, I have access to all of their personnel files. If I can get Karl out of the office for a good long while, I'll use that fancy little spy camera you gave me to take pictures of any important information I find there."

"Excellent idea. Start with Ike. Even if he's not our spy, I'd love to see you find something that would get him fired. And far, far away from you." He paused. "I hope you don't mind that he's going to get away with what he just did," Paul said, brushing a stray curl from her face and then drawing his hand away like it had been dipped in acid. "He should be charged with assault, but there's no way to get the police involved without them finding out that the officer on the scene was a fake. And Ike can't know that he was just face-to-face with an undercover agent. Two of us, actually."

Justine had already figured that out. "It's okay. I know we have to let him get away with it, because I can't do surveillance on him if he's in jail. Tell me, though. After what he just did, do you think maybe he's the one who killed Bettie?"

There was a tiny, uncertain shake of his head. "I doubt it, but I really don't know. The police are sure they have Bettie's killer. This doesn't mean that they're right."

An idea struck her. "Wouldn't Karl keep the personnel files of employees who left? Or died? The person who made me sign a lot of loyalty forms at orientation made sure to tell me that they would follow me forever. Even if I leave Arlington Hall and move across the country, and even if thirty years have passed, the government will come for me if I spill its secrets. How would it do that, unless it kept its files on me forever and ever?"

"Oh, the government's never going to let any of us go," he said, still holding her shoulders like he would never let her go, either, despite all his efforts to do so.

"Then we should forget Ike for now. My next step is to see what those personnel files tell me about everybody in Room 117, especially Bettie and Ed's missing assistant, Mabel Hennessey. While I'm at it, I might as well look for information on Karl's missing assistants."

The sunlight was nearly gone and the trees around them were blocking out the few rays that remained. Finally, Paul leaned back and released one of her shoulders, because he needed a hand to pull off his dark glasses, revealing his face. He usually wore spectacles, so she supposed that she'd never seen him before when he had nothing to hide behind. The policeman's hat and uniform made his eyes look so deeply blue that Justine lost her train of thought.

As if he knew what she was thinking, Paul shoved the sunglasses back on his face. Then he took them right back off again, because even an experienced federal agent couldn't see in the dark. It upset Justine to see him so rattled. She kept her own fears at bay by telling herself that Paul knew exactly what he was doing.

"Wait," Paul said. "Did you say something about Karl's assistants being missing? What are you saying? How many of his assistants are missing? Are they women?"

"Yes, they're both women. Their names are Doris Goldberg and Sandra Stone. You really haven't heard about them?"

Justine found this hole in Paul's knowledge terrifying.

He closed his eyes and that helped her achieve the emotional distance she needed to clear her mind. It was as if she could see him considering possibilities and weighing options. And it was as if she could see this important problem displacing every bit of attraction he felt for her. This man would never stop being someone who could turn his feelings on and off, and Justine was going to have to decide whether she could live with that.

"If the police were investigating any of these disappearances, I'd know about it," he said. "Surely somebody called them. Karl. Dr. van Dorn. Their roommates. Somebody."

"I believe so. Why wouldn't they? I mean, the Army said some mysterious things about them being reassigned, but if I came home and found Georgette and all her things missing, I wouldn't just listen to the Army. I'd do something."

"If anybody did call the authorities, and if the police suspected something had happened to them, then there would be an open case, and one of my informants would have told me. They haven't."

"Do you think maybe they found the missing women but didn't tell anybody at Arlington Hall?"

"Maybe. But it's more likely that they didn't suspect foul play. It's not illegal for an adult to wake up one day and decide, 'I don't want to be here.'"

"But three of them?"

"That worries me. But maybe Karl and Ed are such miserable bosses that their employees want to go without looking back."

Justine would have laughed at the idea of kindly Karl being a miserable boss, if it wasn't making her sick to think about the missing women. "Karl's not that bad. And I don't think Ed is particularly awful."

"There are only a few options left. One, maybe the police have been paid off or are otherwise in on it." He looked down at his uniform with distaste. "Two, maybe they're incompetent. Or three, maybe they're right that there's no crime to investigate."

"Could there be a cover-up?"

"Are you suggesting that somebody official—somebody at Arlington Hall or with the Army or maybe high up in the government—knows what happened to the missing women, but they're not talking?"

"Yes, that's what I'm saying."

"It's always possible."

"I'll see what I can find out," Justine said, taking stock of ways she could do that. "Somebody at Arlington Hall knows something, and I'll find out what it is."

He shoved his sunglasses in his pocket and grabbed her shoulders again, pressing her into the tree. "What if I don't want you to do that?"

At first, Justine thought she would simply refuse to answer him. If she wanted to keep doing her dangerous job, then she damn well would keep doing it. Who was he to tell her what to do?

Then she remembered that, as her boss, he actually *could* tell her not to ask questions about the disappearances.

Unless she quit. But then she wouldn't be able to keep doing her job. Either way, Paul won.

Justine had a slow-burning temper, despite what people said

about natural redheads, but she felt it rising. Paul wasn't acting like a boss who cared about his employee's welfare. He was acting like a man who thought he should be able to control her, just because he cared about her. And he had no right. He wasn't her boyfriend or her husband or her lover. He didn't always act like her friend. He wasn't anything to her, unless she let him be, and he hadn't even asked.

When they'd been coworkers, he had flirted with her, but it had gone no further. He had held her hand once in all that time. He had asked her out once, but circumstances had gotten in the way. He'd never asked again.

She'd kissed him the day he offered her the job, and he had let her. He had more than let her. He had kissed her back like a man who knew she was what he wanted. Then he had retreated behind his impassive I'm-a-secret-agent face for the few weeks they'd had together before she left for the job at the shipyard. It was a handsome face, but it revealed nothing. He'd kissed her twice in all that time, and then he'd pulled away like he hated himself for it.

Gloria had seen how it was. She'd busied herself during those weeks cooking dinner after dinner for the four of them, Justine and Jerry and Georgette and Paul, listening while they talked espionage. She'd watched silently until the young people forgot she was there, as young people do. Then she'd waited until she was alone with Justine and rendered an opinion.

"He's an exceptionally good-looking man, when he wants to be," Gloria had said. "I see why you like him."

Justine had stammered out a response, denying that she was so shallow as to want a man for his looks. "He's also very intelligent. I've never met a man who was interested in my mind."

"You are twenty-one. You've never spent time with a full-grown man before. But I was not suggesting that you wanted this one for his looks, although he is certainly—I believe the term is 'easy on the eyes'—when he wants to be. I have never seen anyone with such complete control of his charisma. And he has a lot of charisma."

Justine had felt rebellion rising, but she'd squelched it. She wasn't a teenager anymore. She didn't have to take Gloria's advice, but she respected her opinion.

"He cares about you, dearest. He probably loves you or he soon will. I suspect he is a difficult man, but if he is the one you want, I believe he will be yours."

Then Gloria's face had changed, taking on the wary look Justine had seen many times before, the look of a fifteen-year-old refugee with nobody to count on but herself.

"But you do not have to decide today. And if you do decide you want him, do not be fooled into believing that you must want him forever. At every juncture, you must ask yourself whether he is worth what you've sacrificed to be with him. And make no mistake, there is always a sacrifice for both parties."

Never content to offer advice without fully driving her point home, Gloria had concluded with, "Your parents had the only fully successful love affair that I have ever seen. Did you ever hear Gerard tell Isabel that she must do things his way?" And then she answered her own question. "No. I don't believe that you did."

Now, here Justine stood, being held against a tree by a man trying to get her to do things his way.

"Are you telling me what to do?"

Paul was smart enough to relax his grip on her. "No. No, I—"

"You're my boss. I work for you, so you actually can tell me what to do. You can tell me not to look into those disappearances, if that's what you want, but that will be the day I walk away. Either I will do this job well, or I won't do it at all. Besides, it seems to me that there aren't many things more dangerous than doing espionage with one hand tied behind my back. If you're not going to let me do my work, then tell me and I'll go."

"I don't want you to go back to New Orleans. I—"

"Did I say that I was planning to go back to New Orleans? Maybe I will and maybe I won't, but I'll be the one who decides. And please don't think I'll tell you where I'm going."

She shook his hands off her shoulders and stepped back onto the path that led to the main road. "I'm sure you're smart enough to give me a head start. We shouldn't be seen together. It's not an acceptable risk."

Chapter 13

As Justine came through the Kansas Hall entrance, she saw Georgette and Jerry sitting next to each other, holding hands. He must have been waiting for her when she got back from splashing in the reflecting pool. A pang of jealousy took Justine by surprise.

She was thoroughly happy for Georgette and Jerry. She was sure of this. She didn't harbor the kind of jealousy that said, "Because I can't have the thing I want, I don't want you to have what you want, either." Why did it hurt her to see them together?

It was because she didn't understand why she and Paul couldn't have what they had.

Jerry patted Georgette on her still-damp knee, then he leaned over and gave her a quick goodbye kiss. "Gotta go, kiddo. Somebody's waiting for me."

This comment tied the choreography of the afternoon into a nice, neat bow for Justine. She had told Georgette that she was going on a walk with Ike to the Lincoln Monument and invited her to come. Georgette had decided that the safer thing to do was to let her go alone and trail her, but to let Jerry know what was happening before she left. Jerry and Paul lived together and were probably both at home on a Sunday, so the decision to send Paul, whom Ike wouldn't recognize, had been made in an instant.

The most interesting thing the afternoon had taught her was that there was a policeman's uniform lying around their house. Justine was distracted for a moment by the question of what other disguises Paul might own, since she was sure he would look quite fetching as a surgeon or a firefighter, but she told herself to focus.

Jerry would have driven the fake policeman to the National Mall to join Georgette in spying on Ike and Justine. In all likelihood, Jerry had then driven back to the Arlington Farms parking lot, where he could wait for Georgette and Justine to return. Once he saw Justine, he would know it was time to pick up Paul at a prearranged rendezvous point that was probably very near the spot where she'd last seen him.

If the three of them could set this operation into action in a matter of minutes, Justine judged that the four of them could do anything, if somebody was so kind as to let her in on the plan.

All this spying had saved her from a dangerous predicament, but the reality of it made her queasy. Had there been an agent spying on her date with Ed van Dorn? If so, who? Jerry? Paul? Somebody she'd never met?

If Ed asked her out again, and she was reasonably sure that he would, would she spend the evening looking in the shadows for peeping toms?

As Jerry rolled himself past Justine, he patted his lips and cheeks with his free hand. "Did she leave any lipstick on me? Please tell me she did. It makes the other guys jealous."

Justine rubbed a finger over what remained of her own lipstick and wiped it on his cheek.

"There you go. Georgette's is red and mine is pink, so now you look like a real ladies' man."

Still rolling, Jerry said, "I know somebody who'll be really jealous."

"If he's not," she said, "he ought to be."

Chapter 14

The corridors of Building B weren't dead silent, but they felt hushed. The raging battle in Europe was on everyone's minds, and this made them live their lives more quietly. They spoke more softly. They walked gently, as if it were an affront to make noise when so many people were fighting and dying.

Typewriters still clacked behind the closed door of the Traffic Records room. Footsteps still tapped on the waxed linoleum hallway floors, and the sound of those steps still bounced off walls newly painted in government beige. The near-constant hum and click that sounded behind a closed door near the end of the hall continued unabated. Justine thought some of the decryption machines that Karl wouldn't admit existed were hidden behind that door, so hearing them run was a comforting sound on an uncomfortable day.

Voices still sounded in each of the rooms along the long hallway that led to her office, but there were longer intervals of silence between the sentences. Perhaps the people in those rooms were holding their breath. Perhaps the whole country was holding its breath, desperate for news from the surprise attack in Europe, but knowing that the answers they needed didn't exist yet.

Who would win and who would lose? Who would die?

There was nothing for anybody to do but work and wait.

Even Karl seemed different. Distracted. He claimed to be satisfied with the work she'd done two days before, but he kept changing the subject when she tried to talk about it. She wondered if she would ever quit feeling that she was being tested and found wanting.

Karl was full of questions, and they all felt like tests.

"You say that your mother taught you the basics of decryption. Tell me what you remember."

"She said that the key characteristics of successful cryptanalysts are perseverance, careful analytical methods, intuition, and luck."

"Good." He let a tiny smile escape. "I should have known that Isabel read Hitt's work."

"She also said that true randomness was impossible to achieve in any cipher."

"Or in anything done by a human being."

Justine knew that this was true.

"Therefore," she said, "repetition will occur, sooner or later. Thus, a long message is, by definition, more susceptible to attack than a short one."

"Agreed."

"My mother also said that humans are creatures of pattern. We open our personal letters with 'Dear.' We close many of them with 'Sincerely' and our names. When we are trying to keep secrets, we intentionally try to break our patterns, with some success. But only some, because nobody's perfect. The Japanese will always need some way to say 'Tokyo,' and their navy will always need a way to say 'ship.' And they will repeat those important words. German messages will, time and again, need to communicate the words 'Berlin' and 'U-boat' and 'torpedo.' We can use those patterns to break their messages."

"And they can use our patterns to break ours."

"Exactly."

Karl leaned back in his chair and studied her face. "Really, my dear, it is as if I have traveled back in time. It is 1920 and I am in Chicago and I am looking at your mother. Your face. Your mind. Gerard and Isabel must have been so proud of you."

Karl was too self-possessed to push them both to tears, so he retreated to rationality. He resumed asking questions.

"You know the most commonly used letters in English."

"Of course. E, T, O, N, A, I, R, S. It's easy to remember the words 'Eton' and 'airs.'"

"For you, perhaps. Do you have experience with numerical cipher alphabets? Polyalphabetic substitution? Diagonal digraphic substitution?"

"Yes to all three."

"It's as if your mother had access to the exact training course we sent to promising students at the women's colleges. Many of the women you see every day are here because they were successful in that course. I'm sorry to tell you that the Germans don't use the ciphers that you've studied, not to speak of. Nor do the Japanese, so you have a lot to learn. However, simply knowing that they exist helps develop your intuition for how ciphers work. For example, your intuition that the rotor-driven machine your mother recalled might be useful was a good one. Both we and our enemies use such machines these days."

This was something that Karl hadn't been willing to tell her just one day before. She really had passed his test.

"Will I be training on those?"

He said, "No," and Justine was disappointed, because the constant noise of the machines behind Building B's closed doors sounded like the future.

"The machines do not eliminate the need for people who work with coded messages by hand, and you are suited to that work. Today, you will tackle recovering additives. I hope you have some tolerance for false math."

Justine didn't know what false math was, but the sound of it rattled her worldview. Math could be trusted. Math was always true.

It seemed that math was *not* always true at Arlington Hall, and this shook Justine more than anything else could.

———

Justine dragged a chair up to the end of the Caféteria table, set down her plate of tuna casserole, and settled herself in the chair. Nora, who had been contentedly writing in a notebook while she ate alone, looked at her like she'd grown a second head, but Justine was determined. Nora was going to have to tolerate lunchtime companionship, unless she was willing to pick up her food and push right past interloping Justine.

And she might be. Nora was certainly capable of doing something that socially odd, but Justine thought that maybe she wouldn't. She positioned her chair slightly right of the end of the table to close up Nora's avenue of escape a bit.

Nora gave her a harried look, but she stayed put. She scooped up a spoonful of vegetable soup and slurped it without a word.

Now that she was closer, Justine could see that Nora hadn't been writing in English. She'd been writing musical notes on five-lined manuscript paper.

Justine leaned closer. "I'm no musician, but it seems to me

that it would take a special talent to write music without a musical instrument handy."

Nora closed the notebook and slid it into a canvas bag full of notebooks like it that sat at her feet. "I'll try it out on the piano tonight, but it's really not that hard. I can hear the notes when I write. Sometimes, I can see them and taste them." Her stare dared Justine to let it show that she thought Nora was strange.

Justine had been surrounded by physicists and other academics as a child. She was used to people whose brains worked a little differently from most people's. She said, "I once knew an astronomer who said that he could hear the stars move while he was looking at them."

Nora gave a little nod and took another slurp of her soup.

Justine heard Georgette and Sally chatting as they passed behind her. She and Georgette had decided to divide and conquer, each taking someone who could theoretically be the spy and seeing what they could find out.

"So tell me, Nora. Did you move here for the job or are you from the area?"

Justine thought she knew the answer, but Jerry had told her that it was good to start interviews with an easy question that had a predictable answer. It was one way to soften up the target. She knew that Nora lived at Arlington Farms, and that was unusual for a woman her age, although it certainly wasn't unheard of. Patsy and Barbara looked about Nora's age. Still, if Nora had already lived nearby, surely she would have stayed where she was. Instead, she'd moved into a residence that was a lot like a college dorm.

As it turned out, Justine was wrong. "My husband and I had a nice little house right here in Arlington. For the first year after he died, I had a cashier job at the grocery store. I counted every penny every month to try to make that house payment. I always did, but some months I had to eat beans three meals a day."

Nora looked at the colorful vegetables in her soup as if she were remembering the brown, mealy flavor of beans at every meal.

"Toward the end," Nora said, "I skipped meals sometimes to scrape together the mortgage payment, and that made the bean months look good. When I took this job, it paid better. I thought maybe I could go back to three meals a day, but they'd still be beans. Or macaroni. Then I heard the other women talking about living in a building that somebody else cleaned, while they ate food somebody else cooked. Somebody else paid for the furniture and the water and the electricity. Somebody else paid for the bus that took them to their high-paying jobs. It just sounded so good. I didn't think about it for even a second. I let my house go back to the bank and got myself a room at Kansas Hall."

"You don't miss having your own place?"

"Not even a little bit. I thought I'd miss my piano, but we've got one in the dorm. I can go downstairs and play it any time, and somebody else pays to keep it tuned. I've got a radio in my room to keep me company in the evenings, too. I don't need anything else but a bed to sleep in and some clothes to wear. I'm as happy as I can be."

Nora's face and voice were devoid of expression as she talked about her life. This gave "I'm as happy as I can be" an unsettling double meaning. What was Nora saying, really?

Had she chosen to live alone in a crowd because it made her happy? Or was it because she wasn't ever really happy, so she might as well live somewhere cheap?

"Oh," Nora said as she solemnly regarded her soup, "and I'm also as happy as I can be with this job, because I like to count."

"What? Do you mean you like numbers? I love math, too."

"Nope. Math's fine, but I really just like to count. You have seven freckles on the back of your left hand. There are three *A*'s in this bowl of vegetable alphabet soup. There are forty-four hundred floor tiles in this room. Only twenty-five hundred ceiling tiles, because they're bigger and it doesn't take as many of them to fill the same space. There were nine carnations in the bouquet I brought to work this morning."

"That's impressive. I must count slower than you, because it would take me forever to check your numbers. I'm going to take your word for them."

Nora scooped the three *A*'s into her soup spoon and ate them. "That's how I got this job, you know. Numbers. Dr. Becker interviewed me in his office, and he saw me counting the pins stuck in his wall maps. He asked me how many floor tiles there were in his office and your office and the hallway. Ceiling tiles, too. He also gave me some tests, but I think I got the job just because I like numbers. When Dr. van Dorn hands me a coded message, it's just pages full of numbers, but I like them all. If I see a string like maybe '9687 3255 8902' on the first page, it feels like meeting an old friend when I see it again on the fifth page."

Justine wondered how many old friends Nora had. She couldn't decide if the woman seemed lonely, or whether it was more accurate to think of her as happily alone. Nobody who could break codes at an elite level could possibly have an ordinary brain, so Nora probably wasn't the oddest person at Arlington Hall. The notable thing about Nora was that she didn't mind letting her oddness show.

"They give me the flowers at church, you know."

A bemused "What?" slipped out of Justine's mouth.

"They don't pay me for being the church pianist, but they do let me take the flowers home after the service."

"The ones you bring to work?"

Nora nodded. "The church arrangements are really big. There's always enough flowers to bring some every day, plus some to have in my room. I keep them next to a picture of my husband, Arthur."

Justine was relieved that Nora didn't live in her wing of Kansas Hall. As each week dragged on, her room must smell more and more like a funeral home chapel.

"I keep a candle next to Arthur's picture, too. I light a candle for him every night."

Living in different wings within the same dorm would not save her from Nora's open flame. Justine hoped the woman was careful when she burned her candles in a building where hundreds of people lived. The little shrine to Nora's husband sounded sweet, though.

"Well, I've finished my soup, and I'm out of saltines. See you later."

Before Justine could answer, Nora, her Caféteria tray, and her overloaded bag full of handwritten music were gone.

———

"Where'd your lunch partner go?" Georgette asked.

"Did you chase her away?" Sally chimed in. They stood beside Justine's chair, carrying empty plates on their trays.

"If you're talking about Nora, she enjoyed as much of my company as she could stand, and then she scrammed."

Justine swallowed her last bite of mock apple pie and drained her water glass. "Are you two going back to Building B? I'll walk with you."

"I'm not sure I've ever seen Nora chattering like that," Sally said. "She must like you."

"It's hard to tell. I like her, though. She's had a hard time and she kept going. It must have been awful to lose her husband like that."

"Did Nora tell you that she's a musician?" Sally asked.

"She was writing music when I sat down," Justine said, "which I thought was really impressive. She said she plays at church. I guess she plays for herself in the evenings, too."

"Well, she's not playing for the other women in Kansas Hall, that's for sure," Sally said. "She plays really strange stuff."

"I don't know about that," Georgette said. "I listened to her play last night, and I really liked it."

"The other women say that Nora's music sounds like a kid banging on the piano with both hands," Sally said, patting the pocket where she'd stashed her apple, as if to make sure it was still there. "But there must be some order to it. Nora spreads her sheet music out on the piano's stand, and she acts like she's reading it. She stops playing and scribbles notes on it. It has to be real music, even if it does sound awful."

"My parents had friends who loved that kind of music," Justine said. "Twelve-tone compositions, atonal music, serial music—the weirder the better. Gloria had recordings of some of Schoenberg's string quartets and piano music. None of them had a tune you could whistle, but I enjoyed listening to those records when I was in the right frame of mind."

"Schoenberg. Huh," Georgette said. "Is everybody you ever knew German?"

"Schoenberg is Austrian."

"Same thing," said Georgette, who knew perfectly well that they weren't the same thing.

"Nora tells people that her music is absolutely current, right out of Europe," Sally said, "and that you have to have the right kind of ear to appreciate it. So maybe you're right about it being

Schoenberg's music. I do know that she listens to it on the radio every night, because the women on her hall complain about the noise."

Nora did not sound like any of the church pianists Justine had ever known.

"Music is a kind of code," Justine said.

"So are Ike's crossword puzzles. And Dr. van Dorn's contract bridge puzzles." A grin dimpled Sally's cheeks. "Samantha tells me you had a date with him."

"I did. He seemed nice, but I don't know if he is. Not really."

"He's nice when he wants to be. But do you want a word of advice?"

Justine did, very much.

"I've talked to women who've gone out with him, and this is what I've learned. You're going to have to be in charge of how fresh you let him be."

"He hasn't been particularly fresh yet."

"Just wait. He will try anything if you don't tell him no. And you'll have to be firm about it. Loud, maybe. And also…"

It was nerve-racking enough to hear that she was going out with a man who was notoriously fresh. What else did Sally have to tell her?

"Make sure you tell him that you don't play bridge, even if you do. If you get him started talking about notrumps and grand slams, he won't talk about anything else all evening."

"Even while he's groping me?"

"You got it."

Chapter 15

Karl had been in and out of his office all afternoon, but never for long. Justine had used the time to peruse her filing cabinets with an eye toward espionage, one quick peek at a time.

Her sole filing cabinet victory had been to locate the personnel files for everyone who worked for Karl and, within those drawers full of overstuffed folders, the files for the people who worked in Room 117. She would have loved to spread them out on her desk and dive in, miniature camera in hand, but she couldn't risk it.

Karl never gave her any inkling of how long he'd be gone. He had a habit of sticking his head in the door, drifting away again, and returning at irregular intervals to ask her to make him some coffee. At any time, she might hear his key in the lock, a signal that she only had a couple of seconds to cover her tracks.

But she'd learned that the seconds that it took him to unlock the door gave her just enough time to do a few things. They were time enough to slam a drawer closed and step away from a filing cabinet where she had no business looking, if she choreographed those movements and was ready to execute them instantly.

That choreography could even include a confused expression that said, "I'm new here and I forgot which filing cabinet was which." But no choreography and no amount of feigned confusion would help her if Karl caught her photographing Ike's or Thelma's or Nora's personal information. That work would have to come later, when she got Karl out of the way long enough for her to see what was in the thick files of the people who worked for Ed van Dorn.

As if to underscore this problem, she heard the singing of metal on metal as, once again, Karl thrust his key into the lock on her office door.

"How's your dictation?" he asked. "I need you to type a memo for me."

———

Justine had the nuns who taught her stenography to thank for the fact that her shorthand was good enough to transcribe Karl's random musings. Her typing muscles needed exercise, but factory work had kept her hands and forearms toned. She was still able to bang the old iron typewriter's keys hard enough to create even, attractive text.

As she yanked the memo out of the typewriter carriage with a satisfying spin of the platen and stood to take it to Karl, a quiet tap sounded on her door.

She opened it and, conscious of security, stepped into the opening. She wondered if she should suggest to Karl that he install a screen like the one that guarded Room 117 from prying eyes. It would have the added benefit of giving her an extra second to get her hands out of the personnel files whenever Karl returned unexpectedly.

Instead of a determined intruder, Dr. Patryk Kowalski waited patiently in the hall, a cup of coffee in each hand and a parcel tucked under one arm. She had forgotten that they were supposed to have coffee together.

She heard Karl's office door open behind her. She didn't turn around, but she heard him say, "Patryk. What a nice surprise."

Again, she wondered whether Karl had a handgun to guard his secrets, like Ed did. If so, she wondered whether he kept it in a desk drawer or in a pocket of the loose suits he wore to camouflage his bulk.

Dr. Kowalski's gaze shifted from Justine to Karl, as he said, "The pleasure is mine." Then his eyes shifted again, flicking briefly toward the pin-studded wall map of Europe on their way back to Justine.

"I neglected to ask what time you took your break when I made our appointment," he said to Justine. "Would this be a good time for a cup of coffee? There are tables in the lobby where we can sit and sip."

Justine looked over her shoulder at Karl, who nodded, took the memo she'd typed, and withdrew into his office.

Picking up her purse, Justine stepped into the hall, and locked the office door behind her. Dr. Kowalski handed her one of the coffee cups. As he escorted her down the hall, he held up the parcel and said, "Shhhh. I have a surprise."

His tone was fatherly. No, it wasn't as intimate as that. If she had to describe the older man's manner in three words, it would have been "Like an uncle." Justine's father had been an only child and her mother's brother had died young, so she had no uncles. Still, she had a sense of what having an uncle would be like, because she'd spent so much time among her parents' professor friends, who were mostly men.

Long ago, one of them had been Karl. This was what he had been to her when she was small.

Uncles liked their nieces and nephews to be excited about their surprises, so Justine said, "Do I have to wait until we get to the lobby to find out what's in the bag?"

It was a brown bag with telltale grease stains seeping through the paper. Justine smelled something savory, so she wasn't actually pretending to be excited about whatever was inside.

"Ah, but we will enjoy a few moments of anticipation!" he said, waggling the bag in front of her face and then playfully drawing it away. "In the meantime, you must tell me more about your godmother. Dr. Becker says that she is from Poland."

"Her name is Gloria Mazur. She's a physicist, like my parents were. She's been in this country a very long time. More than thirty years. Maybe more than forty. Her life in Poland was very long ago."

"Poles sometimes leave. Sometimes we must leave. But we are still Poles."

"She doesn't talk about Poland much, but that doesn't mean she doesn't miss it. I know that. I just think it's easier for her to look forward at what's coming, instead of back at what she's lost."

His expression was carefully blank. If she were thinking as Justine-the-human-being, she would regret referring to the home Gloria had lost, since this man had lost it, too. Thinking as Justine-the-covert-agent, a person who needed to slice through the defenses of a group of people who kept secrets for a living, she thought that poking at this man's weak spot was probably the smartest thing she could do. And his weak spot seemed to be Poland.

"It might be better to forget," he said, "but this presupposes that one is capable of forgetting." Then he arranged his blank face into a smile, waggled the paper bag again, and said, "You will be glad that there are things I have not forgotten."

When they reached the lobby at the end of the hall, he led her to a table in the corner and pulled out her chair for her.

"We will have privacy here," he said, nodding toward the security guard posted by the exterior door on the other side of the room. The guard was far away enough that he wouldn't overhear their conversation, and there was nobody else in sight.

When she was seated, he settled himself in his chair and placed the bag in the center of the table delicately, as if it held an infant or a Fabergé egg. Ceremoniously, he reached in and pulled out two folded linen napkins and offered her one.

"For your fingers," he said.

Then he reached into the bag again and lifted out two bundles wrapped in cotton napkins, one red and one white, and set them on the table.

Gently tugging at the red napkin's folds, he revealed something brown and crumbly. "*Placek z kruszonka,*" he said. "Perhaps your godmother made this for you when you were young."

A sweet, yeasty aroma made Justine smile. "She did. And when I was older, she let me help her."

"I could not get raisins or plums, but my grandmother often made it plain, without fruit."

"I like it better that way," Justine said. "There's nothing to get in the way of the butter and sugar and crunchy crumbles."

"Perhaps you are part Pole." He unfolded the white napkin to reveal more pastries, each one rolled into a snail shape.

"Oh, my goodness," she said, breathing in the scent of onions, cumin, and coriander. "Is that *pierekaczewnik*?"

"It is. Perhaps your godmother has some Tatar ancestry? Do you know where her home was?" He checked himself. "I should have said 'Do you know where her home is?' I make it a practice to assume that my country and its towns will be there when the war is done."

"I'm sorry, but I don't know the name of Gloria's hometown." It occurred to her that there could only be one reason she didn't have this information, and it was that Gloria couldn't bear to talk about it. "But she certainly makes *pierekaczewnik*."

A smile lit his face, the first one she'd seen from him that was without a tinge of sadness. "You say it so well. Americans often have difficulty with my language. I enjoyed making these for you so much. They bring back happy memories, and I see that they do the same for you. We need those memories to get through times like these."

Justine could feel the dough—both kinds of dough—on her hands, and she could hear Gloria directing her in how to handle it. *Placek z kruszonka* was a crumble-topped coffee cake, but it differed from American versions because it was raised with yeast. Strong hands and forearms were required to mix the dough by hand, knead it, punch it down, and shape it.

By contrast, *pierekaczewnik* was made of six layers of tender dough, rolled thin and layered with seasoned ground lamb. She'd learned to use a rolling pin by rolling out that dough, again and again, until it met Gloria's standards. Mixing the dough with a wooden spoon, rolling it out, layering it, rolling it up like a jelly roll, baking it, and slicing it into the traditional snail-shaped pieces—these things took time and care. Hours and hours of labor were bound up in the delicacies this man was sharing with a total stranger. His loneliness hung in the air along with the scents of spices and sugar.

"This is like a holiday feast," she said. "How kind you are to share these with me!"

"It has been a very long time since I had anyone to cook for," he said, spreading a clean napkin in front of her and gesturing for her to help herself.

As she took a piece of the *pierekaczewnik*, he said, "It was impossible to find lamb, so I made it with minced beef," then he watched anxiously as she took a bite.

"The lamb isn't the important part. The spices and the pastry—crunchy on the outside and moist on the inside—that's what makes these so delicious. You're an artist with a rolling pin."

"You make me blush." He flapped his hands at the *placek z kruszonka*. "Please. The cake. You must not save it for last. It is all the sweeter when you have a bit of the salty food and then take a bite of the sugary food."

Justine happily took a piece of the crumbly cake.

"Surely you don't just roll out Polish dumplings. Your godmother would have taught you to speak my language?"

"A little. Only enough to sound like a three-year-old. I do know '*Proszę*' and '*Dziękuję*'—please and thank you. And I can say 'How are you?'"

"*Jak się masz?*"

"Exactly. It sounds better when you say it."

"No, your pronunciation is good. It is obvious that you learned from a native speaker."

"Unfortunately, you've heard most of my vocabulary. Except for food. If Gloria cooked it for me, she made me say it before she let me have any. *Schabowy. Racuchy. Placki ziemniaczane. Makowiec.*"

"You always did love *makowiec*."

"Excuse me?"

"Remember? Your mother always knew where to get the best poppy seeds."

"I'm sorry…what?"

He had taken her hand. The pastries had left his fingertips oily and covered with crumbs.

"I've missed you, Viktoria."

"Dr. Kowalski. My name is Justine. Is something wrong?"

He dropped her hand like it was a cold, dead fish. "Is something wrong? Is something wrong? What could be wrong? A dead wife. A dead son. A dead you. Viktoria, where have you been? *Gdzie jesteś?* I cannot even get back into Gdańsk to look for you."

Justine had always heard that it was dangerous to wake a dreamer, sleepwalking through an imaginary world. Was it dangerous to drag a man away from an imaginary life and back to reality?

It might not be dangerous, but it felt cruel. This man had lost a wife, a nameless son, and somebody named Viktoria. She didn't want to drag him back to a world where they were dead, but it was the world they both lived in. She couldn't be his Viktoria.

"Dr. Kowalski," she said softly, slowly, clearly, "my name isn't Viktoria. It's Justine. And this isn't Poland. We work together at Arlington Hall in Arlington, Virginia. Do you understand me?"

He brushed the crumb-covered fingers of both hands lightly through her hair. "Like strands of sunshine. Your hair was always such a happy color, from the day you first opened your eyes. And here you are, a grown woman now."

"Dr. Kowalski," she said in a slightly louder voice, "I am not Viktoria."

He retracted his hands abruptly, as if her hair was on fire. "No. You are not. Your eyes are brown and Viktoria's are… were…blue, like the sky and the sea."

He rose to his feet, towering over her. "Why are you pretending to be my daughter?" Now he was shouting. "You must explain yourself."

He reached out to grab her, but she saw his hand coming and pushed hard against the floor with both feet. The back of the chair struck the wall, so she couldn't go far, but the wall also gave her enough leverage to get to her feet.

"Dr. Kowalski, you have to listen to me."

His answer was interrupted by a burly arm encircling his throat and the security guard saying, "Are you all right, Miss?"

"I'm fine. He's—"

The security guard bent the older man forward at the waist, and Justine was afraid he meant to throw him to the ground.

She crouched to get into the guard's line of sight, waving her hands. "Look at me. Listen to me. I'm fine. I'm really fine. Please don't hurt him. He's just...he needs help."

In a single fluid motion, the guard twisted Dr. Kowalski's hands behind his waist, the same hands that had touched her hair so gently. With a harsh double-click, a pair of handcuffs closed around his wrists.

"Officer, there's no need. I'm not afraid of him. Please."

Dr. Kowalski had stopped struggling. Actually, he'd never truly struggled. He stood, head down, like a man who had accepted his fate.

"I'm sorry, Viktoria. I just...I just miss you. And I'm so sorry."

As the guard led him away, he kept his eyes on Justine until the door shut between them.

———

Justine slipped into her office, hoping for a quiet moment. She wanted to lay her head on her desk for a few minutes and try not to think, but Karl had other ideas. He was standing beside her desk before her rear hit the chair.

What did he want? Did he want her to take more dictation? File something? Type something? Did he want her to spend another day trying to answer a trick question? Whatever it was, she didn't want to do it.

She was still clutching Dr. Kowalski's oily paper bag and her fingers were still dusted with crumbs and flour and sugar. How could their conversation have gone bad so quickly? And why had she brought his carefully made pastries back to her office? She would never be able to make herself eat them. Her mouth was bone-dry, and it tasted like a broken man's grief. The pastries would stick in her throat, but she couldn't bring herself to throw them away. What if he saw his gift, the product of hours of labor, in a trash can?

Maybe Georgette would eat the pastries.

"Your time with Patryk did not go well?" Karl's voice was quiet.

"How did you know? Nobody saw what happened but the security guard. And he's—" It felt like a violation of Dr. Kowalski's privacy to say, "And he's hauling him away in handcuffs," so she let her voice trail off. "He and Dr. Kowalski are still together."

"You only left a few minutes ago. I knew that something must have gone wrong."

She couldn't speak, but he must have seen something in her eyes, because he simply said, "Well." Then he cleared his throat and went on.

"Patryk is not himself. I suppose that I do not know the old Patryk, the original Patryk, because he has not been himself since I met him. Still, he manages to get through the days. One by one, he survives them. It is better for him to be here working among people than to sit at home, alone with his thoughts. And it is better for those of us who would like the Axis to lose this war, because Patryk is very, very good at everything I ask him to do." He looked at her even more closely. "But I sense that he may have come to the end of being able to use work to get through his days. Perhaps I may soon have another friend whom I need to visit in the hospital."

"What happened to his family?"

Karl dropped into one of the guest chairs across from her desk. "Oh, dear. If his family came up in the short time you were gone from this room, then Patryk is truly at the end of his rope. I should have known by your pale hair that your time together would not go well."

"He called me Viktoria."

Karl turned his head away and cleared his throat.

"Ah, Viktoria. Hers is a sad story. All of Patryk's stories are sad."

"So it seems."

"Patryk was a mathematics professor in Warsaw. He and his wife, Magdalena, had two children, Viktoria and Jakub. It became clear that they needed to leave, so they booked passage to England. They escaped Poland and got as far as the Free City of Danzig, but Magdalena fell in the fracas when so many panicked people fought to disembark from the train. Both her legs were badly broken and she could not proceed."

Justine didn't want to listen, but she owed it to Dr. Kowalski—to Patryk.

"He was able to carry her to a hospital, where he was told she could not travel for two weeks, at the least, and only then in a wheelchair and with help. So the two of them sat together. They considered the factors and weighed the odds. Numbers are, after all, what mathematicians do."

Numbers were so cold. They were so hard.

"Patryk and Magdalena saw four options. One, they could all stay in Danzig for two weeks, risking all of their lives until Magdalena could leave with their help. Two, Patryk could take both children to England, with no knowledge of when Magdalena would recover sufficiently to travel alone or whether he would be able to come back to help her. Three, they could send the children ahead to England, with fourteen-year-old Viktoria, a responsible girl, in charge of seven-year-old Jakub for two weeks until their parents could follow. Or four, Patryk could take Jakub to safety, leaving Magdalena with Viktoria, who was large and strong enough to help her mother to the ship in two short weeks."

"What did they decide?"

"I believe they were swayed by horror at the thought of both children losing their lives, but they could not bring themselves to put Viktoria and Jakub on a foreign ship bound for a foreign country during a time of war without a parent to look after them. Thus, the best of their bad options was for Patryk to take Jakub to England, leaving Viktoria with her mother. Two weeks is, after all, not a very long time, and Patryk was able to secure tickets for Viktoria and Magdalena before he left. It was a reasonable plan, but it was August 1939, and nothing in the world was reasonable then."

"They haven't been reasonable since." Thinking of a woman and her daughter, left behind in a blitzkrieg, she asked, "What happened to Magdalena and Viktoria?"

"For a year, he did not know. Then he received a letter from a family friend saying that they had perished within weeks of his departure. He has told me no further details, and I hope he does not know them. Poles suffered terribly when Danzig was taken. Execution. Torture. Terrible things."

"But he got Jakub to safety?"

"Yes. Patryk found work at a university in London and they lived there for three years, until a German bomb destroyed their apartment building. Patryk was knocked unconscious. When he awoke, Jakub was lying beside him, dead."

He paused, but Justine couldn't speak, so he went on.

"It is not easy to leave England these days, but Patryk was

determined to leave Europe, leave his family's memory, leave everything. And mathematicians will always have a home at Arlington Hall. He wrote a letter to a colleague and was here within a month."

Justine leapt to her feet. "We have to find him. The guard doesn't know why he's acting like this. He won't be gentle with him. Where would he have taken him?"

"I will make a phone call, and then I will go retrieve Patryk."

He rose and shuffled to his office door, his age and bulk slowing him far more than usual. As he passed Justine, he rested a hand on her head.

"I have seen a photo of Viktoria. You don't resemble her in the least, my dear, other than your pale hair, but I don't think that matters to Patryk. I believe he sees her everywhere."

———

Justine sat at her desk, unable to think about anything but Patryk, Viktoria, Magdalena, Jakub, and the fragrant pastries in her desk drawer. The moment came when she couldn't bear the scents of cumin and cinnamon for another minute. She needed to take her mind off the doomed family, so she might as well do her job. She might as well go take a look at the people in Room 117.

Sally answered the door with her customary smile. "Come in! Are you here to see Samantha or did Karl send you?"

Justine gestured at the file folders in her hand. "Karl sent these to Ed...I mean, Dr. van Dorn."

She lowered her eyes and was gratified to feel the warmth of a real blush. She also felt the eyes of Ed's employees on her. She could tell by their faces that they'd been gossiping about her and their boss.

Instead of waiting for her to walk down the aisle of desks to reach his, Ed picked up a stack of files of his own and hurried to meet her. "Wonderful. I'd been waiting for Karl to send me those folders. If you don't mind taking these to him, that would be a big help."

Before Justine knew what was happening, he had her by the elbow, leading her toward the door. In all likelihood, he was angling for a few minutes alone with her in the hallway, but he was costing her time with her suspects. Trying to make the most of the seconds left to her, Justine swept the room with her eyes.

Nobody sat at Patryk's desk, and his empty chair made her heart hurt. Nora was working quietly, but there were a few flower petals at her feet to show that she'd brought her daily bouquet. The absence of flowers on Ike's desk showed that he'd already given Nora's gift away.

Other than the petals and Patryk's empty chair, little had changed since her last visit. Everyone was bent over their work. All the desks were piled with paper. And all that paper was facedown.

Ed pulled the door shut and gestured for her to follow him. An instant after they passed through the exterior door, he reached in his breast pocket for a pack of cigarettes, shook one out, and lit it.

"I heard about the scene with Patryk."

"But it just happened. How could you already know?"

"Beulah was standing at the door, too horrified to come into the lobby to help you and too horrified to walk away. I'm sorry that happened to you. If it makes you feel any better, it's not the first time." He sucked in a lungful of smoke. "No, I guess there's really no reason for that to make you feel better. I should have realized it was coming when I saw your head of beautiful blond hair. I owe you an apology for not warning you."

"How is he?"

"The SSA will put him in front of a doctor, if they haven't already. The doctor will talk to him, and Patryk will lie. He will tell him that he caved in during a weak moment, but that he's perfectly fine. The doctor will send him home in the care of Karl, who is assuredly sitting in the waiting room by now. What else can anyone do? There are no medicines for diseases of the mind, no pills to ease Patryk's pain. His only alternative is electric shock therapy."

"That sounds—"

"It sounds awful, because it *is* awful. Can you imagine someone with Patryk's mind allowing it to be disrupted that way? And what about his memories? What if he lost some—any—of his memories of his family? He has nothing else left of them. I hate the idea that it might come to the point that he'd have to take the risk. Living without your family is hell, but living without your feelings and memories is a different kind of hell."

He reached out his hand and used his thumb to gently trace the angle of her jaw.

"If Patryk comes back to us..." he said. "I mean, *when* Patryk gets back, please stay away from him. You're not good for him, and a torn-up Patryk isn't good for anybody, not for him and not for you. "

"I certainly don't want to make things any worse for him than they are."

Ed shook his head. "I don't think you make things worse for Patryk, so you shouldn't carry that guilt. If it wasn't your hair, it would be a child's toy in a store window or a wedding ring on a woman's hand."

"But what will he do?"

"As long as Patryk can hold himself together, like a battered puppet tied together with twine, he'll do that. He'll be here tomorrow. He may even paste on a smile. What are his other options? Should he stay home? Would you want to be alone with his thoughts?"

There was nothing for Justine to say but, "No."

Ed tapped his cigarette, until its cylinder of ash fell to the ground. "Nobody can change things for Patryk, not unless they have a time machine. His world is as dark as it can be."

Chapter 16

At the end of the workday, Justine met Georgette in the hallway outside Room 117. The flood of people hurrying to get in line for the bus carried them down the hall, through the lobby, and out the door.

As they passed from the warm building into the cold winter air, Justine heard a familiar voice calling. "Samantha! Justine!"

Jerry had parked his wheelchair beside the sidewalk to wait for them. "May I see you home?"

He was already wheeling away from them, so they followed his lead.

"I don't always have ration stamps for gas, but you ladies can be assured that my old car is your chariot when I do," he said, loud enough for anybody nearby to hear. "Especially you, Samantha," he said, flashing a dazzled grin at Georgette. "It's a little bit of a walk to where I've got it parked. I hope you don't mind."

Justine could see that Jerry was enjoying his role as Georgette/Samantha's infatuated swain.

Not to be outdone, Georgette gave him a shy giggle and said, "I'd walk to the White House and back if it meant I got some time with you, Alan."

Steering his chair between the two women, Jerry said, "I like the sound of that. I guess you two can't tell me much about your day, what with all of Arlington Hall's government secrets and all, but how did it go? Can you at least tell me what you ate for lunch?"

Justine told Jerry a tale of eating tuna casserole with Nora and her vegetable alphabet soup that kept him laughing all the way to his parked car. He waved Georgette off when she offered to help him get his chair in the trunk, then unlocked the front passenger door for her and reached in to unlock the rear door for Justine.

"I'm sorry you have to sit in the back," he said to Justine as he opened it, with a wink she didn't understand.

Then she heard the other passenger door open as Jerry rolled away. Someone got out and extended an arm to help Jerry get himself into the driver's seat. Settling herself in the seat behind Georgette, Justine peered through the car's rear window, but she couldn't see the face of the person handling the chair. All she could make out was a torso and a pair of gloved hands folding it and stashing it in the trunk.

In front of her, Georgette scooched across the front seat to get closer to Jerry. They were so happy to see each other that their faces were phosphorescent. She looked away to give them a moment of privacy.

Then the rear door opposite her opened and a man slid onto the seat. Pulling off his gloves and putting his gray fedora and muffler in his lap, Paul said, "Hello, ladies. And Jerry."

Jerry put the car in drive and pulled out onto the street.

While Jerry may have wanted to hear their funny stories about Caféteria food and eccentric coworkers, Paul did not. He spoke like a man with no time to waste.

"The news out of Europe isn't good. Our failure to foresee this last-ditch attack could be devastating."

Justine had been comforting herself for months with the hope that the war was nearly over. Surely, the successful attacks on Normandy's beaches had signaled the Allied Forces' coming victory. Paul was in a position to know far more than she did, and it scared her that he didn't look like a man who thought the war was going his way.

"Our analysts had been watching an uptick in radio traffic. We knew it meant that an attack was possible, but we had no indication of where or when. Europe is a big place. If we could have reinforced all our positions, we would have. It wasn't possible."

That was the reality of overstretched supply lines. No army is big enough to be in all places at all times. And if it was, it wouldn't be able to feed itself. This was how empires fell.

"I don't want you to see this problem as something that's far away in Europe," Paul said. "Don't think of it as something that you can't do anything about. You two are in the right place at the right time. Putting you at Arlington Hall at the time of the attack may be the luckiest thing I've done lately."

"Not lucky," Jerry said. "Smart."

"If I were smart, I'd have had them there a month ago. Maybe they could have made sense of that uptick in radio traffic. But I can't change the past. I'm here to tell you that finding the leak in Room 117 is critical to making sure that the fighting in Europe goes our way. There's plenty of classified information in that room already—"

Justine thought of the mountains of paper on all the desks in Room 117. Every sheet was an exposed secret.

"—and we have to presume it's all compromised. We are diverting everything important away from those people, so their talents are wasted until the situation is rectified. And we have to do it without alerting the traitor to the fact that we're on the trail. People like that tend to be very dangerous when cornered."

Justine imagined the faces of the people in Room 117: Sally, Nora, Dr. Kowalski, Ike, Ed, Thelma, The Bees. None of them looked like people who could swing the outcome of a battle. Or a war. They certainly didn't look dangerous.

Paul opened a briefcase resting at his feet and pulled out a stack of papers. "You both remember what I told you about the unexplained attack on a pontoon bridge in Poland."

Justine and Georgette nodded.

He handed a stack of papers to Justine. "Here are the messages we sent on the day that we think the leak occurred. Some are in English. Others are in German because we were pretending to send them to a German double agent. They passed through the hands of radio operators based in four countries. Do you see anything noteworthy?"

Here was a real-world chance to put the things she'd learned from Karl's test to good use. Justine grabbed the papers before the words were out of Paul's mouth.

As she read, Jerry drove slowly through Arlington and into the rural area beyond, where he drove a quarter mile down a deserted dirt road and parked. She remained conscious that Paul was watching her flip back and forth between messages that intrigued her, but he could wait. She took her time, and he let her. Jerry and Georgette talked quietly in the front seat. Nobody rushed her as the landscape outside her window dimmed and went dark, except for the rising moon. Paul handed her a flashlight and she kept reading.

When she was finished, she squared the papers into a neat stack, except for a single sheet that she held in her right hand. "At first glance, these messages are unremarkable."

"At first glance?" Moonlight reflected off Paul's glasses as he leaned closer.

"One message stands out. This one. It's written in German,

and it gives the location of the pontoon bridge. The date is written in the American style. Like this—October 30, 1944." She held up the message and pointed to the date. "All of the other messages are dated in the European style—30 October 1944."

She could see Jerry's eyes in the rear-view mirror. Georgette had turned in her seat to face her.

"Justine," Paul said, "do you think that one of our people intentionally constructed this message with that American-style date? Do you think it was a signal to attack the station?"

"I do."

"We think so, too."

Justine was holding a typed copy of the message, with no other identifying information. What had the original looked like?

"People who do cryptanalysis are pretty stubborn about records and paper trails," she said. "How else will they check their work? And the military likes its paper trails, too. Surely you know who drafted this message. I imagine that you have the original. I'd like to see it."

"We have the handwritten draft in English. It bears the initials of a woman named Thelma Dickens. The draft bears only the message, with no date, so it tells us nothing about the American-style date you noted. There's nothing odd about it at all, not even a stray pencil stroke. From Thelma's notes, we know that she gave it to Edison van Dorn so that he could translate it into German, because it was supposed to be going to a German double agent, but we don't have the document he created. Karl Becker, who is not above rubbing Edison's face in his own status as a native speaker, double-checked his German. He very likely threw Edison's work away and substituted it with his own. He does that from time to time."

"I bet that made Dr. van Dorn crazy," Georgette said.

"That," Paul said, "is likely an understatement, but we have no documentation of it. We do, however, have Dr. Becker's notes that say he received the document, checked it, and returned it to van Dorn."

Justine laughed. "You can spot their rivalry from twenty paces."

"No kidding," Georgette said. "I'm waiting for them to challenge each other to a duel."

"It gets better," Paul said. "Sometimes van Dorn gets so angry with the interference that he tears up Becker's work and throws it away. We think he did that with this message. The upshot is that we know for a fact that they both worked on the message, but we have no physical copies of their work."

"So Karl and Ed destroyed each other's work and broke the chain of custody for this message?" Justine asked.

"Shattered it. But a woman named Nora saw Karl's final message, because she was the one who encrypted it. Of course, we have no way of knowing whether she encrypted what she read word for word—"

"Because Dr. van Dorn tore Dr. Becker's work up after she translated it." Georgette looked embarrassed when she realized she'd interrupted him, but she kept talking. "Isn't that the most unprofessional thing you've ever heard of? And I've got to work for that man."

"It's more than unprofessional," Jerry said. "It should be a firing offense. The fact that Dr. van Dorn still has a job tells you something, although I'm not sure what it is. Maybe he's so good that the government is willing to put up with his foolishness. Maybe nobody's paying attention. Maybe he's got friends in high places. But maybe those friends are traitors, too. All of these things are also true of Dr. Becker."

"Exactly," Paul said.

"What happened after Nora encrypted the message?" Justine asked.

"A woman named Sally Tompkins checked her work, made a clean copy with the telltale date, and initialed it. This copy is the only one that survives. It has the altered date, but we can't be sure whether it came to Nora and Sally that way. Then, a woman named Bettie—"

"She's the one who got murdered a few weeks back," Georgette said.

"Yes," Paul said. "I've heard about the murder. And it's worrisome that the woman who was murdered was the one who routinely carried encrypted messages to the Traffic Records Unit for typing and filing. It's possible that she noticed the changed date and that she was killed by the person who needed to make sure it stayed secret."

Justine was startled to think that a life could end because of something so prosaic as a misplaced number.

"All we have on paper," Paul said, "is Thelma Dickens's handwritten original message in English, which is not dated, and Sally Tompkins's final version with the altered date, which was carried to Traffic Records by Bettie Mountford, typed by Patsy Young, and filed by Linda James."

"Because the two men in charge ignored procedures so flagrantly, any person in Room 117 could have put their hands on the message at any time. Nobody can be excluded."

She wished Paul would tell her that she was wrong, but he said only, "Yes. So what do I want you to find out?"

"You want to know who the traitor is, obviously. That's why we're here," Justine said. "Eventually, though, you're going to have to figure out why they blew up that port. There were only two rational ways for the enemy to respond to that message. If our fake traffic fooled them into believing that we were planning a major offensive in the area, the response should have been an all-out effort to push us back from our targets. If the fake traffic didn't fool them, they should have lain low so we wouldn't know they'd broken our code. They did neither."

"Exactly. So tell me everything you two have found out about the people who work in that room."

Justine looked at Georgette, who had spent two full days in Room 117. She should be the one who answered him.

Georgette had plenty to say. "I've spent the most time with Sally Tompkins. She seems real nice, but maybe spies usually do. She says she's twenty-one, but she don't look it. The word is that she's really, really good at all that code business. I heard Ike say she could pick up a coded message and read it like it was English. I think it's like the way Justine's mind works when you put a math problem in front of her."

"Or when you pick up a dress pattern and can tell how to sew on the sleeve by the markings on it," Justine said.

Georgette blushed. "Well, that ain't the same as the things you and Sally can do. Anyway, the most interesting thing about Sally don't have a thing to do with her work." She turned to Justine and asked, "Did you notice that she was wearing three necklaces, all of 'em lockets and all of 'em shaped like a heart?"

"I did."

"She says she's loved and lost three men that died in the war. She says she was engaged to all three of 'em."

Justine sucked in an involuntary breath. "I can't imagine what that would be like."

"Me, neither." Georgette's eyes flicked for the tiniest instant in Jerry's direction. She tried to hide it, but Justine saw. She wondered if her eyes had gone to Paul.

"If it's true," Paul said.

"I want to believe it's true, because I like her, and she don't seem like a liar," Georgette said, "but I guess we can't believe a thing we hear. Not in our business."

Georgette had been a spy for all of three months, but she seemed to be enjoying it a whole lot.

"If her story's true, I'm guessing that's the real reason she keeps telling Ike to keep his distance," Justine said. "She's going to need time to heal from all that pain."

"You would think so," Georgette said, "but she didn't take much of any time after the first two. She ain't old enough for that, and the math don't add up. She says that she's twenty-one. Say she was engaged to the first one and he died at Pearl Harbor. That would've made her eighteen. Then say she spent a year feeling all that pain you're talking about and met another man when she was nineteen. Give her a year to get engaged to him. Even if he's killed right away, now she's twenty. Let her pine for him for a year and she's twenty-one. No matter when her birthday is, that means she would've had to get engaged to that last man and then have him die on her in less than a year. Maybe a lot less than a year. He would just now be dead, and ain't nobody mentioned it, so maybe she was even faster about going from one dead man to the next."

"Your math checks out," Jerry said. "Right, Justine? You're the one that likes math."

Justine nodded.

Georgette had some feelings about Sally's frenetic acquisition of fiancés. "Yeah, the math checks out, and you'd think that it adds up to somebody who's pretty dang cold-blooded. But Sally don't seem that way."

Justine thought Georgette had a good point. "I don't think Sally seems cold-blooded, either. I'm not sure what her list of dead fiancés means, though."

Paul said, "Nor am I."

"Anyway," Georgette said, "Sally ain't the only one that Ike likes. And there's somebody he don't like, but who does like him."

Justine remembered what Sally had said at lunch about one of Ike's admirers. "Are you talking about Nora?"

"Yep, Nora is Ike's not-so-secret admirer. She's…"

Georgette was silent for a moment, until Paul prodded her. "She's what?"

"Nora's just…I like her, but she's strange in lots of little ways. She talks to herself while she's working, which makes the rest of us nuts. When Dr. van Dorn gets fed up with it, he starts talking to himself, too, and he does it in three or four languages. Eventually, he tells Nora to stop talking. So she starts humming. I think it's really highbrow music that she's humming. It's certainly odd. I might even like it sometimes, but Ike don't. I ain't sure he's going to be able to stand Nora for one more day."

Now Justine was curious. "Because she hums strange music?"

"It's not just her humming. She stares at him a lot. And she brings him flowers. Sally says she brings 'em every day. She's sure done it since I've been there."

Jerry was looking at Georgette like he'd never heard anything so odd as a woman bringing a man flowers. Justine thought Georgette should buy him some posies, just to see how he would react.

"At lunch," Justine said, "she told me that the church pays her in flowers and that she brings some to work every day. She didn't say anything about bringing them to Ike."

"Well, that's what she does." Georgette's nod was emphatic. "Watchin' the two of them and those flowers is like watching square dancers go through their moves. Both days since I got here, Nora came to work with a little bouquet in a paper cup. Sometime in the middle of both mornings, she took a break and put her little cup of flowers on Ike's desk. Then she went back to her desk and started working again like nothing ever happened. I ain't never seen her say a word to the man, but she sure spends a lot of her time looking at him all moony-eyed. And it don't seem to bother her that he don't keep her flowers."

"Does he throw them away?" Jerry asked. "That's not very gentlemanly."

"It's worse than that. He never thanked her and he never looked at them, neither day. When it came time for his break, he just picked 'em up and left the room. Both days. Came back empty-handed. The first day, I thought it was what you said, Jerry. I thought he threw them pretty flowers away, but no. I followed him this morning, and he walked down the hall to Traffic Records. I watched him go in and, right before the door closed, I saw him set them flowers right on Linda's desk. If I was Nora, that would've happened exactly one time."

"If some woman, like maybe this one sitting next to me, were to bring me flowers, I wouldn't give 'em away." Jerry elbowed Georgette.

Georgette raised her hand as if to swat at him, but she just ended up ruffling his crew cut.

Paul had no time for teasing. "What about Dr. Kowalski?" he asked.

"There's a sad story there," Georgette said, "but I ain't been able to get anybody to tell it to me yet. I think they're afraid he'll hear us talking."

"I heard it today. I just haven't had time to tell you about it. It's…it's just awful. He lost his wife and daughter early in the war while they were trying to leave Poland. Then his son was killed by a bomb in London. He came here right after that, and he's been here ever since."

"What about Dr. van Dorn?" Paul asked.

Georgette shook her head. "I don't know much about him.

He don't smile, and he gives a lot of orders. He acts like a real mean boss, and maybe that's the way he is all the time. I can't tell, but Justine knows him better."

Justine hated herself for blushing when Paul and Jerry turned their eyes on her.

"I can tell you a little bit about him," Justine said. "He took me to dinner at the Mayfair on Saturday night, so I learned a few things to tell you about him."

"Nice place." Paul's face was expressionless, but this was not new. She was pretty sure he knew about her date, since Jerry would have told him about it at the first opportunity, but he was going to make her tell him. Well, fine. She would do just that.

"I found Ed—Dr. van Dorn—to be a man who keeps his cards close to his vest." She heard the words come out of her mouth and they made her laugh. "I guess that's only natural for a serious bridge player. He did take off his 'mean boss' face when we were together, but I couldn't tell you whether the face he showed me was any less of a mask. He's intelligent, but we could have inferred that from what he does for a living. He likes to play bridge. He doesn't get along with his father. He has a brother in the war, but he didn't mention his mother. He likes jazz."

"None of that's earth-shattering," Jerry said.

Paul was still silent.

"That's about all I learned," Justine said, "but he said that he wanted to see me again, so tell me if there's anything you particularly want me to find out."

"You're going out with him again?" Jerry asked.

Justine shrugged. "We're here to find out what's going on in Room 117. I've got a chance to have another long conversation with the man in charge. Shouldn't I take it?"

"You're not required to—" Paul cleared his throat and tried again. "Your safety is—"

"I can take care of myself. And didn't you and Jerry take us on this little drive to tell us how critical it is that we find the person leaking sensitive information?"

"We did." Paul's voice regained its edge. "With the German attack going on right now, our troops in Europe are at risk of losing the ground they've gained since Normandy, yet the situation in Room 117 is forcing us to route messages around our most valuable analysts. The two of you need to find the enemy agent who has put us in this corner."

"Even if it means spending more time on the dance floor with Edison van Dorn's hands on me?"

Paul didn't say yes, but he didn't say no.

———

When Jerry parked the car in the Kansas Hall parking lot, Georgette stayed in the front seat long enough to give him a lingering good-night kiss. She missed him, and she never knew when, or if, she would see him again. She could see that Justine was already out of the car, and the man in the back seat had his eyes on the papers in his lap, so she felt comfortable displaying this much affection, but no more. One day, they would have some time alone, but it might not be for a very long time.

Jerry put his lips near her ear and murmured, "Wouldn't you know that he'd manage things so that I'm busy driving, and he's in the back with his girl?"

"Is she his girl?"

"Pretty sure he wants her to be."

Georgette's hand brushed the back of his neck as she whispered, "I couldn't tell that he took a bit of advantage of the situation."

Cutting a glance at the man behind him, Jerry said, "Not sure he knows how."

Georgette kissed him on the cheek and retrieved her purse from the floorboard. As she got out of the car, she flung her reply over her shoulder. "I sure do, sugar." Then she shut the door.

She was watching him through the window, so she saw him laugh right out loud. Then he bellowed his answer loud enough for her to hear him through the glass, and never mind that Justine or the man in the back seat would hear.

"So do I, honey. So do I."

———

Justine waited in the cold for Georgette to get out of the car. Paul had skipped his opportunity to tell her not to go out with another man, so she supposed she was going to keep going out with Ed van Dorn until there was nothing else that her country needed her to learn about him. She hoped that Paul hated the idea, and she hoped he spent a lot of time stewing about it.

She wasn't sure how long she'd leave him to stew before she reported on what she learned on her next date. She guessed it would depend on what she had to tell him. She didn't have an immediate, secure way to communicate with him, other than to ask Jerry to relay a message. She cringed at the idea of describing a date with one man to a second man, who would then turn around and tell a third one.

She had envied Georgette, sitting comfortably beside Jerry. They had behaved perfectly respectably, sharing only an occasional glance or touch on the hand. Paul, on the other hand, had barely looked at her, except for that one instant when she'd shaken him with talk of her dinner with Ed.

Still, the car's back seat was small and there had been no way for him to avoid touching her for the entire ride. Whenever

Jerry had rounded a corner, Paul had been forced to lean toward her or her body had been forced toward his. Whenever Paul had reached down for his briefcase, the back of his forearm had brushed her knee, and she had felt it through her stockings. She couldn't have said how she knew that he felt her nearness, too, but she did know it.

When Jerry put the car in park, Justine had leaned down to get her purse and her hand had accidentally brushed Paul's thigh. She had felt his response and known it to be real. Or perhaps it hadn't been an accident at all. Perhaps her body had done it for her.

Murmuring "Good night," she had reached for the door, but he'd moved to stop her.

Grabbing her hand, he'd said, "Be careful when you're alone with a man like Dr. van Dorn. Be careful all the time, but be especially careful then."

She had nodded to show that she'd heard, but all she'd said was, "I understand." Still holding his hand, she'd gotten out of the car, and he'd leaned over, hard, to maintain contact as long as he could. Then, slowly, she'd backed away from the car and pulled her hand away.

As she closed the car door, Justine could hear Paul saying, "I'll see you soon." She answered him, but there was no way to know whether he heard. Then Georgette got out and slammed the door shut, still joking with Jerry, even through the car window. As the car slowly pulled away. Georgette and Justine stood alone in the dark and watched it go.

Chapter 17

The lobby of Kansas Hall was oddly empty, reminding Justine that it was "No-Man Monday." She was inordinately grateful to the housemother for her policy of giving the women their privacy once a week.

"It's late and I'm exhausted. You probably are, too," Justine said to Georgette. "Let's just grab some sandwiches we can eat in the room."

Five minutes later, she and Georgette were leaving the service shop with their sandwiches when they saw Sally ahead of them, two steps up a staircase. Waving, Justine called out, "Hi, Sally! How was your day?"

At the sound of Justine's voice, Sally jerked her head like she was startled, but she was smiling by the time she turned to look down at them. "It was just like all the other days. A lot of work. Not a lot of reward."

"I wasn't just talking about work," Justine said. "Samantha's new boyfriend took us for a drive in the country after we got off work. Did you do anything for fun this evening?"

"A drive sounds really nice," Sally said, but she didn't answer Justine's question.

Turning away and grasping the banister, Sally said, "You two enjoy your sandwiches," but she didn't start climbing again until Justine and Georgette had moved away.

Justine was halfway up her own stairs before she remembered that Sally lived on the first floor of Kansas Hall, in the same wing that she did. It probably meant nothing that she was climbing the stairs of another wing. Anybody in the dormitory could have friends in any wing and on any floor, but something about Sally's behavior had seemed wrong somehow.

Gregarious Sally was always interested in chatting. She was warm. She laughed. She asked questions to keep a conversation going. But on the staircase, her single-sentence replies to their questions had been brusque, almost rude. They had been designed to make them shut up and go away.

What was at the top of those stairs?

———

Georgette studied her friend, lying flat on her back and still wearing her work clothes. Justine had collapsed onto her bed without even eating her sandwich, and Georgette didn't think it was just because she was tired from working all day and then sitting awkwardly beside the man she was crazy about while he asked her to work some more.

"I'm not sure I can keep doing this job," Justine had said, one arm flung across her face. "If you could have seen Patryk's face..."

Georgette had known all evening that she needed to ask Justine to tell her more about her time with Patryk Kowalski. So she asked. Then she held Justine's hand and listened while Patryk's story erupted out of her—the full story, not the bloodless his-family-died-in-the-war version she'd told to Jerry and the man beside her in the back seat. There had been tears, and there had been a lot of questions.

"How can people do such things to each other?"

"How could anyone go on after suffering through something like that?"

"What makes us think that we can do anything to make a world like this one any better?"

Georgette didn't have any answers, so she'd offered to go get Justine a Coke. Justine had declined, which was worrisome. The woman simply loved Coca-Cola, any time of the day or night.

Georgette had suggested a hot shower. She had absolutely not offered her the *placek z kruszonka* and *pierekaczewnik* hiding in the drawer of her bedside table. She'd taken them off Justine's hands as soon as she'd heard Patryk's story, promising that she would either eat them or give them away or throw them away.

Having run out of ideas for helping her friend cope with the terrible fate of the Kowalski family, Georgette had finally admitted defeat.

"I think you need to stay home from work until you feel better. Maybe you just need to ask What's-His-Name to find you another job. You're too torn up to think straight. That's when people make mistakes."

For reasons that Georgette didn't fully understand, this was the thing that calmed Justine.

"No," Justine said, shaking her head as if the motion would clear out the images of Viktoria, Magdalena, and little Jakub, all of them dead. "My work is important. *Our* work is important. If I don't do my job, then I'm not doing anything to make sure that no more families suffer what the Kowalskis did."

Georgette didn't know what had changed for Justine. Maybe, sometimes, a person just needed to let the tears do their job.

"You could call Gloria," she suggested. "She'll know how to help you feel better."

"Nope. If I were foolish enough to cry to Gloria, she would explain to me how ridiculous I was being, in excruciating detail. That would embarrass me into thinking clearly, but you managed the same thing without all the humiliation, so thank you for that."

Justine hopped out of bed and started gathering her towel and pajamas. "If Nora can get up every day and go to work after losing her husband, and Sally can do the same thing after losing three fiancés, and Ike can do it after getting blown up on a battlefield, and the people in Room 117 can do it after losing their friend Bettie, and Dr. Kowalski can do it after losing…everybody…" She grabbed her bathrobe off its hook and stuck her shampoo and soap in its pocket. "If they can do those things, I can do some light stenography for Karl while I try to figure out whether he—or any of the people who work for him—have betrayed our country."

"That's the spirit."

"Can I borrow your hair dryer? For victory?"

"Yes, *chère*, you are welcome any time to use my hair dryer to fight the Nazis."

———

Sally had known the risks when she started walking the hallways of Kansas Hall, moving from hallway to hallway and wing to wing. This was her second time through the dorm. She'd walked through the whole thing after dinner, listening, and now she was doing it again, so late at night that she hoped nobody saw her and wondered why she wasn't in bed. If her suspicions were right, she would get proof during this second tour of the dormitory. She was exercising as much caution as she could manage as she moved nonchalantly up and down staircases with a smile, as if visiting an old friend. This time, at the top of this staircase, she heard a distinctive noise that made her think she'd found what she was looking for.

Sally lingered on the landing, hoping that she could hear enough from that vantage point to know for sure.

Alas, but no. She needed to get nearer.

Step by step, she crept down the hall, but the sound remained at the very limit of her hearing. There were too many women still listening to their radios and phonographs, despite the hour, and the voices of the singers, actors, and newscasters battled with each other. Sally needed to get closer.

All the way down the hall, she passed doors to the women's rooms. They came in pairs, with the door of the room on the right directly opposite the door of the room on the left. The only room that broke this pattern was the last one, and that room was the source of the sound she was tracking. Its closed door faced an enclosed stairwell that gave the residents of that hall a second way to get downstairs. This was an excellent fire safety measure, but it was more than that. If anyone who lived in Kansas Hall needed to access that room, they had an easy, discreet way to do it.

Actually, it wouldn't have to be someone who lived in Kansas Hall. Sally knew for a fact that women routinely smuggled men up those fire escapes. It was a dormitory, not an impregnable fortress. Anybody could be sitting in there with the room's resident. For all she knew, the room didn't have even have a permanent resident. A few dollars slipped into the hand of the dormitory's registrar would keep that room open for anybody who needed a place to do something they shouldn't do.

The fire escape might be convenient for whatever person or

people were in the room at the end of the hall, but Sally would not be entering the far stairwell. If the room's occupant heard a telltale sound, Sally had no desire to be trapped in the stairwell, just the two of them. Her plan was to hear what she needed to hear, then to retrace her steps and descend the open staircase she'd come up, the one that ended in the very public dormitory lobby. Then, she planned to unobtrusively ask around and find out who spent time in that room.

Setting her feet down gently to keep the tap of her saddle shoes to a minimum, Sally crept down the hall.

She was within a few feet of the last door when she could finally hear clearly the sounds emanating from the room behind it. Earlier in the evening, she had walked this hall and heard nothing but the perfectly melodic sounds of a normal, everyday radio. Now, she heard the characteristic "hollow" distortion of shortwave radio. She had worked for the Signal Security Agency long enough to know the difference. She'd also worked there long enough to know the reasons why a listener would switch to shortwave late at night, when the reflection characteristics of the ionosphere improved reception at some frequencies.

The message she heard was coded, and she didn't know the code. She just knew that she shouldn't be seen outside the door listening to it.

Her saddle shoes sounded their *tap...tap...tap-tap* as she did her best to back away quietly, but her ears told her that she had failed. A click signaled that the shortwave radio and its quiet broadcast had been turned off, and the softer taps of two horseshoe-clad feet followed.

Sally knew that her only hope was to disappear down the far staircase and blend into the crowd in the lobby below. Turning, she abandoned any pretense of walking quietly and flung herself headlong down the hall at a full run. And she almost made it. She had already begun to descend when she heard the door yank open. Even though it slowed her down to turn her head and look, Sally couldn't help it. When she did, she made eye contact with her pursuer, and she knew.

She knew that she wasn't safe. She wasn't safe at all.

Chapter 18

Justine's alarm clock interrupted her dreams. She groped for it, forcing her eyes open through sheer willpower. She wanted to go back to sleep, but she wanted breakfast more. By the time she was ready to go downstairs, Georgette was, too.

The dormitory's public space, still relatively empty at that time of day, was scattered with companionable groupings of bamboo-trimmed furniture upholstered in electric blue, scarlet, and chrome yellow, and you could actually see them when the lobby wasn't filled with the usual throngs of hopeful men. The bright colors and sleek lines of the furniture screamed, "Hey! We're new and modern!" Justine rather liked the look.

The tinkling of a piano in the music room only added to the pleasant atmosphere. Women chatted as they stood in line for their mail. They waited in line at the housemother's desk to check out irons and vacuum cleaners, tapping their feet while the harried woman scrounged around in her desk drawers for carbon paper and pens.

Linda was the first familiar person who caught Justine's

eye, and she stood out among the relaxed and smiling women, because she was weeping. Patsy stood beside her, dabbing at her own eyes. Something was wrong. Justine grabbed Georgette's elbow and dragged her along as she hurried over to them.

Linda was standing with a hand on Thelma's elbow, and Thelma was crying, too. Tears would have been a little extreme for matter-of-fact Beulah, the older, gray-haired half of the pair of The Bees, but the worried furrows between her dry eyes said as much as the other women's tears. Barbara hovered nearby, damp-eyed and trying to get someone to take the handkerchief she was offering. It occurred to Justine to wonder if Bettie, too, had been one of The Bees. If so, these two women had lost a close friend.

"What's wrong?" Georgette asked. "Are all of you okay?"

Patsy turned her face their way, but she said nothing. Thelma was outright sobbing, gulping for air, so she too said nothing. Barbara spread her hands as if to say, "I don't know why they're crying, but here's a hanky, if it will help." It was left to sweet, pretty, featherbrained Linda to deliver the news.

"Sally is missing. Thelma just woke up, and she can't find her anywhere."

"Could there be a reasonable explanation?" Justine asked.

She heard a flash of Thelma's usual personality in her acid tone. "You think I'm not reasonable?"

Justine resolved to never try Thelma's patience again.

"I was just trying to think of possibilities. Maybe she took an early bus to work?"

"That wouldn't explain why she never came home. Her bed hasn't been slept in."

Justine offered, "Maybe she had a date that went really well?" and braced herself for another blast of sarcasm, but Thelma's braggadocio collapsed under its own weight.

The weeping woman dropped her face into her hands.

"Sally just lost her fiancé a month ago," Thelma said, her face in her hands. "If she'd decided to start dating again, she would've told me. I haven't seen her since before dinner last night, so that's more than twelve hours she's been gone. She left her purse in the room and her wallet's in it, so she doesn't have any money. She doesn't have a car. She couldn't afford a cab even if she did have her purse. If she's gone anywhere, she did it on foot and in the dark. I can't imagine why she'd do that, not after what happened to poor Bettie."

"The trolley?" Justine asked.

"Her tokens are in the purse she left in our room." She didn't finish that sentence with "dummy," but Justine heard it anyway. "But let me humor you and say maybe she put a token in her pocket and used it to leave this dump, but left the other tokens behind because…you tell me. And maybe she even took a couple of bucks out of her wallet and put them in her pocket, too, although it makes no sense to do that and leave the rest of her money behind. Along with the rest of her tokens. But say she did. Where does that get her? As far as I know, Sally hasn't spoken to her family since we got here three years ago. If she has friends outside the people right here, they don't write her letters. Where would she go?"

"Did you call the police?"

"They didn't stay long. When they found out she was twenty-one, they said that a grown adult has a right to come and go as she pleases."

A couple of voices in the crowd piped up with "Sally's twenty-one?"

Thelma gave a weary nod. "Believe it or not, she's of legal age. Anyway, the police said that they don't intend to do a thing, unless I can give them some indication of foul play. And do you know what else?" The biting edge was returning to her voice. "I saw them winking at each other. They think she's run off with a man."

She pulled away from the women hovering around her and ran across the lobby and down the hall that led to the room she shared with Sally. Linda, Patsy, and Beulah followed her. Barbara took a few uncertain steps after them, then retreated to the ladies' room, leaving Justine and Georgette standing alone.

——

As she waited in the breakfast line with Georgette, Justine watched Barbara emerge from the bathroom and begin a slow, deliberate tour of the dormitory lobby.

Tentatively, Barbara approached a cluster of young women exiting the Caféteria and spoke to them briefly. Still hesitant, she approached two more women taking off their coats and hanging them in the cloakroom by the main entrance. Again, she spoke to them briefly, then moved on. She seemed to have a goal of speaking to every woman in the dormitory.

Justine and Georgette were sitting down to breakfast when Barbara approached them. She was tentative, even apologetic.

"Hi, Samantha," she said. "And Justine. We've met, but I'm not sure you remember me. I'm—"

"It's good to see you, Barbara," Justine said. "Would you like to join us? We're a little dazed by the news about Sally—"

"Thank you, but no. I've got something I need to do. I need to ask everybody a question. It's about Sally."

Justine could feel herself sitting up straighter. Georgette did the same.

"Ask away," she said.

"I'm trying to find out if Sally said anything to anybody about going to the library."

As Justine shook her head, she looked at Georgette. She was shaking her head, too.

"No," Justine said. "She never said so to me. Did you ask Thelma?"

"She said no. She said she wasn't sure if Sally even had a library card." Barbara looked deflated, but Justine noticed that Thelma's response hadn't prompted her to quit asking her question. Code breakers were, after all, persistent people.

"Why do you think it's important to know that?" Georgette asked.

"Because it's the last thing that two of Dr. Becker's assistants, Doris Goldberg and Sandra Stone, said to me before they left. Or quit. Or disappeared. Or whatever you want to call it. The same thing happened with one of Dr. van Dorn's assistants, Mabel Hennessey. They all said they were going to the library, and then I never saw them again."

Georgette let out a low whistle.

"But what about Bettie? The one who was murdered?" Justine asked.

"I don't know if she went to the library, but I never heard her say anything about it."

"Do you know which library?" Justine asked.

"The one on Columbia Pike."

"Did you tell the police?" Georgette asked.

"The police didn't come to talk to us about Mabel and Doris and Sandra the way they did about Bettie. I did call them, but all I got every time was, 'She is not considered to be a missing person.' I asked Dr. Becker if he could get them to take me seriously, but he said, 'The SSA does not consider them to be missing.' That's all I know."

Within minutes, Barbara was back to her dogged tour of the

Kansas Hall lobby, moving methodically from one information source to the next as only a code breaker could.

———

Linda walked slowly through the Kansas Hall lobby, carrying a sandwich and some potato chips, constantly aware of how she looked to others. Head high, she made sure that her impeccable posture showed her figure in its best light. As she passed women she knew, she made it a point to bend her head over the food in her hands and murmur, "For Thelma," so that everybody would know that she was intimately involved with the day's exciting event.

Barbara was still moving through the lobby with purpose, so much so that she almost bumped into Linda and made her dump Thelma's food on the floor. She said she was sorry, but Linda didn't think her tone indicated that she was sorry enough.

"I need to ask you a question," Barbara said. She was so nervous that she trembled all over. Even her curls trembled. This made Linda wish that the woman would put some color on the gray threads winding through those curls, because she was tired of looking at them. She'd almost convinced Patsy to color hers, and it would be a relief when she did.

"Did Sally say anything to you about going to the library recently? Or ever?"

Linda could not imagine why anyone who had graduated from high school would want to borrow more books to read, so this question made her impatient. "No. Never. I don't know why she'd do that, and I don't know why she'd tell me."

And then she swept away from Barbara, saying, "I've really got to get these to Thelma. She's quite prostrated."

Barbara watched her go as if she had something to say to her, but Linda really didn't want to hear it.

Chapter 19

The Tuesday morning ride from Arlington Farms to Arlington Hall had been grueling for Justine. It wasn't because the bus had no functioning shock absorbers, although it didn't. And it wasn't because the body heat of a few dozen women had been stifling, although it was. Justine had hated every minute of the ride because every word out of those few dozen mouths had been about Sally.

Thelma was sitting across the aisle from Justine, and her head had drooped lower every time Sally's name was mentioned. Justine didn't know whether to tell her a stupid joke or pat her on the hand. Instead, she sat there looking like somebody who didn't care, until she saw a tear crawling down Thelma's cheek. This was a problem with a solution, so she knew what to do. She pulled a handkerchief out of her purse and handed it over.

The only thing she could think of to say was, "Have the police found out anything about Sally?"

"I should have lied to them."

"Lied about what?"

"I should have told them all about some scary man she'd been seeing, somebody like the man they arrested for killing Bettie.

Instead, I told the truth. Sally didn't have any scary boyfriends. She didn't have any boyfriends at all, although I'm not sure the police believe that. She didn't drink. She didn't curse. She went to work. She saved her money and paid her bills." Her hand flew to her mouth. "Oh, God. I said all that in the past tense. Have I already given up on her?"

Now the handkerchief was mopping a flood of tears. "I think the police believe she ran off with some man, and that's that. They think that it's her right to do it, and they have no interest in interfering. But I know she didn't do that."

Justine took her hand and gave it a squeeze. She was surprised when sardonic, unfriendly Thelma put her other hand on top of Justine's hand, holding it there for a couple of seconds and then letting it go.

Without meeting Justine's eyes, she whispered, "Where is she?"

———

Karl met Justine at the door, carrying a heavy armload of files and saying, "We have much to do this morning. Much to do."

She caught several files before they slipped out of his arms. Checking their labels, she saw that each one bore eight digits that meant nothing to her.

On her desk, she saw six tall stacks of files. She began a seventh stack with the files she'd taken from Karl. Taking the rest of the folders that Karl was holding, she added them to that seventh stack.

From her mother's lessons in cryptanalysis, Justine knew that code breakers work from educated guesses that they call "cribs." The number "7" can enumerate a lot of things, but one of them is the days of the week. She'd been required to take stenography at her all-girls high school, and the nuns had emphasized the utility of a filing system organized by date. Thus, her crib for answering the question of what-is-this-thing-that-Karl-wants-me-to-do? was that it involved a week's worth of files organized by date.

She looked again at the labels on the files and at the eight-digit numbers typed on them. A date can be identified by two digits for the month, two digits for the day, and four digits for the year. Two plus two plus four, always and forever, equals eight. She was reasonably certain that the files were arranged by date.

However, none of the numbers typed on the files ended in 1944, or anything close to it, so the dates were encrypted. Maybe that mattered to her and maybe it didn't. She'd know when she saw what was in the files, but this was a start.

"We must prepare for the weekly liaison meeting," he said.

"Who are we having a liaison meeting with?"

"The Navy. They have a whole outfit for code breaking in the city. They even took over a women's college, just like Arlington Hall."

"Doesn't anybody worry that the Army and the Navy might be duplicating effort?"

"One would think so, but the various branches of the American military can be a little…hmm…contentious."

"I guess that's in the nature of organizations that were created for fighting."

Karl sank to a seat on the edge of the desk. Breathing heavily, he continued explaining Army–Navy relations. "The Army had a good claim to be in charge of breaking codes from the start. It was, after all, the home of the Signal Intelligence Service, which was founded to do cryptanalysis and recently became the Signal Security Agency."

"Our beloved boss, the SSA."

Karl might have been out of breath, but that didn't keep

him from chuckling. "Exactly. But the Navy, all along, felt that it needed its own code breakers. The situation came to a head with this war, with the Army and Navy sometimes forgetting who the enemy was in their hurry to be the first to break an important code or message."

"That's absurd."

"Indeed. These liaison meetings are a tremendous improvement. We discuss intercepted messages. Captured codebooks. Duplicate messages that can serve as cribs for ciphers we haven't broken yet. And we hear from units who do important work in less obviously critical areas. For example, we have a unit that monitors commercial communications. They stay on top of the codes used by banks and corporations in the private sector. This is more important that it might seem."

"Surely we need to know who Hitler's doing business with."

"And it is good to know what they are doing for him."

Justine looked at the seven stacks of files. "This can't possibly be everything your people did this week."

"Now you know what I do on Sundays. I sort the week's business and decide what must be shared at the liaison meeting. The Navy has never complained about the material I choose to share. I do not waste their time or mine, but I do not—as far as I know—omit important information."

The seven stacks of files rested on her desk. If she'd been sitting in her chair, each one of them would have reached past her chin. Karl pressed his palm to the top file in each towering pile, each in turn. "Sunday. Monday. Tuesday. Wednesday. Thursday. Friday. And Saturday. Our critical work of the week is all here."

"How are we going to move it all? Do you have file boxes?"

"I am so happy you asked. I do have boxes. They are small ones, because I can no longer lift what I once did, and I have no interest in injuring your young back. I also have a cart that will handle three boxes at a time, at most, without suffering a flat tire. We will thus have to make three trips, even with the cart, but we can get the information where it needs to go. When I am between assistants, there is always a danger that I will not move the files in time. I have not failed yet, but it is so much more efficient when I have help."

Justine was studying the stacks of files, and she was developing a plan.

"Where's the meeting?"

"In Building A."

Perfect. The meeting room was in the building next door, not just down the hall. If she played her cards right, she might be able to finagle some time alone with the filing cabinet full of personnel files during the meeting, with no risk of Karl interrupting her. She'd have two windows of time, one when she took the cart back for the second load and the other when she went back for the third.

Justine had never in her life been glad that there were seven days in the week, and not six.

———

Georgette had her eye on Dr. van Dorn. He was always difficult, but he was having a bad, bad morning. As his assistant, she supposed it was her job to protect him from himself. As a government agent trying to ferret out a spy, though, it was her job to find out what had pushed him to this point.

Guilt? Fear? So far, she couldn't tell.

He had snapped at poor Thelma before she'd even gotten to her desk. Georgette had taken him aside and told him about Sally, thinking that he would apologize. Instead, he'd doubled down.

Not at Thelma. Only a fool would keep yelling at a woman on the edge of tears, but he hadn't apologized to her, either. He'd retreated to the other side of the room, so that Thelma could get herself together while he harangued somebody else for working too slowly. At the moment, this was Beulah, who had been the first one there and who was not working slowly at all. Georgette was tempted to withdraw from all the conflict, sitting at her own desk and doing her own work while her boss put a match to the powder keg that was Room 117.

But no, she couldn't do that, not when his next target was Dr. Kowalski. It hadn't been twenty-four hours since Justine had come home all torn up about Dr. Kowalski's dead family. Georgette had been shocked to see him turn up for work, as if nothing had happened. He sat quietly at his desk, doing nothing but shifting papers from one side of it to the other, but he was there. If Dr. van Dorn started yelling at him, he might send him straight to the hospital, never to come out.

To keep that from happening, Georgette had to sprint half-way down the long aisle between the desks, past her own desk and Ike's. She ran like her brothers had taught her, arms pumping and legs driving hard like she was running for the home plate they'd made out of a flour sack and a shovelful of sand. Unfortunately, she was doing it this time in Cuban heels and a straight skirt. She hoped she didn't have to slide.

Just in time, she reached Dr. van Dorn, grabbing him by both shoulders and turning him away from Dr. Kowalski while she hissed, "No, no, no, not him. Not today."

Something—maybe her words or maybe her vise grip on his shoulders—got through to him. He turned his eyes to hers like a man who was just waking up and said, "You're right. Not Patryk. Never Patryk. I have let myself lose control and that is not acceptable."

Then he shook her hands off him and straightened his shoulders. He paused just long enough to say, "Thank you, Samantha, for saving me from myself," and then he walked away as if she didn't exist.

———

Justine hefted the third heavy file box onto a table. She and Karl were alone in the conference room, but nameplates were already in place for the liaison meeting. The only names she recognized were Karl's and Ed's, but some of the seats had no nameplates. She figured that assistants like her would sit there.

As Karl placed a notebook and pen at his place at the table, Justine steered the empty cart out the door, expecting Karl to stay behind. She was flummoxed when he hurried to catch up with her.

"Wait! Wait, just let me lock the files up safely, and I'll go with you. We'll load three boxes on the cart, and I'll carry one. It will save you a trip."

And it would also completely eliminate Justine's time alone with the files. Did Karl know how badly she wanted this time?

"Don't you need a minute to review your notes?"

"I typed them myself yesterday, so I know them quite well. You should thank me for that, actually. I have the option to require my assistant to work with me on Sundays, but I like my quiet time with the files, and I assume you enjoy your day of rest."

"I'm grateful, Karl," Justine said as she racked her brain to find a way to distract Karl from "helping" her.

She failed. Karl trailed behind her as she pushed the cart out of the conference room.

Justine had never noticed Karl's hands trembling quite so much. They wobbled to and fro as he tried to select the right key and aim it at the conference room's keyhole. She itched to make a clean getaway, taking off with the cart at a jog that he could never match, but it wouldn't fix her problem. He would eventually get to the office where she was snooping through his files, and she couldn't let him catch her at it.

She racked her brain for something to keep Karl where he was, but she came up with nothing stronger than "You can't leave those files alone."

All that got her was an exasperated look and a terse retort. "How do you think I manage when I lack an assistant?"

This made her want to ask, "Why do you keep losing assistants?" but she held her tongue.

Karl turned the key and it was done. There was nothing to stop him from coming between her and those filing cabinets...

...except for the navy-blue wall sauntering toward them.

A gaggle of Navy officers approached, five of them filling the hallway from wall to wall. The two men were clad in winter dress uniforms that looked startlingly like the police uniform Paul had worn to rescue her. Beside them were three women in crisp WAVES uniforms, navy-blue suits with skirts and jackets designed so beautifully that Justine knew women who claimed they'd signed up just for the chance to wear them. The hats were chic enough to make Justine want to volunteer herself.

The WAVES walked toward her, pump-clad feet clacking on the polished floor. Karl had told her that they'd been instrumental in breaking Japanese codes with war-changing results. They looked powerful. They were powerful. There was no deference in them. Reluctantly, Karl turned his key again, unlocking the conference room door that he'd just locked and throwing it open for the five Navy officers.

Justine stood there, obviously a clerical worker assisting an older man with the transportation of his paperwork, while they sailed past her to their seats at the table. Part of her wanted to call out, "Hey! I'm doing important war things, too," but the rest of her silently cheered them on.

She looked at Karl. "We can't possibly leave the Navy standing here in the hall, and we can't possibly leave them alone with your paperwork. You're going to have to babysit them while I go get another load of files."

He heaved a heavy sigh. "I hate for you to move such heavy boxes without help, my dear."

"Oh, don't worry," Justine said as she maneuvered the cart around the naval invasion. "I'll make as many trips as it takes."

———

Karl's "Please hurry!" was ringing in Justine's ears as she skidded to a stop outside the door to their office suite. In her hurry, she scraped her key across the plate surrounding the dead bolt's keyhole, leaving a shallow scratch in the metal.

Would this scar give her away?

No. She had a legitimate reason to be in a hurry. Still, there were so many moments and actions in a day, and any of them could be the slipup that revealed her.

She turned the key, flung the door open, and shoved the cart through the door. It banged against the doorframe, bounced off it, and banged against the other side of the doorframe, leaving more scars to chart her progress but, again, she was in a legitimate hurry. Karl would be furious if she left him left to stare the Navy down while he waited for his files.

Even worse, he might come looking for her. She could only afford a few moments with the personnel files before she took him the second cartload of boxes.

She yanked open the drawer and pulled out the file that was first on her list. It was labeled "Ike Grantham."

Chapter 20

Georgette had typed Dr. van Dorn's notes for the progress report he would present at the liaison meeting, and she knew that this was a good thing. His handwriting was abysmal, and he was stingier with words than a telegraph operator, but the information was there. It told a coherent narrative of what the German section had accomplished in the past week, and it presented a plan for the next one. It was just too bad that all that work would be meaningless until she and Justine rooted out the spy working for Dr. van Dorn in Room 117.

Carrying an attaché case full of everything her boss might need, Georgette walked a few steps behind him and thought meek thoughts, hoping that this would help her be invisible. Wasn't it the dream of every important man to have a secretary who made him look good while she herself faded into the woodwork?

She must be doing a good job of it because everybody was talking pretty dang freely. It was as if she weren't even there.

She didn't like what she was overhearing. Hitler had blitzkrieged his way into someplace called the Ardennes Forest, and something terrible had happened in Antwerp. Communication was spotty, due to horrible winter weather and just the general chaos of war. The Navy people seemed to blame the Arlington Hall people for this because of their association with the Army's Signal Corps, which Georgette didn't think was fair, since nobody can control a snowstorm.

She gave Dr. van Dorn a silent "Attaboy!" when he cut off that line of conversation with a crisp, "Perhaps the Navy might want to keep its opinions on how to fight a land battle to itself?"

This didn't even upset her on her brothers' behalf, despite the fact that four of them were still in the Navy, and the other one was only home from the sea because he was badly wounded. The only feeling she had about the Army versus the Navy is that she was glad that her brothers weren't fighting in the snow. And she wished the Army's soldiers weren't, either.

Up ahead, she saw Justine pushing a cart away from her at top speed, like an ambulance attendant trying to get a dying patient to the doctor. Her skinny legs made Georgette think of the crawdads she'd chased when she was a hungry little girl. She knew Justine's plan was to rifle through the personnel files while Dr. Becker was busy chatting with the Navy, so Georgette sent a silent "Run, Justine, run!" in her direction.

Then she followed the naval officers into the meeting room and settled herself into the unmarked seat next to Dr. van Dorn. She waved at Linda, sitting on his other side. She supposed that the man sitting on Linda's other side was her boss.

She was surprised to see Linda's friend Patsy standing behind them. Did their boss rate two assistants for this meeting, while hers only rated one? Dr. van Dorn would not be happy about that. She braced herself for the eventual explosion.

Then Patsy leaned over and whispered to them, "If you need me to run back to Room 117 and get anything for you, I'm here to help all the SSA people."

So they did have help. Maybe her boss wouldn't explode after all, although he might have some acid things to say over the fact that the assistant didn't come from his own staff.

The Navy people were lined up on the other side of the table, and all that navy-blue wool made them look like united and... well, military. The SSA people on Georgette's side of the table were dressed in neat business clothes, but they were made of all kinds and colors of fabric. It made them look scattered and unprepared and nervous. Dr. van Dorn's feet, tapping nervously under the table, did not add any sense of calm competence to the group from Arlington Hall.

To cover her nerves, Georgette opened the attaché case, which to be honest made her feel fancy and businesslike, and pretended to organize its already organized contents while she waited for the meeting to begin.

And while she waited for Justine to complete her mission.

———

There was a clock on the wall of Justine's office, hung high over the pin-studded maps. Its dangling electric cord hung over a map of Africa, an inconvenience that made Karl curse in three eastern European languages, but Justine liked the inconvenient gray cord. It meant that she didn't have to remember to wind the clock.

The clock might not need winding, but it still had machinery to move the hands and that machinery ticked. There had been times when its constant "tick tick" had made Justine want to scream, but not now.

Now, the ticking meant that she didn't have to watch the clock while she worked.

She had decided to allow herself to spend sixty ticks of the clock to search the personnel files, but then she'd need to go. The arrival of the naval officers meant that the meeting was about to begin, and she still had to make another round trip to and from the conference room.

Tick.

She yanked her camera out of her purse and pulled off the wooden covering that made it look like a matchbox.

Tick.

She riffled through the papers in Ike's file, fighting back the urge to rush. There wasn't much time, but she had to be shrewd about how she used her resources. She only had enough film to take thirty-four exposures, and Ike was far from the only suspicious character in Room 117.

Tick.

Ike's file was organized into three stacks, each paper-clipped together. The first stack contained his personal information. The second stack was comprised of his annual performance reviews—one for 1942, one for 1943, and a crisp, fresh review for 1944 that was just a few weeks old. The third stack held three letters to his file—all reprimands. She hated to waste so much film on one person, but Ike's behavior was disturbing. He was a reasonable suspect, and she had to check him out thoroughly. She needed all three reprimands. As for his personal information, she opted for the first page—his personal information on the day he was hired—and the last page—his current contact information. There went five of her thirty-four exposures.

Tick.

Her camera clicked, and she hoped that she was holding it at the proper distance to ensure a focused photo.

Tick.

Her camera clicked four more times while the clock ticked four more times.

Who else did she desperately need to know more about? Sally.

Tick.

Hands shaking, she ripped Sally's file open. She could see at a glance that Sally's annual reviews were monotonously enthusiastic. There were so many commendations that Sally must have gotten bored by them. It seemed to Justine that Sally's personal information was the critical part of her file. If she hoped to find Sally, she needed information like the addresses where Sally had lived, her parents' address, and the locations of her high school and college. That information was spread over six pages.

The camera clicked six times and the clock ticked right along with it, but now she was losing count. One more file, and then she'd have to go. Who would it be?

Bettie? Being dead certainly made her important.

No, she would get to Bettie next. First, she should take a look at Mabel Hennessey.

Sally was missing, and her danger grew with every minute she was gone. Mabel, too, was missing and she had worked with Sally in the very same room. Justine needed to know if the two women had anything in common.

Mabel's file had five pages of contact information, but no commendations, no reprimands, and only one annual performance review. Justine decided to photograph it all. The clock's ticks seemed to accelerate as she snapped six photos, one by one.

In a single motion, she slid her camera back into its matchbox camouflage and dropped it into her purse. Stacking each pile of documents neatly, tucking them in the proper files, and slipping each one into the right drawer took up every tick of the clock that she had left, plus a few more. She banged the drawer closed and plunked three boxes on the cart.

Then she took off for the conference room as fast as her legs would take her.

———

Georgette heard the door bang open behind her. She could tell by Dr. Becker's face that Justine was the one who had flung it open and that he was very, very displeased with her.

"Three boxes? You could find no way to bring the last box?"

"Sorry, no. You said that the extra weight might give the cart a flat tire," Justine said, heaving the boxes onto the table and heading for the door. "Back in a second."

The door slammed behind her, but Dr. Becker yelled his frustration at Justine anyway. "We cannot keep these people waiting."

"We've got a coupla minutes left," Georgette offered. "That guy who was sitting next to you went—" She was embarrassed to say that he went to the bathroom, although she was pretty sure that was where he had gone, so her voice trailed off.

She tried again. "We can't start until he comes back."

Dr. Becker didn't look mollified, but he stopped talking. Nobody else said anything, either. The silence meant that there was nothing to distract them from the ticking of the clock on the wall. Nothing, that is, except for the nervous tapping of Dr. van Dorn's feet under the table.

Georgette wished she could tap her feet under the table, too, but she needed to look calm, serene, carefree.

Without warning, Dr. van Dorn shoved his chair back from the table and stood.

"I need to—"

She wasn't sure who he was talking to, but maybe it was her. She waited for him to finish his sentence.

"I'll be back in a minute."

And he was gone.

———

Ed van Dorn didn't know why he'd left the conference room. The meeting would start at any moment. When it did, he needed to be there.

The trouble was that he didn't think he could stand being there.

His mind was churning and he couldn't make it stop. It fixated on his failure to make headway on decrypting a nettlesome message that had resisted every attack he'd made on it. It dwelled on the infuriating egotism of Karl Becker and others like him. Sometimes, it darted other places, but they scared him, so he called it back.

He felt separated from his own body, as if he were far away and watching himself lumber like a bear down the hallways of Building A, looking for something.

Not something. Someone. He was looking for Justine. He didn't see her anywhere, but he knew where she was going. He could find her.

———

Justine banged the cart through the office doorway, holding the door open with one hand and using the other to maneuver it toward her desk. Using one hip to close it, she grabbed the last box, set it on the cart and turned toward the filing cabinet where the personnel files lived. She saw that she'd left the critical drawer open just a finger's-width in her hurry to leave, which could have been a deadly mistake if anyone had been around to notice it. She was about to expend one minute and her last eighteen exposures on the contents of that drawer, and then she would close it firmly and leave.

Arguing against that plan was the sound of a man's voice saying, "Justine."

First, she froze. Then she turned slowly to see a well-shod foot thrust between the door and its jamb. She swung her hip at the open drawer and hoped that it stayed closed.

A well-manicured hand gripped the door and pushed it open as the voice said again, "Justine."

The door opened and Ed van Dorn's face appeared. "I know we only have a minute to spare, but can we take that minute?"

She stood beside the cart, one hand on the file box, and willed him to look at her instead of the file drawer that might or might not be open. "Karl may kill me just for taking that minute, but—" Hoping that sexual attraction would keep him looking where she wanted him to look, she met his eyes and gave him a slow-burn smile. "But I'm willing to risk Karl's wrath for you. Let's talk while we walk."

She grasped the handle of the cart with both hands to signal that it was time to leave her office with its traitorous file drawer. He responded to the cue by grasping the cart from the opposite side. Together, they guided it through the door without bumping the doorjamb once. It was amazing to Justine what teamwork could do.

Once in the hall, he waited while she locked the door. As they passed through Building B, he said, "It's very good to see you again. And to talk to you. I would have liked to call you this weekend, but those damn government dormitories don't see fit to give grown women private phones in their rooms."

He shot a nervous look at her to see whether she was prim enough to be upset by the word "damn." She just smiled and let it pass, saying, "Since I left my parents' home, I've lived in a rooming house and a dormitory. I've never had a private phone, and I'm not sure I could spare the money for one, anyway."

They reached the exterior door. He opened it and, again, helped her maneuver the cart through the opening. Once outside, he pulled it off the sidewalk to a spot under a tree and said, "Can we take that minute now? This is as private a spot as we're going to get. Until somebody else decides they want to get from Building A to Building B, that is."

She shrugged and smiled, as if to say, "Big, strong men like you always get what they want." At this point, she didn't care whether she got to the meeting in time and she didn't care if Karl was angry. This wasn't her real job, and he wasn't her real boss. Ed had torpedoed her file-photographing operation, so she might as well take the opportunity to learn more about him. Besides, she'd had a sudden idea of what she could do with the rest of the film in her camera, and it would only mean a few extra hours before she could pass it to Jerry for developing.

But none of this answered the question of what on Earth was wrong with Ed van Dorn. His eyes kept seeking out hers and darting away. His jaw was clenched. His nostrils were flared. His arms were crossed so tightly across his chest that she wondered how he could breathe.

As if he'd noticed her looking at his crossed arms, he unfolded them. Smiling, he tapped at the pencil spearing the bun atop her head, and said, "You look very businesslike. This pencil would make any other woman look like a schoolmarm, but not you."

Fumbling in the breast pocket of his charcoal-gray suit coat, he pulled out a cigarette case and lighter. "Cigarette?" he asked, holding out the open case in a hand that had the shakes.

When she shook her head, he said, "No, of course. You don't smoke."

He lit one, then pocketed the dull aluminum lighter and matching case. Holding a deep drag of smoke in his lungs, he held the cigarette out at arm's-length and stared at it.

Still looking at the cigarette and not her, he said, "I'm sure it's too late to ask a refined woman such as yourself whether she's free tonight."

What should she say? Dropping her plan to finish up the roll of film in her camera seemed like a failure. She'd just made the plan, but it was a good one. And Ed seemed like the kind of man whose interest might cool if she made herself too available. Thus, Ed needed to wait.

"I do have plans, but you'll laugh."

The cigarette stopped being too fascinating to smoke. He put it to his lips and the tip flared red. "I promise you, sweetheart, nothing is funny to me today."

"The truth? I'm going to the library. The nearest branch only has evening hours one night a week, so I was planning to check out a few books to last me until next Tuesday."

"Lucky for you, I like eggheaded women, so I'm not insulted. How about tomorrow? I wasn't thinking we'd go any-place fancy, just a soda shop I like. The burgers are juicy and it reminds me of the one where my brother and I worked in high school."

She smiled and nodded. "It sounds relaxing, and that sounds just right. Tomorrow, then."

He brought the cigarette to his lips and inhaled so much smoke that she thought his lungs might burst.

"I shouldn't say this. I should just pat myself on the back that you've agreed to a second date and keep my mouth shut, but I have to tell you this." With a practiced motion, he tapped a short cylinder of ash off the cigarette. Its acrid odor tickled her nose. "I got some news this morning that made me want to yell at everybody in my vicinity. Or to run away from everybody I know. I wasn't sure which."

She was afraid to ask the obvious question, but it was wrong to leave it echoing silently in the air. "What news did you get?"

"My father called to tell me that my brother's not where we thought he was."

"Where is he?" she asked, although she had a pretty good idea of the answer to that question.

"We thought he was in Africa, but we were wrong. He's in Europe. My father has connections, and they got us this information that we're not supposed to know."

Justine said, "The Ardennes Forest?" and the words were incongruously beautiful, like they described a lovely place where one might encounter wood nymphs and picnicking bears, instead of bombs and bayonets.

"Probably. Or someplace nearby. That's really all I know. My mind hasn't been working well since I got that call. The only clear thought I've had all day was that I wanted to see you. I hope that doesn't scare you away. I wanted to see your face. It is the only one I have ever seen that is utterly without guile."

"I don't have to go to the library. Let's go get those burgers."

"I wouldn't hear of it. All I want to do tonight is smoke another pack or two, while I think of you doing something so sweet and so ordinary as going to the library. You're probably going to bring home something heavy—Dostoevsky, maybe—but don't tell me that. Let me think of you checking out something light and happy. Let me picture you and Samantha laughing as you settle in for the evening to read your romance novels. I want to imagine the two of you sleeping the sleep of the innocents."

He crushed the cigarette under his heel. "Shall we go to our meeting, where we will be discussing how to read the enemy's mail, so that we can blow him up before he blows us up? Or, rather, before he blows up our brothers, who are doing our fighting for us?"

He gently removed her hands from the cart, then he pushed it for her all the way to the conference room. When Justine appeared at the conference room floor, inexcusably late and in the company of his intellectual foe, Karl refused to even look at her.

He hissed three words. "Where were you?"

When she tried to answer him, he hissed a few more words. "Never mind. I don't want to hear it."

The meeting lasted for the rest of the day. Karl kept her busy all that time, demanding that she find this document and put away that one, but none of his busywork occupied her mind. This was not a good thing.

All day long, she shuffled paper and thought about what Ed had said to her. On this terrible day, as he wondered whether his brother was alive or dead, he had wanted to be with her. He'd said that she was totally without guile, which struck directly at Justine's heart, because she knew the truth.

Everything that she had ever said to him had been, in some sense, a lie.

Chapter 21

"How'd you like that liaison meeting?" Georgette asked.

Justine rubbed her eyes. "Do you even have to ask? If I'm never locked up with that many egos in the same room, it will be too soon. I'm officially dreading Tuesdays for the duration of my time here."

"You and me both."

They walked side by side out of Building B toward the checkpoint where Jerry sat at his post.

Justine jerked her head in his direction. "Tell him you want to see him tonight. Ask him to come to Kansas Hall at…say… nine o'clock."

"I'm going out this evening. You remember. I'm going to watch Nora practice with her church choir."

"Well, I'm going to be waiting for Jerry in the lobby at nine," Justine whispered, "because I have a matchbox I want to give him." She smacked her hand on the purse where her matchbox/camera was.

"Oh. Oh, okay. I think Nora and I will be back by nine, but if I'm not, you two can…um…chat until we get there."

They made their way through the checkpoint, where Jerry

agreed to a last-minute date, then they parted ways. Georgette asked, "Where ya going?" as Justine passed up the Arlington Farms bus stop in favor of the trolley stop.

"The library on Columbia Pike," Justine said, waving goodbye and hoping that Georgette would figure out that her library trip had something to do with the film she wanted to pass to Jerry.

The trolley ride was short. She could have walked it, but Justine needed every minute in the library that she could get, because she didn't know what she was looking for. All she knew was that three women had visited this branch of the Arlington Public Library system. And then they had disappeared.

———

The librarian greeted Justine from the circulation desk, where she was speaking with two patrons. Justine could see several more browsing the stacks. This was a large crowd for a building that had started its life as a modest house.

Justine saw nothing about the library itself that looked out of the ordinary. The main room was warm, so she shrugged off her coat and hung it on a rack near the door. This gave her a chance to survey the room. The patrons looked like the people she would expect to see in a small-town library. A few parents loitered while their children browsed picture books. A few bookworms carried armloads of books while they looked for just one more fun thing to read. A man in a battered hat sat in the reference section studying maps. A woman in a WAVES uniform sat at a worktable nearby, surrounded by several volumes of an encyclopedia.

Justine wondered where she should start. Maybe she should just browse the shelves and hope something jumped out at her.

As she moved to do that, the librarian called out, "Miss?" and beckoned her over.

Was she supposed to check in at the desk before using the library? Justine had never visited a library that worked that way, but she obeyed the beckoning hand.

"Is there anything I can help you with?"

Justine flailed around for something to ask for. "Um...I'm new to town. Do you have anything about Arlington that I could read?"

The woman glanced at Justine's lapel. "You work at Arlington Hall. I've seen badges like that one before. People come in from all over the country to work there. They come in asking for information on their new home all the time."

The librarian rose and said, "Let me take you to our general travel section first, so you can get the tourist perspective. I'd start with that." She moved toward a shelf at the back of the room and pulled out a book wrapped in a green-and-cream cover for Justine.

From there, the librarian led her past the children's section, past the man in the hat, past the WAVE, and into the next room.

"This is where we keep our books about Arlington itself, if you want to learn more about local history."

The room had been a bedroom when the library had been a house, and a well-used fireplace was centered on the exterior wall. The two of them were alone.

"There's a carrel in here so that you can read in peace," the librarian said as she studied the books, plucking one after another off the shelves and stacking them on the carrel, a small wooden desk constructed with wooden walls to give its user privacy. Last, she placed the green-and-cream book in the back, up next to the carrel's rear wall.

"There. One of those should tell you what you need to know."

As she passed through the open door that led back into the library's main room, the librarian paused and turned. "We locals hear things, you know. We heard about the poor woman who was murdered and... Well, we hear things. Please be careful."

And then she left Justine alone with a stack of books that didn't interest her nearly as much as the warning did...

...except for the green-and-cream volume that the librarian had picked up so casually and yet so deliberately. It interested Justine a whole lot. She dragged it toward her, wondering what she would see on the cover.

She didn't know what she'd been expecting, but it wasn't *Tennessee: The WPA Guide to the Volunteer State.*

———

Justine had spent an embarrassing amount of time with *Tennessee: The WPA Guide to the Volunteer State.* She had found nothing.

Well, she'd found that about a third of the book was devoted to the history of Tennessee, but she couldn't imagine how that would be useful to her. Another good chunk of it was devoted to tourism in the bigger cities of Tennessee, and the rest of the book gave information on driving tours through the countryside. Why did the librarian think she should see this book?

Was it an accident? Had she intended to give her a book about Virginia?

No. If she closed her eyes, she could see the librarian study the shelf and deliberately choose this book. She'd reached out with intention. She could hear the woman cautioning her to be careful, because she was a local and they "hear things."

There was a reason that Justine was holding this book. She just didn't know what it was. Her matchbox camera sat in her purse, useless, because she'd failed to find anything worth wasting any film. She was no closer to learning what had happened to Doris and Sandra and Mabel after they visited this library branch.

Closing time was approaching, and Justine had planned to leave well before that. She wanted to at least walk through the library, studying the books and hoping for a miracle. It was time to give up on *Tennessee: The WPA Guide to the Volunteer State.*

Justine carried the armload of books back to the circulation desk. She thanked the librarian, who looked at her with a question in her eyes. Justine didn't know exactly what answer was in her own eyes, but it was something like, "I'm sorry I'm too dumb to know why you gave me this book."

"We like to keep track of how our books get used," the librarian said, holding out a pencil. "It helps us know what to buy with our limited funds. Would you mind signing the checkout record for me?"

She opened the back of the book, where a flap of paper was glued to the inside cover. It was lined, and there was a signature on each of the first five lines.

Three of those signatures were Doris Goldberg, Mabel Hennessey, and Sandra Stone.

"Can I help you with anything else, Miss?"

Trying to mimic the librarian's light, cool tone, Justine said, "No. I've got everything that I need," as she signed the book.

"It's dark out there," the other woman said. "You be real careful getting home."

Chapter 22

Georgette was a little surprised by how much she enjoyed Nora's company, first at choir practice and then over dinner at a local diner. For one thing, she'd learned that Nora could be hilarious when she chose to use her sharp wits that way. Her impersonations of Dr. van Dorn and Linda were wicked, complete with an I'm-so-smart-and-a-doctor-too aura for the doctor and an I'm-so-pretty-and-that's-all-you-need attitude for the filing clerk.

Nora's piano playing had been impressive. So had the diner. Georgette gave the chicken and dumplings on her plate an appreciative sniff. In her head, she knew that the point of dumplings was to use flour and grease to stretch a chicken as far as it would go, but that didn't mean the dumplings weren't delicious. Her bowl of flour, grease, chicken broth, and a few shreds of chicken meat tasted like home, because her mother had known a hundred ways to feed seven people with nothing much. Her mother would have used more black pepper, though.

"How's your salmon croquette?" she asked.

"Mostly cracker crumbs," said Nora, "but I like cracker crumbs. And the French fries are great. So's the stewed tomato."

Nora had insisted that they wait a few minutes extra to be seated, until a table for four opened up. Otherwise, there would have been no space for the tremendous floral arrangement that she'd brought from the church. Even so, its pink dianthus, white chrysanthemums, and burgundy snapdragons crowded their plates and silverware.

"They don't like me to take the flowers when I leave on Sunday, because there are still people there, so I bring them home after choir practice on Tuesdays." Nora brushed a loving hand through the trailing greenery that spilled over the base of the arrangement. "You'll see these flowers the rest of this week and on Monday and Tuesday, too. I'll be bringing some of them in every day."

"I like it when you bring flowers. They sure brighten up the room. And they smell good," Georgette said.

Neither of them mentioned the fact that they only brightened up the room for part of each morning, until Ike carried the bouquet down the hall to Linda. According to the German section's gossips, this had been going on for months. Since Ike still didn't like Nora, and Linda still didn't like Ike, the flowers were not successfully wooing anybody, but they kept people entertained.

"I sure enjoyed your piano playing today. Did you take a lot of lessons?"

"When I was a girl in Connecticut, I didn't do much else but play the piano." Nora's plain face was transformed by a smile that went beyond just her lips, lighting her eyes. The thought of her music warmed her voice when she said, "My parents sent me to lessons for years and years, and then they sent me to the Malkin Conservatory of Music in Boston. I studied piano performance, voice, music theory, composition, everything they offered. Then I stayed after graduation to teach while I prepared for a career performing in concert halls."

"But you didn't do that?"

"No. I met Arthur." And Nora's face transformed again. There were no more harsh lines around her mouth. Her neck and shoulders relaxed. Her hand lifted to run her long fingers through her short locks.

"You loved him a lot to give up your dreams for him."

"He was everything. He still is everything. He was younger—younger than me and young enough to interest the Army—with golden-brown hair and a smile that never went away. I guess he'll always be young. He died almost as soon as his feet touched the ground in Africa. It was like he…I don't know. He was here, and then he was gone like a puff of smoke. It happened so fast that I still have moments when I forget he's gone."

Georgette didn't know what to say. The only thing that popped into her head was, "That's just terrible, Nora."

Nora nodded. Her eyes were focused on the salmon croquette she was shredding with her fork.

"It didn't take long after he died for me to figure out that I needed a job. My parents were gone by that time, so there was nobody I could ask for help. No place to go. This job and the cheap rent at Arlington Farms saved me. I survived it all, but there will always be a void here"—she put her hand over her heart—"where Arthur should be."

"Does it help your feelings to play the piano? When you play, it sounds like you're pouring out your whole heart."

"Not all of it. If I poured my whole heart out, everybody in the church would be terrified." Her laugh tinkled, a brittle echo of the sound of her fork on the heavy stoneware plate.

"I wish I could play like that. My grandmother showed me how to find Middle C and read some notes. And I can play a hymn or two, but that's all."

"I'll teach you. If you can do that much, you'll move right along. You'll be surprised at how fast you'll learn."

"Oh, I wasn't asking you to… That's a kind offer, but…" Georgette's voice trailed off. "I'd love to learn, but I can't afford lessons."

"Don't be silly. You don't have to pay me. Come down to the music room in the evenings, and I'll show you a few things every night. I'll lend you a book for beginners, so you can practice, but you'll have to save your practicing for when I'm not around. I don't need money, not now that I've got this job, but I need my piano time." She slapped her palm on the table. "I need it. Sometimes, it's all I need."

Georgette said, "Oh, I wouldn't never want to get in the way of your music. Anything you teach me would be a real gift. I would be so grateful to you."

Nora's nod was quick and brusque and designed to cut out any discussion of emotions, even gratitude. "Then I'll expect you. Let's head back to the dorm, and I'll give you some things to practice."

Justine felt uneasy waiting alone at the trolley stop. She'd stayed at the library all the way until closing time, and the after-work crowd was already home eating dinner. It wasn't a long walk to Arlington Farms, and it was entirely possible that she could get there before the next trolley came along. Somehow, she felt safer as a moving target, so she set off walking.

Was she even a target? If she understood what she'd just learned in the library, Doris Goldberg, Mabel Hennessey, and Sandra Stone had left Arlington of their own free will. She had no idea why they might have gone to Tennessee, but women who were kidnapped did not generally have time to research the place where their kidnappers would be taking them, so any theory of kidnapping was no good. If they'd all gotten fed up with their bosses, quit their jobs, and left town, would they all go the same place? It seemed more likely that the SSA or the Army or somebody important had sent them to Tennessee, but why?

The streets were well-lit all the way back to Arlington Farms, but the light on the sidewalks grew murkier as she approached the dormitory complex. The shade trees that she loved so much in the daytime plunged Justine into the shadows.

Someone was waiting for her in those shadows.

———

Georgette was sitting with her fingertips on smooth piano keys, and she was happy. Excited. Nervous.

Nora had listened to her play the hymns she knew, then she'd spent an interminable amount of time getting Georgette positioned at the keyboard. She had scooted the bench forward and back, stopping between each movement to examine the angle of Georgette's forearms. She had tapped Georgette's shoulders time and again, reminding her to pull them back so that she wouldn't slump. She had made sure that the soles of both Georgette's shoes stayed flat on the floor.

Georgette couldn't even manage to hold her head up well enough to suit Nora, who was constantly adjusting the angle of her jaw. Finally, though, her posture met Nora's high standards and she was allowed to press down the keys and listen for a noise.

"I want you press down your fingers one at a time and nothing more. You can't hear yourself when you're trying to play those hymns that are too hard for you. Strike the keys and listen. That's all. Listen."

She did, and the sound was beautiful. Bell-like. Melodic. Georgette wanted to stay at the piano all evening long.

———

A faint rustle was Justine's only warning. Her assailant emerged from the pool of darkness at the foot of an old oak tree. If the tree hadn't spent the autumn dropping crisp dead leaves, she would have known nothing before she felt two hands around her throat. Her assailant stood at her back, squeezing the life out of her.

Her instincts begged her to grab at the hands around her throat, but her mind said that there were better things to do with her hands. She had two of them, so she should go for two targets.

No, wait. She had also two feet, one to stand on and one to stomp with. She was going for as many targets as she could reach, and she was doing it quickly.

Justine knew that she had only seconds to defend herself against a strangler. If she lost consciousness, she was gone.

———

"How do I know which keys to push when I'm playing a song I don't already know?" Georgette asked Nora, pointing to the sheet music on the piano. "And how do I know which fingers to use?"

"Never mind those things," Nora said, picking up the sheet music and firmly folding it closed. "We'll worry about them later."

She rested her hand atop Georgette's and said, "Follow my fingers. We're going to play a C scale." So they did, and it sounded like music, not just random notes.

"Now give me your other hand. Until we work together

again, I want you to play a scale with each hand every time you pass the piano. Sit down and make sure you're using proper posture, then play the scale and listen. Just listen."

Georgette did. With Nora's help, her other hand played a C scale, too, and it was lovely. The notes sounded lovely and the keys beneath her fingers felt lovely. For the rest of her life, Georgette would do her best to live with a piano and, when that wasn't possible, she would do her best to live near a piano that somebody else would let her use.

Nora looked at her with an amused smile. "I recognize that look on your face. You're going to practice, and you're going to play, and you're going to play well. I promise to teach you something new every day, if you promise to never interfere with my practice time."

"Oh, I promise," Georgette said, so quickly and so loudly that she embarrassed herself. She hid her blushing face by taking the music book out of Nora's hands and opening it, hoping it would give her some clue about how pianists looked at a page full of black dots and, miraculously, knew exactly which keys to play.

This particular sheet of music was covered with so many black dots that Georgette knew that it would be a long time before she'd have the slightest chance of being able to play it, and it was likely that she never would. Raking her eyes over the page, the composer's name caught her eye. It was Nora Moore.

"You wrote this?"

"I write a lot of stuff."

"And somebody publishes it?"

Nora gave a rare laugh. "Not all of it, no. Nobody's publisher is that generous. But, yes, I've been publishing my compositions since I was at the conservatory."

Georgette had never felt more like an uneducated, uncultured little girl from Des Allemands, Louisiana.

"Holy mackerel," she said, sliding off the bench. "Well, I promised I'd let you have your practice time. Maybe could you write something I might be able to play one day?"

And then she hurried away, wondering how a little girl from Des Allemands had found herself in the nation's capital, conducting espionage and brushing elbows with honest-to-goodness music composers.

She checked her watch. It was ten past nine. She'd kept Jerry waiting for ten minutes, but surely Justine was out there keeping him company. Justine was the one who'd asked for him to come by Kansas Hall at nine, so she must be bending his ear about whatever she'd been doing with her camera. Justine hadn't had time to say why she'd wanted to go to the library before she handed her film over to Jerry for developing, but Georgette was about to find out.

As the lobby came into view, her eyes went immediately to the spot where she and Jerry always sat, because the settee was positioned to make it easy for Jerry to park his wheelchair close enough to hold her hand. Sure enough, he was sitting there waiting for her. Alone.

As Georgette approached, the same question was on both their lips: "Where's Justine?"

———

In an instant, Justine had planned her attack. Now she had to execute it.

She twisted her body to the right as far as it would go, gouging at her assailant's eyes with the fingernails of her left hand. Her heart sank when her hand sailed through the air and she knew that she had missed.

Shifting her balance onto her left foot, she stomped the heel of her right dress shoe on her assailant's instep. This time, she felt herself make firm, solid contact. She heard a sharp grunt, almost a groan. The pressure on her throat didn't ease, but she hoped she'd inflicted enough pain to distract from her next move.

She used her right hand to pluck Gloria's pencil from her updo and the left one to slide the wooden sheath off its concealed spike. With this, she could do some real damage.

Now, she twisted to the left and let the motion add power to the sweeping motion she was making with her right hand. She felt the spike make contact, but it was a glancing blow. She wasn't able to embed the spike in her assailant's body, but she heard fabric tear. It was entirely possible that she'd struck the flesh beneath it hard enough to draw blood, because she heard a shriek of pain and she was glad.

The hands gripping Justine's throat loosened enough for her to draw a breath, so she'd achieved her first goal. Unfortunately, she'd failed at her second goal, which was to disable her assailant. She felt a fist strike her jaw and she went down with one of her assailant's hands still squeezing her windpipe, but she went down fighting. She struck out with the spike and was rewarded with another grunt of pain.

Darkness was gathering around Justine, but the hand on her throat slipped away as she fell. She retained just enough awareness to make sure she didn't land on her weapon, putting the spike through her own chest. Once on the ground, she drew her right hand beneath her chest, protecting the weapon with her body. This person might yet be able to kill her with her own weapon, but it would require lifting her torso and prying the handle from her grip.

A hard blow to the back of her head knocked that thought and all others clean out of Justine's mind.

Chapter 23

Justine couldn't remember why she was playing dead. She couldn't remember why she was lying on her belly with one hand gripping...something. Was it a knife?

A memory started to stir. Had she unsheathed Gloria's weapon-disguised-as-a-pencil? She thought maybe she had. Why?

It hurt to swallow. The pain brought back the feeling of two hands encircling her throat as someone did their best to choke her to death. Maybe this was why she was playing dead. Maybe she was trying to convince someone that they'd succeeding in killing her.

One thing was for sure. Her brain wasn't working well. Justine judged that she should continue playing dead until she figured out what was going on.

———

"Are you sure she was planning to take the trolley home?"

It was a reasonable question, so Georgette resisted the urge to yell, "I don't know!" at Jerry as they hurried outside.

"She said she was goin' to the Columbia Pike library. I saw her get on the trolley. I don't know how she planned to get home."

"Then we might as well head for the trolley stop. Even if she walked home, she'd have to come right past it to get to Kansas Hall." Jerry gave his wheels an extra hard spin. "How late is she?"

"Late enough. The library's been closed since eight thirty. It's well on past nine. She should be here."

"Maybe she had to wait for a trolley. There's no need to panic unless the next trolley comes and she's not on it."

The next trolley arrived as they reached the stop. She wasn't on it. They were alone at a trolley stop surrounded by trees and a streetlight, and there wasn't a soul in sight. Georgette gave herself permission to panic.

"Justine!" she called out. "Justine!"

She set out walking, searching along the sidewalk that would have brought Justine home if she'd chosen to travel on foot. Jerry followed her.

"Are we going all the way back to Kansas Hall, calling her name?" he asked.

"It's the best idea I got," Georgette said. "You got a better one?"

———

Justine heard her name. Then she heard it again in a lower pitch.

Two people were looking for her. What did that mean?

To the best of her memory, which was pretty damned raggedy, the person who'd tried to strangle her had been alone. Was this someone else, or had her assailant come back with reinforcements?

If so, she was doomed. However, these people were not behaving like they were trying to cover up attempted murder.

They were walking down a public street bellowing her name at the top of their lungs. They were looking for her. They seemed safe enough.

She tried to call out to them, but all that came out was a soft, breathy groan.

————

Georgette stopped dead still on the sidewalk and Jerry had to swerve to keep from running into her. They'd been going out for a few months and he'd learned to expect Georgette to do the unexpected. Keeping this in mind had significantly cut down on the frequency of collisions.

"Did you hear that?" she asked.

"Hear what?"

She answered him by sprinting off the sidewalk, into some tall grass, and down a sharp incline. There was no way he could follow her in the chair in that terrain, and there was no way he could walk that far through all those obstacles. All he could do was wait.

A long minute passed before he heard Georgette's voice again. "I found her. She's alive."

He heard her grunt, then he saw her stand, hauling Justine's limp form to her feet. Bringing Justine's right arm across her shoulders and wrapping her left arm around Justine's waist, Georgette took a step forward, and Justine took a tottering step along with her. Then she took another and another. Her head lolled with each step, but she was holding it up on her own. Jerry was encouraged.

Then the two women reached the sidewalk and the dim light of the streetlights, and Jerry saw the dark smear of blood on the front of Justine's blouse.

"I don't think it's her blood," Georgette said, holding up a bloody spike. Its handle was tipped with an incongruous pencil eraser. "This is her weapon, and she's not bleeding anywhere I can see. I think Justine did some damage to somebody with this thing. Might've saved her own life." She settled Justine on the trolley stop bench and sat down beside her.

"You have a hard head," Jerry said to Justine, checking the lump on the back of it. It was impressive, but there was no sticky blood matting her hair. "Most people would be bleeding like there was no tomorrow."

"Think I got in a good lick." Justine pantomimed a stabbing motion. "Not sure where. Shoulder…leg…both, maybe."

"Do you know who did this? Man? Woman? Somebody you know?"

Justine took a deep breath. "…came up from behind. Could've been anybody." She ran her fingers over the lump.

Jerry rolled his chair back a foot and sat there looking at the two women sitting on the trolley stop bench. Justine was leaning against Georgette's shoulder, but she was coming around. Her eyes were focused. She was in control of her movements. As if aware that he was assessing her condition, she lifted her head off her friend's shoulder and sat up straight.

"You go get the car," Georgette said.

"What? You've got to be kidding me. No."

"I can see your brain working. You're trying to figure out what to do now. Maybe Justine could walk back to Kansas Hall. She's got us to help her. But it would be a lot to put her through, and what will we do if she faints on us? We could put her on your lap and I could help you by pushing, but we'd attract a lot of attention that we don't want. Speakin' of which, we probably don't want to take her to the emergency room, do we?"

"Well…"

"No. We don't. Here's what we're gonna do. I'm gonna sit right here with her. You're gonna go to Kansas Hall, ask to use the phone, and call what's-his-name. You people have got to have doctors you trust, so you're gonna tell him we need one. Then you're gonna get in your car, pick us up, and take us to wherever the doctor is."

Jerry didn't like the sound of this. "No, I'll stay with her. You go—"

"You think I'll be safer on this dangerous sidewalk all by my lonesome self? Where somebody attacked her and left her in this condition? And then what will I do? You know I can't drive a car."

"I need to fix that."

"Well, you can't do it tonight. We'll be fine. We've got our Stingers. And she seems to be pretty good with that pencil-spike-thingie."

Jerry reached into the holster strapped to his lower leg and handed her a snubnosed .38. "Remember how to use this?"

"I do," Georgette said. "We both do."

Leaving those two women alone in the dark was the hardest thing Jerry had ever had to do.

As he rolled away, Georgette said, "Don't worry, sugar. I've got your back. And I've got her."

———

Justine's head hurt and her throat hurt. The car ride had been hard, as every pothole had jostled her aching body. But none of this mattered, because Jerry was pulling the car into a driveway and Paul was there, pacing as he waited for her. He yanked her door open before the car had even stopped rolling.

"Are you okay?" spilled out of his mouth about five times

as he palpated the lump on her head. The finger marks on her throat made curses flow. As he helped her to her feet, she felt his lips brush her temple. Then she felt him turn her toward him and press those lips to hers for a long moment.

Leaning on his arm, she made it into the house, where an easy chair, an ice pack, and a footstool waited for her. Once in the chair, Paul put the ice pack in her hand and guided it toward the painful lump on the back of her head.

"Hold this here," he said. "It'll help." Then she felt him wrap a blanket around her, waving away her protests that she wasn't cold.

"You could go into shock. Better to be too warm than to let yourself get chilled. Let me make you a cup of tea."

And he was gone, walking with the loose-limbed, natural gait of a man who was younger than he seemed. His business suit was replaced by a powder-blue seersucker shirt, dungarees, and loafers. He'd shampooed away the hair cream that kept his daytime hair in rein. He looked like the carefree, bookish factory worker she'd fallen for in New Orleans. Here, in his home, Paul looked like himself.

Perhaps. Which version of Paul was "himself"? Wouldn't he be himself in the privacy of his home?

Georgette sat on a sofa across from her, and Jerry rolled his chair right up next to her. Justine waited for the pang she always felt when she saw them holding hands, but it didn't come, because Paul had just kissed her. She could still feel his protective arm around her waist.

Georgette cut her eyes toward Jerry. "Does he fall over himself to take care of every agent that gets banged up a little?"

"Nope. He's got people to do that for him. And he sure as heck don't kiss 'em."

Justine looked around the room, so that she wouldn't have

to watch Georgette and Jerry laughing at her. So this was where Jerry and Paul lived.

It was a modest house, and it was furnished like somebody's grandmother lived there, with lots of dark woodwork and lots of furniture upholstered with horsehair. It was a little large for two men, perhaps, but these two men appeared to need room for things most bachelors didn't. A wardrobe of disguises, for one thing. How else could Paul have donned a police uniform at the drop of a hat?

Somewhere in the house, there was probably another room stuffed full of their arsenal—guns and knives and bombs and brass knuckles and such. She fervently wished that she and Georgette had an arsenal of their own. Her roommate talked big, but Justine noticed that she'd given Jerry his gun back without even negotiating another Stinger in exchange.

The house also had a darkroom. Justine knew this because she could smell the chemicals. Jerry had disappeared to the back of the house while she was telling Paul everything she remembered. He'd still been sitting beside her when the doctor arrived.

Now, Paul stood across the room, watching the doctor's every move. Justine missed having him close.

"She'll be fine," the doctor said to Paul, after he'd shined lights in her eyes, made her walk a straight line, and checked reflexes she didn't even know she had. Continuing to speak as if she weren't even there, he said, "She should rest for a few days. She should avoid hitting her head again for a lot longer than that. If I had my way, she'd never bump her head again, but I know how you people operate." Then he packed his instruments into his black leather doctor's bag and left them.

"Let me refill your tea," Paul said. "And you should eat something with some nourishment in it. We have... I don't know what we have, but I'll bring you something," Paul said. Then he looked sheepishly at Georgette and Jerry, saying, "Would you two like anything?"

"If we decide we want something," Jerry said, "I'll go get it. Right now, we're enjoying your angel of mercy act. It's quite a spectacle."

"He ain't wrong, *cher*."

As they listened to cabinets and drawers open and close, Jerry said, "We keep the kitchen stocked like two bachelors live here. I have no idea what he's planning to feed you. Some tuna, maybe?"

"I've seen her eat it right out of the can," Georgette said. "She ain't fussy."

Justine luxuriated in the comfortable home and the good friends and the suddenly attentive boyfriend. Maybe it was the head injury, but she was beginning to think that her life was going okay.

Jerry excused himself to go finish up in the darkroom, so he missed the expression on Paul's face when Georgette shook her head at the plate of peanut-butter-and-crackers that he'd made for Justine.

"I'm sorry to have to tell you this, sugar, but she was hoping for an open can of tuna and a fork."

Justine shot her a "Be quiet!" glare, then said to Paul, "I adore peanut butter, and I have no idea what she's talking about." Then she commenced eating peanut-butter-and-crackers with a vengeance, despite the messages she was getting from her queasy stomach.

Seven crackers later, Jerry emerged with prints of documents from Karl's personnel files.

"I wish I'd gotten a photo of those names in the library book," Justine said, "but they're right there in the public library if we need them."

"Based on what you learned there," Paul said, "Doris, Sandra, and Mabel are probably in Tennessee, safe and sound, working at something that the government doesn't want anybody to know about. Bettie is certainly dead. That only leaves one of our missing women unaccounted for."

"Sally," Georgette said. "Do we have any leads yet?"

Paul shook his head. "Do those photos tell you anything?"

Justine riffled through the prints and pulled out the images she'd taken of pages from Sally's personnel file. "I see that her home address is in Iowa. It looks like both of her parents are living, or they were when she took this job. She graduated from high school at the top of her class."

"No surprise there," Georgette said.

"Not in the least," Justine said. "Her background check uncovered no convictions, so she's not a secret thief or murderer."

"Or she's good enough at stealing and killing that she hasn't been caught."

Justine could see that Paul's comment didn't sit well with Georgette.

"I don't like thinking about Sally that way," Georgette said. "It feels like you're speakin' ill of the dead. She may've been kidnapped. She may be in danger."

"Maybe she kidnapped herself," Paul said. "Maybe she's our enemy agent."

"I can't make myself believe that," Georgette shot back.

Justine stayed silent, flipping through the photos one by one. "Everything else about Sally's paperwork looks ordinary. So do Mabel's documents." She picked up the next stack, photos of documents from Ike's file.

"You said you paid special attention to Ike," Paul said. "Do you see anything noteworthy there?"

She held up a finger that said "Wait a second," and kept paging through the photos of Ike's personnel file. When she reached the end, she squared the stack on her lap and looked at Paul.

"In answer to your question, Ike has certainly not been Employee-of-the-Month. He's been reprimanded three times for disrespecting his superiors. Sometimes he neglects to come to work on time. Or at all. None of these things speak to whether he's an enemy spy."

"A traitor," Georgette said.

"A history of poor attendance at work could be useful to a spy who sometimes needs to be elsewhere," Paul said.

Justine nodded to concede his point. "The thing that catches my eye are some details where Ike has flat-out lied, either to me or to the government."

"What did he lie about?" Paul asked.

"His parents. He told me they died when he was in high school, but his background check showed that his parents were living when he took the job at Arlington Hall. So that's one definite lie that he told me. He also told me that he'd spent his growing-up years with them in West Virginia, but their address in his file is in Washington, DC, which contradicts what he said when he told me that he didn't have any nearby relatives. I don't know the truth about Ike's parents, but I know that he didn't tell it to me. Or else he didn't tell it to the government."

"People lie about relatives they don't get along with," Paul said. "This lie may mean nothing, but we should keep it in mind. Do you think he might have been the person who knocked you unconscious? Ike has already attacked you once."

"All I can tell you is that it was someone taller than me. Lots of people are taller than me. Ike's one of them, but so are Sally and Linda. Thelma and Nora, too. And Dr. Kowalski and Ed. Even Karl is taller than me. The Bees and Patsy may be shorter, though."

"Nora was with me tonight," Georgette said. "She couldn't be the one who attacked you."

"There wasn't much time between when you left Nora and when we left Kansas Hall to look for Justine," Jerry said, "but there were a few minutes when Nora could have run down the sidewalk toward the trolley stop and found Justine. It doesn't take long to bang somebody on the head."

Justine shook her aching head. "Yeah, but how would she have known how to find me? Even I couldn't have told you where I would be at 9:10 in the evening. I think the person who attacked me followed me from Arlington Hall to the library, waited outside, then struck when I was on my way home."

The others all nodded, but Justine could see that the men weren't as sure as Georgette that Nora was innocent. She didn't know what she thought.

"You did a good job of defending yourself," Jerry said. "You drew blood, for sure. Do you remember anything about the struggle, maybe what part of your assailant's body you struck?"

"I was just flailing. I think I grazed...something—an arm? a chest? a shoulder?—while I was still standing. I believe I did some more damage as I was falling. I have the sense that I gouged the person's leg pretty well on the way down."

"That may be why you're alive," Paul said. "You sustained a solid blow to the head, but we didn't find anything like a rock or a stick that was used as a bludgeon. Our best guess is that it was the grip of a handgun. We think that the intent was to strangle you, which is a nice, silent approach for an attack right there by a main road. The handgun was a backup plan, but shooting you was just too risky once you stabbed the assailant's leg. You removed the chance of a speedy getaway, so your assailant fled. Or, more likely, limped away."

Justine ran her fingers lightly over the lump on her head. Was it made with a handgun that had come close to ending her life?

"Here's what I think," she said. "I think we're getting close to the truth. That's the most dangerous time, right? When your quarry senses that you're closing in. So let's take the eccentric geniuses in Room 117 one by one. What have we learned?"

"Well, Sally's gone and nobody knows why," Georgette said. "And Thelma is all torn up about it. Or she seems to be."

"That's true," Justine said. "And then there's the library, where I got information that Doris, Mabel, and Sandra may be in Tennessee. I only knew to look there because Barbara pointed me in that direction."

"Makes Barbara seem innocent, don't it?" Georgette said. "Beulah doesn't seem real guilty, either. And don't forget all the stuff I learned about Nora. She's a heckuva piano player and a published composer. She worshipped her husband and every sign says that she worships Ike now."

"But Ike sure doesn't worship her," Justine said. "Ike rejects her in a really humiliating way. Nora has every reason in the world to turn on him, although that's neither here nor there when it comes to finding the spy."

"Nora has every reason to hate Germany, too," Georgette said. "And so does Dr. Kowalski. Ike, too."

"Are you saying that there's no way that Nora, Patryk, or Ike could be spying for the enemy?" Jerry asked.

"Can't say," Georgette said. "I don't know that they love our country. I just know that Nora and Dr. Kowalski hate the people who took away the people they loved. Ike's gotta hate the people who broke his body. I wouldn't spy for the country that did those things to me. I guess they could be workin' for Japan, but that pontoon bridge was in Europe. Besides, Japan's in cahoots with Germany. I just don't see how Nora, Dr. Kowalski, or Ike could stand to work for either of 'em."

"Ed van Dorn is hard to figure out," Justine said, with one eye on Paul. If he had any thoughts about her date with Ed, he hadn't said so. "He prides himself on his emotional control and his intellect, but he's got a brother in combat, so he can't like Germany much, either. Add that to his high-pressure job, and he's like a ticking bomb that could explode any minute. I may get to watch him explode, because I've got a date with him tomorrow night."

"No, you don't," Paul said. "Well, you do, but you're not going to keep it. I'm shutting this mission down."

His tone was professional. His posture was almost prim, sitting as he did in a straight-backed dining chair pulled up close to Justine's armchair. "You've been attacked twice. This time, you were targeted. Somebody followed you, looking for a chance to—" The professional tone slipped. The voice cracked. "—to take you out of commission. They wanted to do it in the same way somebody killed Bettie. Deep down, I've never believed that her death was just a date gone wrong. And now you're planning to be alone with a man who's showing signs of—of instability?"

He took a second to gather himself. "I can't in good conscience continue to put you in this kind of danger."

Justine wasn't looking at Paul when she asked her next question. She was looking at Jerry, because she thought he was more likely to tell her the truth.

"Is it normal to pull an agent off a case that they're on the verge of cracking? Because I do think we're close. Jerry? Is it?"

Jerry looked like he wished she'd direct her questions at their boss.

"It's an honest question, so please answer it," she said. "It seems to me that a job like ours naturally grows more dangerous when the bad guys are afraid of being pushed into a corner.

Does he ask everybody to quit when they're about to get to the truth? Or just me?"

Jerry suddenly found the ceiling very interesting.

"If I'm never going to be allowed to see a job through, I might as well quit. No, wait."

Justine turned her eyes to Paul and made him look at her by refusing to continue talking until he did.

"I refuse to quit this job, and I refuse to quit this mission. If you don't want me at Arlington Hall tomorrow, doing what you sent me there to do, then you're going to have to fire me."

Georgette had sat quietly while Justine did the talking, but she saw her opening. "You might as well fire us both at once. It'll save time."

Paul's face was blank. The affable and charmingly awkward man who had been sitting in his chair had gone somewhere else. If Justine thought she'd seen him fully put on the face of a spy before, she'd been mistaken.

Here it was. Here was the unfathomable nature that made her fear falling in love with him.

No, she didn't fear it. It was too late for that. This was the unfathomable nature that almost made her sorry she'd ever fallen in love with him. She believed that it hid his fear for her. But could she ever be sure?

"I see that the two of you have missed an important detail." His tone was icy. "This is to be expected. You've had an eventful night. But consider this."

He put his hand to his head, mimicking the moment when Justine saved herself with a fake pencil hiding in her hair.

"We can all thank Gloria for the weapon she gave you. It saved your life. But that weapon revealed you. If your assailant was the traitor we're chasing, and I think that's the case, then your cover is blown."

"Didn't we already know that?" Jerry asked. "Why else would she be attacked?"

"Her attacker could have thought she was just another woman who didn't even know she'd learned something dangerous."

"That's what I think happened to Bettie," Jerry said, and Paul gave him a quick nod of agreement.

"Or you could be a nosy amateur," Paul continued. "Or even an undercover cop. None of these people would be armed like a government agent."

Justine put her hand to her mouth. "I knew it when I pulled the pencil out of my hair, but it seemed necessary to defend myself. Then I just…forgot…that I'd unmasked myself. How could I forget something like that?"

"Your brain has been shaken up pretty bad." Jerry's voice was kind.

"I'm sorry," Justine said. "So sorry. I should never have used it."

"Of course, you should have used it," Paul snapped. "Keeping you alive is what it was designed to do. But using that camouflaged blade changed everything."

She could hear Paul trying to make his voice kinder, less businesslike. "I think you should stand down and wait for another assignment, but if you insist on walking into the lion's den tomorrow, I won't stop you. I believe you're a day away from unmasking the traitor, and the fate of our troops in Europe rests on stopping that information leak. Nevertheless, please know that tomorrow is the final day of this operation, no matter what. After tomorrow, I'm pulling all three of you out."

Now Jerry was sputtering his own protests.

"One day. That's all you get," he said. "The person who attacked Justine—presumably, the same person we're trying to identify—is wounded and can't know what other dangerous toys she carries. Tomorrow will be for regrouping, but after that, our adversary will have had time to make a plan to take Justine—and maybe all three of you—out of commission. If you watch each other, I think you will probably survive one more day, but then you're leaving Arlington Hall and never going back. Because I will fire you. And I do mean all of you."

This time, his glare was for Jerry, who looked like he was preparing for a ferocious protest. Paul cut him off.

"This decision is not a personal one. I would say the same thing to three strangers. Now take them home, Jerry, so they can get a few hours of sleep. You get some sleep, too. Your odds will be better if you've all had some rest."

Oddly, Justine found herself thinking of Ed and the game that he loved so well.

"The cards are dealt," she said in a voice that seemed to come from somewhere outside herself. "It's time to play the final hand and see who takes the tricks."

———

Thelma crouched behind a bush as the car pulled to a stop in the Kansas Hall parking lot. It was far past midnight and getting on toward dawn. She'd waited until she thought nobody would see her, but she apparently hadn't waited long enough to creep out into the open.

The front passenger door opened, and the new girl, Samantha, got out. Thelma supposed that the driver must be the handsome blond man who'd been chasing her around in his wheelchair. Samantha didn't seem the type to be out at four in the morning. Then the door behind Samantha's opened.

When she got a good look at the second woman leaving the car, Thelma rocked back on her heels in surprise. She wasn't expecting to see Justine, but her blond updo was unmistakable.

Neither of these women seemed like they went for all-night dates. Well, they'd moved to the big city, so she guessed that they were trying out big-city ways.

Thelma cradled a tote bag in her lap. It held the entire contents of the housemother's pencil drawer—stapler, scissors, pens, pencils, erasers, carbon paper, and a banana. She hadn't had time to pick and choose. She'd just upended the drawer over her bag when nobody was looking, then hurried away.

Thelma waited for the women to enter the dormitory and for the car to pass out of sight. Then she waited some more, just to be sure.

———

"Tomorrow's going to be a hard day. Sally's still gone, and we don't know why," Justine said from the bed where she lay flopped, still in her street clothes and still clutching her purse. She'd been there ever since they came upstairs.

This was to be expected after an attempt on her life, but Georgette was worried about her. "Yep," she said. "Everybody at Arlington Hall's going to be talking about Sally again tomorrow. She's got a million friends."

"There's a good reason for that," Justine said. "Nice people usually do have about a million friends."

"Maybe that's where she's been all night and all day, with one of her friends. Maybe she's comin' in the lobby right now, and we're all gonna laugh tomorrow about how scared we were."

"Yeah." Justine's defeated voice broke Georgette's heart. "How did things go with Nora this evening?"

"I didn't learn much important—at least, not much that what's-his-name would say was important—but I did enjoy her company."

"Things can't always go our way, I guess."

"Naw," Georgette said, but she didn't really mean it, because things really did seem to be looking up for her. She felt guilty about it, though, because Justine was so down in the dumps.

Georgette knew that things with their mysterious boss weren't going the way Justine wanted, although she never came out and said so. For a while that night, it had looked like he was ready to let down his guard and let her in. And then he wasn't.

Justine's stone-faced almost-boyfriend made Jerry look like the best boyfriend in the world. To be honest, though, Jerry probably *was* the best boyfriend in the world. Georgette was a good enough friend to wish that Justine could find the other best boyfriend in the world, whoever he might be.

Georgette also felt like things were going her way because she could still feel smooth ivory keys under her fingertips. She could still see how the long shiny strings looked when Nora lifted the piano's lid to show her how its hammers and dampers worked. She could still hear the percussive, resonant sounds of those hammers hitting the strings and the soft thud of the dampers as Nora used a brass pedal to raise and lower them.

Georgette couldn't believe that she was going to learn to play the piano. She was going to really play with both hands, and she was going to learn to read music instead of just mimicking her grandmother's memorized hymn-playing. Even when she was a little girl, she'd understood that her parents would never be able to afford lessons, so she'd never asked for them. She hadn't wanted them to know how badly she wanted something that they couldn't give her. Georgette was afraid of the danger that would come with the sunrise for all the usual reasons, but she was also afraid because dying would take her away from Jerry and from Justine and from pianos and from all the things that the wide world outside of Des Allemands offered.

Georgette didn't say any of this. She just said, "You should hear Nora play the piano. And she writes her own music. It's published and everything."

"Really? That's nice." Justine's voice was sad, and that made Georgette sad.

"Do you know how to play the piano?"

"No. We had a piano and Mama liked to play, but I was never really interested. I like to listen, though."

Georgette had figured the answer would be yes, because Justine could do everything. She could do all kinds of math, even calculus. She knew so much about physics that they couldn't even talk about most of it, because Georgette didn't know the language. Justine could weld. She was really good at German, and she could talk to Gloria pretty well in Polish. She said her French was terrible, but Georgette didn't believe it.

She started to tell Justine that Nora was going to teach her to play, but something stopped her. Maybe it was because she was afraid that she would fail, and she didn't want Justine to know it if she did. Maybe it was because she was afraid that Justine would decide she wanted to learn to play, too, and that it would only take her a week or so. And maybe it was because she knew she was a terrible person to feel this way.

Instead, she just said, "Get up and grab your shampoo and bathrobe. That's what I'm gonna do. There's a lot of shower stalls in Kansas Hall and plenty of hot water. It's the best thing about this place. You'll feel better after you wash off the dirt of the day."

Not to mention that Justine would feel better after she'd washed off the last traces of somebody else's blood.

"And then, after the shower, you need to sleep."

———

Thelma felt the disappointment in her whole body. Her head sagged. Her shoulders drooped. Her stomach heaved.

She'd been so sure that she knew where Sally was hiding.

Thelma had spent hours creeping through the hallways and stairwells of Oklahoma Hall, the Arlington Farms dormitory that was under renovation. She'd been hoping to find a frightened young woman curled up on the floor under her winter coat. She'd found construction debris and some unidentifiable footprints on the dusty floor, but no Sally.

This was a disastrous turn of events.

Either Sally was somewhere else, and Thelma had no idea where that would be, or else Sally...

Or else Sally wasn't anywhere.

Thelma almost dropped to the dirty floor of Oklahoma Hall in despair, but she didn't. If Sally was hiding somewhere else, then she couldn't help her. And if Sally was...gone...then she couldn't help her. But if she was hiding here in this building, then she wasn't beyond the help of someone who cared about her.

Rosy light was seeping in the windows of every room that Thelma passed through. She needed to go before the sun rose and revealed her.

She passed into the stairwell. There, she set down the tote bag filled with the housemother's stolen possessions. Into the bag, she dumped the contents of her purse—five sandwiches, an orange, a letter, all of the money Sally had left behind, and all of Thelma's cash. She had some crackers in her room that would keep her alive until payday. She wasn't hungry, anyway, and she wouldn't be until Sally was found.

Was this enough money to get Sally someplace safe? Thelma didn't know, because she didn't know why Sally had run. Maybe there wasn't enough money in the world to make her safe.

Chapter 24

Justine woke after sleeping like a woman who had been bashed in the head.

She'd dreamed dreams—she knew that—but they had slipped out the window when daybreak came. The dreams left nothing behind but a certainty that she knew more than she realized. So many things nibbled at her mind, asking her why she couldn't decipher the messages they were sending.

Nora's piano playing bothered her.

Sally's lockets bothered her.

Ed's bridge playing bothered her.

Ike's daily snub of Nora and her flowers bothered her.

Linda's makeup bothered her.

Patsy's slavish copying of Linda's makeup bothered her.

Thelma's insistence that Sally was missing mere hours after they'd been together bothered her.

Karl's maps with their pushpins bothered her.

The Bees' miniature clotheslines, clipped with classified military secrets, bothered her.

Patryk's status as a mathematician, the science of codes and symbols, bothered her.

What did it mean, really, to pass information in secret? Passing information was an act of communication, certainly. But the secrecy…that required a shift in the mode of communication. Either the message had to be completely hidden from bystanders, or it had to be communicated in a way that was not understandable—not even recognizable, ideally—to anyone who didn't share the secret language of the two people passing the message.

This was the very definition of a code. But it applied to written music. And spoken languages. It applied to the private cipher known only to her and Georgette, but it also applied to the implicit understanding between roommates that signaled a problem when a bystander would see nothing but a young woman enjoying her night out a little too much. This same understanding had brought Jerry and Georgette to her as she lay unconscious in a ditch. It may well have saved her life.

And wasn't makeup a symbolic way to speak to potential mates from across the room, saying, "I'm available, honeycakes, and I'm looking for someone *just like you*"?

The Victorians had sent messages with flowers, and this meant that Nora could be doing the same with her daily bouquets.

Messages clipped to clotheslines could carry messages in the way they were arranged, like semaphore flags.

Pins stuck into maps could signify places, but their colors and patterns could send an entirely different signal.

The world was full of coded messages. But how was she to know which ones were deadly?

———

Justine felt wobbly on her feet. Maybe she really did have a concussion. Well, she hoped she still had enough of her wits to carry out the plan. She fluffed up the frilly collar hiding the bruises on her throat and kept moving across the campus of Arlington Hall

Jerry had picked up Justine and Georgette at Kansas Hall, giving the three of them a chance to speak freely in the car. They had a plan. They had an exit strategy if things went wrong. They were armed, even if this meant nothing more than two skirt pockets loaded with Stingers, pepper gas spray, and noisemakers. They had no weapons in their hair, unfortunately, because Paul had taken their pencil blades. She guessed he'd put them in his home arsenal. Now that the fake pencils' real purpose had been revealed, there was too much of a chance that their adversary would amble by and pluck their weapons from their coiled locks.

Unsteadily, Justine walked to the door of her office and opened the door. Karl was there, rearranging the colorful pins scattered over the map on the wall behind her desk.

She'd rehearsed her lines. Now she had to say them casually, as if they weren't rehearsed at all. "Dr. van Dorn's assistant—you know her, my roommate Samantha—has asked if I can come help her for the day. She has a huge backlog of filing to do. If I help her, she'll have a better chance at being ready for the next liaison meeting."

Karl grumbled and harrumphed, then he waved her out of the room.

Thus, she had accomplished Part One of the day's plan. What did she hope to accomplish by the end of the day? She intended to find the traitor who was passing the Allies' secrets to the enemy. She intended to make the treason stop.

———

"Here let me help you with that," Ed said, grabbing a corner of the desk she was dragging across the room. "Let's put it right here by Samantha's desk, so you can work together."

Her heart clenched when she realized that the desk—bare-topped, empty-drawered, and tucked in a corner—might have been Bettie's. At least it wasn't Sally's. Sally's desk sat in its usual spot, covered with papers and pencils. She wondered if anybody had checked its drawers to make sure that Sally hadn't left any apples behind. If not, the sickly smell of rotting fruit would fill Room 117 within days, unless Sally came back to eat the apple or throw it away.

"I'm so glad you're here," Ed said. Then he looked around the room and added a quick, "Because we can use the help," for the benefit of his gossiping employees.

Nora entered, her tote bag slung over her shoulder. She carefully cradled a bouquet of pink dianthus and yellow daisies in both hands. Proceeding down the aisle to her desk, she looked straight ahead, which allowed her to avoid everybody's eyes but Georgette's. For Georgette, Nora had a small smile. Georgette returned it with a big one.

"You're enjoying this," Justine whispered as Georgette dumped pile after pile of loose papers and neatly labeled file folders in front of her.

"Karl gave you permission to work in here all day. I might as well make the most of your time," Georgette chirped sweetly. "Here's a copy of the file list." She handed Justine a multi-paged document. "Here's a stack of tracking forms. And here are some sharpened pencils. You'll need a few."

Justine had learned to file in school. She had hated it just as badly as she'd hated learning to keep a neat lab notebook. She wasn't a naturally organized recordkeeper, and she knew it. The nuns who had taught her filing had been insistent on meticulous recordkeeping in an office, and her mother had been equally insistent on meticulous recordkeeping in the lab, so she knew how to keep track of details. She just didn't like it. She sighed and spread her pencils and documents out in front of her. It was going to be a long day.

Patryk shuffled down the aisle, a dreamy expression on his face. She kept her eyes on her work. She had forgotten that her presence might cause him to break down again.

Thelma's shoulders slumped as she dropped into her desk chair and lit a cigarette. The Bees looked almost as despondent as they took their own seats. None of them looked at Sally's empty seat.

Ike wasn't there. And the same thing was true thirty minutes later, when Justine had finished entering filing numbers on her first stack of documents. More time had passed while she'd slid most of them into file folders. Finally, Ike appeared. He was dressed as eccentrically as usual, with his woolen peacoat swinging open over an open-necked white sports shirt. His customary knit cap was on his head.

With Ike finally at his desk, the suspects were assembled. Nobody looked like they'd been stabbed by the blade that she'd kept hidden in a pencil, but they were all wearing conservative business wear. (Except for Ike and his out-of-place outerwear.) Thus, Ike's arms, legs, shoulders, and chest were covered, and so were everybody else's, except perhaps the lowest twelve inches of the women's legs.

Nobody was limping and nobody was favoring a bad shoulder, but she needed to keep a close eye on whether that changed. People got tired as the day passed. Wounds started to ache. At any moment, somebody's pain could give them away.

Nora fussed with her flowers. She snipped off the tips of the stems over her trash can, then she put the trimmed stems back into the paper cup of water that served as a vase. Three yellow daisy petals fluttered away from her hands. Wet, they stuck to the metal side of Nora's wastebasket.

Beulah stood and picked up a box of long paper strips, as narrow as cellophane tape, and commenced clipping them to a taut string hung between wooden posts. She hung a few strips, adjusted them to be just where she wanted them, then hung a few more. Barbara was doing the same thing on another string. From a distance, it looked like they were hanging quarter notes on a musical staff.

Patryk stared abstractedly at the ceiling, his pencil eraser tapping out a syncopated beat. Every few minutes, Ike glanced at Patryk like he wanted to yell at him about the racket. Once, he even opened his mouth to speak, but he backed down rather than dragging Patryk back to the real world, where his losses waited for him. Even Ike was sensitive enough to deal gently with Patryk.

Justine was sitting close enough to Ed to sense that he was fidgety. She knew this was a problem for him, because breaking codes is not a task that lends itself to being fidgety. When his nerves became too much to bear, every ten minutes or so, he would stand up and make a circuit of the room. He probably thought that he looked like a supervisor managing his people, but Justine knew him better than that, even after a single date and a few intense conversations. He didn't look like a conscientious manager to her. He just looked nervous. It crossed her mind that a nervous man should not keep a revolver, presumably loaded, in full view on his desk.

The clock in Room 117 ticked as loudly as the one in her office. It was a sound that faded into the background when she was calm and focused, but she was not, in fact, calm and focused. She was on the verge of jumping out of her skin.

———

Justine would always wonder if anyone saw her face when the first light of realization began to dawn. In particular, she would wonder whether the person who had brought a Browning Hi-Power 9mm semiautomatic handgun to work saw her then or whether recognition came later.

She wasn't sure that it was possible for anyone to suppress the fierce light that shone from their face when they finally put two and two together and got four. On that morning in Room 117, when Justine was looking at Ike and thinking about how awful it must be to be the only survivor in his company, the word "survivor" rang in her head for a while. It made her think of the attack on the pontoon bridge that had kicked off this investigation. There had been no survivors at all.

Perhaps she stared at Ike a little too long while she thought this through, but by the time she looked away, she had finally grasped what the phrase "no survivors" really meant.

It meant that nobody had lived to tell the tale.

And this meant that the truth could be easily concealed, especially when it was an unexpected truth. In the case of the destroyed pontoon bridge, an army that left no survivors could be any army at all.

It had seemed odd to Justine from the outset that the Germans had revealed the fact that they'd broken an Allied code, just to blow up a small bridge. Why hadn't they pursued their advantage, pummeling the Allies while they still could? The clock was ticking for the Axis powers. In particular, the clock was ticking for the Germans. Enemy troops were knocking on their door. There was no reason for them to blow up one bridge and then stop…unless it wasn't the Germans who did it.

What if somebody else had killed all the soldiers stationed

there and—dear God—everyone in the beautiful family that had been so unfortunate as to live at the crossroads of history? Did all those deaths serve to conceal the identity of an entire army?

If it wasn't the Germans who blew up the bridge, then who? Who else had an army in Poland? Well, the Allies did, obviously, but who were the Allies? There were many countries in the alliance, but they were dominated in Europe by the United States, Great Britain, and Russia.

Russia didn't fit comfortably into the alliance, and it never had. While Justine didn't know anyone who wanted to be at odds with the Russians, she didn't know anybody who trusted them, either. Gloria, a Polish refugee with a long memory for Russian perfidy, had been grousing to anyone who would listen about the foolishness of allying with the Soviet Union.

But, perfidy aside, why would the Russians care about that one tiny bridge? And then it came to her. The bombing wasn't about the bridge. It wasn't about the bridge at all.

Blowing up the bridge hadn't been an act of military strategy. It had been about establishing communication. It had been a signal to the very person that Justine was tracking down.

A message had left Arlington Hall with a subtly altered date. Subsequently a small, inconsequential bridge was destroyed. The effect? Now the spy at Arlington Hall knew that communication had been secured with an entity that was probably Russia.

An explosion the size of a bridge would be one way to say, "We got your message. Stand by for more instructions." If this bombing was accomplished in a way that implicated another army—the German army—then the question of why the attackers would give away the fact that they'd deciphered the Allied code became moot. Of course, it was moot. The attackers *were* Allies, untrustworthy Allies.

This only worked if the attacking army killed everybody. Thus, someone had thought that establishing communications with Arlington Hall was important enough to leave no survivors.

Again, the word "survivors" echoed in her ears. There had been no other survivors of the attack that had wounded Ike and, as she'd just realized, leaving no survivors makes it possible to hide information.

Involuntarily, her eyes darted back to Ike. Did he see her when she let that happen?

An attack's sole survivor was free to tell his own narrative, as long as an inconvenient set of parents wasn't around to contradict him. What if Ike was telling the truth about his growing-up years in West Virginia with parents who had died, but what if his name wasn't actually Ike? What if Ike had died when this man was wounded, enabling him to assume Ike's identity? The people in the battlefield who could have said otherwise were dead. Perhaps the new Ike had even killed some of them to make sure that this was so. When he got home, who could contradict him, as long as he stayed away from people who had known the real Ike?

———

When the knock came on the door to Room 117, nobody rose to answer it. That was Sally's job, and Sally wasn't there.

Hesitant, Georgette rose to her feet. "I'll get it."

Every eye swiveled to watch her go. Every body revealed the tension in the room, hands pressing into desks, shoulders hunched, lips pursed.

Georgette passed out of sight around the screen, then she came right back.

"It's Karl. He's here for you, Justine."

"Thanks, Samantha," she said.

She walked the long aisle between the desks, passing Georgette walking back to her desk.

Behind the screen, Karl looked distracted. He looked burdened. He beckoned for her to come into the hall with him.

"What does van Dorn have you doing in here? Does he seriously expect for you to be here all day?"

"He's not the one who asked for my help. Not directly, anyway. I told you that Samantha needed help getting ready for the liaison meeting next week. We thought you might not mind if I worked with her, since those meetings are so important."

"Yes, yes, they're important," he muttered. "As is the work you do for me. It's just that…well…my office is very silent. The silence bears hard on an old man when the news from the war is so bad. There is nothing I can do for those boys and nothing I can do for you. It grieves me to hear that young Sally is missing. Arlington Hall has become a dangerous place for women, it seems. You're…are you quite all right, my dear?"

Wondering whether Karl could possibly know about the attack on her, Justine answered cautiously. "I'm perfectly fine. Why do you ask?"

"Young people move with such ease and grace that it is not hard to notice when that ease ebbs. I saw it this morning in the short moment you spent telling me you'd like to spend the day away from me. I see it now. Are you in pain?"

Justine cast about for an answer that would cut off this line of questioning, but Karl did it for her.

"Perhaps it is not a physical pain. I well remember the traumas of young love. Please do not tell me about any of that."

He gently cupped her chin with the exact gesture her father had used. "Take care, my dear, with the pains of youth. I feel different ones at my age, and one of them is isolation, but I can do without you for a day, if I must. I charge you to work so hard that Dr. van Dorn never recovers from his jealousy that I am the prime beneficiary of your labor."

He trudged away.

Justine went back into Room 117 to walk its aisle again, trying to put a spring in her step. Did it matter if anyone realized that her head had been throbbing since the night before? The person who injured her knew that it had happened. What did it matter if the others in the room thought she had a hangover?

Thelma ignored her as she approached. So did Nora. Patryk's eyes were focused on the far wall.

The Bees were carefully arranging strips of paper on strings that were strung as tightly as a violin's.

Ahead of her sat Georgette and Ed. Georgette was focused on her work, or she was trying to look focused. Beside Georgette, Ed was focused on Justine. He was watching her approach him like a man who didn't realize he was staring. Or perhaps he knew it, but he still couldn't look away.

Ike's eyes were on her, and they leered. She wanted to look away from him, but she refused to give him the satisfaction. She held his gaze. This made him angry. She could tell by the way he swiveled his body, keeping his shoulders squared toward her. The twisting motion caused his peacoat to swing open and it pulled the open neckline of his shirt out of shape.

Peeping past his collar was the edge of a bandage that didn't quite cover an inflamed area of angry red skin. This was where her first glancing blow had landed when she had lashed out at her attacker with her pencil spike. Somewhere on his leg she had left another, deeper wound, or she missed her guess.

Did he know that she'd seen? She didn't think so. She shifted her eyes to the other side of the aisle, fully away from Ike.

On that side of the room, the daisy petals that Nora had

dropped remained stuck to her wastebasket. Unwilted and still bright yellow, they caught Justine's eye. To hide her face as she mulled over the wound on Ike's chest, Justine reached down and plucked the damp petals off the metal receptacle. Her intent had been to throw them away, until she felt their texture. She rubbed them between her finger and thumb, but they refused to wilt in her hands. Something was wrong about the daisy petals.

They were made of silk.

Justine's eyes darted to the bouquet on Nora's desk. The dianthus were clearly natural flowers. No human could duplicate such blooms, no two alike, some of them only buds beginning to swell. Tucked among them, the spray of daisies looked almost natural, but not quite. Nora's bouquets had been all been different—snapdragons, carnations, dianthus, chrysanthemums—but all of them had contained yellow daisies.

Did Nora have a stash of silk daisies in her room? Why? Georgette said that the church gave her a huge number of fresh flowers every week. She hardly needed more.

The simple shape of a daisy leapt into Justine's mind's eye, a circular center surrounded by a single row of petals arranged in a radial pattern like the numbers on a clock. It was a pattern that could support a code as sophisticated as any alphabet. That code could be learned as readily as reading music or reading German or playing contract bridge.

Remove the petal at the one o'clock position, and you could communicate the number one. Or the letter Q. Or "We ride at dawn." That missing petal could say anything you wanted it to say. All you had to do was teach the code to your recipient.

Remove the petal in the six o'clock position at the bottom of the flower and you could communicate a different number. Or a different letter. A spray of daisies could communicate the letters in a word or the digits of a date.

You could even remove a specific pattern of petals and trigger an attack on a bridge in Poland by signaling, "Today's the day. When you type the message at the top of the stack, change the date, just as I told you to do."

This wouldn't work with natural flowers, which might have any number of petals. But with artificial flowers? Oh, yes.

Using identical stems of artificial daisies with identical petal counts, it would be easy to establish which petal was "up" or "twelve o'clock" because the leaves, too, would always be in the same place. The person receiving the daisies would know how to hold the flower and read the message, just as a bridge player knew what it meant when their partner made a bid that said, "We can take all the tricks."

Justine's steps never faltered. She did nothing but walk and think. The only thing she did to give herself away was glance at the petals as she walked.

She'd seen Nora snipping at the bouquet with scissors, pretending to freshen the stems so that they'd take up the water better. The loose petals in her hands made her think that Nora had actually been snipping at the silk daisies' petals, and fake flowers didn't need freshening. She'd been changing the message they were sending.

It had been a huge risk for Nora to do this in public.

Justine reached her desk and turned around to take her seat. She glanced around the room and asked herself what had changed for Nora since she had left home that morning. What had driven her to take the risk of changing the message?

Room 117 looked as it always had, with the exception of Sally's empty desk, and the fact that Sally was missing wasn't news to anyone in the room. The only thing that was new since the day before was Justine. Nora had been frantically snipping at her daisies, signaling that the adversary was in the room. Justine was the adversary and Nora was the spy, or rather, Nora was a spy, because she was not working alone. The flowers and their hidden messages were not winging their way overseas. They were sending messages to someone in Arlington Hall.

Was it Ike? He and Nora were never ever seen speaking to each other. Was the flower code their way to pass information while maintaining that silence? Possibly.

But the flowers reliably went down the hall, so Justine had to presume that there was a third conspirator, probably Linda. Could Ike read the messages in the flowers, or was he just the muscle of the operation who moved messages and beat up women when the situation required it?

Justine tried to ignore the soreness of the bruises on her throat. Did Ike also kill women when required? What had really happened to Bettie? To Sally?

And Linda? Did she understand what she was doing when she followed Nora's instructions and filed a message with a subtly altered date? Did she know about the bridge and the soldiers and the family?

Justine didn't know. But she did know that Nora was the one snipping the daisies to create the messages. She was the one who was in charge.

Justine raised her head from the petals and saw Nora's eyes boring into her. Because of the yellow scraps of silk in her hand, Justine knew too much and Nora knew it.

As Nora's hand eased into her tote bag, Justine reflected that a bag big enough to hold several music books was also big enough to hold a gun. It might not have held a gun every day, but guards get slack when they see a nondescript middle-aged woman carry the same bag of music through the gates every day for years. Justine knew in her bones that, today, Nora's bag held a firearm. Her first thought was to drop to the ground and use her desk for cover, but it was replaced by another, more important, thought.

Georgette didn't know about the danger. Justine had to protect her friend. Her partner.

As she lunged toward Georgette, intending to drag her down behind the desk with her, Nora yanked a Browning Hi-Power 9mm semiautomatic out of the tote bag and took aim. Justine might have only had a few measly weeks of training as a federal agent, but she recognized the gun, and she knew that "High-Power" referred to its extra-large thirteen-round magazine.

Nora could kill everybody in Room 117 and have five rounds left over. Six, actually, since she wouldn't need to kill her partner, Ike.

Justine's tackle of Georgette didn't go as planned. They bounced off the desk chair and ended up draped across the desktop. Papers carrying state secrets floated to the floor.

They were not safe from the coming bullet. If anything, they were more exposed. Firing at point-blank range, Nora could hardly miss them.

Chapter 25

In the hallway, walking past the Traffic Records room on the way back to his office, Karl sensed something behind him. He wasn't sure what he'd heard—a scuffle of sorts, perhaps—but it was coming from Room 117. He wasn't surprised, not really. He'd been expecting the situation in there to explode for quite some time, but he couldn't have known that Justine would be in the room when it blew.

Karl turned. He needed to go to Justine.

———

Without an instant's thought, Ed lunged for Justine and Georgette when he saw Nora pull her gun. It was a gentlemanly thing to do, but it took him out of reach of his own revolver lying on his desk.

———

The room was absolutely still. The people of Room 117 were calm by nature, rational to the core. Their reactions were measured. Even Patryk, whose emotions were ripped and scarred and would not ever heal, would never be a person who ran screaming from a crisis.

None of them were. They just weren't.

But they were human. Even brilliant people can be stymied when confronted by a situation that doesn't make sense, and it doesn't make sense to see someone you know train a gun on you. They watched Nora as if hypnotized, as if they hoped to make it easier for her to pick them off one by one. Nothing in the room moved except their eyes, until the second that she pulled the trigger.

Even for one more moment after that, they sat and watched in shock, so everyone heard what Nora said when she took aim on Ike and what she said afterward.

"The jig's up, and you're too irrational to take with me."

The bullet struck him in the center of his throat. Ike sprawled bleeding on his desktop.

"That's for Bettie. I told you she didn't know anything. There wasn't any need to kill her."

And then Nora was moving, backing down the aisle between the desks and panning her weapon back and forth to pin them in their seats. As she edged around the screen, the gun lingered on Justine. The eyes, too, lingered, as if calculating the ballistics necessary to put a bullet in her head. They locked on Justine's face as Nora gave a barely perceptible nod and backed out the door without pulling the trigger.

Justine couldn't be certain what that nod meant, but it felt like Nora was saying, "You caught me. I'd kill you if I had to, but I don't." The nod felt like an acknowledgment of respect, and Justine was puzzled about why Nora's respect meant anything to her at all.

Because, in the end, it meant nothing. If Justine knew anything, she knew that Nora would kill her in a heartbeat if she got in her way, but only then. Nora was a woman who had reasons for the things she did. And the reason she had decided to ally herself with the Russians was because she thought that they would be the most likely to utterly crush a defeated Germany, far more likely than the Americans or the British. And she believed that they would keep the Germans crushed. Germany took her husband, and Nora wanted them shown no mercy.

Justine had been right to discount Nora as a suspect when she thought that the spy was working with Germany, an entity that Nora had every reason to hate. Nora only made sense as the suspect when allied with Russia.

But what did Nora want now, right now? She wanted to escape, and she wanted to protect any Russian secrets she'd shared with her co-conspirators. Or, more likely, her fall guys. If Justine had to guess, Ike had been nothing to Nora but a helper who could offer muscle and an utter lack of scruples. There was someone else that she had used just as surely as she'd used Ike, and Justine was as sure as she could be that Nora was on her way to kill the other one. Linda was in utter peril.

After Linda was dead, then what? Nora would disappear, and Justine couldn't have that. Nora was a traitor who had to be brought to justice. She knew things that she couldn't be allowed to take to a foreign government. The coded flowers could only carry a small amount of information per day. Justine clung to the hope that Nora hadn't had time to share everything she knew.

Still sprawled on top of Georgette's desk, Justine leaned hard and reached for Ed's revolver, but it wasn't there. It was in Ed's hand, and he was sprinting around his desk, ready to chase Nora down.

Justine wasn't about to cede responsibility for stopping Nora to Ed, even if he did have a gun. She didn't know for sure what side he was on, anyway. Clapping her left hand against her thigh, she made sure she still had the Stinger and the weapons Gloria had given her. They were right there in the pocket that Georgette had sewn.

She spun on her rear on the desktop, swinging her legs to the other side. When her feet hit the floor, she was running. Even in her impractical dress shoes, she was five steps ahead of Ed, because he'd taken the time to go around his desk. That gap widened with every step. Neither Justine nor Ed was an athlete, but she was a government agent with twelve whole weeks of training and experience. She had a pocket full of weapons that were vaguely useful. She knew in her soul that she could do a better job of taking down an enemy spy than a college professor with a gun that he probably didn't even know how to use. There was no way she was going to let him beat her in a footrace.

Justine dodged around the screen and out the door of Room 117.

———

Ed van Dorn had never pictured himself careening down a hallway, gun in hand but with no idea whom to shoot. Justine was ahead of him, moving with astonishing speed for a woman wearing a skirt that hobbled her at the knees. She clearly wasn't satisfied with her speed because she lengthened her stride, and the skirt's back seam responded by ripping at least a foot up from her knees. He had no idea what Justine, who didn't even have a heavy purse to use as a weapon, planned to do when she caught up with Nora, whom he had just seen commit murder. He could hear Samantha coming up behind him, despite the fact that she was equally encumbered by her clothes and, he presumed, equally unarmed.

Karl was ahead of them all, standing stock-still in the dead center of the hallway that ran between the doors of Room 117 and Traffic Records. Ed had no idea what he was supposed to do about Nora, Justine, and Samantha, but he knew what to do about the old man in danger of being trampled or shot.

"Karl! To the wall!" he shouted, using his free hand to gesture wildly to the left, so that the confused man wouldn't have to choose a wall. "Then hit the ground."

Never steady on his feet, Karl lurched to the wall, then sank to his knees.

"All the way down, like an air raid!" Ed barked. "Head in your lap and hands holding the back of your head!"

Karl complied, and Ed was satisfied that the old man now offered as small a target to stray bullets as a man his size could manage.

Samantha passed Ed at a dead run, and there was absolutely nothing he could do about that.

———

Justine watched Nora shoot at the lock on the door to Traffic Records. The door was tottering, but it was still doing its job. Nora drew aim again while her pursuers advanced, making it clear that silencing her accomplice behind the door was the most important thing in her world at that moment. It might even be more important to Nora than her own survival.

Justine was counting bullets and there were two gone, but Nora had that damnable extra-large thirteen-round magazine. The rounds weren't dwindling fast enough. There was still going to be ammunition left in the gun when Nora finished blasting the door open. When that happened, Linda was going to die. What could Justine do to stop it without dying herself?

She reviewed the contents of her left pocket. The Stinger would do her no good unless she was an arm's-length from Nora, which wasn't going to happen while her target was holding a Browning Hi-Power that still had rounds in its magazine.

Two of the weapons that Gloria had given her would work from a distance, however. They weren't deadly, but Justine didn't see that she had any other choices.

She palmed Gloria's noisemaker, giving it a twist. An ear-splitting noise erupted. Nora flinched, but recovered enough to take aim at the lock again.

Justine felt the thud more than she heard it over the din. She felt something hit the floor behind her, just as Nora took her second shot at the door, and she looked to her right just in time to see something slide by. It was Georgette, the tomboy who had played baseball with her brothers, executing a slide so illegal that it would get her kicked out of a fair game. The ear-splitting racket of Justine's noisemaker, coupled with the fact that Nora was focused on the door and not on her pursuers, had convinced Georgette that it was time to strike. With one leg raised high, she crashed into Nora. Her lower foot swept Nora's feet out from under her, and her upper foot went for the gun.

Justine couldn't see whether Georgette had managed to disarm Nora, but she also couldn't leave her to do hand-to-hand combat with an enemy agent alone. She was scraping the bottom of her barrel of tricks, so she hoped her last one worked.

———

A ruckus behind Ed made him turn his head to see Patryk burst through the door of Room 117. Around Patryk, Thelma and The Bees were clutching at his hands, his elbows, his shoulders, anything they could reach. They were begging him to come back in Room 117 and sit down, but he showed no sign of hearing them. He lurched away from their grasping hands, calling out a single word, over and over.

"Viktoria…Viktoria…Viktoria…"

The sound was searing, more searing than the racket Justine was somehow making. It made Ed want to clap his hands over his ears. His head whipped from Patryk behind him to Samantha and Justine ahead of him.

What was he to do? He had been trained from birth to take care of women, but these two were intentionally flinging themselves into danger. They had rendered his firearm useless, as he wasn't a good enough shot to be sure he could pick off Nora without hitting one of the other women.

He'd had the sense from the moment he met them that they knew how to take care of themselves. Patryk, however, was in no state to care for himself. He needed a friend to do it for him. Ed turned around and walked toward Patryk, left hand held out in friendship and right hand held behind his back. Patryk did not need to see him brandishing a gun.

Patryk skidded to a halt. "Ed? Will you help me find Viktoria?"

"I will do whatever I can to help you with anything you need. First, though, let me do this one thing."

He turned away from Patryk and yelled Justine's name. She didn't acknowledge him, which was understandable, since she was focused on staying alive. Part of her efforts to stay alive included fumbling in her left pocket. He had no idea what she was looking for, as there was no way her snug skirt could be hiding a gun, which was what she really needed.

Unsure what to do, he froze in place, staring at Justine as she stood staring at Samantha grappling with Nora on the floor.

With no warning, Justine ripped her eyes off Samantha and responded to his voice by whipping her head in his direction, and Ed took his chance. He stooped low, set his gun gently on the ground, and gave it a mighty heave.

The revolver slid on the waxed floor toward Justine like a hockey puck on ice, heading for the goal. As it moved, Ed turned to the terrified man huddling against the wall.

"Karl. Very slowly, crawl away from the people waving guns around. Make your way down the wall toward me. You and I and Thelma and The Bees are going to make sure our friend Patryk is safe."

———

As Justine fumbled with the contents of her pocket, the door at the end of the hall swung open and Jerry rolled through it. She'd hoped that the sound of gunfire would bring him. He held a handgun in his outstretched arm, but there was absolutely nothing he could do with it, not while Georgette was wrestling with his target.

Justine gave him a here-goes-nothing shrug, closed her eyes and twisted to look behind her, shielding her face. Just as she pointed Gloria's fake pen toward Nora and Georgette, releasing a cloud of pepper spray, she saw Ed put his gun on the floor and slide it toward her. But she only saw the sliding gun for a second. When the pepper spray hit her, it was as if her eyes had caught fire. How was she going to gain control of Ed's gun now?

Struggling to see through tears, she dropped to the floor, arms flung wide, and slithered forward on her belly toward the last spot when she'd seen the gun. Her prone position offered a difficult target for Nora, also suffering from the pepper spray, and her outstretched arms maximized the possibility that the gun would slide right into her.

The moments while she waited to feel Ed's gun reach her were the longest of her life. She had been suppressing the memory of Ike, collapsed on his desk. Now, when her burning eyes could see nothing, the only image in her mind was of Ike, dying. At any moment, it could be her, writhing, groaning, struggling to breathe. It could be Georgette, Karl, Ed, Patryk, any of them.

She didn't want that for anyone. She clearly didn't want it for Linda, because here she was risking everything for her, despite the fact that she was a traitor. She didn't even want it for Nora. She certainly didn't want it for all the soldiers who risked violent death every day. She wanted them all to come home. In the end, that was why she had taken this job and it was why she had stayed.

Justine's nose was streaming. Her mouth was burning. Her throat was burning. Her eyes were burning. She could see nothing but lightness and darkness and shapes, but she could hear the groan of something heavy sliding on the slick linoleum floor. The groan told her exactly where Ed's gun was.

At the same time, she heard a clang in the general direction of Georgette and Nora as something metallic and heavy hit that same linoleum floor. It sounded like a gun and it could have been a gun, but she wasn't certain and she certainly couldn't see it. She was just going to have to trust that her partner had succeeded in disarming Nora. Groping for the grip of Ed's revolver, Justine rose to her knees and aimed it at the sound of Georgette struggling with Nora. She couldn't pull the trigger until she knew where Georgette was, but she could be ready.

———

The instant that Jerry saw Nora drop her weapon, he was in motion. Speeding down the hall, he felt the cloud of pepper spray envelop him, but he got to the gun before his vision blurred completely. Diving for the weapon, he left the wheelchair with such force that it went flying down the hall behind him. He hit the ground hard, viciously hard, but he got both hands on the Browning Hi-Power. Georgette was still doing hand-to-hand combat with a woman who would kill her and never look back, but at least that woman was now armed with just her fists.

———

A leg-shaped patch of darkness flailed ahead of Georgette's burning eyes. She reached for it, but only managed to catch hold of the foot. Still, holding the enemy's foot was slightly better than having the enemy's foot stomping at her face. It wasn't really like holding a human leg. It was more like getting hold of an octopus leg and trying to ride it like a bucking bronco while the other seven legs slapped her in the face. Was there a Browning Hi-Power being held by one of those other octopus appendages? Georgette had no idea. She hoped not.

Hanging on to Nora's foot with her right hand, Georgette groped in her pocket with her left. Pulling out her Stinger, she rolled onto Nora's leg and used the whole weight of her upper body to hold it down. Then she used her left hand—not her strong one, but strong enough—to press the Stinger into Nora's thigh and trigger it.

There was a scream and a spray of something wet that was surely blood, but that one bullet, the only one Georgette had been trusted to carry, did what it needed to do. Georgette wished for a second Stinger, so that she could render Nora's other leg useless, but she figured even one leg with a gunshot wound would keep Nora from getting away. Even if Nora retained control of her handgun, and even if she used it to blow Georgette away, she still wasn't going anywhere. Georgette had done her duty.

She couldn't see Justine. She couldn't see anything, but she could shout.

"That door's gonna come down any second. You people need to be ready for Linda to come running out."

———

Justine heard what Georgette was saying, but she'd been thinking about Linda. She'd been thinking about how proud Linda was that she knew her filing system and nothing else. Linda didn't type the messages she filed. Patsy did. And Patsy sat in the desk next to Linda's, close enough to read the coded messages that Nora hid in her daisies.

"It's Patsy."

Georgette, still pinning Nora to the floor, said, "Patsy? What?"

"Trust me. The other spy isn't Linda. It's Patsy."

Justine didn't have much strength left in her legs. Her bruised head and throat ached. Her arms trembled. But she still had her desire. She still had her will. Trying to blink the pepper spray out of her eyes and clutching Ed's revolver, she rose to her feet and pointed it at the door to Traffic Records. It was rocking on its hinges as the third and last spy did her best to operate the bullet-ridden lock, trying to create an opening through which she could flee.

The door flew open and a panicked crowd tried to push through the opening, but they were met with the business end of a revolver wielded by a woman whose platinum-blond updo was falling down fast.

Justine's vision had recovered enough for her to recognize faces at such short range, and the first one she saw was a familiar one. Linda was pushing her way to the front of the pack, but she froze, open-mouthed, when she saw a gun being held mere feet from her face. Patsy, beside her, had come prepared. She raised her right hand, which held half of a disassembled pair of desk scissors, slinging her left arm around Linda's neck as if to take her hostage.

Before Patsy could get the blade to Linda's throat, Justine placed the muzzle of the revolver on her forehead and belted an instruction in a loud, deep voice that was unfamiliar even to her.

"Drop your weapon."

And Patsy did.

As Justine held Patsy at gunpoint, she heard Jerry's voice from somewhere below her. It said, "And don't move!" Her eyes were still unreliable at that distance, but she was pretty sure that the dark blob she saw waving in the direction of his voice was the Browning Hi-Power.

Holding Ed's revolver steadily against Patsy's forehead, Justine said, "Patsy. Nora. We don't want to hurt either of you, but you're not going anywhere. Stay right where you are while we get a doctor to look at Nora's leg. It's over."

———

Building B was a place of havoc. Patsy had been hauled away in handcuffs, so there was suddenly nothing for Justine to do. She stood with her back pressed hard against the wall, letting it hold her up as she inched down the hallway, desperate to get away from the sight of Nora, bleeding. Her eyes still burned from the pepper spray, but she could see well enough to know what a tiny little Stinger had done to a living person's flesh.

Justine was trying to get to Georgette, who was trying to get to Jerry. She was having trouble pursuing this goal, because her legs weren't cooperating. Georgette was in the same condition, swaying on all-fours as she tried to crawl. Jerry had pushed himself to a sitting position and was reaching out to steady her.

It was too much. Justine's bruised head ached as the world spun around it. She heard her name being called from far away, but she wasn't sure whether it was coming from this world or from the abyss at her feet. She decided to let herself fall into that abyss, sliding ever-so-slowly down the wall into nothingness, but someone caught her in their two strong arms.

They were Paul's arms and they were wrapped around her. They steadied her. They held her close while he kissed her with none of the reserve of a government agent who kept his secrets to himself.

For a moment, she kissed him back. And then she fainted.

———

Paul had found a comfortable place in Building B's lobby for Justine, Georgette, and Jerry to sit while he did secret agent things. Justine wanted to put her aching head on the table and sleep, but she was hampered by the condition of her eyes, nose, throat, and sinuses. Jerry had put the word out that handkerchiefs were needed, so she was well-supplied whenever residual pepper spray forced her to blow her nose, which was often.

It had been hard to sit there and watch two stretchers go by, both carrying someone she knew. One stretcher, carried by armed guards, was carrying Nora, motionless and staring at the ceiling. The other carried Ike, his lifeless face covered by a sheet. More armed guards were stationed in Room 117, where Paul was conducting interrogations, and still other guards were waiting with the people in Traffic Records.

Even in the heat of battle and even when choked by pepper

spray, Georgette's voice sweetened when she spoke to Jerry. "Do we think that it was just the three of 'em?"

"That's what my roommate is trying to find out."

"I think it was just Nora," Justine said. "Well, almost. Ike and Patsy helped her and Patsy deserves whatever the government does to her, but I think they were just tools for Nora. They did what she said and she paid them."

"But Nora wasn't quite able to control Ike," Georgette said. "That's what happened to poor Bettie."

"Exactly. But when he did what he was told, he was able to keep Nora from ever speaking to Patsy, the one who actually passed the messages."

"That makes sense," Georgette said. "But where was Nora getting *her* information from? How did she know what to tell Linda to put in the messages?"

"I think she got it from the radio. And I think there are coded messages in her music, all of it. The music she plays. The music she writes. The music she listens to on the radio. Remember that the atonal music that she plays and writes doesn't follow the repetitive patterns of more familiar forms of music. You'd never know that you were hearing a coded message. I have a theory that even her music publishing career is tied into her espionage activities. If she sent messages coded as musical notes to a contact at a music publishing house, they could be printed up and shipped to agents anywhere in the world and nobody would suspect a thing. It's not a convenient way to move information around, but the war's got lines of communication so throttled that we're using things like carrier pigeons."

A voice came from behind her. "She did get her messages from the radio. And she did use music for her code." It was Thelma.

A guard stood beside her. He said, "I know you people wanted us to keep the Room 117 people together until you could question them, but this one convinced me that she had information that you needed now. And I mean you three in particular, not just any of the mysterious folks running around this building."

Thelma said, "It's obvious from what I just saw that you three aren't who you say you are. You work for the government, for sure. You came here to catch some people who are…terrible is the word, I guess. I heard Nora say that Ike killed Bettie. And to think that I sat there looking at him every day, and I never knew." She swallowed. "Anyway, I think this might help you get to the bottom of things."

She handed Jerry a single sheet of paper. He held it so that Justine and Georgette could see the handwriting covering its face.

"That's Sally's handwriting," Georgette said. "Did you find her? Is she okay?"

"She's been hiding in the vacant wing of Oklahoma Hall, the one that's under construction. I thought she might be, so I left a bag of food and some money there for her. Oh, and some scissors and carbon paper that I stole from the housemother. When I went back to check, this note was in the empty bag."

"Were the scissors and carbon paper for a disguise?" Georgette asked.

Jerry looked baffled.

"You can color your hair with carbon paper," Georgette said, "if you've got a lot of it and if you take your time about it. With short, dark hair, Sally would've been a lot harder to recognize while she was on the run."

"What about your escape?" Justine asked, eyeballing dark-haired Thelma.

"You're right. I was planning to go with her. I stole some bleach from the laundry room and was going to do my best

334 *Mary Anna Evans*

with lightening my hair tonight after everybody went to bed. I'm pretty relieved I won't have to do that. Now Sally can come home to our room in Kansas Hall, and it will be as if none of this ever happened, as long as you people keep the contents of this note to yourselves."

Jerry, Justine, and Georgette huddled around the sheet of paper.

It's not safe for us in Arlington, Thelma. I'll get things arranged and then we'll leave together. You'll find a note here when it's time to go. Until then, don't do anything to attract attention, but stay as far from Nora as you can. I've thought for a long time that she might be passing secrets, but I couldn't figure out how.

Now I know. She listens to music on the radio every night, just like she says she does, but late at night she switches to a shortwave radio. I'm sure the information she receives on those frequencies is encrypted into the broadcasts somehow, and my guess is that the music played on the programs she listens to is the actual message.

Nora is a musical genius. It would be the easiest thing in the world for her to listen to something on the radio, write it down, and reconstruct the message by decoding the notes. Think about that weird music she listens to. Atonal, I think she calls it. You wouldn't even have to disguise the message by making it into a melody that you can sing. You would just translate the numbers and letters into musical notes that sound random to the rest of us. But not to Nora. She's a very valuable asset for them, whoever "they" are.

Nora knows that I know. That's why I had to disappear without a word to you. If she doesn't leave immediately, it will be because she needs to pass critical information first. So if anything happens to me, you have to take this information to Karl. You can never be absolutely certain that it's safe to trust anybody, but I'm as close to sure about Karl as I can be. When we're safely away, I'll write and tell him what I know.

I love you, Thelma. I'll come for you. I promise. And then we'll never have to be apart again.

Justine lifted her eyes from the page and Thelma's eyes met them.

"I'm so glad you found each other," she said, and she finally saw solemn Thelma's full smile.

"Disguises don't have to be hard," she said. "Carbon paper. Scissors. Three heart-shaped lockets to commemorate three lost loves who never existed. After all that heartache, who will blame Sally if she chooses to live her life as a spinster? Who will wonder why she lives that lonely life alongside an old friend like me who's too much of a sourpuss to ever attract a husband?"

"You shouldn't have to pretend," Georgette said.

"The world is the way it is. Maybe it'll be different someday, and maybe we can change it, but Sally and I have decided that we'll find a way to be happy, no matter what."

Chapter 26

The days after Nora was apprehended were blissful for Justine. She and Georgette couldn't exactly go back to work and hope nobody had noticed that they'd been carrying experimental weapons of the secret agent variety in their skirt pockets. They couldn't even keep living in Kansas Hall, so Paul had sent somebody to pick up their things and to give Justine two notes. The first one was written in an ornate, old-fashioned script by someone whose hand trembled a bit.

Dearest Justine,

It seems that you have come back into my life only long enough for me to rue losing you again. I don't understand everything that happened today, but I understand enough. And I have sufficient connections with various intelligence agencies that I am reasonably certain that this note will find you. As you will see, I have used those connections to help someone else who very much wanted to reach you.

I have said it to your face, but I want to say it to you

again in writing, so that you can keep this page for those times when you need reminding. Your parents would be so proud of you, so very proud. You are in every way what I would expect a child of theirs to be. Even as an imperfect substitute father—grandfather, I suppose?—I am very proud.

You are evidently employed in a career that keeps you very busy, but this war will be over someday and perhaps you will want to do something else. And perhaps you will want to spend time with your family. I hope that you will think of me thus. Consider this an open invitation to stay in the guest apartment over my garage for as long as you like. Perhaps you would like to stay there while you pursue an education at my institution. I can arrange for tuition and all of your expenses. You would have no worries. You would begin your program of study already having received credit for an advanced course in logic, based on the work I've seen you do in the past week.

You have accomplished another thing in this week. You have reminded me of a time in my life when I was very happy, and you have made me think that I could feel that way again. Take care, my dear.

> Your imperfect but devoted
> substitute grandfather,
> Karl

The second note was written in a decisive hand.

Dear Justine,

After the events of the day, I cannot imagine that you will return to Arlington Hall, and this deprives me of the chance to say goodbye. However, I am not known for giving up easily, so I refuse to say that the events of the day will deprive me of ever seeing you again. This note will show that I am so devoted to the goal of reaching you that I humbled myself enough to ask Karl for help in sending it.

You are a singular individual whom I would like very much to know better. In addition, I devoutly believe that you would be the finest bridge partner a man could ever find. Therefore, I intend to find you. If you're inclined to make this task easier for me, so much the better, but don't make it too easy. Where's the fun in that?

Until we meet again,
Ed

Justine had tucked the notes into her purse and walked out of Kansas Hall forever, with no knowledge of where she and Georgette would sleep next. It turned out that secret agents at Paul's level could secure two studio apartments in a lovely building in Arlington, with kitchens and bathrooms and telephones and everything.

"Can I afford this?" she asked him.

"The organization is covering it until you get your next assignment. And, of course, we'll pay the rent on wherever you live then. Ours is a remarkably carefree existence."

"Oh, I don't have a worry in the world, except for whether there's a bullet out there with my name on it. Or Georgette's. Or Jerry's. Or yours."

"All jobs have drawbacks."

He told her to use this time between assignments to do absolutely nothing, saying, "Most people with head injuries spend a little time resting."

And so she rested. She slept late. She celebrated having her very first kitchen of her own by baking a spice cake to share with Georgette and Gloria. She read novels. She napped. She soaked in the tub for an hour a day, without the first worry that one of the women down the hall would be impatiently banging on the bathroom door, because nobody had access to Justine's bathroom but her. She helped Georgette with her math, and Georgette helped her with her Choctaw. They made pancakes for breakfast every single day. They worked on their private cipher so that they could always keep their communications between just the two of them. They saw Jerry and Paul every day, sometimes for dinner and sometimes just for an afternoon soda. They cooked a Christmas dinner and the four of them feasted, then played cards for hours. They shopped for the perfect New Year's Eve dresses, and Justine held on to Paul's promise that the evening would include time for just the two of them, alone.

Justine allowed herself to pretend that it would always be this way. Paul would always wear his off-duty seersucker shirts. He would always sit beside her while the four of them talked after dinner, his arm casually slung around her shoulders. He would always have the lopsided smile that had charmed her from the first. He would never again forget how to laugh.

And then came the afternoon when Georgette didn't come to the door when Justine knocked. In a panic, she used her very own phone to call Jerry, who didn't know where she was, either.

This was an immediate crisis. Georgette was a government agent with twelve whole weeks of training and experience. She knew that it was critical for someone to know where she was at all times. She couldn't just wander off. She wouldn't.

They had nobody to interview about her disappearance. Georgette no longer had coworkers. She no longer lived in a dormitory with a host of women who could be asked whether they'd seen her. If Justine didn't know where she was, and if Paul didn't know, either, then nobody did.

Paul was at their apartment building in minutes, pale beneath the slight black stubble of a seven-hour-old shave.

The only witness they could find was the apartment manager, who may or may not have worked for Paul. He said, "She walked through the lobby bright and early this morning, wearing her winter coat and smiling, as usual. She wasn't carrying nothing but her purse." He unlocked Georgette's apartment, where they found all of her possessions but not Georgette.

Paul immediately had people, lots of people, out doing things like talking to cabbies, bus drivers, and train conductors, but Justine could see that he was worried. She knew that Paul reported to people who were high up in the government. If Georgette had been transferred, as she suspected Mabel, Doris, and Sandra had been, and if Paul hadn't been told about it, then his authority over Georgette had been trumped by someone high-ranking indeed. And if his authority hadn't been trumped, then Georgette had been taken by the enemy. Justine could see no other options.

"I've only got one thought about how to find out where she is," she said to Paul. "Walk me to the library?"

"Considering how things went the last time you went to the library, I'm certainly not going to send you alone."

———

The same pleasant-faced librarian sat at the circulation desk with no patrons in sight. Justine hoped this meant she could speak freely.

Approaching the librarian, she said, "I don't know if you remember me, but—"

"Oh, I do. I heard that there was a ruckus at Arlington Hall last week and that a blond-haired woman was at the center of it. The town gossips say that she accomplished something important, but nobody knows quite what. I remembered your badge and your hair, and I was pretty sure it was you. I also heard that the woman who went missing last week showed up, safe and sound. Sally was her name, I think."

"It is and she did. Speaking of missing women, has anybody else come in lately to look at travel books?"

She was disappointed to see the woman shake her head.

"No, but I'm not always here. Why don't you take a look?"

Justine didn't even bother to go to the carrel to work. She stood in front of the WPA Travel Guides and pulled the Tennessee volume off the shelf. She hoped that it would tell her that Georgette was safe with Doris and Mabel and Sandra, doing whatever top secret work they were doing, but there were no new names inscribed on the check-out slip.

Justine was deflated, but she refused to be defeated. She went back to the beginning of the series and started with the Alabama volume. She opened it to the back inside cover, hoping to see a signature reading "Georgette Broussard."

Nothing.

She moved on to the Alaska guidebook. Nothing.

She checked all the books in order—California, Florida, Maine, Nebraska, and all the other states in between—and with each one, she was disappointed. Tears were pricking her eyes, but she refused to cry in front of Paul. She just kept doggedly opening books and showing him the signatures in the back.

They had looked at thirty books, and even stubborn Justine's hope was starting to fade, when she opened *New Mexico: A Guide to the Colorful State* and hit paydirt. Samantha Ogletree's name, written in Georgette's careful loopy handwriting, was waiting there for her. Beside it was a pattern of dots and lines written in light pencil strokes that represented the number 280 in their private cipher.

Justine hugged the book. "I knew she wouldn't leave without a word."

She turned to page 280 and hugged the book again. In the margin of that page, she saw more pencil marks that read "*ant pisa*," also written in their private cipher. "*Ant pisa*" meant "come and look" in Choctaw.

But where did Georgette want her to come and look? All she knew to do was to study page 280.

On that page was a description of adventures available in New Mexico to intrepid travelers so interested in remote desert landscapes that they were willing to risk roads described as "unimproved," "hardly passable for cars," and "hardly recognizable." Justine held the page up to the light, hoping for more, and was rewarded with a faint indentation that looked like it was made with the scrape of a fingernail. It underlined two words that Justine had never seen before.

She turned to Paul.

"Georgette wants me to come and look for her. She wants me to come to a place called Los Alamos."

AUTHOR'S NOTE

Winston Churchill published the words quoted in the epigraph in his 1951 book, *The Second World War: Closing the Ring*, recalling them from a November 1943 session of the Tehran Conference (code-named Eureka), attended by Stalin, Roosevelt, and Churchill.

ACKNOWLEDGMENTS

I'd like to thank all the people who helped make *The Traitor Beside Her* happen. Tony Ain, Rachel Broughten, Anne Hawkins, and Chris Aurelio read it in manuscript form, and their comments were incredibly enlightening. A conversation with Chris that he claims not to remember was the genesis for an important part of the spy plot that Justine unravels. Whether he remembers it or not, I am grateful.

Dora M. Wickson of the Chahta Anumpa Aiikhvna School of Choctaw Language gave me valuable assistance as I wrote the lessons in the Choctaw language that Georgette gives Justine. I'm grateful for her help in making such a beautiful language part of this story.

I am also grateful to the internet for preserving such things as menus for The Mayfair Club and a description of its interior that helped me bring Justine's date with Ed into period-appropriate focus. The July 1942 issue of *Architectural Record* included a floor plan for a typical dormitory at Arlington Farms that I adapted for the scenes set in Kansas Hall, and a number of photographs taken on the Arlington Farms and Arlington Hall campuses that are available through the Library of Congress website helped me with the outdoor scenes. Floor plans of the buildings at Arlington Hall in 1944 are not, to my knowledge, available, so I created my version of those buildings based on surviving photographs of the interiors and exteriors of the buildings.

The National Park Service's website preserved a description of the CCC-camp-turned-spy-training site that history-minded readers will have recognized as the predecessor of Camp David. Those same readers will also have realized that the surprise attack in Europe described here would be known to history as The Battle of the Bulge.

Liza Mundy's book *Code Girls* provided valuable background on wartime activities at Arlington Hall and alerted me to the existence of the German section, which was said to be populated by eccentric geniuses. (The eccentric geniuses I portray in the book are, however, wholly fictional.) *Code Girls* is an incredible look at the wartime work of women who deserve all the recognition in the world, and I wholeheartedly recommend it.

These people and resources helped me avoid many errors, and any that slipped through the process are all mine.

As always, I am grateful for the people who help me get my work ready to go out into the world, the people who send it out into the world, and the people who help readers find it. Many thanks go to my agent, Anne Hawkins, and to the wonderful people at Sourcebooks and Poisoned Pen Press who do such a good job for us, their writers. Because I can trust that my editors, Anna Michels and Diane DiBiase, and my copy editor, Beth Deveny, will help me make my work shine, I can stretch myself creatively and try new things. That's a wonderful place for a writer to be. Anna Venckus does an amazing job of helping my work find new readers, for which I am eternally grateful. I'm also grateful to the University of Oklahoma for providing the opportunity for me to teach a new generation of authors while continuing to write books of my own.

And, of course, I am always (always!) grateful for you, my readers.

ABOUT THE AUTHOR

© Nadia Lombardero

In addition to holding a master of fine arts in creative writing, Mary Anna Evans holds a bachelor of science in engineering physics and a master of science in chemical engineering, and she is a licensed professional engineer. All of these things come in quite handy while she's writing about Justine. She is also the author of the Faye Longchamp Archaeological Mysteries, which have received awards including the Oklahoma Book Award, the Benjamin Franklin Award, and a Will Rogers Medallion Awards Gold Medal. Her essays on science and the environment have appeared in publications including *The Atlantic's Technology Channel*, *EarthLines*, and *Flyway*. She is an associate professor at the University of Oklahoma, where she teaches fiction and non-fiction writing and she studies the work of Agatha Christie. She is the coeditor of the *Bloomsbury Handbook to Agatha Christie*.